PATRICIA CORLIS

A

RSE

AMONG

THE

THISTLES

ISBN: 978-1-4866-2645-8
eBook ISBN: 978-1-4866-2646-5

Word Alive Press
119 De Baets Street Winnipeg, MB R2J 3R9
www.wordalivepress.ca

WORD ALIVE
—P R E S S—

Cataloguing in Publication information can be obtained from Library and Archives Canada.

ACKNOWLEDGEMENTS

PHILIPPIANS 4:13 SAYS, *"I can do all this through him who gives me strength."* This book is the result of the Holy Spirit's inspiration and the Lord's guidance. Whenever people ask where my ideas come from, I often tell them that it all began with a dream—one that persisted until I finally wrote it down. From there, the journey unfolded, with pauses and detours along the way, as certain pieces had to fall into place. Leaning on Him has allowed His message to come through in this work, creating a spiritual connection that guided me throughout the writing journey.

I want to give special thanks to my dear friend Sue G, whose invaluable feedback and constant encouragement significantly contributed to the completion of this book. Her regular question—"How's the book going?"—was the gentle nudge I needed to keep moving forward. My heartfelt thanks to Jackie A, who started a "Zoom" writer's life group at my church during the challenging times of COVID-19. Though I had already begun writing this book, the group provided the accountability and structure I needed to stay on track. These amazing women have been my greatest cheerleaders throughout this journey.

I am also profoundly grateful to my many friends who read through parts of the manuscript and provided insightful feedback, particularly regarding areas requiring further research. To all those who took the time to read and offer feedback, your contributions are deeply appreciated. This labour of love has finally come to fruition. Your long-term commitment and dedication have been instrumental in this journey.

So I leave each of you with a KISS—keep it simple, silly. Without you, I wouldn't have been able to do it. Lots of love.

ONE

KATHARINE STANDS ON the shore, her cloak billowing in the breeze. The wind caresses her face, carrying the salty scent of the sea. She tilts her head back, hugging herself to ward off the chill. With her eyes shut, she inhales the crisp air, a blend of sweetness and saltiness. The rhythmic crash of the waves against the rocks below fills her ears, and the mist from the water splashes gently on her face. Despite the wind's howl and the wave's roar, tranquility permeates the air.

"Ms. Katharine. Ms. Katharine."

She senses that she's being shaken.

"Ms. Katharine, please wake up. You're needed."

Still foggy from the dream, she whispers, "What is it, Lois?"

Lois's voice, filled with urgency, ceases her shaking. She utters, "It's Mr. Collins' brother-in-law, Mr. Leland. He has arrived to fetch you. It's time."

"Thank you, Lois. I'll need a few minutes to dress and collect my things. Have Mr. Leland get Sebastian ready in the stable, and I'll be down forthwith." Her words carry both authority and a deep sense of trust.

"Yes, Ms. Katharine." Lois hurries from the room to take her mistress's message to the man downstairs.

Katharine throws back the bed covers, takes a deep breath, and steps out of bed, moving toward her bureau with a heightened sense of urgency. She has completed this routine countless times before; it's second nature to her. Her brown hair is already in the braid she keeps for these occasions. A few of her natural curls have escaped, but it will have to do for now. She dresses swiftly, each movement purposeful and efficient.

Out of the room, she strides down the hall to the door on the right. She enters. In the corner to her left is a cloak rack. She retrieves a full-length cloak and swiftly puts it on, drawing the hood up. Automatically, she bends to pick up the bag on the floor beside the cloak rack. She exits as quickly and quietly as she entered. Down the hall, she proceeds to the back door. Before she steps out into the darkness, she lights a lantern. She says a quiet prayer for what lies ahead this night, then lifts the lantern to light her way to the stables.

The full moon shines brightly in the darkness below, and the thunder from the horses' galloping feet pound the road as the riders urge their mounts toward the farmhouse ahead. The silhouette of the man standing before the farmhouse grows more prominent, and the lead rider pulls back on the reins to slow the horse down. The second rider does the same.

The man looks up to the hooded rider and smiles. "Good evening, Ms. Katharine."

"Good evening, Thomas. How's she doing?" Katharine asks as she dismounts her horse.

A scream is heard from within the farmhouse.

"You'll see for yourself," he says as he moves to take the horse and places the bag in her hand.

"The girls, where are they?"

"I sent them over to my sister's place earlier today. Thought it would be best." He nods to the second rider, his brother-in-law.

"You're a wise man, Thomas."

"I'll look after Sebastian for you, Ms. Katharine, and be in shortly."

"Of course. See you inside." She turns to enter the farmhouse.

Katharine lets herself in. She knows her way around. Poppy is the sister she never had. They've known each other since childhood. When Poppy married Thomas, this became their home. Katharine has visited numerous times, both personally and professionally. Another scream comes from the bedroom.

"Poppy, I'm here. I'll be in as soon as I wash up."

Katharine moves through the motions. She moves the chair at the head of the table in the kitchen to put her bag on it and throw her cloak over it. She takes a quick look around for a wash basin. *Oh good*, she says to herself.

An apron and a washcloth are the top items in her medical bag. As she grabs the washcloth, she moves to the wash basin. It's clean, warm water. "I'll have to thank Thomas," she says to herself. Dropping the washcloth in the water, she rolls up her sleeves, grabs a bar of soap, and begins the task ahead. Once washed up, she takes the washcloth and throws it down by the chair where her cloak is. She dons her clean, crisp apron, grabs the bag from the chair, and hurries to the bedroom.

"It's about bloody time," growls the woman in the bed.

"It's only been thirty minutes, my friend."

"Well, from my position, it feels like forever," Poppy replies as she lies back on the bed.

"Poppy, you've had five other children. You know by now how this works."

"Katharine, seriously, you need to work on your bedside manner; this is not helping."

Katharine smirks at her friend's comment and moves closer to examine Poppy. "If you prefer, I can have Mr. Leland get Dr. Wylie. He may arrive sometime tomorrow."

"Oh my goodness, you would do that to me?"

"You're the patient, Poppy." They look at each other and then burst into laughter.

"Thank goodness you're here. You know exactly what I need."

"Yes, I do. So let's see how baby number six is doing."

Katharine examines Poppy. The baby is in position, and now it's a matter of time. Thomas has now entered the room. Katharine looks up to see that he had washed up before entering the room.

"Thomas, can you help me position Poppy and sit behind her?"

All three work together as they've done before. When a contraction comes, Katharine encourages Poppy to push, and Thomas supports her.

"Poppy, I need you to give me one more good push. Ready?"

Poppy moans, squeezes her husband's hand, and screams as she bears down. Out comes the baby into Katharine's experienced hands. A strong and hearty cry is heard. Poppy falls back into Thomas, who kisses her forehead and says, "You did it, love."

Katharine places the child on Poppy's chest and wraps the bed sheet around the mother and child. "Poppy and Thomas, say hello to the newest member of the family, your son."

Poppy looks up into the face of her newborn and then looks at Thomas, who is beaming with joy. "Katharine, I never could have done this without you."

Katharine winks at Poppy. "Thomas, can you bring me a basin of warm water and clean rags?" she asks.

Thomas moves from behind Poppy, placing the pillow to keep her propped up. A short while later, Thomas returns with a basin of hot water and the box of fresh rags made ready for this moment.

"Here you go, Ms. Katharine," he says as he sets both on the bureau to one side.

"Could you hand me a rag?" asks Katharine. He hands her a rag, and she wipes her hands and then takes the instrument needed to cut the cord. Once Katharine is done with the cord, she takes the newborn from under the covers and cleans him up. Afterwards, she wraps him in a blanket and gently lays him in his father's arms.

"Thomas, if I may have a few minutes with Poppy."

"Yes, of course." He moves over to his wife. Bending down with their son in his arms, he kisses Poppy's forehead. "We will be out by the fire." He leaves the room with a smile.

Katharine closes the bedroom door slightly and then turns her attention to Poppy.

It's nearly 3:00 a.m. when Katharine returns home from delivering Poppy's baby. She slips in the back door and finds her way to the office. Removing her cloak, she places it on the rack. Her hand brushes against the brooch attached to the cloak. Her uncle had given it to her when she started apprenticing with him, as he saw she had a gift for healing. Her aunt had passed the cloak down to her, as her mother had done to her. She came from a long line of women with the gift of healing.

The cloak was deep burgundy, hooded, and ankle-length. It protected them from the elements when travelling to see patients but was also a way for the people she visited and cared for to know who she was.

"If you could talk, the stories you would tell," Katharine says lovingly at the cloak as she swipes the brooch with her hand. "Now to finish up before bed," she says to herself. It's automatic for her to take her medical bag and place it on top of a clean cloth on the cabinet. She reaches up to take down a tray and a disinfectant bottle, checking off the list of things she must do in her head. *Make sure the apron and wash-cloth go into the wash basket. All instruments go into the tray and soak in disinfectant.* Katharine grabs a clean washcloth from the cupboard and pours disinfectant onto it, wiping down her bag. Inside, outside, the handles, and the bottom. She then hangs it on the cloak rack to dry. Grabbing the dirty cloth the medical bag is sitting on, she throws it and the one in her hand into the wash basket. "That should do."

Katharine has learned over the years that keeping her instruments, herself, and others clean means less infection, giving all her patients a fighting chance. The medical profession would say she goes overboard or doesn't need to do it at all, but in the community she takes care of, her mortality rate is extremely low. If it's working, keep on doing it.

"One last thing," she says to herself. She discards her dress and throws it in the wash basket too. A pitcher of water with a matching basin is located by the window leading into a small waiting room. It sits here so she can wash up before or after meeting with a patient. Tonight is no different. Once her hands, face, and neck are washed, she takes disinfectant and uses it on the same areas. "Back to bed I go." She takes the light housecoat she keeps on the hook nearby for these occasions, ties it around her waist, and gingerly closes the office door into the main house behind her so as not to wake the others. Tiptoeing to her bedroom, she goes for, hopefully, a few hours of sleep before the day's routine begins.

TWO

THE FIRE BURNS brightly as the crackle of the dry wood is heard. Ethan Stuart sits in his favourite winged-back chair, staring into the flames while he sips his scotch. "It's good to be home," Ethan says to himself. He has removed his top coat to dry by the fire. He may have to dress like a businessman, but he prefers to wear a clean shirt and pants at home. It's much more comfortable.

The last two weeks in town to deal with an issue at the shipyard was necessary, but this Friday evening, he could return "home" with the other tenant shipbuilders. Ethan Stuart is a young man but wise for his age. He knew growing up that he would inherit the "Laird" title as the oldest son. His father had taught him the business side of town and the labour side of the estate, so he's no stranger to working with his hands, whether on the land or with the ships. If he had his choice, he'd much prefer to work with his hands, so any chance he can, he does.

He may hold the title "Laird," but Ethan has learned to rely upon his other siblings, who each have their strengths at Stuart Holdings. Reid is an excellent businessman who's passionate about the ships their well-known, family-owned company has built. Reid stays in town to run that part when Ethan is home on the estate.

His sister, Bonnie, is in charge of the estate when he's away in town. She has a love of the land, which you can see in her gardens, both floral and vegetable. He tries to spend as much time as he can here in the country, but duty calls, and at least once a month he goes into town to catch up with Reid at the shipyards.

A large number of the shipbuilders are tenants on the Stuart estate. They come home on Friday, spend the weekend with the family, and then return to town on Monday to stay for the week. A handful of men specifically stay to work the land, but for the most part, the wives and children help them get the crops in while the husbands are away. It's been done for generations and helps families financially. Along with Bonnie, Ethan has Ty, the Stuart steward. He's in charge of all the work done on the Stuart estate. He works closely with Ethan and Bonnie to ensure the tenants and land are looked after.

Ethan sets his drink down to remove his boots. "Aye, that feels better," he says. He runs his hands through his thick, black hair. "I'll need to see if Mrs. Jones can trim it tomorrow," he says to himself. He takes a look around the room, which has always been referred to as "the study." To him, it's his sanctuary. Primarily, it's used as an office where he handles all the paperwork associated with the estate, just like his father and his father before him. But it's also where he can be alone, enjoy a good drink of scotch, soak in the warmth of the fireplace, or talk to a friend at the end of his day. You'll most likely find him here if he's not out checking on the estate and any tenant matters.

The room hasn't changed much over the generations. The main focal point is the large executive desk. It's beautifully crafted out of mahogany with drawers on each side, and a sheet of glass protects the top. Ethan, with the help of Bonnie, has made a comfortable sitting area around the fireplace to make it more inviting. Here he and Ty have their evening meetings.

Ethan settles back into his chair and looks across the other side of the room. You see what looks like a bureau and chair, but the bureau pulls down and can be used as a desk. His mother would sit there for hours and write letters to family and friends to keep her husband company while he was doing business at the oversized desk. Ethan smiles at the memory. "One day," he says, thinking his wife will sit across from him at the desk while he works there.

A systematic knock is heard three times at the door. "Speak of the devil," says Ethan, and in comes Ty. There's no need for an invitation. Ty knows he's always welcome, and the three knocks are his signal to Ethan as to who it is. He's only six months younger than Ethan. Looking at them side by side, you'd think they were brothers more than you'd think he and Reid are. They have the same height, build, and black hair; once you get to know them, you discover that they have a wicked sense of humour. The things they would get up to as children! Those stories are for another day.

Ethan and Ty have known each other since they were both starting to walk. Ty's parents were tenants on the Stuart estate. His father, now deceased, was the Stuart steward before him. Most days, Ty's father would bring him to work. Ethan and Ty grew up together. Ethan trusts Ty implicitly, which doesn't hurt. Ty is in love with Bonnie, so they may not be blood brothers, but soon enough, they'll be kin.

Ty sees the pile of papers on Ethan's desk, expecting to find him sorting through them. Instead, he's enjoying a drink in his "thinking" chair.

"We'll both need another after this conversation," says Ty to himself.

"Good evening, Laird," greets Ty.

"I'm not going to like this conversation, Ty," replies Ethan as he sips his drink.

"That depends. Do I speak to you as your steward or friend?"

"Friend, please."

Ty moves to sit in the chair opposite Ethan at the hearth.

"Very well, Ethan. As you may have heard, the deaths that occurred two nights ago were the result of us not having experienced medical personnel nearby. It seems that medical emergencies are much too complicated for Liam and Tamara. You have two workers who are still healing broken bones, which may not have been set properly, and with the change in weather, we're looking at the usual ailments taking over. We have to do something, Ethan."

"I am well aware of the situation, Ty." Ethan slams his hand against the arm of the chair to illustrate his frustration. He rises from his chair and moves to the cabinet behind the desk. He pours a glass of scotch for himself and one for Ty and then returns to the fire, hands Ty his drink, and sits in his chair.

"I've made an inquiry to Walter Bennett in this regard. In my dealings with him, I remember him mentioning that his family handled the 'doctoring' in their community of Brookville, England. Since he has a large note owing regarding the last ship we provided to him, I have offered to consider it paid in full if he can find us someone to come and work for a year. Their main focus is to raise experienced medical help for our people."

"The tenants may not take to an outsider, especially an Englishman. Are you sure about this, Ethan?"

"No, I am not. But desperate times call for desperate measures. It took us long enough to find the last doctor in our area, and he wasn't with us long enough to teach Tamara and Liam. We already know he wasn't keen on teaching Tamara." Ethan takes a sip from his glass.

"You figured it might be easier to get someone from outside."

"Yes, and to be honest, Ty, I thought bartering the note would incentivize Mr. Bennett to make sure we get a proper doctor. With his family connections, I thought it was an option I had to look into."

"When will you hear something?" questions Ty as he sips his drink.

"I was hoping to hear something by the end of the week. If not, I was going to send another telegram."

"Let's hope having the note paid in full is enough incentive for Mr. Bennett to find us a good English doctor to look after us Scots," says Ty sarcastically.

"You and I both." They clink their glasses together.

They both sit back, lost in their thoughts and staring into the flames dancing in the fireplace. It looks as if the flames have something to say as they twist and turn up the chimney.

"Our community needs to be healthy and strong, Ethan. Losing both child and mother for the third time in as many months is not helping the morale. People are concerned. As their Laird, you need to address this with them."

"Aye. I want to be sure I can tell them something good."

"I would encourage you, my friend, to tell them something. Perhaps you could communicate the progress tomorrow night at the monthly tenant supper. It may help to ease the tenants' concerns."

"I hope by this time next week, Mr. Bennett has found us a doctor and that he's on his way here."

"May I point out, Ethan, that if Mr. Bennett can get a doctor to agree to these terms, we have no guarantee of how good this doctor is."

Ethan takes a drink, looks at his friend, and says, "Ty, are you trying to cheer me up? Because it's not working." It takes a moment, and then they both laugh.

"Ethan, how long have we known each other? Since the age of five?"

"If not earlier," chuckles Ethan as he recalls some of their antics.

"In all that time, who's been the one to tell you to look at both sides of the coin?"

"You," replies Ethan as he takes a drink.

"Yes. And because of that, you've made me steward over your estate. You know I always have your back and the best interest of the Stuarts in mind. That's why I can speak with you regarding your decisions—to make sure you've considered all options."

"There's hope that you won't need the opportunity to do so one day."

"One can always hope, my friend," snickers Ty as he raises his glass to Ethan. They both sigh, take a drink, and return their attention to the fire as the last of the glowing embers snap, crackle, and pop.

THREE

"MS. KATHARINE, YOUR brother has asked to speak to you," says Lois as she pokes her head into Katharine's office.

"Did he say what it was regarding, Lois?" Katharine asks as she finishes writing her note.

"No, Ms., he did not. He asked you to meet him in his study at 11:00 a.m."

Katharine glances up at the clock on the mantle. She has fifteen minutes. "Very well. Thank you for relaying the message, Lois."

"You're welcome, Ms. Katharine," she says as she returns to her kitchen duties.

Katharine rises from her desk and stretches. Updating her patients' files takes time, and she's a bit behind due to the house calls she's had to make over the past several weeks. She straightens and heads to see what Walter wants.

It's not often that Walter calls on her. Having been raised together and with only five years difference between herself and Walter, most people are surprised to learn that they don't have the same mother. Walter's mother was their father's first wife, but she passed away, and Katharine's mother married him a year later. Upon their father's death five years ago, Katharine and her mother moved to the small cottage near the estate home. As per her father's will, this is where they were to live for the rest of his wife's life and until his daughter married. Katharine serves as the doctor in the area, mainly at no expense. It's been a long and arduous journey to get the people of Brookville to accept her as their doctor, especially in the last three years when it's been just her.

Her mother receives a monthly income, and Katharine, in her own right, is a wealthy woman. She generates a substantial income from her uncle's estate. About three years ago, her uncle and aunt died. Since Katharine was the closest living relative, he left the estate, mostly land for agriculture, to her. To ensure it passed without issue, Mr. Robert was left to oversee the property until Katharine married or turned thirty, and then she'd inherit it free and clear. The wonderful thing is that Mr. Robert is a man before his time. He believes women are equal to men and should be allowed to run their affairs. Katharine gives him instructions, and he's happy to ensure that they're followed. He doesn't have to do the work because she's so good at what she does.

Katharine walks from the cottage over to the estate home. When she arrives, the butler answers the door.

"Good morning, Ms. Bennett."

"Good morning, Mr. Hynes. How are you?"

"I'm well, Ms., thank you. Mr. Bennett is in his office, Ms.; he expects you."

"Thank you, Mr. Hynes."

She lifts her skirt to move up the stairs to Walter's office.

"Ms. Bennett."

"Yes," Katharine replies as she stops and turns toward him.

Mr. Hynes bows his head, takes a deep breath, and swallows. As he lifts his head, she sees the beginning of tears in his eyes; his hands shake slightly.

"I never had the opportunity to say how grateful I am for all you did for my wife … I don't know what would have happened had you not been there."

She steps down and places her hand on his wrist. She looks at him, smiles, and says, "Mr. Hynes, you don't have to thank me for doing what I've been called to do. But if it makes you feel better, you're welcome." She slightly squeezes his wrist. To most, he and his wife would be but "the help," but to Katharine, they are people needing her medical skills, and she wouldn't deny anyone her assistance. They both nod at each other. Katharine turns and takes her skirt up again to move up the stairs toward Walter's office.

Katharine arrives at Walter's office door. It's slightly ajar, but she knocks and waits for Walter to acknowledge her before she enters.

"Come in, Katharine."

Katharine enters to see Walter behind his desk.

He looks up from behind his round glasses. "Please have a seat." He motions to the soft, winged-back chair.

"Lois said you wanted to see me."

"Yes, I did." Walter removes his glasses and pushes his chair back from his desk. There's an awkward silence before Walter clears his throat to speak. "I'm not sure how to say this, Katharine, so I'm just going to spit it out. I need your medical expertise to help the family business get out of debt."

Katharine needs clarification and wonders if what he said is what she heard. "Sorry, Walter. You said you needed my medical expertise to get the family business out of debt?"

"You're correct, Katharine."

Still perplexed, she looks at him and says, "I don't think you're talking about me delivering a ship, so perhaps you could be a bit more specific, Walter."

"Bennett Import & Export Trading Business holds a large note with Stuart Holdings, a shipbuilding company in Scotland. It's for the last cargo ship we had built, the *Grand Olympia*. They're one of, if not the, best shipbuilders in Europe. Many of their ships are used for voyages to the Americas. Sorry, I got off-topic there. The note we owe is substantial. However, an offer for it to be paid in full within a year has been handed to us. The stipulation from the Stuart family is that we secure a doctor to go to Scotland for a year. For the year, they require a doctor's services to provide medical assistance to their community and to train the individuals who've been doing it since their last doctor died. That's where you come in."

Katharine leans back into the chair and takes her right hand to support her chin. "You want me to leave my home and my patients, travel to Scotland, and be their doctor for a year. You know there's no love lost between the English and the Scottish, and add on the fact that I'm a woman." She moves forward in her chair. "It's taken me these past three years to finally get the community of Brookville to accept me as the doctor, and now you want me to go to another country and do the same?"

Walter gets up to walk over and sit in the chair beside Katharine. "Katharine, having this note paid off will provide the company with a greater cash flow, the ability to obtain credit from the bank at a lower interest rate, and a better asset-to-liability ratio. This, in turn, means the business generates the necessary funds for you and your mother to live in the cottage in the manner you've been accustomed to. I know I'm asking a lot from you, Katharine. If you wish, I can show you the books so you can see for yourself."

"I must do so, Walter, to entertain your proposal."

"Of course," Walter says, looking up at the clock on the mantle. "It's almost lunch. How about we meet back in my office at 3:00 p.m.? I'll have everything for you to look at then."

"Very well, Walter. I can finish a few things at the cottage and return here."

"Excellent, see you at 3:00." Walter returns to his desk as Katharine rises and leaves the room to return to her office to finish work before her return this afternoon.

On her way back to the cottage, Katharine is very curious as to why the Stuart family in Scotland are willing to ask an Englishman to come and be a doctor, especially when the English and Scottish don't exactly get along. "You know what needs to happen, Father. May I be willing to hear and obey." Katharine walks to the kitchen to find Mrs. Florence and her daughter Lois working away.

"Good afternoon, Mrs. Florence. You're just the person I wanted to see. I'll have lunch in my office today. I need to finish some work."

"Certainly, Ms. Katharine."

"Lois, could you put a sign on the door around 3:00 p.m. inviting anyone who needs medical assistance to come to the estate home? I'll be meeting with my brother, Walter, for a few hours this afternoon."

"Of course, Ms. Katharine."

"Thank you both. What would we do without you?" They all laugh, knowing how much each depends on the other.

"The lunch tray will be delivered shortly, my dear. Off you go," says Mrs. Florence.

Katharine moves down the hall toward the seating room, where she sees her mother sitting in her favourite chair by the window. Today she knits while watching the animals' activity outside.

"Mother, good afternoon."

"Afternoon, Katie." This is a nickname only her mother has used since Katharine's childhood. "How are you doing, sweetie?"

"Tired, but what do you expect when you're out till 3:00 a.m. delivering a baby?"

"How is Poppy doing?"

"She and her new baby boy are doing well."

"A boy! After five girls, they get the boy they've been praying for."

"Yes, they do. His name is Arthur, after both their fathers."

"Good, good," her mother replies, knitting away without looking at her hands.

"I'll take my lunch in my office to catch up on paperwork. Then I'll meet Walter at the estate house for a few hours this afternoon."

"Very well, my dear. Do you think you will be back for tea?"

"I'm sure I will be, Mother. If not, I'll have someone come tell you."

"Thank you, love. We'll catch up at tea then."

"Have a lovely afternoon with the ladies and your cards."

"You know we always do," says her mother, winking.

Katharine turns down the hall to her office, where she will finish the task she started earlier in the day.

Upon Katharine's return to Walter's office at 3:00 p.m., she takes about an hour to review the company's books. Walter is available to answer her questions, but the solution is in black and white. Paying this note in full will put the business back in good financial standing. It's up to Katharine to decide if she'll accept the proposal of going to Scotland to provide medical training.

"I agree with you, Walter, regarding the business. Now, as for the Stuart family, why would they even ask you for something like this?"

"I spoke of you to them while building the latest cargo ship."

"You told them you had a sister who was a doctor?"

"No, I don't believe I specifically told them who it was. But I did indicate that my family had provided medical assistance to the community of Brookville for well over ten years."

Katharine is shocked to learn that Walter spoke so highly of her. She clears her throat and asks, "Can you clarify the specific request?"

"Certainly. One moment, I believe I have Ethan Stuart's correspondence here." Walter moves to his desk and looks through one of his drawers. "Ahh, yes, here it is." Walter picks up his glasses and places them on. In the note, Mr. Stuart indicates that his parish recently lost their doctor. In the meantime, those with some knowledge are doing their best but need someone with more experience to care for those in need and train those working together to fill the position. He seems to feel that with a doctor's expertise, along with his people who are already doing the work, a year is sufficient time to get them on the right track. "Here, you can see for yourself," he says as he passes the note to her.

Katharine takes it and asks, "So Mr. Stuart is not going to be upset to find a woman filling this position?"

"I don't know, Katharine. He doesn't specify. I sense an urgency in his letter."

Once Katharine has finished reading the note, she responds, "As do I. If I may, Walter, I must think and pray on it."

"Yes. I understand. But I do need to give him a response by the end of the week."

"I believe I should be able to have an answer for you by then."

On her stroll back to the cottage, Katharine takes her time to think. She knows money is not a factor in her decision. She can look after her mother and herself with the income she earns from her uncle's estate. The question she keeps returning to is why the Stuart family is in dire need and why they'd ask for someone from England. The Scottish and English aren't exactly friendly, so Mr. Stuart's request for assistance from Walter indicates they really must be in need. But why?

"Enough of that, Katharine," she says to herself. "I'll have to deal with that later. Right now, my concern is the people of Brookville. I'll need to speak to Dr. Wylie tomorrow to see if he could handle looking after the community while I'm away."

Dr. Wylie and Katharine work well together to ensure that the neighbouring communities are cared for. When one is away, the other takes over, and vice versa. However, with her being gone for so long, this may be a problem, but she must at least ask. "Tonight I can speak with Mother. The rest I leave in your hands, Lord."

Katharine arrives in the dining room, where the evening meal is taken. It has a beautiful bay window that allows them to see out into a meadow with a small pond off to the side. Here they watch the sunset and sunrise and the animals in the area congregate for water. It's always entertaining and a source of discussion. Katharine's mother arrives and they both take their seats.

"How was your meeting with Walter?"

"Interesting, Mother."

"Oh, and what pray tell does that mean?"

"Well," begins Katharine, but then Mrs. Florence and Lois enter with trays of food and place them on the table. They take their seats with Katharine and her mother. Mrs. Bennett says grace, and as food is passed around the table, Katharine returns to finish her story.

"I was just about to tell Mother about my meeting with Walter this afternoon. As this will affect you both, I wanted you to know what's happening."

Everyone fills their plates. The tray is put back down, and Katharine moves to fill the wine glasses before she continues.

"Are we going to need this?" says Mrs. Florence as she sips.

"I'm not sure, but I thought it would be best if it were available," laughs Katharine as she sits back down. She too takes a sip of her wine and begins to tell the tale between bites and sips. All participants sit and listen tentatively as they consume their meals. Everyone listens as she speaks, and when she finishes, there's a look between all three as they turn toward Katharine.

Her mother sips her wine and says, "I'm concerned, Katie, love. However, I also know you'll be guided to make the right decision. I ask you to take time to pray on this and be sure this is the path you're meant to take. The Bible says, *"I know your deeds. See, I have placed before you an open door that no one can shut."*[1]

"I can speak for both of us," Mrs. Florence says as she takes her daughter's hand and squeezes it. "We'll continue to take care of this home and your mother if you choose to go to Scotland, Ms. Katharine. Your mother is wise to counsel you to ensure this is what you must do."

"I told Walter this when I left him. I wanted to be sure you're aware of what's happening. One of the things I have to look into is ensuring that everyone in Brookville is looked after in my absence. I'll be going to see Dr. Wylie tomorrow."

"Whatever you decide, Ms. Katharine, we support you and will do whatever we can to assist you," says Lois.

---

[1] Revelation 3:8a

"Thank you, everyone. I know I can count on you." She tips her glass to them and sips like everyone else does. She looks out the window to see the sun setting. She smiles and is reminded of the scripture, "*From the rising of the sun to the place where it sets, the name of the Lord is to be praised.*"[2]

"So who's ready for dessert?" asks Mrs. Florence.

---

[2] Psalm 113:3

FOUR

THE WEATHER IS brisk on her ride to the Wylie residence, so she has time to think and enjoy the peacefulness of the morning. Katharine makes sure her horse, Sebastian, is tethered. Lifting her skirt, she climbed the steps to the front door and uses the knocker to make her presence known.

Mrs. Wylie welcomes her. "Good morning, Katharine."

"Good morning, Mrs. Wylie. Is Dr. Wylie home? I'd like to speak with him."

"He's with a patient at the moment."

"May I wait for him? I need to speak with him about something," Katharine asks.

"Of course, Katharine. Please come in." She shows her to a small sitting room opposite Dr. Wylie's office. "I finished making a fresh pot of coffee. Would you care for a cup while you wait?"

"That would be lovely, Mrs. Wylie."

"Please make yourself at home. When he's finished, I'll let him know. Be right back with your coffee."

Forty-five minutes later, Dr. Wylie enters the sitting room where Katharine has been waiting.

"Good morning, Katharine."

"Good morning, Dr. Wylie."

He laughs as he takes a chair beside Katharine. He reaches for the coffee pot and pours himself a cup. "Katharine, you know you're to call me Roger. We're colleagues."

"I know. I'm not comfortable calling you by your first name, especially when you're a licensed doctor and senior to me."

"You may not have a degree, but you have over thirteen years of experience working in this field. I'll take you over someone right out of medical school any day."

"You're so kind, Dr. W—" She stops mid-sentence. He lifts his eyebrow and takes a sip. "I mean Roger."

"Now, what can I do for you, my dear?"

Without getting into too many family details, Katharine explains that she may need to be away in Scotland for a year. However, she needs to know if he'd be willing to take on her patients in Brookville during the year's absence.

Roger puts his coffee cup down and looks at Katharine. "You, my dear, are an answer to my prayers."

"How so?"

"You remember my nephew, Ian?"

She nods.

"He's finishing his medical degree. Just like you with your uncle, he's been 'apprenticing' with me. But it's hard for my patients to take him seriously on his own. I've been trying to find a way for him to get more experience. This would be a great opportunity for him to learn and start handling your patients from scratch."

Katharine is overjoyed. A sense of peace floods over her. "Dr. W … Roger, I'm so glad to hear we can all help each other. Perhaps in the next few days, I could take you and your nephew around to meet the people in the area so they can get to know him. He'll handle any medical needs in my absence, with you as his mentor."

"That sounds like a splendid idea. He's coming today to do a few house calls with me. I'll speak to him, and we can both come by tomorrow to see a few of your patients."

Mrs. Wylie comes in to let her husband know he has another patient.

"Thank you, sweetheart." He rises from his chair and kisses his wife's forehead. "Katharine has just given me wonderful news." He tells his wife the purpose of Katharine's visit.

She claps her hands together and grins. "Katharine, this is wonderful news."

"Yes, it is, Mrs. Wylie." She looks at the doctor and says, "I have appointments around 11:00 a.m. Could you come at 10:30 a.m.?"

"I believe we can."

"I'll see you then. Thank you, Roger." She rises and extends her hand to shake, as if to indicate an agreement.

"For an answered prayer, may I hug you instead?" he asks.

"You can." Katharine hugs Roger.

He passes his wife, whom he winks at, and then moves out the door to attend to his patient.

Mrs. Wylie moves in to get a hug and says, "Katharine, you have no idea how much this is going to assist Ian—and Roger, too. I also sense it allows you to make a decision you need to make."

Katharine smiles and says, "Yes, it does."

With a lightness in her step, Katharine follows Mrs. Wylie down the hall and out the front door, where she's greeted with the brilliant light of the morning. There's a soft breeze on her face. She takes a moment to breathe. "Thank you, Father." She skips down the steps. Untethering Sebastian, she climbs aboard, and with a movement of the reins on his neck, she guides him to head home, where she can give the good news to everyone.

When Katharine returns from meeting with Dr. Wylie, Mrs. Florence has morning tea in her mother's receiving room. She enters, removes her cloak, sits in the chair, and begins to pour herself a cup of tea. She then sits back and sighs. Mrs. Florence looks at Mrs. Bennett, who looks at Lois, who looks at Mrs. Florence, and then finally, Mrs. Bennett says, "Come now, Katie, tell us what has happened."

She takes another sip of tea, leans forward, and begins her report. "Dr. Wylie can't take care of my patients."

"Oh dear," says Mrs. Florence.

"However, under Dr. Wylie's guidance, his nephew Ian will do it instead."

"That's wonderful, love."

She talks about how going over to speak with Dr. Wylie was also an answered prayer for him. It's a win-win for everyone.

Mrs. Bennett takes a sip, winks at her daughter, and says, "Doors are opening for you, my dear."

"Yes, they are, Mother. Ian and Roger will be here tomorrow at about 10:30 to attend to some patients with me. This will allow me to see how he interacts and assure the people they're in good hands."

"I'm sensing then, Ms. Katharine, that you have decided."

"I think so, Lois. I believe God has prepared a way for me to entrust my patients to someone who will do the type of job I do. I'll wait until after tomorrow, when I can see for myself how Ian deals with two of my most 'difficult' patients. Then I'll know for sure."

"My goodness, child, if you want him to take the job, start easy on him."

"Mrs. Theo and Mr. McCloud are the two; if he can win them over, the rest of the people in Brookville will follow suit. Ian can handle Mr. McCloud, but Mrs. Theo will be his biggest hurdle."

"We will see," says Mrs. Florence.

"In the meantime, ladies, I suggest you do extra praying tonight; it never hurts."

"Amen, Ms. Katharine, Amen," says Lois.

They all continue to sip their tea and hope Ian is prepared for what awaits him tomorrow.

FIVE

KATHARINE IS WORKING on patient notes in her office when Roger and Ian arrive the following day. Lois escorts them to the office.

"Katharine, this is my nephew, Ian. Ian, this is Ms. Katharine."

"I've heard so much about you. A pleasure." He takes her hand and shakes it.

She turns, winks at Dr. Wylie, and says, "You can't believe everything you hear, Ian."

"Even if it's all good?" says Ian.

"Well, in that case, maybe. Before we start, let me show you around. This is the office, and here's an exam room. For the most part, people come here to be seen. You're more than welcome to use it in my absence. This will allow the patients at least a sense of familiarity. It's off the back of the house, so you can access it from the stable, where you can keep your mount.

"There are some patients I tend to visit with. Today we'll see two. If you follow me, I'll show you both to the stable." She moves to the cloak rack to retrieve her cloak and bag and moves out the door. "Dr. W—I mean, Roger—can you get the door, please?"

"Certainly, my dear."

She leads the way out, and the two doctors follow behind. It's a short distance to the stable where Sebastian is kept. Katharine indicates that while she's away, Ian is welcome to Sebastian. He's a faithful companion and familiar with the places she goes. "I'll meet you up at the front at your buggy, and we can be on our way."

Katharine checks the saddle, mounts Sebastian, and leads him toward Roger and Ian, who are waiting in their buggy at the front of the cottage.

It takes about twenty minutes to arrive at the McCloud farm. Katharine gives them a little background on the patient on their way there. Mr. McCloud has a bad leg. It was severely damaged in a farming accident. He's fifty years of age and a widower. He can't work the farm anymore, so his son has taken over. He lives in the farmhouse with his son, daughter-in-law, and two grandchildren.

Ian gets out of the buggy to assist Katharine in tethering her horse and getting down. When he arrives at her side, she's already down and has the horse tied. He looks at her, and she responds, "I'm sorry. I'm not used to a helping hand."

"Quite all right, Ms. Katharine. Shall we?" He motions toward the house.

Katharine knocks on the door, and Mr. McCloud's daughter-in-law greets them.

"Good morning, Ms. Katharine."

"Good morning, Evelyn. How are you today?"

"Very well, thank you." She sees the two men with Katharine.

"Evelyn, I want you to meet Dr. Roger and Ian Wylie. I need to deal with a family matter that will take me to Scotland for a year. Ian here," she says, turning to him, "is going to be taking over the patients in the area, and his uncle will be mentoring him in my absence. We wanted to see Mr. McCloud, if it was convenient."

"Welcome, Dr. Wylie." She nods to them both. "You know where to find him, Ms. Katharine. Excuse me, I must tend to something on the stove. Just yell if you need anything."

"This way, gentleman." Katharine leads them down the short hall to the left as they enter a parlour room. Mr. McCloud sits in his rocking chair, looking out over the fields.

"Good morning, Mr. McCloud. How are you on this bright and sunny day?"

"Bored and stiff," he growls as he looks toward Katharine.

"Did you go for your walk this morning?"

"No, I did not. Who are these two?"

"Why, where are my manners? Mr. McCloud, this is Dr. Roger and Ian Wylie."

"Why are they here?"

Ian moves to take Mr. McCloud's hand to say hello, but Mr. McCloud gives an icy stare and folds his hands to show that he's not going to extend his hand to greet the visitor. Ian goes to take his hand back, and he sees the interesting chess set on the table beside the rocking chair in front of the window.

"Mr. McCloud, do you play chess?"

"So what if I do, sonny? What is it to you?"

"I'm a good player myself. My Uncle Cole taught me everything I know; this set is unique. May I ask where you got it from?"

"I made it. With my own two hands," he says as he lifts his hands and shows them.

"May I?" says Ian as he puts his bag down and moves to the chair opposite Mr. McCloud. He picks up a pawn and the knight and notices the board.

"Did you make the board as well, sir?"

"Yes, I did. I need something to keep me busy during the day. The pieces and the board are all handmade from wood found on the farm."

"Mr. McCloud, this is an exceptional chess set." He looks to his uncle, who moves over to take a look.

"I would agree, Ian. This is an exceptional chess set," says Dr. Wylie.

"Mr. McCloud, have you ever thought about making more chess sets? With this workmanship, you'd fetch an excellent price." Ian looks at his uncle and says, "I bet Uncle Cole would love a set. We never know what to get him for his birthday. He loves to play, and it would be perfect for his games room."

"That is an excellent idea, Ian," responds his uncle.

"What do you say, Mr. McCloud? Do you think you could have a chess set made for me, say, within the next three months?"

"Six months, and yes, I could."

"Very well. Sold."

"You haven't even asked me how much, young man."

"Mr. McCloud, I know good workmanship when I see it. I also see that you're a fair and honest man. I expect the amount to be that as well."

With that comment, Mr. McCloud sits up straighter and seems to have lost his gruff and growl.

Ian explains to Mr. McCloud that he may be unable to work on the farm with his leg, as he gestures out the window, but he can certainly use his hands to make the chess sets to sell. It keeps him busy, uses his talents, and adds to the household.

Katharine is impressed with Ian's down-to-earth approach to the patient. He doesn't consider himself superior or the doctor they must listen to. Instead, he recognizes that one reason for Mr. McCloud's sour disposition is that he doesn't feel he contributes, and his stiffness is due to spending too much time sitting in his rocking chair.

"You know, Mr. McCloud, to help with the stiffness, you could go out and do some walking to strengthen your leg and look for the perfect wood for your chess sets."

Katharine has to cover her mouth with her hands to stop the chuckle that wants to escape. She had suggested he get out and walk to help with the stiffness. Ian gave him the same recommendation but put a different spin on it. Watching Mr. McCloud transform from a cranky old man to someone who now knows he can make a difference is very rewarding. The two continue with their conversation.

Roger turns to Katharine and says, "I believe we just witnessed a checkmate, and not a piece was moved."

"I was thinking the same thing. Ian is very good with Mr. McCloud."

"Very well, Mr. McCloud; I'll return in a few weeks to see how you and my uncle's chess set are doing."

"That sounds like a plan, son. Katharine, I hope you have a safe trip to Scotland."

"How did you know?"

"Small house and voices carry. I heard what you said to Evelyn when you came in. I'll look after Master Ian for you until you return."

They all laugh. Roger says, "In that case, I don't think I will be needed. Good day, Mr. McCloud."

Mr. McCloud gets up to shake both Roger's and Ian's hands. Then he walks to Katharine and hugs her. "Safe passage, my dear, and we look forward to your return. Be sure to write to your mother so she can keep us updated on how you're doing."

"For you, Mr. McCloud, anything."

They take their leave. Roger and Ian climb into the buggy as Katharine untethers and mounts Sebastian. Katharine looks to Ian and says, "You'll find most of your house visits are more of a social time. It allows them to get to know you, and you get to know them. Once you get past the niceties, you can address the issues, as you did with Mr. McCloud. When it's a medical emergency, someone will find you." With that being said, Katharine uses her reins and turns Sebastian's head to lead him toward Mrs. Theo's home.

SIX

IT TAKES ABOUT fifteen minutes to slowly ride from the McCloud farm to Mrs. Theo's home. Again, Katharine informs Roger and Ian about Mrs. Theo during this travel time. She's a widow who loves her plants and flowers. She also likes the attention. "When you arrive, there will always be something. The last time I was there, she complained of sinus congestion."

They're impressed with the landscaping and plants outside as they enter the cottage. A large variety of hostas circle the house. Mrs. Theo is out walking around the plants and checking things out. You can hear her sneezing as they approach.

"Good morning, Mrs. Theo," says Katharine as she waves.

Mrs. Theo waves back and then sneezes into her handkerchief. "Oh dear, not again."

"What seems to be the problem, Mrs. Theo?"

"This constant sneezing and feeling congested. I come out here in the morning, and within minutes I'm hachew, hachew, hachew."

"Oh dear, let's go inside then, shall we?"

"Yes, let's. Once I'm inside, it takes a while, but usually in a few hours I'm back to normal."

"How long has this been happening?" questions Ian.

"Oh, Mrs. Theo, I wanted to introduce you to Dr. Roger and Ian Wylie."

"Nice to meet you. Hachew, hachew, hachew."

"Do you have any allergies you know of, Mrs. Theo?"

"Cats. I'm allergic to cats."

24

"I see," says Ian. "Didn't we see a few cats on our way here?" Ian asks his uncle and Katharine.

"Yes, now that you mention it, we saw several of them," responds Roger.

"Oh, they're from the McCloud neighbouring farm," says Katharine.

"Let me check something out." Ian looks around the hosta bushes before returning to the house. "It would seem the cats use your garden, especially around your hosta bushes, as a litter box. Their fur and dander can accumulate on the large, flat leaves in and around the foliage. Then when you go out to tend to them, it transfers to you and activates your allergies."

Mrs. Theo looks at him as it to say "Who are you" then turns to Katharine as she sneezes again.

"My apologies, Mrs. Theo. I've brought both doctors here to meet with you. I'll be away in Scotland for a year and want you to meet Ian, who will take over in my absence."

"My apologies as well, Mrs. Theo. I should have mentioned something earlier, but I wanted to be sure about what I thought was the culprit in your breathing issues. It's a pleasure to meet you." Ian extends his hand, and she takes it.

"Katharine, would you mind putting the kettle on? We can show Mrs. Theo how to ease her symptoms with a simple bowl of hot water and a towel," asks Ian.

"Yes, of course. We can drape one of the kitchen towels over her," says Katharine.

"Mrs. Theo, I highly recommend that you stay out of the hosta bushes for the next week so that we can be sure this is the case," Ian advises.

Katharine has the bowl set, a kitchen towel, and a chair ready for Mrs. Theo to sit in. She pours a small amount of hot water into the bowl. "Ian, would you like to show Mrs. Theo what we need her to do?"

"Yes. Mrs. Theo, I need you to sit before the bowl."

Mrs. Theo moves over and takes the chair in front of the bowl.

"Now place your head over the bowl about halfway. Excellent. Now take the towel, place it over your head and the bowl, and pull it together at your neck so the hot air doesn't escape." Ian helps her while he provides instructions. "Take a few deep breaths. Good. Let the hot, moist air do its job."

Roger winks at Ian, and Katharine does a little curtsey to say well done. Ian tries to suppress the chuckle inside of him.

"How are you feeling, Mrs. Theo?" asks Katharine.

"Oh my, this is wonderful. How long should I keep doing this?"

"I'd give it no more than five minutes. Uncle Roger, do you have your pocket watch?"

"I do, Ian." He pulls out his pocket watch to time it.

"I'll tell you when to remove the towel, Mrs. Theo."

Once the time is up, Mrs. Theo lifts her head and removes the towel. She takes a deep breath. Her smile of contentment says it all.

"Better?" says Katharine.

"Much better," says Mrs. Theo. "Now, what is this about you going to Scotland?"

"It's a family matter, Mrs. Theo. I couldn't leave without someone I trust taking over, and I wanted to ensure I had your approval regarding my replacement. So what do you think, Mrs. Theo? Does Dr. Ian pass the test?"

"With flying colours, my dear. I will do as you requested, young man. When you return next week, we can go from there."

"As you wish, Mrs. Theo," replies Ian.

They take their leave. Katharine mounts her horse, and Roger and Ian get into the buggy. Roger takes the reins and says, "Those are the two easiest house calls I've ever made. I could get used to this."

Katharine and Ian both laugh. "It's good you came so they could get to know you. I'm sure you both will need to take over for each other now and then through the year."

"Yes, you're quite right, Katharine," says Roger.

"Ian, may I say you did an excellent job with Mr. McCloud and Mrs. Theo. They are the two most influential people in Brookville. For everyone else to accept you, they had to give their blessing. You have it from the mouth of Mrs. Theo—passed with flying colours. When we visit others, they'll already know you've won over these two, so all is good."

"Katharine, you threw me to the wolves on my first day."

"Yes, and you were brilliant in taming those wolves without them even knowing it."

Roger lets out a roar of laughter. "Katharine, I believe Ian will do a good job in your absence. He has the gift of a diplomat and the social grace of a healer."

"Agreed. Gentleman, you've done well this morning. It's almost lunch. Let's return home and see what Mrs. Florence has for us today. Ian, why don't you lead the way."

Ian takes the reins from his uncle. He turns the buggy around and starts down the path to lead them back to the Bennett estate and the cottage he will call his office for the next year.

They arrive back home, and taking her time to enjoy the stillness of the afternoon, Katharine ventures over to the estate house to meet with Walter. As is the routine, Mr. Hynes greets her and informs Katharine that her brother is upstairs in his study. She nods and climbs the semi-spiral stairs leading to Walter's office door. Today, in a bold move, instead of waiting to be let in, she knocks and, as she enters, says, "Good afternoon, Walter."

"Good afternoon, Katharine," says Walter, a bit surprised at her entering without being asked. "From the smile on your face, I can tell you're bringing me good news." He leans back in his chair and looks up and over his glasses.

Katharine doesn't close the door completely but leaves it slightly ajar. She steps over in front of the desk. "I believe it is good news for both of us, Walter. My biggest concern was ensuring someone took over for me while I was away. Under his uncle's mentorship, Dr. Wylie's nephew Ian will handle any medical issues in the community of Brookville for the year. So with that being said, I'm willing to fulfill Mr. Stuart's request to go to Scotland to be the doctor in their family parish."

You can see the joy light up Walter's face.

"However, I do require one thing from you," she says as she lifts her hand and raises her index finger.

"What is it, Katharine?" he asks eagerly as he removes his glasses and puts them on the desk.

"I require at least two more weeks. This will allow me and Dr. Wylie to work together to ensure the community of Brookville is informed of the change, and it will allow me to get medical supplies ready for the travel."

"Consider it done, Katharine." He smacks his hand on the desk. He jumps from his chair, walks around, hugs Katharine, swings her around, and kisses her cheek. "Katharine, thank you so much. You can't begin to know how much this means to me."

"My goodness, Walter!" She laughs as she swings around. "I think I like this brother much more. If my going to Scotland allows you to come out from behind that desk and live more, I know I'm making the right decision."

He releases her with a hearty chuckle. "This calls for a celebration." He goes over to the side table, where a decanter of sherry and glasses sits. "Care to join me, Katharine?"

"Yes, I think I will," she replies as she sits at the desk.

He pours two glasses and carries them over to where Katharine is sitting. He hands Katharine hers and raises his hand. "Here's to new beginnings." They clink their glasses together and drink up. Walter takes his glass, places it on the desk, and then says, "I'll let Ethan Stuart know and make all the arrangements for your travel." He leans against the desk, crosses his legs, and turns his chin up, as if trying to remember something. "I believe we have a shipment going to Dublin in about three weeks. We can have them deliver you to Scotland on their way."

Katharine laughs. She's never seen her brother this relaxed, playful, or animated. She likes what she sees. "You can provide me with the details of when the ship is leaving, and I'll work with that date. It's for a year, so I'll probably need at least two trunks, one for medical supplies and the other for personal. Also, is there any way for you to find out the area of Scotland I'll be going to, or do you already know? Just to have some frame of reference."

"I'll look into that for you. We have some information regarding when the ship was received. Give me a few days, and I'll have someone bring you the details of when the ship is leaving and reference material of the area of Scotland you'll be travelling to." He moves away from his desk and says, "I must send Mr. Stuart a telegram immediately so that he knows."

"Of course, Walter." Katharine rises and puts her glass on the desk. "I'll have Mr. Hynes come up as I let myself out."

"Yes, please do. We'll talk in a few days, all right?"

"Yes." She nods and closes the door behind her. Walter sits behind the desk, pulls up his chair, and puts his glasses back on. Taking pen in hand, he begins to draft a telegram to be sent to Ethan Stuart.

SEVEN

FOOTSTEPS ARE HEARD as they hit each stair leading to the study door. Ethan enters his study to deal with the week's correspondence. He sits and surveys the stack of envelopes and papers on his desk. With a sigh, he pulls his chair back, sits, and opens the right-hand drawer of his desk. Inside is a letter opener. It was inherited with the desk and duties of the Stuart estate. He takes hold of the letter opener, starts at the top of the pile, and works his way down. After reviewing the contents of envelopes and various papers, he puts them into piles. As he opens the letter in his hand, he sees a telegram from Bennett Import & Export Trading Business and begins reading:

> I have found an individual with over thirteen years of medical experience who has agreed to your one-year term. They require at least another two weeks for their replacement, who is taking over in their absence, to get acquainted with the community. They will travel on our *Grand Olympia* cargo ship, heading for Ireland. I anticipate you can expect the doctor to arrive in about a month.

He looks at the date on the telegram. "Darn, why am I only hearing about this now?" He grabs the paper, checks the calendar, and sees that in two weeks, a doctor will be arriving. He gets up from his chair to take the information to Ty. He needs to go into town tomorrow and ensure a telegram is sent to confirm receipt and get an update.

As Ethan walks down the hallway, he sees Mrs. Jones. "Mrs. Jones, I received wonderful news today," he says as he waves the paper. He then picks her up and swings her around. "We have a doctor on the way. He should be here in a few weeks. Can you get the room off the kitchen ready for him?"

"Of course, Laird." She laughs as she smacks his arm. "Next time, young man, how about you keep my feet on the ground and hug me?"

"Yes, Mrs. Jones," he says as he blushes slightly. Mrs. Jones has been with the family since Ethan's parents married. She's been a constant in his life.

"This is wonderful news. Everyone will be so happy," says Mrs. Jones.

"Yes, I believe they will be. When you can, please ask Liam and Tamara to come to my study this evening. I'd like to speak to them directly about this."

"Of course, Laird. I'll inform them myself."

"Thank you, Mrs. Jones." He smiles and continues down the hallway, out the door, and into the stables, where he will find Ty to deliver the news.

Ethan enters the stables and walks to the back, where one of the old stalls has been converted into an office. Ty can be found here if he's not out checking on the tenants, crops, and equipment, or ensure the workers are brought back and forth from town. Ethan knocks on the door panel as he sees Ty filing away papers, his back turned to him.

"Ty, great news!" He waves the paper. "Mr. Bennett has indicated that he was able to find a doctor. He should be arriving soon."

Ty takes the paper from Ethan's hand to read it for himself.

"Tomorrow morning, I'll need you to telegram Mr. Bennett. Confirm we received his telegram. Have him provide us with up-to-date information regarding when the doctor is expected and the cargo ship schedule—the usual information."

Ty has moved to his desk to pick up a pen and write notes on the telegram to execute the instructions. "Of course, Laird. I'll go to the station first thing in the morning when the telegram office opens."

"Excellent," Ethan says as he rubs his hands together. "When you return tomorrow, please come see me immediately. I want to be able to get the word out, so to speak."

"As you wish, Laird."

"Ty, I have a good feeling about this."

"I will reserve my judgement until I meet the good doctor."

Ethan blows on his hands to keep them warm and then nods to Ty. "I'll see you later this evening. Oh, and I've asked Liam and Tamara to meet with us after dinner. I want them to hear the news from me directly."

"Have you told Bonnie?"

"No. If you see her, please ask her to see me in the study. I was still working on the paperwork pile when I found Mr. Bennett's telegram. By the way, do you know who put the telegram on my desk?"

"No, Ethan, I don't."

"Very well. From now on, if any correspondence is brought back, please have whoever has it give it to you, and then you can give it to me. I'll also ensure that Mrs. Jones and Bonnie know that all correspondence must go to you first and then to me."

"Yes, Laird, and speak of the devil, your sister is right behind you."

"I thought you were in your study catching up on paperwork," Bonnie jokes as she hugs him.

"I was. Can you walk with me back to the house? I have something to discuss with you."

"Aye."

As Ethan turns to exit the stable with Bonnie, he sees Mr. Holmes and gives him a nod. Mr. Holmes nods to acknowledge Ethan's presence. "I knew I should have destroyed that telegram instead of burying it in the pile of paperwork on his desk," Mr. Holmes says to himself as he returns to work.

Sitting around the fire in the study that evening, Ty and Ethan catch up on the happenings on the estate, issues to be addressed, and conversations between friends. During their friendly banter, a knock is heard on the study door. "Come in," says Ethan. The door opens, and hesitantly, Liam and Tamara enter.

"Good evening, Laird. Mrs. Jones told us you wanted to speak to us," says Tamara.

"Yes, I do; please come in."

Both walk into the study. Ty gets up to let Tamara sit. She sits in the chair. Liam sits on the arm, and Ty stands slightly behind Ethan's chair. Ethan notices they're both uncomfortable. He tries to put them at ease right away.

"I have great news for you both. Ty will be obtaining the details in the next day or so. I wanted you both to hear the news directly from me. A doctor will be arriving from England shortly."

Liam and Tamara hear an intake of breath and look at each other as if to say "What?"

"I need you both to work with the new doctor. However, if you have any issues, please know that Ty, Bonnie, and I are here to support you. Don't hesitate to come and speak with any of us."

"Yes, Laird," they say in unison.

"Liam, Tamara, you've been doing a wonderful job filling in for Dr. Bell with what little time you had to learn under him. The main purpose of this new doctor is to mentor you both to become more confident and knowledgeable in medical situations. This will allow you both to take over after the year of service is complete."

Now their faces show confusion. Ty says, "I think we should start at the beginning. What Laird is trying to say is that the new doctor is not going to be here permanently. He's coming for only a year. We intend that he will teach and mentor you both to handle all types of medical situations for the community."

Tamara is the first to speak. "I mean, we're grateful for this opportunity, Laird. However, this doctor may not appreciate teaching a woman." She is well aware that Dr. Bell didn't hide his disdain for having to teach Tamara.

"I'll speak to the doctor when he arrives about this. Liam, what about you?"

"I'll have to wait and see, Laird. I don't want to make a judgement call before I've met or dealt with the new doctor."

Ethan looks at Ty and says, "Someone else said almost the exact words, Liam. Wise, very wise of you."

Tamara speaks again. "I'm sure you've already thought of this, Laird, but it may be difficult for an Englishman to be accepted here. It's one thing if he was Scottish, but he—"

"You speak the truth, Tamara. I know it may not be easy. I also believe the community will be more grateful for someone to help with medical issues than they'll be concerned about where they came from. I intend to take you and the doctor around to the tenants to introduce him and let everyone know I have their best interest at heart." Both nod in acknowledgment. "Very well. We'll let you know once we have the details. Remember, this is your home, your people; make the most of the year you have to learn what you can."

They both say, "Yes, Laird," and show themselves out of the study.

"Tamara will do well. Liam must step up if he's serious about medicine. For now, we'll have to wait and see what happens with the new doctor," says Ty as he moves back to the chair. They both stare into the fire and watch the flames rise, trying to reach the sky.

EIGHT

THE TWO WEEKS to get Dr. Ian settled with her community and arrange for travel to Scotland went quickly. Katharine looks up at the *Grand Olympia* anchored at the docks in Whitehaven, where Bennett's Import & Export Trading Business is located. The ship is a full-rigged clipper and can hold up to four hundred tons of cargo and sail at seventeen knots. The journey from Brookville to Whitehaven took about forty-five minutes.

When Katharine and Walter arrive at the dock to get her trunks onto the ship and get situated, she's overwhelmed by the enormous size of the ship. Once the trunks have made their way over the gangway, which is sturdier than it looks, she's taken on a ship tour. The *Grand Olympia* is a cargo ship consisting of three decks. The first is the very bottom. The captain and crew refer to it as the "hold." Here is where the cargo is stored for the trip or, as they say, passage. The depth of the ship is overwhelming. It's strategically arranged to ensure the proper balance of the cargo weight for the ship.

The crew cabins are located on the second deck. Each cabin is a standard-size room. When you exit the cabins, you enter a communal area where tables and chairs are set up. Meals are taken here, and the crew can unwind together after duties. This deck includes the galley and extra rooms for use at the captain's discretion. Then you have the top deck, the working deck. This is where the crew works to get the ship to and from the ports to pick up and deliver their precious cargo. Four huge masts are on the top deck, including the long one out the front of the ship for the sails. In the middle of the top deck, a small platform has been constructed, enclosed for safety from the elements for those working during brutal weather on long-distance expeditions. The wheel to steer the ship is located on the enclosed platform, as is all the necessary equipment used to determine direction.

Katharine tries to listen to what's being said but struggles to keep her balance and not fall due to the ship's movement. "If this is what it's like when anchored, what will it be like when we got out into open waters? It's best not to think about that right now." She smiles politely as the captain continues the tour. He and the crew know who she is but not why they're delivering her to Scotland. Thank goodness her family business only sails cargo ships. They don't deal with travel for passengers and have never considered using the ships for slaves. The company makes a better profit with a crew big enough to get the ship there and back with only cargo. They only have to worry about the crew and cargo, not all the other passengers.

Katharine takes over the two extra rooms on the second deck for this voyage. Depending on the weather, this will be her home for the next five to seven days of travel to Scotland. When Katharine is shown to her room for her stay, she takes a moment to sit on the bed. She feels slightly better with her legs now adjusting to the ship's movement. She notices that although the cabin is tiny, the bed has a mattress, and the room is furnished with linens, a washbasin, and some drawers. The ventilated door opens directly into the common area for eating and socializing. She's surprised at how neat the cabin, and the entire ship, are. She'll have to mention to the captain how impressed she is with its tidiness.

Even sitting on the bed, Katharine begins to feel the ship's movement. It's like a wave. It moves forward but pulls you back just as fast. She stands for a minute to get a feel for it and realizes that standing that way doesn't help her keep her balance. She moves her feet further apart, one in front of the other. When the ship moves forward, she bends her legs slightly and moves her weight to her right leg, and when it pulls back, she moves to her left. It will be a balancing act to learn to move with the ship and not try to stay neutral.

"I might as well see how this works while trying to find my way up to the top deck." She convinces herself to move. She strategically moves to the ship's rocking motion, using the railing along the cabin walls. She attempts to feel the rhythm of the "dance," and the rails up the stairwell from the deck are very helpful in ensuring she gets from one to the other. She emerges from below to meet with her brother and the captain before the ship sets sail. Walter and the captain are in deep conversation as Katharine approaches.

"Ms. Bennett, I hope you'll find your cabin adequate for the short time you'll be with us."

"I'm sure I will, Captain. Thank you. I'd also like to say that I'm impressed by how well this ship is kept. It's neat, and there's a sense of order."

The captain bows to her. "Thank you, Ms. Bennett. A cargo ship needs to run on order. Everything has its place. The crew works in rotation; no person always does the same thing. So everyone works together to ensure the next person is ready for the job. I'll let the crew know."

"The captain tells me that with the good weather ahead, you should arrive in Scotland in about five days," Walter tells Katharine.

"Where will we be landing, Captain?" asks Katharine.

"We'll pass by the larger port where passenger ships dock. We'll go into Talisker Bay, which is an inlet port, and drop you off with some cargo, pick up more from the distillery, and then go off to Ireland."

"The captain has assured me, Katharine, that someone from the Stuart estate will collect you before he leaves port."

"Of course, Mr. Bennett. I have dealt with Ethan Stuart. He's a fair man. I don't doubt that his steward, Ty, will likely be there to meet us."

"Thank you, Captain. I have full confidence you will deliver me safe and sound to Scotland."

He turns slightly to Katharine and then says, "I need to check on the last-minute details before we depart in an hour. Please excuse me."

"Captain, thank you, and safe passage," says Walter as he shakes the captain's hand. The captain then takes his leave.

"Walter, I wanted to ask, did you indicate to Mr. Stuart that it was a woman you had found as a doctor?"

Walter looks at her with a blank face.

"So I can take your look to mean Mr. Stuart has no idea that I, a woman, will be arriving to be the doctor for the next year, does he?"

"Katharine, I'm sorry. I don't think so. You've cared for the Brookville community for so long that it didn't occur to me to tell him I was sending a woman. Oh my, oh my." He puts his hand on his hip, rubs his chin with his other hand, and paces.

"Walter, it's fine; we can't go back on our word. Both of us sensed an urgency in Mr. Stuart's letter. He needs a doctor. It shouldn't matter. The worst that happens is that the captain has to stop and pick me up on the way back. In the meantime, while I'm there, I do what I can. Besides, Walter, it's not like I haven't been down this road before. I already know what to expect."

Walter takes his hand to run it through his hair as he looks to Katharine. "I am truly sorry, my dear. I didn't think. If you need anything, or if it doesn't work out, don't hesitate to send a telegram, and we'll make sure you get back home as soon as possible."

"Walter" — she moves over to take his arm — "it will be fine. I've already fought this battle once. I can do it again."

"Yes, you have, haven't you? All right, so you have everything, do you?"

"Well, no. I had hoped I could have brought Sebastian with me. However, that wasn't feasible, and Ian will need a mount when he visits patients. I can only hope they have as good of a horse for me to use when I'm there."

Walter chuckles. "You were always the one to make sure everything was in order from start to finish, weren't you?"

"Yes, I am."

"Remember when you used to come to play with my soldiers? You'd line them all up so close to each other, row after row, to ensure your lines of defence were always intact."

"It worked, didn't it? You took one look at what you had to fight and marched off for tea."

They both laugh. "You are so right, Katharine. It was a bit intimidating."

They chat for a few more minutes. Katharine assures Walter that she has everything she needs. Her medical instruments and necessities have been stored in the crew deck's extra room.

"I'll write as soon as possible, but I'll have the Stuart family send a telegram to confirm that I arrived safe and sound."

With a hug between brother and sister, Walter takes his leave. He walks down the gangway. When he steps off the dock, it's promptly pulled onto the ship. He turns and waves to Katharine, and she returns the wave.

NINE

THE CREW IS moving about quickly. It's time for the ship to leave port. One of the deckhands indicates that Katharine should move up to the ship's bow to watch as they prepare to take the ship out to sea.

"The bow?"

"My apologies, Ms." He points to the front of the ship. "The bow is what we refer to as the front of the ship. The stern is the back." He then moves his other arm to indicate the back of the ship.

"Bow is the front; stern is the back. I'll try to remember. Thank you, Mr."

"I am called Kennedy, Ms."

"Mr. Kennedy."

"No, Ms., just Kennedy. You'll find that the crew only refer to each other by their last names, except for the captain, who is called Captain."

"Thank you, Kennedy. I'll move up to the bow," she says, moving her arm to the front of the ship.

"Yes, Ms." Kennedy rushes to the stern to work with the other crew members.

She passes the enclosed platform, which she finds out is referred to as the bridge. This is from where the captain directs the ship. It's also where a vital piece of equipment for any ship is located: the binnacle, the stand on which the ship's compass is situated.

As Katharine passes by, the captain looks out the window and says, "Ms. Bennett, you can sit on the bench, which is just up on the port side."

"Port side, Captain?"

"Left side, Ms. Bennett. The right is called the starboard."

"Very well, Captain." And she thought medical terminology was complex.

She moves up to the bench and takes a seat. She turns to see that Walter is still standing on the dock. She waves to him, and he waves back. She notices several men on the pier removing the large ropes anchoring the ship to the dock. For each rope, two men on deck pull it in and secure it into place.

The captain bellows, "Anchor up."

In unison, crew members reply, "Aye, aye, Captain," and start pulling on the rope they hold while another turns a large handle to raise the anchor.

Once the captain sees that it's up enough, he turns to the stern and again bellows, "Bring to back halyard."

"Aye, aye, Captain," is said in unison again as Kennedy and his mates work to hoist the back sail.

Katharine watches this well-choreographed dance. The captain gives the orders, and the crew executes the manoeuvre. She feels the water take control to roll the ship out of port. Then the wind and sails push it into the open waters and on to Scotland.

The view from the bench is breathtaking. She looks back to see that the land is quickly fading. Open blue skies, blue-green waters, and a shining sun are ahead. Katharine tilts her head up to the skies. She closes her eyes and quietly prays for a safe voyage for the ship, crew, and herself. She breathes in, opens her eyes, and keeps in mind that she should move with the ship, so she adjusts how she stands, moving her feet apart with legs bent. She has the next several days to take time for herself and enjoy the soft swaying of the ship. She can enjoy the beautiful view, relax, and catch up on medical journals she wants to read.

She asks one of the crew members if she can return to her cabin, and he gives her the okay. She retrieves her journal and a few books. Navigating on the ship is more complicated than she expected, but as she learns to walk with the movement, she can return to her seat on the bench at the front of the ship to watch as they move closer to her destination.

For the first night of the passage, Katharine sits at the table with everyone, including the captain, to have dinner. She doesn't want to be rude, but she explains to the cook that she's not used to the movement and feels a bit queasy. After checking out a few medical references to see what will help the seasickness, she asks the cook if it would be too much trouble to get a pot of hot water to pour over her ginger for tea, and if she could have some simple oatmeal. The cook considers this a straightforward request and obliges Katharine.

The crew suggest that she try sitting at the dining table in the middle of the ship, where there's less movement. Also, she should try to be up on deck as much as possible for fresh air. They advise her to keep her eyes on land, when there is some, and sit in the stern (back), where the movement is better than up in the bow (front). That may be why she feels the effects today, as that's where she sits most of the time. She's grateful for the advice. Over the next few days, things improve once she starts to take the advice and concentrates on adjusting to the movement.

On the third day, Katharine decides that she needs to get her mind off the constant movement of the ship; she inquires where the medical supplies are kept. Kennedy tells her, "If you need medical assistance, you should talk to the cook; he's the one we go to."

"Thank you, Kennedy; I'll go speak to him."

Katharine rises from the table and moves to the window, from which you can see into the galley and where the crew get their food.

"Cook, so sorry to bother you, but where are your medical supplies kept?"

"Is everything all right, Ms.?" asks Cook. He puts down the spoon he's using to stir his soup, wipes his hands on his apron, and moves over to the window.

"Oh no, I'm doing well, thank you. The crew's advice has been helping greatly. I feel I need to do something, so I thought I could look at your supplies, arrange them, and add to them if possible."

The cook gives her a look that says "What?"

"My apologies; I didn't explain myself well. Back home, I'm the doctor in my community, so I'm used to being busy. Here on the ship, I'm feeling unproductive. By your leave, I'd like to check out the medical supplies you have on hand.

"It's right here, Ms." The cook moves to the wall beside the window, takes down a bag, comes out of the galley door, and hands it to her.

"I'll take a look through it at the table."

She moves back to the table and checks the supplies. Like the ship, they are neat, but some supplies could be topped up.

"Cook, I have some extra supplies I was bringing with me. Would you mind if I added a few things to your kit?"

"No," he shouts back from the galley.

Katharine goes to the cabin where the trunks are kept. She takes out what she can spare and brings it over to fill up the medical kit. She brings it back over for the cook to return to its place.

"Cook, where are the ointments you use to clean wounds?"

He shrugs. "I use water."

"But don't you have rum or beer on board, or even the vinegar?" She points to it.

"Yes, we do; I just don't think to use it."

Kennedy comes rushing down the stairs, yelling, "Cook, we need you up top. Brett has cut his eye. It looks bad."

"Kennedy, remove the pot from the stove to ensure nothing will burn in my absence."

Cook grabs the bag, and Katharine follows them to the top deck. Brett is sitting and holding a rag on his face.

"What have you done, lad?"

"The end of the sail rope caught me."

"Let's have a look."

He removes the rag to show a deep cut over his left eye.

"Cook, may I?" asks Katharine. He steps aside.

Kennedy returns. Katharine looks up at him and asks, "Kennedy, can you please run to the kitchen and grab the vinegar?"

"Ms. Katharine, I need that for meals," inserts the cook.

"I'll only be using a small amount, I promise, Kennedy."

Kennedy looks to the cook, who nods and returns to the kitchen to retrieve the requested item.

Katharine moves to the medical bag and takes out a needle and thread she had added from her supplies.

Now out of breath, Kennedy returns with the bottle of vinegar.

"Do you have some clean rags?"

The crew look at each other.

"Very well." She bends down to tear off a piece of cloth from the bottom of her skirt and then pours a bit of vinegar on it. She cleans the needle and thread and then uses them to close the cut.

"Brett, this is going to sting. I need to stitch the cut up." She takes the cloth and places it on the cut.

You can hear Brett taking a deep breath.

"Oh wow, that stings," he says.

"I did warn you," she says as she uses the cloth to clean around the wound. She threads the needle and turns to Brett. "I need you to stay still. Can you do that for me?"

"Yes, Ms."

Taking the skin on either side of the cut, she pushes it together and meticulously sews it to close the wound. It takes about ten stitches, and for the most part, it's bearable. The start and finish are the worst. Once done, she uses the other end of the rag to pour more vinegar onto it and clean the now-stitched wound and her instruments before returning them to the medical bag.

"I'll put a bandage on it for now. We'll remove it tomorrow when you come to see me to check on it, okay? You'll have a headache, and it might be best if you can do any jobs that require you to sit for the rest of the day."

"Yes, Ms."

Kennedy helps Brett up.

"If you should feel dizzy or nauseous, come get us right away."

"Yes, Ms. I'm good; I just feel stupid that I didn't move quicker."

The cook looks at Katharine and says, "I would have just put a bandage on it and called it a day. Why did you sew it up?"

"Because I could see the bone, so I knew it wouldn't heal unless we gave it a little help. A needle and thread in your kit can help you look after these wounds. It means he doesn't get an infection and possibly lose an eye."

"I'm not good with stitching, Ms."

"If you want, I can show you how the next few evenings after the meal. It's easy. Think of it like tying two pieces of stew meat together."

"I could do that. Very well, Ms. Katharine. I'll try after the evening meal. We must inform the captain of what happened and that Brett is to sit out the day."

"Lead the way, Cook."

After the evening meal, the cook comes to the dining table and sits across from Katharine. He brings with him six pieces of raw meat.

Katharine lifts her eye to him. "I take it that's my evening meal portion tomorrow?"

Cook grins. "Nay, Ms., I think there's enough that these won't be missed."

Katharine and the cook sit at the table for the rest of the evening while the crew watches and is entertained. One wouldn't think threading a needle is hard, but it seems complicated when you're not used to it and have hands that aren't used in delicate ways. Cook is a good student, and by the end of the evening, the stitching to connect the raw meat is done relatively well for his first try. The banter between the crew is filled with laughter and love.

Katharine adds in, "Gentlemen, may I remind you that he's the one who will be using the needle on you."

They laugh.

"You're a quick learner, Cook. I suggest you work with these pieces for a few more nights and get more practice."

Cook nods at her. Katharine then shows Cook how to tie off and cut the thread, and she explains the importance of cleaning the needle and his hands before and after using them on the crew.

A few nights later, Cook can put what he's learned into practice. Kennedy cuts his left hand when securing the sails at the front of the ship. When he comes to Cook to see what he can do, Cook takes a look, and Katharine agrees that a few stitches wouldn't hurt. He sits Kennedy down at the community table and follows what he's been taught. Five stitches later, his cut is cleaned, closed, and bandaged. Katharine observed only. She is very impressed.

"Kennedy, stop using that hand for a day or two. I'll let the captain know."

"Thank you, Cook, Ms. Katharine." He gets up to return to the deck.

"Well done, Cook. Your crew is in excellent hands with you, both as a cook and for medical purposes."

"I have my reasons for ensuring everyone can do their job. If they aren't, guess who has to—me."

"So who does your job as a cook?"

"Whoever I replace. It happened once, Ms., but only once. The crew can only go so long when the food is bad, and I mean bad."

"So you're telling me you heal them through food as much as tending to their physical needs."

"Yes. We all work hard on this ship. We can do that because we have good meals to nourish us. A good meal makes you feel good and fuels the body to do its work."

"Cook, you are a wise man."

Cook rises from the table. "Thank you, Ms. Katharine. Years of experience. Excuse me, I must see the captain about Kennedy."

"Of course. May I return those items to the medical kit you have in the kitchen?"

"Please. I'll be back to check on lunch once I've talked with the captain."

He nods to her and takes the stairs two at a time. Katharine picks up all the items, cleans them, and returns them to the medical kit, ready for when they'll need to be used again. In a few short days, Katharine has gained the respect of both the crew and the captain. She has taken their advice regarding getting her "water" legs and is understanding all the ship jargon they use. She, in turn, has shown them that she's a good doctor and teacher. The cook has been learning new things from her and putting them into practice to help the crew. It has helped pass the time on the voyage and takes her mind off where she is going.

TEN

"MS. BENNETT!" SHOUTS the captain.

Katharine looks up from her book under the cover of her bonnet.

"We're about two hours out. Looking to your starboard side, you can see where we'll be coming into port."

Katharine looks up to see the clear blue sky with its fluffy white clouds moving ever so gently as they pass over what looked like peaks. She moves forward and can see the outline of what looks like mountains. Instead of being covered in white, they look like a very dark green. The peaks and valleys are also noticeable, and she notices the colour variation on each mountain. The rock and greenery move fluidly together, almost as if they're one but still separate.

The ocean today is calm, and when she looks down, she sees a distinct line of colour change; it goes from light blue by the ship to a darker blue and then to an almost blue-green closer to the land. Katharine takes a moment to breathe in the fresh air. There's something about it; it reminds her of something. But what is it? She sits for a few more minutes to enjoy the ship's movement and see the landscape come into better focus.

She rises and turns. "Thank you, Captain. I'll go and make sure everything is ready for transport off the ship and then come back up so I can watch as we enter the port."

The captain nods to her as he continues to look ahead and give orders to the crew.

Katharine already had everything done before she went up earlier, but now she double-checks to ensure she has everything and that the cabins she used are neat, tidy, and clean. She secures the locks on the trunks and dons her cloak. As she does so, she feels she should also ensure she has her medical bag with her. She unlocks the trunk with the medical supplies where her bag is on top, takes it out, and then relocks it. She places the medical bag with her carry-on, which contains a change of clothes. With a quick sweep of her cabin and the other one, she turns and heads up to the top deck to watch the show of getting the ship into port.

Katharine sits where she was before to watch as the ship is brought into port. Just as when they left port, it's a well-rehearsed dance between the water, ship, and crew. They work together to get the ship safely into port, tied off, and anchored. Only then will she be able to leave the ship along with some of the cargo.

The captain leaves the wheelhouse once the orders are heard that the ship has been secured. He approaches Katharine and says, "Ms. Bennett, thank you again for assisting in the medical attention my crew needed. Both Kennedy and Brett are healing well."

"It was my pleasure, Captain. Cook did a good job stitching up Kennedy. I hope teaching him how to sew up cuts will help everyone out. In that regard, Captain, I apologize if I overstepped my bounds. I didn't speak to you before I took it upon myself to add to the medical bag or, for that matter, show the cook some new techniques."

The captain grins. "I'll overlook it this time, Ms. Bennett." He winks at her. "I think Cook will enjoy stitching up a few of the crew."

"Good. I want to be sure everyone stays healthy so that in a year, when you come back to bring me home, the crew can hear about my adventures on the wild Island of Skye, Scotland."

The captain bows. "As you wish, Ms. Bennett. I'll be down on the dock waiting for Mr. Stuart's man, Ty."

"I believe Kennedy and Brett are getting my trunks. I'll wait for them here." Katharine stands, stretches, and then moves down near the gangway.

Before she'd left England, the information given to her indicated that the Stuart family's parish was on the Isle of Skye. It's an independent island of Scotland but still considered part of the country. From Walter's information, the estate is about a forty-to-sixty-minute ride from the shipbuilding yard, which takes up a large part of the port where they'll land. She takes a glance from where she stands on the deck. There is a hustle and bustle all around her. It's not chaotic like in the city, but it's still busy and seems so organized. It's like when the captain and crew work as a team to get the ship out and into the port. Everyone is working to accomplish something. It's well-organized and timed. Katharine takes a minute to close her eyes and breathe in the fresh salt air. She feels the breeze upon her face and is taken back to the dream she had months ago, the day Poppy gave birth to her son, Arthur.

"What were you trying to tell me, Lord?" she says to herself as she continues taking in the salt air, the breeze on her face, and the sounds around her.

ELEVEN

THE WAGON DRIVEN by Liam arrives at the dock, and Ty immediately sees the name *The Grand Olympia* painted on the front of the ship as it sways against the pier.

"The ship has already docked." Ty climbs down from his seat beside Liam. "Let me talk to the captain, and then I'll return for you, Liam."

"Yes, Mr. Ty." Liam puts the brake on the wagon and eases up on the reins to give the horses some allowance to move. Ty moves down the pier, arriving at the gangway leading off the ship. It takes a few minutes, but then a man emerges from the ship and starts down the gangway.

Ty recognizes the man. He waves and shouts, "Good morning, Captain."

"Good morning, Mr. Ty," he replies as he reaches the end of the gangway in front of Ty.

"Aye, it's good to see you again, sir," says Ty, extending his hand to shake with the captain.

"It's been a while since we were last in port, Mr. Ty. If I think of it, it was to pick this beauty up."

"Yes, I believe that's correct. How is she holding up?"

"She's a very reliable ship, Mr. Ty. It's a privilege and honour to command her."

"I'll let Mr. Stuart know, Captain. He'll be pleased to hear good reports about how the ships are handling. But I'm here for a different reason."

"Oh yes, the young doctor. She's assisting the crew in bringing up the trunks containing medical equipment and supplies."

"She? I'm sorry, Captain, I must have heard wrong. Did you say 'she,' as in a—" He's not able to finish, as he sees two crew members carrying a trunk, and a lovely young lady walking beside it.

"We were lucky she was on board with us. She had to stitch up Brett there, and she trained our cook how to do the same, and he worked on Kennedy. They're both healing well. Ms. Bennett, please come meet Mr. Ty; he's the steward from the Stuart estate."

Katharine is standing on the ship's top deck, just off the gangway. She waves to acknowledge that she heard the captain. She waits for Brett and Kennedy to take the second trunk down, and then she follows behind. The captain extends his hand to help her off the gangway. She steps down onto the dock. She's now on dry land, and her legs feel different. She's had to adapt to the ship's movement for the past five days, and now she must regain her land legs. As she orients herself on the pier, she looks up to Ty and says, "Good afternoon, Mr. Ty. It is a pleasure to meet you." She extends her hand to shake his. Ty takes it but still has not spoken; he's been thrown off and has not yet righted himself.

"Kennedy, Brett, thank you for taking such good care in carrying the trunk off the ship."

"Our pleasure, Ms.," says Kennedy. "It may take you a few days to get your land legs."

"Thank you, Kennedy. I was thinking that. It feels different standing here on the dock."

"Wait until you get on land. The dock here is still built to move with the movement of the water."

"Oh yes, I see what you mean," she says as she looks down. "I look forward to seeing you both in a year, and try not to keep Cook busy with stitching."

"We'll try, Ms. Good day," both say, tipping their hats and hurrying back up the gangway to continue their duties.

Katharine's attention is turned back to Ty. He looks at Katharine and opens his mouth to speak, but nothing comes out. While she'd been interacting with the crew, he'd seen how naturally graceful, kind, and beautiful this young woman is.

Before he can speak, Katharine says, "May I call you Ty, or is it Mr.?"

"No, Ty is fine; thank you, Ms. Bennett."

"Ty, if we're going to be on a first-name basis, then you must call me Katharine. From the look on your face, I can see you weren't expecting a woman. My brother and I didn't try to deceive Mr. Stuart. You see, back in Brookville, I was the doctor in our area for well over thirteen years. It didn't come to our minds until I was on the ship, and we both realized—"

Ty puts up his hand in a gentle manner to interrupt. "Ms. Katharine, I can assure you, I had a mother and sister who are both healers. There's not a woman on this island who hasn't had to deal with sickness in one way or another, and they're the ones who deal with most, if not all, of the births. I, for one, don't care. But I should warn you—there will be others who don't have the same opinion as I do. I won't lie. You weren't what I was expecting. Please accept my apologies if I seemed rude in not responding to you, but for the lack of better words, you have, no pun intended, blown the wind out of my sails." Ty winks at her.

Katharine smiles and responds, "Ty, you and I will get along wonderfully. It's refreshing to meet someone who speaks honestly and directly."

Ty moves his arm to point toward the end of the dock. "The wagon is this way. If you come with me, we'll load you and the trunks into the wagon and be on our way."

"Lead the way, Ty."

He offers his arm to help guide her off the dock. She takes it, as her legs don't feel very sturdy.

Liam, who had stayed with the wagon as instructed, is curious about what's happening down the dock. He can see but is too far away to hear anything. Mr. Ty is now approaching him with a young lady on his arm.

"I wonder if the new doctor has a wife and she has accompanied him," he says. "Did we know there would be two coming?"

"Liam, this is Dr. Bennett."

"Ms. Katharine is good enough. Nice to meet you, Liam."

"Ms. Katharine." This is all he can get out as he nods.

"Ms. Katharine, Liam and I will get the trunks off the dock and into the wagon. May I suggest you sit on the benches along the waterway. I'll come get you when we're ready."

"Thank you, Ty. I'll walk around to get my land legs back, but I'll stay near the benches so we can see each other."

"Aye, as you wish, Ms. Katharine."

Katharine walks off the dock, and Ty moves beside Liam to take the reins.

"Mr. Ty, what?"

"Yes, Liam, our doctor is a woman."

"But I thought ... we all assumed it was a he."

"Yes, we did. In any event, she's here now. We'll retrieve the trunks and return to the estate."

Ty manoeuvres the wagon back down to the end of the dock. Then he and Liam collect the two trunks from the pier and secure them in the back of the wagon. Katharine is standing by the bench as they're about to pull the wagon away from the dock.

"Ms. Katharine, you can sit up here with Liam."

"There's no need for that, Ty. I can sit in the back of the wagon with the trunks on this bench."

"Are you sure?"

"I'm quite sure, Ty. Can a telegram be sent to my brother, Walter, before we leave, just to let him know I've arrived in Scotland safely?"

"I think we can do that, Ms. Katharine."

"Very well then, Ty. How long of a drive is it to the estate?" she asks as Ty assists her up and into the back of the wagon. She takes her seat at the end of the bench. There's plenty of room for her. It would seem this wagon has been constructed for several people to sit along this bench and the one on the other side.

"It usually only takes about forty-five minutes, Ms. Katharine."

"I look forward to enjoying the ride."

Ty nods to her. He closes the wagon gate and climbs up beside Liam. After a slap of the reins on the horse's back, the wagon lunges forward. For a minute, Katharine thinks she's back on the ship, the way it moves, but the feeling is very different. Katharine looks back to take one last look at the ship that has delivered her to the Island of Skye, Scotland. She closes her eyes to calm herself, takes a deep breath, makes a silent prayer, and then watches as they move away from the port. They take a road that leads them to the telegram office. They stop long enough for Ty to go inside, have the telegram sent, and return to the wagon. Then it's out of the city and they move from the urban to the rural area into the country toward the Stuart estate.

TWELVE

THE EARLY EVENING is beginning when the wagon pulls up to the Stuart home. Standing to greet them is a man and woman with an older lady and a small boy. Ty jumps off the wagon, moves back to open the gate, and helps Katharine down. She slightly stumbles when she touches the ground, and Ty has to catch her.

"Ms. Katharine."

"I don't seem to have land legs yet, Mr. Ty."

"Aye."

Once she feels more secure standing, she approaches the group waiting to greet her. The bewilderment on all the adult faces awaiting her is very noticeable.

Ty says, "Laird, may I present Ms. Bennett to you."

"Good evening, sir. It's very nice to meet you. My brother, Walter, speaks very highly of you," says Katharine as she extends her hand to Ethan to greet him.

"Your brother? What kind of joke is this? He said he was sending a doctor."

"I am a doctor, Mr. Stuart. Perhaps if we can go inside, we can discuss this further."

Katharine had prepared herself for this. It was always the way. How could a woman be a doctor? Ethan Stuart is a dominating figure. He has jet-black hair and is clean-shaven. This says that he's a businessman first, yet his build says he isn't afraid of manual labour. What stands out to her, even as they were approaching, are his eyes. They're so piercing—not frightening, but beautiful. They say the eyes are the windows to the soul of a person. In Mr. Stuart's case, he may be rough on the outside, but he's gentle and kind on the inside.

She has no sooner finished her own internal assessment of Mr. Stuart when a lone horseman comes riding up.

"Laird, Laird, Mr. Randall sent me. Mrs. Randall is in labour, and she requires medical assistance."

Liam moves quickly. "I'll get Tamara." He jumps down and runs into the house.

Katharine picks up her skirt, turns around, and says, "Ty, can we take the wagon to the Randall home?"

"Yes, why?"

"I think we may need it, and the trunk with the medical supplies is in it. There's no point in taking them off the wagon."

Liam returns with Tamara behind him.

"Everyone into the wagon," orders Katharine.

Liam takes the reins, Ty moves up beside him, and Katharine and Tamara climb into the back of the wagon and sit on either side of the trunks. Just before the wagon begins to move, Ethan comes up, closes the gate on the back of the wagon, and then hops in and sits on the wagon's floor.

Ty turns around and nods to Ethan.

"Let's go, Liam," says Ethan.

Liam steers the horses in the necessary direction, and the rider follows behind.

Katharine introduces herself to Tamara, who gives her the same look she's been seeing all day. She smiles and leans back to say a quiet prayer and calm herself, all the while feeling the presence of Ethan's eyes upon her, which isn't giving her a good feeling.

It's a bumpy ride to the Randall house. Once they arrive, Liam hands the reins to Ty, who stays with the wagon. Liam and Tamara leave the wagon with Katharine, who has her medical bag. Ethan follows behind. Tamara leads them into the Randall home.

"You're here. Good," says Mr. Randall. "And who might you be?" he asks Katharine directly.

"I'm the doctor, Mr. Randall." She extends her hand to shake his. It seems like forever, but it's only a few moments. He looks her up and down, and the anger in his face is apparent when he hears her English accent.

"I will have no English in my house. Get out. You are not welcome."

"Mr. Randall, I understand your apprehension." A scream is heard from the bedroom. "Your wife needs medical assistance to bring your child into this world. It shouldn't matter what or who I am, but I have the experience of being a midwife to assist her. Liam and Tamara from the Stuart estate are also here. I ask you to allow us to be of service, sir."

Another scream is heard from the bedroom. Katharine spots the three young children huddled together on the stairs, terror in their eyes from their mother's screams.

"Mr. Randall, I have a call to help those in need; your wife is in need. So unless you intend to physically remove me from your house, I suggest you stand aside and let us tend to your wife and child."

"Tend to her," Mr. Randall orders.

She looks at Liam and Tamara. "I need you to find fresh, clean water and rags or towels. Mr. Randall, is this fresh water?" He looks at her. She checks it and determines it will work. She removes her cloak, opens her bag, and begins the routine.

She sees Liam and Tamara still standing there. "You need to get the water and rags now, please. Once you have them, Liam, I'll ask you to please put a pot on to heat up. Tamara, you will wash and clean before you come in." She sees that Tamara has on a dirty apron. "You'll need to remove that dirty apron first. Liam, you're welcome to attend as well, but you'll need to do the same. Remove any of your outside clothes and wash up."

She turns to the basin and begins her routine. She takes her bag and moves to the bedroom. Liam and Tamara do as they're told. Tamara goes into the bedroom to be of assistance. Liam stays out to make sure there's warm water and clean rags. Mr. Randall returns to his chair by the fire, and Ethan sits at the table. The three children Katharine had seen go unnoticed by the others until Ethan hears a baby cry.

Mr. Randall bellows, "Charlotte, quiet your sister."

Ethan notices the young child rise and go upstairs, soon returning with a babe in her hands. She sits on the stairs with her other siblings, rocking the babe. It seems like hours until they hear another crying baby. Tamara comes out to get the warm water and rags and returns to the bedroom. About sixty minutes later, Tamara and Katharine emerge from the bedroom. Tamara goes to Liam, and they both work to complete the instructions provided by Katharine. Katharine moves to stand in front of the fire in the direct line of Mr. Randall's chair. During the birth, Katharine noticed several things that concerned her.

"Congratulations, your son and wife are doing well, Mr. Randall," speaks Katharine as she wipes her hands with a clean rag and looks up to the children to let them know all is well.

He beams with pride.

"Mr. Randall, are you aware that your wife has a heart condition?"

"Heart condition? How could she have a heart condition?" he responds as he continues to rock in his chair as though he has no care in the world.

Katharine stays calm. Talk about a stupid question. Inside, she wants to roar like a lion, but she must be as sweet as honey to deal with Mr. Randall. "Your wife lives and breathes, sir. As such, she would require a heart. Therefore, it's very possible she could have a heart condition."

Liam and Tamara stand in the kitchen looking at each other, as if to say, "I can't believe she just said that." They move quickly to gather all the dirty rags and clothes to take outside. Sitting at the table behind Mr. Randall, Ethan is having a tough time containing a smirk of amusement, as he finds Katharine's swift comeback entertaining.

Katharine takes a deep, silent breath before she begins. "I'll make this as simple as possible for you, Mr. Randall. Your wife has a weak heart. The added stress of carrying a child, delivery, and caring for the newborn as well as the other children will weaken it even more."

You could hear a pin drop. She took advantage of Mr. Randall having nothing to say to her. "Have you not noticed that she's tired most, if not all, of the time? She needs to catch her breath, and I would bet the farm, please excuse the pun, that she is constantly cold."

Ethan raises his right hand, making it look like he's coughing while trying to hide the chuckle that comes out.

"Well, I thought it was just due to the day-to-day stuff she had to do," responds Mr. Randall as he makes a sweeping gesture with his hand.

Katharine's frustration has hit its limit. She moves to place both her hands on her waist. She tilts her head to the left slightly and looks directly at Ethan to signal him to please help her out, before she looks back to Mr. Randall. "Sir"—she speaks in a controlled voice, having had years of experience dealing with his type, but her patience has been stretched very thin with the long travel—"your wife cannot look after herself, you, four other children, and the newborn and do her day-to-day stuff."

Before he can open his mouth to respond, she puts up her hand to stop him mid-sentence.

Katharine looks over Mr. Randall's shoulder and says, "Mr. Stuart, do you have room back at the estate for the Randall children to spend at least a week while Mrs. Randall rests and recuperates?"

"I'm sure we can find room," Ethan says, trying not to sound like he's enjoying this show.

"Now wait just one minute, young lady. You have no right to come into my house and start giving orders."

Katharine smiles. In a very polite voice, her hands move in front of her. She says, "My apologies, Mr. Randall. Were you intending to stay home, look after your wife, your newborn, these four, and yourself for the next week?"

There's no response. Ethan can barely contain himself and moves to the door to exit the house. Mr. Randall looks at her, turns to Ethan, and then looks back at

Katharine, who has folded her arms across her chest and raised her eyebrows, waiting for him to respond.

Ethan reaches the door, opens it, and leaves. He says, "I will ensure Ty has the wagon ready for the children, Ms. Bennett." He nods at her and looks at Tamara and Liam, who have left the cottage with their Laird.

As Mr. Randall hasn't responded, she says, "Well, Mr. Randall?"

"No, I have to work at the shipyard, miss."

"I thought you might. I was trying to serve you and your wife in having the children come to the estate. They can be looked after by myself or others while your wife recuperates, and you can continue to work."

"Only for a week, Ms. Bennett."

"Only for a week, Mr. Randall." She nods. "Children, please grab your coats and meet Mr. Stuart, Liam, and Tamara at the wagon."

"Father," says the oldest boy.

"Do as you're told, lad."

He and the others climb the stairs, grab their coats, and help each other get them on. Katharine opens the door for them and calls Liam and Tamara to help the children into the night.

Katharine will keep the children at the estate as long as possible so that Mrs. Randall can regain strength. She has a week to convince both of them to take it week by week. Mrs. Randall will need at least three weeks. Katharine busies herself doing her usual cleaning routine and puts on her cloak. Before she leaves, she pops into the bedroom to say good night to Mrs. Randall and checks on them both. She assures Mrs. Randall that the children will be well taken care of and that she'll be back tomorrow to check on her and the new babe.

Before she opens the door to exit the house, she closes her eyes and says a quiet prayer. It feels just like it did almost thirteen years ago. She had to prove herself to the community in Brookville. It took her that long with her people to get where she is. Tonight, necessity took over pride and prejudice. It may be a long year if this is what it will be like every time. With the bag in hand, she turns the doorknob, and a wisp of salty air hits her. She sees the children in the back of the wagon, who are frightened and uneasy. Lifting her cloak and skirt, she pulls the door behind her and moves toward the wagon.

Ethan extends his hand to help Katharine into the back of the wagon. She moves over beside one of the young Randall children, who's holding a sleeping sibling. She takes the sleeping child in her arms and sits on the bench. Ethan hops into the back of the wagon and sits on the floor again. Ty looks back to be sure everyone is ready to go. Ethan and Katharine nod to Ty at the same time. He acknowledges the signal, makes the clicking sound, and gently moves the reins to let the horses know it's time to move and return to the estate.

Katharine introduces herself to help settle the older children, who are looking fearful.

"Good evening, children. My name is Katharine. You can call me Ms. Katharine. Your father agreed that it would be best if you came to stay at the estate for a while to allow your mother to recover from delivering your brother."

"We're not in trouble then, Ms. Katharine?"

"No, you're not, child." She places her hand on the cheek of the boy she took for the youngest. "It's to help your mother recover, that's all."

The boy nods to Katharine and pulls his other sibling to his side.

Katharine turns to see that Ethan has been observing her. She moves her eyes from his unsettling stare as she rests her chin on the head of the sleeping child in her arms. She would close her own eyes, too, but the rhythm of the wagon may put her to sleep, just like the one in her arms. Instead, she silently watches the house disappear behind them into the night and concentrates on keeping the child in her arms there.

The Randall children fall asleep on the ride back to the estate. Katharine is barely awake herself. Exhaustion has overtaken her from her travels, attending a difficult birth, and handling an even more difficult Mr. Randall. She soon sees the older lady who was out to greet them earlier.

"Mrs. Jones, the Randall children will be our guest for the next week," directs Ethan.

"Aye, Laird. We can put them in with William for now. Bring them in. I'll go find more blankets."

Ethan and Ty carry them into the house and place them in the room where William is sleeping, as Mrs. Jones suggested.

"Is there some place where we can clean up from the night?" asks Katharine.

"Follow me," says Tamara.

They follow Ethan and Ty as they take in the last Randall children. Tamara shows Katharine to the back room, where anyone coming from the stables or farm washes before entering the kitchen.

"This will do," Katharine says. She shows and explains to Liam and Tamara her procedure to ensure the safety of her patients and her own home. Even though they're exhausted from the evening's events, this must be done. She starts by removing her cloak and hanging it on a hook. She then places her medical bag on the floor, underneath her cloak, to deal with in the morning when she can get to the supplies. She washes up and then has Liam and Tamara do what she has done.

"Good night, Ms. Katharine," says Liam.

"Good night."

Liam and Tamara leave the back room to head for their rooms. On nights when they're called out, they have rooms at the estate.

Ty passes Katharine as he leaves the house to take the wagon and horses back to the stable.

"Katharine, your trunks have been put in your room. Mrs. Jones will get to you in a few minutes. She's just finishing up with the children."

"Thank you, Ty. Good night."

He nods and heads to the wagon.

Mrs. Jones comes to get Katharine. "Ms., follow me; I'll show you to your room."

"Yes, thank you."

She's led through the kitchen, and her room is just off to the right.

"Good night, Ms. We'll see you in the morning." And off she goes.

Katharine steps into her room. Her trunks have been placed at the foot of the bed. She moves in, closes the door, and looks around. *So this is to be my room for next year*. She sighs and moves to sit on the bed. The events of the day have finally taken their toll. Her head finds the pillow, and sleep overtakes her.

The wind is blowing, and waves are crashing and knocking. What? Her automatic response is to say, "What is it, Lois?" She opens her eyes to orient herself. This is different from her room; again, there's a knock at her door. She gets up to open the door.

"Good morning, Ms. Bennett. I'm Mrs. Jones, the cook. You were asking for Lois?"

"My apologies, Mrs. Jones. Back home, our housekeeper's daughter, Lois, was the one who would get me for medical emergencies; when I heard the knock, I—"

"Aye, you thought Lois was back home waking you. Thought you might like something to start your day." Mrs. Jones, a stout woman with a warm smile, offers a tray with tea and freshly baked biscuits with butter and jams.

"My, that smells delightful, Mrs. Jones." Katharine moves to take the tray from her. "This is unnecessary, Mrs. Jones, and please call me Katharine." She sees the look on Mrs. Jones's face. "Or Ms. Katharine, if you would prefer."

"Yes, Ms. Katharine will be lovely. I want to apologize for last night when you arrived. I was shocked to see you arrive. It's just, you know, that we were told a doctor was coming. We assumed it was a man, so you, well—"

"Mrs. Jones, no need to explain."

"But after what Laird and Mr. Ty said of you last night, I think you'll do well here. How is the room?"

"I don't know, Mrs. Jones. I sat down and then fell asleep. I haven't had a chance to truly look around. I'm sure that once the trunk containing medical supplies goes elsewhere, it will be very spacious."

"You'll need to speak to Ms. Bonnie regarding where the trunk will go. I'll leave you to your breakfast, Ms. Katharine. The Randall children are in the kitchen having theirs."

"Oh, in that case, can I bring this out there and enjoy this with them?"

"Of course."

Katharine moves to take the tray, not realizing she's still in the same clothes she arrived in yesterday. "Oh dear, I was so tired I fell asleep in the clothes I arrived in. If you don't mind, I'll be there in but a minute, and you can show me the way to the kitchen. Last night was so dark when we came in, I didn't see where I was going."

Mrs. Jones backs out and tells her she'll be outside the door. Katharine quickly opens her trunk, takes out the first-day dress she finds, and strips off the one she's had on for more than a day. She twists her hair and takes cold water to wash her face and hands. She opens the door and says, "Lead the way, Mrs. Jones; I'll follow." She grabs the tray and turns to leave the room.

Mrs. Jones is taken aback; she realizes that this isn't someone who will expect to be catered to. A smile comes across her face. One less thing for her to worry about. This puts Katharine in a positive light with Mrs. Jones right away, and since she's the person who runs the house, that's a good thing. Katharine follows Mrs. Jones into the kitchen. It's large and homey. There's a little nook off the side, like at her house, but no window.

The three older children sit and eat breakfast while Tamara feeds the youngest. Katharine places her tray on one of the prep tables in the middle of the kitchen. She pours a cup of tea, takes the biscuit and butter, and moves to the table with the children.

"Good morning, children."

"Good morning," is spoken back in a choir of voices.

"We didn't have the opportunity to be properly introduced last night. You know my name. With whom do I have the pleasure of eating?" She looks at the far end of the table to see who she thinks is the oldest.

"My name is Colin; I'm the oldest. This is Charlotte, Lucas, and Bree."

"It's very nice to meet you all. Later today, I'll be going out to check on your mother and your new brother. I'll let her know you're all doing well."

"You talk funny," says Charlotte, her eyes wide with curiosity.

"Yes, I'm from England and have an English accent. Just as you have a funny accent to me because yours is Scottish," she says as she taps the tip of Charlotte's nose.

"Can we go with you to see Mummy today?" giggles Charlotte.

"Not today, my dear. Perhaps in a few days. I'll be sure to let you know."

"Have we done something wrong that we can't be at home with Mummy and the new baby?" asks Colin.

"Children, none of you have done anything wrong." Katharine pauses, not quite sure how to address this matter. "It was your father and I who decided your mother required some time to recover from this last birth. Mr. Stuart, the Laird, was kind enough to let you come here and stay while your mother recuperates. I promise you, you'll be able to see her in a few days. How's that?"

Three heads nod simultaneously, with the youngest smacking her spoon on the table.

"Good. Let's finish our breakfast, help Mrs. Jones with the dishes, and see what we can have you do for the rest of the day. What do you say?"

Eagerly, they all finish their meal. Then they help to tidy up the kitchen with Mrs. Jones's instructions. Charlotte asks to stay and help Mrs. Jones like she does her mama in the kitchen. Katharine discovers that the young man who stood beside Mrs. Jones last night is William. Mrs. Jones has taken him in. His mother died a few years ago, and his father was killed in an accident at the shipyard about a year ago. William and Colin work together to get wood for the kitchen stove in the house for the day. Lucas is led by Tamara and Liam out to the back door into a courtyard where there's a chicken coop. He cleans the coop, gathers eggs, and feeds the chickens.

Katharine returns to her room to retrieve her cloak and bag. She'll start her day by going to see Mrs. Randall.

As she's coming out of her room, she hears, "G'day, Ms. Bennett. My name is Bonnie, Ethan's sister."

"How nice to meet you, Bonnie." Katharine recognizes her as the woman who stood beside Ethan last night. "Please call me Katharine," she says as she reaches out to shake Bonnie's hand.

"I see we have some guests with us," Bonnie says as she shakes Katharine's hand and then nods toward the kitchen.

"Yes, the Randall children."

"They're excellent helpers. We should be able to keep them busy while they're here."

"I'm not sure, but would Collin and Charlotte not be of age to go to school?"

"I can't say if the children didn't mention it. You might want to check with Mrs. Randall when you visit her today."

"I will, thank you."

"Aye. Mrs. Jones indicated I should speak to you about putting your trunk with medical supplies somewhere."

"Yes."

"Once it's out, can I get a desk of some sort put in? It will help me to do work in the evening."

Bonnie takes a moment to ponder the request. She moves her head to the side and then raises her right hand. "I think I might have a solution for you, Ms. Ben ... I mean, Katharine. Come with me."

Katharine follows Bonnie as she leads her down a hall and then up a flight of stairs, which leads to another hall. Bonnie goes to the door and opens it. She leads Katharine into the study.

"My brother uses this as his office, but it's also a study. There's another desk over there. Will that work for you?"

Katharine moves over to the bureau and opens it up to see how it can work as a desk. "It will do the trick, and I think it will fit."

"Oh no, I thought you could use the desk here."

"Well, since this is your brother's office too, won't I bother him when I use it?"

"Not likely. There are periods when he's not here, so you'll have time for yourself. Otherwise, the two of you can work something out regarding using it. I think you'll find him over there and you here; there's plenty of room for you both. We can speak to Ethan after dinner this evening if you wish."

"Very well, thank you, Bonnie. Can you show me back to the kitchen and where the stable is so I can see Ty about getting to the Randall place to check on my—sorry—the patients?"

"Aye, follow me."

As Katharine moves out the door, she turns and notices the wall of books. She must see if they will assist her while she's here at the Stuart estate.

Retracing their steps, Katharine is led back to the kitchen.

"That wasn't too bad. I think I can find my way from here to the study."

"If you need someone to help, just ask William."

"I will. Thank you."

"If you're ready, I'll show you to the stables. Once there, I'm sure Ty will be able to find you a mount to ride over to the Randalls."

"How do you know I ride?" questions Katharine.

Bonnie looks at her and says, "Oh, I don't. I just assumed."

Katharine smiles and laughs. "You assumed right. I do know how to ride. I tried to talk my brother into letting me bring Sebastian with me."

"Sebastian?" asks Bonnie.

"Yes, the horse I used at home. He was so familiar with where we'd be going; even if I was tired, he always got me home safe and sound."

Bonnie looks at her and says, "I think we can accommodate you in that regard."

Strolling to the stables through the courtyard out the back of the kitchen, Katharine stops to take a deep breath and says, "It smells different."

Not missing a beat, Bonnie says, "It's probably the horse manure you smell. The stables are this way." They both laugh.

"I know what horse manure smells like, Bonnie. No, the air. It's different from where I come from. Here, it's sweeter and saltier, if that makes sense. Back home, it's more grass and earth."

"I never really thought of it," says Bonnie as she closes her eyes and breathes in. "It smells like home to me."

They arrive at the stables to find Ty and Mr. Holmes.

"Good morning, Ms. Katharine. I'd like you to meet Mr. Holmes. He works in the stables."

"Good morning, Mr. Holmes."

Mr. Holmes nods and continues with his work. She notices the Garrick coat he's wearing. It reminds her of her cloak. It's grey with only one row of buttons up the front, not the usual two. The two ruffles over the shoulder come past his forearms. The collar seems higher than normal. It's a quarter in length, and his gloves and hat are black to complement the colour of his coat. It's functional for the amount of driving he does with the wagon in cool and cold weather. Looking down at his feet, she notices a leather sheath attached to his right leg. She can see a knife handle inside of it. On further inspection, she sees that he walks with a limp. It's not pronounced, but it can be detected if you watch. Katharine turns to Ty. "Why does he limp?"

"Mr. Holmes was originally a shipbuilder. However, he was injured, and another man was killed when there was an accident. They both fell from a scaffold they were on."

"How long ago was this?"

"About a year ago. He's not able to work at the shipyard. Ethan thought he could continue to work here on the estate instead."

"Oh." She takes a moment to watch Mr. Holmes as he walks out of the stable and out of sight. "Perhaps in the future I can inquire about the limp?"

"Unless he comes to you, Katharine, I suggest you leave be."

Katharine nods to show she understands what he's telling her indirectly. "And what's that on his right leg?"

"That's a dirk. Most of us only wear them as part of our traditional Scottish wear. However, since Mr. Holmes drives to and from the shipyards, he wears it for protection. It can be used as a weapon if needed."

Bonnie looks to Ty. "Katharine is here for a horse to ride to the Randall home. I told her you could find her something."

"Aye, I can. We have a fine, reliable horse named Tally. Come, we'll introduce you."

Ty shows Katharine to Tally's stall. The horse comes to the door to greet Katharine, and she likes her immediately. Katharine rubs her nose, and she nods her approval.

"I think we'll get along very well, my friend. Shall we see about getting you saddled and off to the Randalls?"

"Ethan isn't available this morning to take you. He's asked Liam to accompany you, since he's one of the people you'll be mentoring."

"Very well. Can you show me where the saddle is, and I can get Tally ready?"

"Right this way, Ms. Katharine."

THIRTEEN

KATHARINE HAS TALLY saddled in no time, and as she mounts, Liam rides up beside her.

"Good morning, Ms. Katharine. Shall we be on our way?"

"Lead the way, Liam." And toward the Randall home they ride.

"Well, Ty, what do you make of our new doctor?" Bonnie asks as they stand outside the barn, watching Liam and Katharine ride away.

"She handled Mr. Randall well enough last night. I believe she'll surprise us all."

"Aye, we'll see. When you can come in for a coffee, we can discuss the day ahead and a few things we need to deal with this week. Fresh coffee and scones will be available."

"Let me finish with this horse. Grab the books, and I'll be right in."

"I'll see you in the kitchen," says Bonnie as she turns to take one last glance at Liam and Katharine in the distance.

Ethan may be the Laird, but Bonnie and Ty run the estate daily. They coordinate to ensure the tenants working the land have what they need, keeping the animals healthy and machinery in excellent working condition. When Ethan is away, he leaves Bonnie in charge. Ty and Bonnie make a good pair.

It's an excellent visit to the Randall home. Mr. Randall has been taken into town to work at the shipyard for the week, so it's just Mrs. Randall at home with the newborn. Katharine checks both of them but takes more time with Mrs. Randall. Already she has a better colour than last night. Liam tells Mrs. Randall what the kids are up to, and she smiles.

"The children would like to come see you. I told them it would be a few days. I want you to have time to look after your new little one."

She nods to Katharine but doesn't speak.

"Very well then. We'll be back in two days and bring the children to visit. If it's all right, either Liam or Tamara will be by tomorrow to check on you."

Mrs. Randall is moving the rocker the babe lies in. She looks up to smile and nods at them to say "Very well."

"Until tomorrow then, Mrs. Randall," says Liam. Katharine and Liam leave the Randalls' home and mount to return to the estate.

They're about a mile from the estate when Katharine can see all of the beautiful green and vibrant plants. Some she recognizes, like myrtle and heather, but others she needs clarification on. "Liam, can you tell what some of these plants are? I recognize the myrtle and the heather, but I'm not familiar with these two," she asks as she stops Tally.

"This one here is called St. John's wort, and this one is willow bark."

"Do you know if they're used for medicinal purposes?"

"No, Ms. Katharine. I know you can use them, but I don't know what they can be used for."

"Well, Liam, we'll learn together with Tamara. If you have natural remedies, you should use them."

"Yes, Ms. Katharine."

They nudge their mounts to continue on home.

"I noticed several books in Mr. Stuart's study. I'll see if we can find anything regarding native Scottish plants and their properties. I'll also pull out some of my medical books and see what they have to say."

"You mean we may have medical supplies right here in our back yard?"

"That's exactly what I mean, Liam. Back home, we have chamomile, which grows wild and is also gardened because it's a bright and cheerful-looking flower. I use it to give to patients in tea form. It has a very calming effect on individuals. If you have plants that can assist you, you should do your best to use them as a resource."

"Never would have thought of it, Ms. Katharine," shrugs Liam.

"I suggest you and Tamara work together to identify as many of the plants in the area as possible. Be mindful to observe only. Please don't touch it until you know for certain what it is. Then we can work together to see which are most beneficial for medical purposes."

By this time, they've returned to the estate stables. Liam is the first to get down and takes hold of Tally. Once Katharine has dismounted, Liam says, "I'll look after the horses, Ms. Katharine."

"Thank you, Liam. I think I'll walk around and look at the plants and shrubs so we can do some research this evening."

"Aye, Ms. Katharine. I'll mention our discussion to Tamara. Her mother is a gardener; she may know more than we do."

"Very well, Liam." She smiles at him as he leads the horses into the stable.

With her bag in her hand, Katharine turns to move toward the house, but when she sees all the greenery along the way, she decides to take the opportunity to investigate the plants and shrubs that are so close to the estate. If they can use them, they should. "What do we have here?" she says as she squats down to inspect a plant that interests her. It's but a few minutes later when she hears movement behind her. Turning, she sees William, who was part of the welcoming party from the night before. She estimates he's about the age of eight to ten. He has dark, wavy hair that could use a cut. He's wearing well-worn clothes with dirt on them. She thinks he spends much time outside. She also notices that he has a look of curiosity on his face.

Turning slightly, she says, "Well, hello! And who might you be, little man?"

He tilts his head to mimic her and looks at her.

Moving her head back up correctly, Katharine reaches for a handshake and says, "My name is Katharine."

The young boy steps in, but he puts his finger on the brooch pinned to her cloak instead of shaking her hand. "What's this?" he says.

She looks down at the brooch where his finger lies. She takes her hand and moves it to his. "Well, little man, I'll be happy to tell you the story behind the brooch, but first, may I know to whom I am speaking?"

"My name is William."

"It's a pleasure to meet you, William," she says, taking his hand in hers.

"Ms. Katarine."

Oh, he has a hard time with his "th." "No, Katharine. But William, if it's too hard for you, you can call me Ms. Katie."

"I'll try to say Ms. Katarine; I mean Ms. Katharine. I'm having a hard time with some words."

"That's quite all right, William, and as I said, Ms. Katie will be fine."

William gives her a massive grin as a silent way of saying "thank you."

She looks down to where his little fingers had been. "The brooch, or as some would call it, a pin, was given to me by my Uncle Terrance when I was about fourteen years of age."

She moves to remove the brooch from her cloak and gives it to William to look at. He moves it around to see it more clearly.

"It looks like a snake wrapped around a tree branch."

"You're very close, William. It is a snake wrapped around a pole. Do you know what the Bible is, William?"

"It's the book the minister reads from at church, and Mrs. Jones reads out of it every night before bed."

"Well, William, in the Bible, there's a story about how God instructed his servant Moses to make a serpent and set it on a pole so that if any of God's people were bitten by a serpent, when they looked at the serpent on the pole, they would live."

William looks up at her with a confused yet curious look.

"My uncle, a doctor, gave me this brooch when I started to apprentice with him. I learned everything I know today from him and my aunt."

Katharine places her left hand under William's and touches the brooch with her right. "When my uncle gave me this brooch"—she turns it around in William's hand— "he told me the story from the Bible. I wear it on my cloak to remind me that whenever I go out to help those in need, I must look up to God for his wisdom and strength to help me heal and provide healing."

William looks up at Katharine and says, "If I need help, can I just come to you?"

Katharine chuckles. "Of course you can, William." She takes her brooch back and pins it where she always keeps it. "It looks like I should get back. Could you help me find the way, William?"

"Yes, Ms. Katie. This way," he says, taking her hand.

She grabs her medicine bag, rises, and lets him lead her back to the house.

With the sun setting in the background, Ethan sees William leading Katharine, hand in hand, back to the house. The orange against the green is a sight to be seen. Even more pulling is the image of Katharine walking with William, as though they were mother and child. She hasn't been here a whole day and has put one of his most disruptive shipbuilding workers, Mr. Randall, in his place. Now she befriends William, who was adopted by the Stuart community after his father's death a year and a half ago. He's a unique child who wins the hearts of those he encounters and has become Mrs. Jones's charge since his father's death.

Ethan turns from the window with a smile and shakes his head. What is he to do? He was not expecting a woman to be sent as a doctor. He moves to his favourite chair by the fire and ponders if he'll send her back or allow her to stay. The usual knock is heard on his door, and Ty comes in.

"Good evening, Laird."

"Evening, Ty."

He comes in, unbuttons his jacket, and sits in the chair beside Ethan.

"So …"

"So …"

"Ethan, are we going to play twenty questions?"

"I haven't made up my mind."

"What do you need to think about? You remember what she did at the Randall home a night ago, and she's won over the little scamp William."

He grins as he remembers the chastising Mr. Randall got from her, all with a smile. "Oh, I well remember, Ty, and William is drawn to someone who is motherly."

"'Motherly' is not the word I'd use to describe Ms. Bennett, Ethan. Do you need glasses? From what I see, she's more than capable of handling herself and getting the job done. My shoulder has been bothering me of late; I may have to visit her in the morning." He moves to rub his right shoulder and winks at Ethan.

"It would be best if you didn't bother our good doctor with an imaginary illness, my friend. Besides, I don't think my sister, Bonnie, would take kindly to you falling for the new doctor."

"Bonnie need not worry in that regard, or you. So does that mean she stays?"

"For some reason, I feel she's what we need. As much as I assumed it would be a man who'd be sent, watching her barely arrive, be whisked away to deal with a difficult birth, and handle the situation with such grace was quite astonishing."

"Not to mention how she handled Mr. Randall. You did say it was pure entertainment."

"For what it's worth, Ty, I like her. She's more than what she seems. I think we should not underestimate her."

"I agree."

"It's time for supper, my friend. We mustn't be late; otherwise, we'll never hear the end of it from Mrs. Jones."

"Aye, let's be off. After you, Laird."

At dinner that evening, Ethan takes a moment to ask Katharine to meet him in his study after she's finished her meal. Katharine needs to find out where the study is from the dining hall. She takes the last of her tea and sees William coming in from the kitchen. She raises her hand to signal William to come over. "William, Mr. Stuart has asked me to see him in the study. Can you show me how to get there from here, please?"

"Yes, Ms. Katie. I must tell Mrs. Jones where I am."

He runs back into the kitchen, and in the blink of an eye he returns to take her hand and lead her to the study.

"We're here, Ms. Katie."

"Thank you, William."

"Do you need me to stay to show you back to the kitchen?"

She bends down so that she's at eye level with him. "William, you're quite the little man. I can find my way back to the kitchen from here. Bonnie showed me earlier today."

"If you think you can, Ms. Katie."

"Yes, I can, William. Before you go, do you remember the brooch we talked about earlier today?"

He nods.

"Well, a snake makes a 'th' sound. Can you do that?"

He watches Katharine as she puts her tongue between her teeth and makes the sound, and then he does the same.

"Excellent, William. Now when you say my name, use the 'th' sound, so it's Ka—'th'—arine."

"Katharine, Katharine, Katharine." His eyes light up when he hears that he has said her name correctly.

"I never thought I'd say this, but remember the snake when you say my name, William." She takes her hand and places it on his cheek. "I'm sure Mrs. Jones can use you in the kitchen. I'll see you later."

"Yes, Ms. Katharine," William says with a grin of victory and dashes off to the kitchen.

He brings joy to her heart. She smiles contently. Then she rises, knocks on the door, and waits for a response.

"Come in."

Katharine enters to find Ethan sitting behind his desk.

"You wanted to speak to me, Mr. Stuart."

"Yes. Please come have a seat by the fire." He motions to the chairs to his left.

"Can I get you a cup of coffee or tea?"

"Nothing, thank you," he says as she sits in his chair.

He pours himself a cup of coffee and moves to sit in his chair, realizing she's in it. He stares momentarily, and then Katharine realizes she is to sit in the other one. "Oh, this is your chair, isn't it?"

"Well, I usually sit in that one, yes."

"Oh my, well, here you go." She gets up and moves to the opposite side.

Thrown off, Ethan sits, places his cup on the side table, takes a drink, and then turns to Katharine. In the meantime, she's been looking at the shelves of books on either side of the fireplace.

"Do you like to read, Ms. Bennett?"

"When I can, yes. But I was wondering if any of these books have information on the types of plants that grow in this area and their medicinal properties."

"I know there are some agricultural books, but I can't say what they contain. You're welcome to take a look for yourself."

"Yes, that would be helpful. So does this mean I get to keep the position, and you won't send me back to England?"

"Ms. Bennett, I'm sure you're well aware that not only had I, but most of the staff here, assumed a doctor would mean a man." Katharine is about to respond when he puts up his hand to signify he's not finished. "However, we also know that women have been midwives for centuries, and most of our mothers, aunts, sisters—I think you get the idea—were also the ones who tended to the sick daily. I've seen firsthand how you helped a distressed patient give birth to her child and then how you tended to the other household members who needed your help. That's not something most doctors would do." He takes a sip of his coffee, looks at her with a smile, and says, "But to see you deal with Mr. Randall."

"I apologize, Mr. Stuart. I was tired, and my patience was worn thin; I didn't behave—"

"Ms. Bennett, I'm not scolding you. You made Mr. Randall feel like you were doing him a favour; it was a brilliant move. I expect you've learned to deal with the likes of Mr. Randall before."

"Too many times, I might say."

"Having watched you last night, I'm confident you are more than capable of dealing with the medical side of what's expected of you and of providing some life experience to the individuals you'll be mentoring. I'll do my best to help you integrate with the people, but there will be some resistance, as you're well aware."

"Yes, sir, I'm well aware."

"Ms. Bennett, if we're to work together, please call me Ethan."

"Very well, Ethan, and please call me Katharine."

Ethan nods; he likes how his name sounds coming from her. He places his coffee cup down.

"Since we'll be working closely together for the next year, Katharine, and you'll be looking after those on the Stuart estate, please tell me about your background."

Katharine, in short order, explains to Ethan that she started mentoring with her uncle, a doctor, and aunt, who was his nurse, at the age of fourteen. They didn't have children of their own, so she became their "adopted" child, so to speak, even though she was their niece. When she was old enough, her uncle took her under his wing and began to mentor and teach her what he had learned as a doctor. He took her on his visits as a nurse and then had her helping out in his office attached to his home. Soon, it was customary for everyone to see her uncle and her together. She may not have gone to school and received a degree in medicine, but she'd spent eight years working under her uncle and five years handling the duties in her community on her own. With help from another mentor, Dr. Wylie, Katharine has the best mortality rate in her parish.

"My uncle taught me to stay up on medical procedures and not to fix what isn't broken. The biggest part of doing what I do is the people. You have to be able to handle them as well as the situation. Everything else falls into place as soon as you can put them at ease. For the most part, my community has accepted me because they know me and trust me to do what's best for them. The people here don't know me and, therefore, won't trust me. This is going to be the biggest obstacle, Ethan."

"Aye, you're correct, Katharine." Ethan fluidly moves out of his comfy chair to his desk. He opens the bottom drawer and pulls out a piece of fabric. He takes the scissors from the desk and cuts a small square from the fabric. Ethan moves back toward Katharine.

"During your time here on the Stuart estate, it will help if you wear the Stuart tartan on your cloak." He hands her the square match of fabric. "This will signify to all that you have my approval as the doctor for the Stuart community, so to speak."

As Katharine takes the piece of tartan, their fingers touch, and they feel a "spark." Katharine gasps as she looks up into Ethan's piercing blue eyes and feels like she's being swept away into a calm pool of water. Ethan looks at Katharine and is mesmerized as her brown eyes change to black. He smiles back and releases the tartan fabric into her palm, letting his fingertips linger. He notices that her eyes are an intense black now. Interesting.

Katharine nods. "I'll attach it to my cloak when I return to my room."

"Excellent idea," Ethan says, returning to the desk and removing the papers from a folder. "I've drawn up this agreement regarding your stay here in Scotland," he says, returning to his chair. "You're welcome to review the agreement now or take it with you and return it in a day or two. If you have any questions, we can discuss them," he says as he hands the papers to Katharine.

"I thought this arrangement was made between you and my brother as a business agreement," Katharine says as she takes the papers from his hands and another "spark" occurs.

"It is, and I have a signed contract for that. This is for you as the individual who is to complete the work. It's to ensure you're aware of what's expected and agree to the terms that don't benefit you but your family business."

"You are an astute businessman, Ethan. I might as well review it now and have it settled." She returns to her chair to get comfortable and opens the folder to review the contents. Ethan moves back to his chair to finish his coffee. He waits while Katharine reads. She is so engrossed in the agreement before her that she's unaware of him observing her.

She has brown eyes and a warm, inviting smile that sets anyone at ease. She looks younger than she is, but her experience makes her seem older. When Ethan first saw her, he thought a "pixie" had been sent. She's short and small compared to the Scottish, but he's seen with his eyes that she's not to be underestimated. She's like a stick of dynamite. Power is contained in a small package, and you never know what hits you until it's over. He moves his hand over his lips to hide the smile from the excellent analogy. She's in good physical condition and unafraid to get her hands dirty. And she knows how to ride a horse.

"Mr. Stuart—I mean, Ethan," says Katharine as she looks up from the papers, unaware of his surveillance of her, "to assist the community, I will require a place for people to come see me—I mean us, as you have set out in the agreement. I believe the two people you want me to mentor or apprentice are Liam and Tamara."

"Yes, they are. We have a room off the back of the kitchen for now, but your input into where a more permanent place should be would help."

"I'll see what I can do," says Katharine as she stacks the papers in a neat group. "I have one thing to add to the agreement, Ethan," she says, easing out of her chair to stand. "I understand that I'm here to provide medical assistance to your community, specifically the estate tenants, shipbuilding workers, and members in the house. However, anyone who comes to me for assistance will receive the same. I must help all in need who come to me for medical assistance." She hands him the folder.

"I understand, Katharine." He moves to get up out of his chair, and Katharine eases back into hers to give him room. "Most of the other communities do have their own doctors. Once they get to know you after you've been here for a while, they may even request your assistance occasionally, but you'll find that, at least while you're here, we stick to our clans or communities."

"That may be true, Mr.—I mean, Ethan. I must apologize. It's hard to call an employer by his first name; it just doesn't seem right."

"In most cases, I would agree. But technically, I'm not your employer. You're going to be a vital part of this community. Others must see that we respect and trust each other. When we're in the company of others outside of this home, we can address each other as Ms. Katharine or Mr. Ethan; when we're alone, first names will do."

She nods. "I understand. As long as everyone is welcome to call upon me for medical assistance, I'm good to make that small addition to the agreement, and we can finalize the contract."

"Aye, we can make that small addition to the agreement if it pleases you, Katharine." He moves past her. As he does, Katharine feels not a spark but more like a static shock.

What is this spark here and shock there I feel when I'm around him?

Her thoughts are interrupted by three distinctive knocks on the door. The door is opened before Ethan can answer, and Ty sticks his head in.

"Ethan, there was a matter I forgot to mention earlier." He looks up to see Katharine sitting in the chair by the fire. "My apologies, Laird, I didn't realize—"

"It's all good, Ty. Katharine and I were finishing up some business. Suppose you could get Bonnie for us. We want you both to witness the agreement/contract we must sign."

"Of course, Laird, one moment. He disappears behind the door to yell for Bonnie and then moves entirely into the library.

"Ty, really, I could have done that. And since when do you call me Laird after hours?"

"Oh, you wanted me to get her! Sorry, Ethan. Next time, be more specific. He's like that, Katharine, and thinks the rest of us can read his mind."

She laughs as Ty winks at her and moves to the cabinet where the sherry's kept.

"Did someone bellow?" asks Bonnie as she steps into the room, wiping her hands with her apron, and glares at Ty.

"Yes," Ethan says as he moves to hug her. "Katharine and I require you and Ty to be witnesses for this agreement/contract."

"Very well. Katharine, have you spoken to Ethan about using the other desk in the evening for your paperwork?" She motions toward the bureau across the room.

"No, I haven't yet had the opportunity." She looks at Ethan and says, "I try to keep the patients' records as up-to-date as possible, so in the evenings, I tend to make the notes—"

"I think we can work something out, Katharine."

"As much as I'm enjoying this party, Ethan, I still have a few things to finish in the stables; you wanted us as witnesses."

"Sorry, Ty and Bonnie, if you could be our witnesses."

"Katharine." Ethan holds the pen. She moves to take it from him and then signs the contract, followed by Ethan. Ty signs beside Ethan's name, and Bonnie beside Katharine's.

"If that's everything, brother, I must return and help Mrs. Jones with the Randall children."

"Oh yes, I wanted to speak to them about my visit with their mother today. Good evening, gentleman." Katharine turns to Ethan and Ty.

"Good evening, Katharine," they respond in unison.

Bonnie and Katharine leave the room and return to the kitchen. Katharine can tell the children that their newest sibling and mother are doing well and that they'll be able to visit and see them in a few days. With this exciting news, it takes Mrs. Jones, Bonnie, and Katharine to get all of them to bed.

Katharine returns to her room for the evening. With the swatch of fabric in her hand, she takes her brooch from her cloak and pins the fabric through it, arranging it so it's visible for all to see. She smiles, running her hand over it. "What would you think, Uncle Terrance? Will I be taking care of others in Scotland? Oh, how I miss you both," she says as she moves over to the lantern on her side table, adjusting it to low. While she changes from her day clothes into her bedtime dress, she starts to hum. Once she's changed, she climbs into bed. Katharine reaches over to extinguish the lantern and pulls the covers up and over herself, ready for a good night's sleep. It may be dark, but she's excited about what tomorrow will bring.

FOURTEEN

KATHARINE'S NEXT FEW weeks in Scotland on the Stuart estate are much more routine than her first day. William is the one who always seems to be in the right place at the right time to help her find her way. The Randall children are still at the estate house but staying busy with work around the estate. Mrs. Jones seems to be getting extra help from the oldest girl, Charlotte, who enjoys working in the kitchen with her. Colin and William stay busy helping Ty and Mr. Holmes in the stables, or Mrs. Jones around the house. Lucas helps mainly with the chickens and works in the garden with Bonnie, if not following around behind Colin and William. Baby Bree spends most of the day in a makeshift buggy in the kitchen with Mrs. Jones. Everyone takes their turn with her.

Katharine, Tamara, and Liam begin preparing the designated treatment room. Their tasks included cleaning, organizing, and identifying the necessary supplies. They talk about the local flora and its potential uses as they work.

"My mother was going to look up some of her books and let us look at them, Ms. Katharine," Tamara says as she sweeps the floor.

"Wonderful, and Mr. Ethan has indicated we can look at the agricultural books in the study to see what we can find," responds Katharine. Katharine sees a bit of herself in Tamara but hasn't yet figured out Liam. He's very good with people; he's just a little squeamish around blood, which isn't good. It's only been a week, so time will tell. She has a year.

Now that Katharine is more aware of her surroundings, she gets up for early morning walks. It gives her a chance to start her day fresh. She finds a glen on the estate that reminds her of the pond she can oversee from the dining nook at home. This is just on a much grander scale. It looks like an eye to her. One stream runs water into the glen. Here it moves slowly and pools around the shape, but it finds its way to the other end, where a small but rapid brook runs the water into another stream. It provides the water for the tenants and the estate. But in the glen, the stillness of the water is calming and refreshing. It has natural protection from the bushes that grow around it. What look like holes have been carved into the bushes to make a path to gain entrance to the glen. Once you step through, it's like walking into a picture. Green grass, blue water, and the kaleidoscope of colours from the various vegetation and open areas invite you to come to sit, relax, and take in the beauty of nature all around you.

This morning, Katharine wants to take some time at the glen to write a letter to her mother to let her know how things are going. The beauty around her absorbs Katharine. Only when she finishes the letter does she realize that today is Monday. *If I return to the house in time, I can give the letter to Ty when he takes the men into town for work.*

Katharine rushes to put the letter in the envelope, addresses it, and returns to the house. On her way to the stable, Katharine notices someone waiting outside the room they've designated as the examining room. She comes over to the woman and nods as she says, "Good morning."

"G'day."

"Are you here for medical assistance?"

"Aye."

Around the corner comes Tamara with a few books in her hand.

"Good morning, Mrs. Carr," says Tamara.

"Good morning, Ms. Tamara. I was waiting for you."

Tamara looks up at Katharine as though to say, "Did you want to handle this?"

"Excellent, Mrs. Carr. I'm Katharine. I'm working with Tamara and Liam. Tamara, how about you take Mrs. Carr in. I need to give this letter to Ty to post while in town, and I'll be right back."

"Yes, Ms. Katharine. I have a few of my mother's books we can review. I'll leave them in the office. Let me help you, Mrs. Carr." Tamara takes Mrs. Carr's arm to help her up and leads her into the room.

Katharine arrives just in time to get the letter to Ty. When she arrives, the last workers heading to the shipyard are climbing into the back of the wagon. She runs from the house to stop beside the wagon on the side where Ty is sitting up front.

Ty looks down at her, having seen her run up to him. "What is it, Katharine?" he asks, concerned.

"Can you put this letter in the post for me when you're in town?" Katharine asks as she waves the letter in her hand and then gives it to Ty.

Ty nods. "Yes, Katharine. I'll do it myself."

"Thank you very much, Ty." She steps back to ensure the wagon wheels don't run over her feet. "Safe travels, everyone," she says as she waves.

Mr. Holmes signals the team, and off they go. She continues to wave. Some of them wave back. Mr. Randall gives her an angry look.

"Well, some of them waved back, and I think Mr. Randall just has a permanent scowl," she says. "Duty calls." Katharine lifts her skirt and heads back to see if she can assist Tamara with Mrs. Carr.

FIFTEEN

SINCE ETHAN IS away for the week in town at the shipyard, Katharine has Liam and Tamara come to the study after dinner to look through the agricultural books and the books Tamara's mother provided on plants.

"Ms. Katharine, this book says the myrtle and heather you recognized have several medical uses."

"Excellent, Liam; please note what and how we can use them. Tamara, anything in your mother's books?"

"St. John's wort and willow bark have several medical uses, and I was able to identify wooly lamb's ear, a natural bandage for wounds. And there is the allheal plant, those lovely purple flowers you like. The book says they're an 'all heal' plant. They're also good for attracting bees."

"Brilliant. Since we have eight plants, each of you takes four for now. Figure out what we need to extract and the process to use for medical purposes. We'll use them on ourselves first to make sure. When we use them on patients, it will be necessary to make sure no one has any allergies to plants or any respiratory issues, just to be sure."

Both nod and then turn back to their books to write out instructions.

"This is an excellent start," says Katharine to herself. She takes a moment to watch as both of her pupils work to finish their homework. Scotland has given her more than she expected. She turns back to complete her notes for the evening with a smile.

On a morning when Katharine is visiting the glen and reading her Bible, William quietly comes alongside her, playing with the grass before him, and begins to speak.

"If there be righteousness in the heart, there will be beauty in the character. If there be beauty in the character, there will be harmony in the house. If there be harmony in the house, the nation will have order. If there is order in the nation, there will be peace in the world."[3]

"William, that's lovely. Where did you learn it?" asks Katharine.

"My mother, she taught me," replies William.

Katharine places her hand on his and says, "You did a wonderful job of reciting it, William. Your mother would be proud."

William grins at Katharine and returns to play with the grass before him. When Katharine finishes reading from the Bible and closes the book, William takes her hand and says, "This way, Ms. Katie." William leads her through a different opening in the bushes surrounding the glen.

"Why have I not noticed this one before?" she says. As they come to a hill to walk down, Katharine spots a building. William leads her to it. Upon inspection, Katharine figures it looks to be an old shed.

"William, I think you've helped me find our new infirmary location," she says as she squeezes his hand. "Let's take a look." They move in closer to look around. She can open the door and see inside. "It's seen better days. Cobwebs everywhere, dust is thick, and there look to be a lot of broken items, but it just might work."

"What are you looking for, Ms. Katie?" William asks as Katharine leaves the shed.

"I'm trying to determine if this is central to the house"—she points to her left—"and the tenant farms"—she points to the right.

William moves in front of her to mimic what she's doing. Talking to herself, Katharine looks from one end of her hand to the other, saying, "It's in a good setting. It's not part of the main house, which gives people privacy to come and go without being seen. Yet it's close enough to the main house that they can be reached if further assistance is needed. Good find today, William."

"Thank you, Ms. Katie. I'm good at finding things."

"Yes, you are, aren't you, little man?" she says as she puts her hand on his head to mess up his hair.

William giggles and then puts his hair back the way he likes it.

Katharine takes a few more minutes to look around outside. She also notices that the foliage and dirt paths around the building look like they may have once had gardens around them. She makes a note to discuss their find with Ethan when he returns from town at the end of the week.

"Ms. Katie, I'm hungry. Can we go back to the house now?"

---

[3] "Confucius Quotes," Goodreads, accessed January 10, 2025, https://www.goodreads.com/quotes/202222-if-there-is-righteousness-in-the-heart-there-will-be.

"Yes, William, we can. Lead the way."

Off he runs ahead as Katharine follows behind. Hopefully this place will work as the permanent infirmary for the Stuart estate, which Ethan wanted her to deal with. *Thank you, Lord, for having William bring me another way today. If I hadn't been looking for it, I wouldn't have found it hidden behind the thick bushes on the other side of the glen.*

On Friday evening, after Ethan returns from town, he and Katharine are in the study, and she discusses the find with him.

"Ethan, William showed me what looks like an old shed on the other side of the glen a few days ago."

"A shed?"

"That's what it looks like to me. It had what looked like paths around it. I thought there may have been some gardens."

"I think I know what you're referring to." He moves to the shelf behind his desk and takes down a picture. He brings it over to show Katharine.

"Oh yes, this is what I pictured it to look like. I thought it would be a wonderful location for your parish infirmary instead of the room off the kitchen. It's not too far from the estate. It would be easily accessed if further assistance were needed, but it would allow you privacy at the estate house and with the tenants."

"We're a family, Katharine; all are welcome," he says as he returns the picture to the shelf and takes his chair behind his desk.

"I understand that, Ethan. However, when it comes to medical stuff, there are times when people require privacy. Everyone should feel like they can come and see us without judgement or people wanting to know why they're here. That's why it's good to keep visiting the homes until they're established. They feel comfortable and safe in their homes. It allows them to open up about things they may not say if they think someone can hear the conversation or see them."

"Aye, I understand, Katharine. We'll check it out tomorrow."

"Aye, we will," Katharine responds with an awful Scottish accent.

Ethan laughs at her attempt. Katharine turns back to her desk to finish her notes, and Ethan picks up papers to continue working through the pile on his desk.

The following day, William leads the way, with Katharine and Ethan following behind. They arrive at the shed, and Ethan looks around and agrees that it would be a good location.

"What will be done to get it in order?" asks Ethan.

"The outside looks pretty solid. It will need a good cleaning. I took a quick look inside. Once it's cleaned, we can go from there," replies Katharine.

"There's no time like the present. William, can you tell Mr. Ty that we'll need the wagon to bring buckets, brushes, rags, soap, and hot water to do some cleaning?" instructs Ethan.

"Yes, Laird." Off he goes toward the stables.

"We can go back and get Liam and Tamara so they can see what we've found and can help out," informs Katharine.

"Aye, and with William and the Randall children, we'll have this taken care of in no time." Ethan chuckles.

They return to the estate. Ethan goes to the stable to check in with Ty. William and Colin are helping load the supplies into the wagon. Ethan explains to Ty what's happening, and Ty indicates that he's available for a few hours and can go and help.

Katharine goes directly to the examining room set up off the kitchen, where she finds Liam and Tamara. A note is placed on the door for anyone looking for medical assistance.

Tamara and Liam go to the stable to help with the items in the wagon and take them to the shed. Katharine speaks to Mrs. Jones on her way out to tell her where everyone is. She also indicates she thought the two oldest Randall children, Colin and Charlotte, might want to come and help out too.

"Colin is with William in the stable, Ms. Katharine. I believe Charlotte is helping out Bonnie."

"Thank you, Mrs. Jones."

"Ms. Katharine, if you all are going to be there for the morning, send the young lads back around noon. With their help, I can bring out a picnic lunch."

"Mrs. Jones, please don't go to any trouble."

"No trouble, Ms. Katharine. I'm making the meal anyway. Today, it will come to you."

"I'll have William and Colin come back to help you," she says, and off she goes.

Everyone meets at the stable, and into the wagon they go. Ethan lifts the children into the wagon, who giggle and laugh.

"I have some work to finish and will be out to help later," says Ethan.

She whispers to Ethan, "Mrs. Jones said she'd do a picnic lunch for everyone. Can you help her bring it out? William and Colin will be sent back to help."

He replies, "I can do that; see you soon."

She smiles back and then lets out a squeal as the wagon moves forward. She's unprepared and has to grab on to the railing to stay up. The kids laugh again, and Katharine turns red from slight embarrassment.

The morning passes quickly. Many hands make light work. The young ones play more than help, but when asked, they fetch items as needed and help drag items to the wagon to be taken back to the stables.

"Ty, do you have a pocket watch?" asks Katharine.

"I do." He takes it out and says, "It's 11:45."

"Thank you. William, Colin, Charlotte, can you come here please?" She yells to be heard over their playing.

"Yes, Ms. Katie," replies William as he rushes over to her.

Katharine smiles. She enjoys hearing her mother's nickname from William. He uses this more regularly than Ms. Katharine, probably because it's difficult for him to say her full name unless he takes the time to pronounce it correctly.

"William, I need you, Colin, and Charlotte to return and tell Mrs. Jones we're ready for lunch."

"Yes, Ms. Katie. Come on, I'll race you back to the house," says William as he starts toward the estate. Colin and Charlotte join in, and off they go.

"I wish I had their energy," laughs Katharine.

"You and I both. What did you mean by ready for lunch?" Ty asks as he continues to clean the shed's exterior.

"Mrs. Jones offered to bring us lunch out here. We'll have a picnic," says Katharine.

"Wonderful idea. It's good weather, and Mrs. Jones makes the best potato salad. Oh, I hope she makes the salad," says Ty excitedly as he rubs his stomach.

"We'll have to wait and see," says Katharine as she returns to help Ty, Liam, and Tamara finish washing the shed.

They've just completed cleaning one side of the shed when voices are heard. All four turn around to see Mrs. Jones, Ethan, William, Colin, Charlotte, and Bonnie. Bonnie is pushing a buggy with the two youngest Randall children in it, and Ethan is pulling a wagon with all the food for their picnic lunch.

"Who's hungry?" shouts Mrs. Jones.

"We are!" yell William and Colin.

Ty, Liam, Tamara, and Katharine clean up while the blankets are spread and food laid out. Everyone takes a seat and enjoys the delicious picnic. The children run around and play in between eating. The adults survey the progress on the shed while watching the children and laughing at their antics.

The fun must have worn some of the children out. Baby Bree crawls into Bonnie's lap and falls asleep. Lucas plops himself down beside Mrs. Jones and falls asleep up against her.

"Mrs. Jones, the picnic was wonderful. But I'll be doing exactly what they have done if I don't get up and get moving," says Katharine as she gets up from the blanket.

"Yes, we need to get these wee ones back and in their beds for nap time," whispers Mrs. Jones.

It takes a while, but the adults get up and help pack everything away. Ty and Charlotte accompany Bonnie and Mrs. Jones to the house with the younger children. Ethan stays to help wash the other side of the shed with Katharine, Liam, and Tamara. William and Colin stay to fetch the water from the glen for them.

Later that evening when they return to the estate home from all the cleaning, they have a light supper in the kitchen. As they're eating, a tenant arrives to receive minor medical attention. Seeing that both Liam and Tamara are exhausted from the day of physical labour, Katharine says she will handle it.

"Thank you, Ms. Katharine," say Liam and Tamara in unison as they collect their dishes to take to the sink and retire for the evening.

Katharine tends to the farmer, who has minor cuts. Having used the poultice of the allheal on themselves and knowing how well it worked, she decides to use it this evening. Checking to make sure he has no allergies, she explains to him what she's using. She'll have Liam go out tomorrow to check on him and bring more if it works. He nods his approval, says "Good night," and returns to his house.

Katharine sets the room back and finishes her note. Now the events of the day have caught up with her. Instead of going to work in the study this evening, she goes to her room, begins her nightly routine, climbs into bed, and as soon as her head hits the pillow, she is fast asleep.

Katharine wakes the following day feeling refreshed. She yawns, stretches, and says, "My goodness, that was a wonderful sleep." She gets out of bed, gets dressed, and goes out the door for her morning walk to the glen. As she passes the kitchen, she sees Ethan pouring himself a coffee.

"Good morning, Ethan."

"Good morning, Katharine. Is everything all right? You didn't come to work in the study last night."

"No, I'm fine. I looked after the tenant who required medical assistance, and then I was so tired from all the work we did yesterday, I went to my room and fell asleep. I think being outside all day, playing with the children, and overeating at the picnic did me in."

"It was fun, wasn't it?" he says as he lifts his coffee and takes a drink. "I can't remember the last time there was a picnic on the estate. It may have been when Bonnie, Reid, and I were kids."

"I won't hold you up. I'm off to the glen."

"Katharine, please let me know when you require assistance working inside the shed. It would be nice to return to doing what I truly enjoy—using my hands to build."

"Ty said he'd be happy to be of assistance."

"I'm sure he did," whispers Ethan under his breath as he takes another drink from his coffee. "Ty has enough to deal with during this season, Katharine. Take stock of what you need. It will feel good to be working with a piece of wood again that doesn't end up floating." With his coffee in hand, he moves toward Katharine. "When I'm in town, I'll let Reid know that I'll be at the estate for the next few weeks doing some work for you to get our infirmary up and running."

"As you wish, Ethan," she replies. She moves out the door to walk to the glen. Ethan watches as she goes. He turns and heads to his study.

SIXTEEN

IN THE COMING months, Katharine begins to see a pattern in the community on the Stuart estate. When the shipbuilding husbands are in town, those are the families to check in on. The women are much more open to discussing issues, taking advice, and implementing medical assistance while the husband is away. It's more challenging when they attend the homes of the farming husbands, but if they figure out when they're in the fields, they have a better chance.

Tamara takes the lead with the families where there are no husbands around. When the husbands are around, Liam takes the lead. Katharine ensures that they're seen together as a team in all the homes. If one can't attend, it's up to the other. The more the community becomes accustomed to them, the easier it is for them to work alone if they have to. Katharine knows that as an English woman, it will be difficult just to come in and take over. She makes it clear she's there to assist Liam and Tamara and provide medical experience when needed.

One evening after supper, Katharine informs Mrs. Jones that she, Liam, and Tamara will be in the study if needed.

"Yes, Ms. Katharine. William will come get you if anyone should come to the house for medical assistance."

"Thank you, Mrs. Jones."

Mrs. Jones nods to her as she returns to her task, and Katharine moves to the room off the back of the kitchen. They've decided to keep the room as is for now. At night, most people will come to the estate home for assistance if needed. Liam and Tamara keep their finished powders and poultices from the plants they've researched here.

"Liam and Tamara, when you're finished here, can you come to see me in the study?"

"Yes, Ms. Katharine."

Since Ethan is in town this week, Katharine knows she won't be disturbed this evening and can work with Liam and Tamara to start keeping records. Ten minutes later, a knock is heard on the study door, which was left ajar so that people would know to enter.

"Is everything all right, Ms. Katharine?" asks Tamara.

"Yes, of course, Tamara. I want to show you both how to keep patient records. I've noticed that this isn't a practice taken on by any predecessors."

"Dr. Bell? No, he said he had it all up here," says Liam, pointing to his brain.

"Perhaps, but he's no longer here, and you are. With both of you working with patients, records must be kept so you can refer to them. With the two of you working as a team, I suggest you have daily or at least weekly meetings to discuss various cases. Let's take Mrs. Randall, for example. Would you be aware of her weak heart if I didn't mention it or have a record for her?" She lifts the file. "As you can see, each patient has a file. Liam, I'm going to give you this one. Tamara, I'm going to give you this one. Please read them and tell me what you see."

Liam and Tamara review the files, and Katharine sits down at her desk to provide them with a few minutes before she starts questioning them.

"Ms. Katharine, I don't understand what you've written," Tamara says, pointing to what Kathrine wrote in the file.

"Oh dear, I used a type of medical shorthand I've used over the years. I didn't realize until now that you may not understand; f/u means follow-up. Good catch, Tamara. I'll list my shorthand words so you can understand and use them if you wish."

"It seems like this is extra work, Ms. Katharine. Do we have to have a file for every patient?"

"Yes, Liam, you need a file on every patient. It will seem like extra work at first, but once you get into a routine, it won't take long. I tend to do file updates at the end of the day, or if I have time, after I've finished with the patient if they come to see us in the infirmary. Taking a file with us when visiting their homes isn't feasible, so I'll come back here and make the notes."

"Even if it's something as simple as a cut?" asks Tamara.

"Yes."

Liam and Tamara are unconvinced and look at each other, as they didn't anticipate this being part of their duties.

"Let's use your example of a simple cut, Tamara. I'll use Mr. Ty as an example. He cut his arm on a nail from the stable pen. It doesn't seem too deep but it is an extensive cut that bleeds out. He comes to you, Tamara, as you're in the infirmary that day. You check it out, clean it, put one of the poultices on it, and bandage it. You tell him to see you in the next few days to check it and put on more poultices and a new bandage. It's been three days, and he hasn't come to see you. The bandage hasn't been changed, and now it's become infected. It's not you, Tamara, who's in the infirmary when he comes in but you, Liam. How do you proceed?"

"I would do what Tamara did: take the bandage off, clean it, put on a poultice, and put on a new bandage."

"Okay, that might work, but do you know what poultice she put on the cut?"

"No."

"His arm is also covered in a rash. What might that tell you about the infection?"

"He's having a reaction."

"Correct, but you don't know what he's reacting to because you have no reference, and Tamara is on visits and won't be back until the end of the day."

"Oh, I see," says Liam.

"Exactly. If a file is available with the necessary information, each of you has a clear understanding, and, as I indicated, each day you both need to take the time to talk and let each other know what's gone on. In this case, Tamara, you could have mentioned to Liam that Ty was in and you asked him to come to the infirmary to have the cut checked and a new bandage put on. Either of you could have gone to him and reminded him to come to see you."

"But what if he doesn't want the bandage to be changed?"

"It's ultimately his decision, Tamara. However, we must do whatever we can to ensure the patient's health. When we've done everything within our power to do what's required of us, but they choose not to do what they need to do, then you can do nothing, and at the end of the day, you have a clear conscience."

"May I look at a few other files, Ms. Katharine?" asks Tamara.

"Of course. Feel free to look through the files for both of you anytime. I'm having a cabinet put in the infirmary so that they're accessible to all of us. If there's anything you don't understand, please ask."

"When did you want us to start doing what you do, Ms. Katharine?"

"How about right now, if you have the time?"

They both nod yes.

"Liam, you went with me to visit with the Taylor family to check in on Thomas. Why don't you find his file, read it, and we can go from there!"

For the next hour, all three work on updating files, discussing issues, and getting a feel for how notes are to be taken.

Katharine feels very grateful for Liam and Tamara as she walks to her room that evening. They're both excellent pupils who are willing to learn, have a natural way with people, and, most of all, love to help and heal. She couldn't have asked for more. With the two of them, this community will have a fighting chance.

Katharine, Liam, and Tamara have been going out regularly to see Mrs. Randall. The children visit with their mother and newborn brother weekly for a few hours. Although Mr. Randall had said the children would be gone only for a week, they have yet to return home. Since Mr. Randall hasn't pushed for the return of the children, Katharine has extended their stay at the Stuart estate so Mrs. Randall will have more time to recover.

Mrs. Randall is told that the children are helping the Laird with the new infirmary, so their stay will be extended if it's all right with her. It isn't a lie—the children have been most helpful around the Stuart estate and are welcome to stay longer to ensure the best possible recovery for Mrs. Randall.

During the last visit, they discuss with Mrs. Randall the return of the children that Sunday after a little party is given to them on Saturday evening for all the help they've been. All this time, Mr. Randall hasn't argued the point; he comes home to a quiet house with a wife who can attend to his every need. However, it's time to talk with Mr. and Mrs. Randall. This meeting won't be pleasant, but it has to be done. Katharine has already had a discussion with Ethan, Liam, and Tamara about what will be discussed. Ethan accompanies her to show his support. Tamara and Liam come to learn another aspect of what they must know as medical personnel in the community. Sometimes they must have conversations with their patients that might be uncomfortable for both parties. However, Liam and Tamara must learn to tell the patient the truth and be open and honest. Katharine's responsibility, which will be theirs in a year, is to ensure the parties involved know what could, can, and will happen under various circumstances.

They arrive in the early afternoon on a Saturday. Katharine knocks on the door. Mrs. Randall opens it and welcomes her and the others into the house. She moves to the stool by the fire, near the cradle with the new babe in it. Mrs. Randall is looking much better. Mr. Randall sits on the other side, enjoying a pint and reading the paper.

After the niceties are dealt with, Katharine advises the Randalls that, in her medical opinion, Mrs. Randall should consider not having any more children due to her weakened heart.

"Having another child would be too taxing on Mrs. Randall's already weak heart, and the probability of her and the baby not surviving would be extremely high."

Mrs. Randall looks relieved but doesn't say a word. Mr. Randall is a different story. He says, "You have no idea what you're talking about. You have no right to tell me what my wife and I can or cannot do."

His outburst doesn't faze Katharine. She expected it, and she doesn't flinch. She looks directly at Mrs. Randall, who nods in acknowledgment. Katharine then turns her eyes to Mr. Randall and responds calmly but firmly.

"You misunderstood what I was saying to you, Mr. Randall. I wasn't telling you what to do or not to do. I provided you with medical information to ensure you're both aware of the possibilities. You can have another child and risk losing a wife and mother to your already five children, or take the blessing of the five children the Lord has entrusted to you and raise them in a family where they have both a mother and father—it's up to you. My moral and ethical obligation is to advise you of what can, could, and likely will happen in this regard."

Mr. Randall is livid and yells, "I will not tolerate this in my house. The children are to be returned to me immediately. How dare you come into my home and tell me what I can and cannot do!"

"Mr. Randall, it's late in the day. Your children are coming home tomorrow. Mrs. Jones had something special planned for the children this evening, as it's their last night with us. I'll have them back here tomorrow as originally arranged," informs Ethan.

Ethan rises and takes his hand under Katharine's arm to indicate they're leaving.

"Katharine, can you take Liam and Tamara to the wagon, please?"

Slightly confused but taking his lead, she nods and says, "Good afternoon." She moves to the door, and Liam and Tamara follow behind.

Once the door is shut, Ethan pinches the top of his nose between his eyes, takes a deep breath, and then moves in front of Mrs. Randall.

"Mr. and Mrs. Randall, I would like to reiterate a sentiment Ms. Katharine just spoke. She is the doctor for this community for the next year. She's here to teach and mentor Tamara and Liam to care for this community medically. As such, it will be their ethical and moral obligation to provide medical information to patients they may or may not like. As the Laird of this community, they will have my full support. You, sir, are not a doctor. You are a shipbuilder, and a very good one at that. When it comes to building ships, you're an expert. Regarding medicine, Ms. Katharine is the expert, and suggesting she doesn't know what she's talking about is absurd. You may not like what she had to tell you, but it's the truth. Are we clear, Mr. Randall?"

"Yes, Laird."

"Mrs. Randall, good day. I will see you tomorrow when I return the children home."

"Thank you, Laird," she weakly responds as she rocks the cradle beside her.

Ethan moves to the door and opens it, and behind him, Mr. Randall moves.

Liam is already in the driver's seat of the wagon, with Katharine and Tamara in the back. Mr. Randall watches as Ethan climbs up beside Liam. The wagon begins its motion toward the estate. With a final glance back, Katharine can see Mrs.

Randall sitting on her stool beside the crib, rocking it with one hand and looking like she doesn't have the strength to do that. And then the door slams closed. She has four other children coming home tomorrow. Katharine and Tamara have tried to show Colin and Charlotte what they must do to help out their mother for the next few weeks. She's done all she can; now it's up to them. Katharine closes her eyes and says a quick prayer. Then she opens them to see that Ethan has been watching her.

"Mr. Randall goes to work on Monday and will be there all week. Perhaps we could have someone come over a few hours daily to help Mrs. Randall," suggests Liam.

"It would give her another week to gain some strength," adds Tamara.

"It would certainly help, but Mr. Randall won't like it," responds Katharine.

"What about my sister Sara? She's not able to work in the fields this week. Maybe she could come over and help out Mrs. Randall instead. Then she can feel like she's contributing but in a different way," responds Liam.

"Brilliant idea, Liam. You can speak with her tomorrow while Laird returns the children to their home," says Tamara.

"Sounds like we can help two people in this community next week," says Katharine.

"Aye, and it's a good idea too, Liam," says Ethan as he winks at Katharine and Tamara.

"Since we have time to talk on our way back, Liam and Tamara, did either of you have questions about what happened at the Randall house?" Katharine inquires.

There's a pause, as though they're trying to figure out the right words. Tamara is the first to ask, "Was it necessary to have this conversation with them both?"

"Yes, Tamara, it was. As husband and wife, they needed to be told what could happen if she became pregnant again. In this case, you can tell by Mr. Randall's reaction—"

"But why could we not just speak directly to Mrs. Randall? She's the one who'll be getting pregnant."

"Liam, if we told Mrs. Randall, do you think she could converse with her husband?"

"Not likely."

"So if he's not aware of the situation—"

"I see."

"I know it may be uncomfortable, but it has to be discussed. They know what can happen if she becomes pregnant again. I did what was my responsibility as a doctor: to ensure my patients were aware of all possibilities. The rest is up to them and God."

For the duration of the ride back to the estate, there's a heaviness as the realization of what else they may have to deal with this year begins to take effect. The last doctor dealt with all this and taught them the basics. With only a year to learn, they need to know all parts: the good, the bad, and the ugly.

SEVENTEEN

YOU CAN HEAR the scratching of the pen across the paper as Katharine speaks to herself while completing notes from the day. It's been a good week for the three of them working as a team to look after those who came to the infirmary for assistance and those they visited. There was nothing major, just many minor cuts, bruises, a sprain, and a dislocated shoulder, but for the most part, these were great opportunities for Katharine to step back and watch Liam and Tamara work. In the meantime, they were learning to use the plants in the area for medical purposes, effectively keeping notes and restocking medical supplies.

Katharine stops to rub her scalp, temple, neck, and shoulders to reduce the tension. She has a slight headache and removes her braid to allow her hair to fall loosely. She's tired from the day of working in the new infirmary. After a stretch, she leans down to cross her arms on the desk. She lays her head down to ease the headache. She can hear the howling of the wind, the sound of the rain hitting the window, and the crackling of a fire to ward off the damp chill; it soon lulls her into sleep.

"What a miserable time getting home this evening," says Ethan as he takes the stairs to the study. The storm delayed them, and everyone was wet and cold. He should first go to his room to change but knows Katharine will be in the study. He hasn't seen her in a week, and he misses her. He opens the study door and drops his bag on his desk. He looks across to find Katharine slumped over her desk.

"Katharine," he says. She doesn't move. He removes his wet coat, hangs it on the hook by the fire, and moves toward her. Her hair is loose. He has never seen her with her hair loose. Golden thread glistening in the firelight with the red highlights twinkling through is what comes to his mind. It falls just past her shoulders. He moves toward her, squats down, puts one hand on the desk, and the other glides over her mane.

"Katharine, Katharine."

She stirs slightly. He moves his hand to hers and repeats her name.

"Yes," she says as she opens her eyes. She looks straight into Ethan's beautiful blue eyes. She smiles, lifts her head, and feels the coldness of his hand on hers.

"Are you all right?" asks Ethan. He moves his hand to her back to touch the tips of her hair, and the other holds her hand.

Katharine feels both fire on her back and ice on her hands. She pushes up from the desk.

"Yes. I, hmmm, I had a headache and thought I'd put my head down for a minute. I guess I was more tired than I realized. How long have you been here?"

"I just arrived. This storm held us up, but we finally made it through."

"You're cold," she says as she takes his hand and rubs it to try and warm it up. "I can feel it in your hand when you touch me. Go sit by the fire," she says in her I-am-the-doctor tone.

"Aye, good idea," he says, but he doesn't move.

"Ethan, the fire." She nods as she moves to put her hair back in a braid.

Ethan stands to move to the fire and says, "If having your hair down helps with your headache, please keep it down. Besides, I like it that way."

She blushes slightly, tucks it in, and puts her tie in to pull it into a loose tail. It's a compromise, as she doesn't have it down with anyone but her family.

Ethan takes his seat by the fire. He removes his boots and places them by the fire to help them dry.

"Can you stay awake long enough to tell me how the week went? Mrs. Jones is bringing up some tea," he says, hoping that will keep her here for a wee bit longer.

"I think so," she says as she stretches. On cue, you hear a knock, and in comes Mrs. Jones and William.

"Here you go, Laird, a good cuppa tea for you both." She places the tray on the side table. "William has a plate I kept for you from dinner." William places it on the table beside where Ethan is sitting.

"Good night to you both," says Mrs. Jones.

William goes over to Katharine and hugs her.

"Good night, William."

"Good night, Ms. Katie." He turns and says, "Good night, Laird."

"Good night, William."

Katharine moves to the tea tray. "How do you take yours, Ethan?"

"Black, please."

Katharine pours him tea as he takes his supper plate from the table. He takes a whiff of the food and sighs. Katharine brings him his tea and places it on the table where William had left his food. She returns to get her tea and settles in the chair opposite him. Having taken a few bites of food and managed a sip of tea, Ethan looks at Katharine, and before he takes his next bite, he asks, "So what did I miss?"

The next morning, Katharine slept in after staying up late to talk with Ethan. She was in a hurry to visit the glen when Bonnie stopped her.

"Katharine, Ethan wants to see you in the study before you head to the infirmary this morning."

"Oh, thank you, Bonnie." They nod to each other. "I might as well see what he wants now, as I was going to go straight to the infirmary from the glen," she says.

Bonnie heads out the back door toward the stable. The study door is open, but Katharine knocks anyway and enters. Ethan looks up and smiles.

"Katharine."

"Ethan. Bonnie said you wanted to see me."

He nods and motions to the chair in front of his desk. "Please have a seat. I wanted to speak to you about coming into the shipyard on Monday and spending the week there with our workers. Most of them are also tenants here on the estate. But there are about twelve single men who occasionally require medical assistance. Two recently sustained broken bones, so we'd like you to look at them." Ethan moves from behind his desk to lean against the front as Katharine takes the offered seat.

"Can the workers not get medical attention in town?"

"Yes, but then they must pay for it out of their pockets. There's no charge for using the services of the doctor we provide. Unfortunately, when the last two injured themselves, as we had no medical services, we had them go to see a doctor, and we paid for it. They're both back to work and having some difficulties. We'd like you to assess them." Ethan crosses his legs in front of him as his hands grab behind the desk. "We pay our workers a fair wage and try to provide extras. My father and I believe that if you look after the workers, they'll look after the customers. Happy workers mean happy customers."

"I see," says Katharine. "If I may, Ethan, I'd suggest Liam accompany us to the shipyard for the week. The workers will be more receptive to or comfortable with him as a man. The workers should get to know Liam from the start. Let Tamara go in when they're comfortable, and Liam can work with her."

"I never thought of that. You make a good point." He crosses his arms and ponders the point. "Might as well have them dealing with Liam from the beginning. Do you mind letting Liam know?"

"Of course."

"Aye. We'll leave at 7:00 on Monday morning, spend the week in town, and return here at about 6:00 on Friday night."

There's a pause, and just before Katharine speaks, Ethan says, "We'll let Tamara know as well. During your absence, if she requires your assistance, someone can come to get you. We can have you back here in an hour."

"Thank you, Ethan. I'll talk with both of them to inform them of next week's agenda."

Ethan pushes himself off the desk and starts moving back to his chair. "We'll be staying with my brother, Reid. You'll meet him when we get to the shipyard. He's in charge in my absence and will be the person the doctor will ultimately report to, but the supervisor on the floor will have direct contact with you—sorry, Liam. Dr. Bell would come at least once a month to check on all the workers and be available for them. I think we could try to start that again."

"We can see how things go next week. Discuss with Liam and go from there."

"Yes, we can evaluate how things went on Friday evening when we return to the estate."

"As you wish, Ethan. I'll let Liam and Tamara know." She lifts herself from the chair and leaves the room.

"Will I see you this evening at supper?" Ethan sits in his chair and pulls it forward to tackle the papers on his desk.

"I believe so. As long as we're not called away."

"Here's hoping we can all enjoy an evening meal together."

Katharine laughs. Lifting her skirt, she leaves the room. As the door closes, Ethan takes a minute to enjoy the peace he feels from Katharine's smile. He then returns to the work on his desk, which requires his attention.

Making her way into the kitchen, Katharine grabs fruit, bread, and cheese. She puts them in a basket. *Liam and Tamara should be getting back from visiting the tenants' homes this morning. I'll meet them at the infirmary with some food and inform them of Ethan's request.*

On her walk to the infirmary, she sees Liam returning the wagon to the stable; she waves and motions for him to return to the infirmary. Liam waves back and nods to show he understands what she's telling him.

"Good morning, Tamara. How did it go?" asks Katharine as she enters the infirmary.

"It went well once we explained to Mrs. King that you had sent us out to check up on them and that you were available to come out if we thought your expertise was required. I think it also helped that the two of us were together."

"Yes, if the community sees both of you working as a team, they'll feel like they're getting more than just one person helping them."

"Oh, I never thought of that, but aye, it does make sense, doesn't it?"

"Aye, it does."

"What's up, Ms. Katharine?" asks Liam as he enters.

"Ethan spoke with me this morning, and I wanted to share the information with you both. Liam, can you put the kettle on for tea while I set out the goodies I brought? Then we can talk."

Both respond with an "aye" and then set about preparing their working lunch. With the door open to signify someone is in the infirmary, they all sit to enjoy their tea and food. Katharine fills them in on her morning discussion with Ethan about what will happen.

"To be clear, I understand what you're saying. You want me to go with you on Monday, spend the week in town, and play the doctor, and you will play my nurse."

There's a pause while Katharine finishes drinking her tea and realizes what he said. They will be switching roles next week.

"I wouldn't say 'playing,' Liam. You are learning, and what better way? The men in town will be more receptive to you as the doctor and me as the nurse. We can work things out as we go along, and if you're unsure of anything, you could say, 'Ms. Katharine, can you come to take a look, please?' Then, once I've assessed it, we can work together to deal with the matter, just as we do here."

Liam takes a bite of his bread and cheese. "I think I can handle it."

"This will allow you to bring Tamara along so you can work together, and as they grow accustomed to you, you can each fill the position."

"I see what you mean, Ms. Katharine. It's just like what you're doing now. You're teaching us to deal with tenant issues, but we know you're available if needed."

"May I say you are both excellent learners. As you can see, most of your job isn't about the ailments but about assuring the person you're looking after and putting their concerns at ease. When you have confidence in what you do, it shows. But remember, above all else, the health and welfare of everyone is your responsibility. Sometimes the ailment may affect more than one person, so you must also keep that in mind."

"Like the Randall family," says Tamara.

"Yes, and why is that, Liam?"

He takes a minute to think about it. "Mrs. Randall has a heart condition. If she had to take care of the newborn and her other children and do her regular duties, she wouldn't have the chance to recuperate and may not be with us today."

"Exactly. That's why keeping records and, most of all, keeping in touch with your patients professionally and personally is important. Going out to see them regularly shows them you care and allows you to make sure things are okay, and if something is to be addressed, it can be."

There's a knock at the door. "May we come in?" a low voice says.

"Aye. What do we have here?" says Liam as he moves out the door to help the father bring in his boy, whose left pant leg is ripped open.

"My boy was helping me cut some firewood when a piece of wood with a branch caught him."

"Bring him in and let's take a look."

Tamara and Katharine clear the area of the food, and the father brings the boy in to place him on the examination table. Katharine steps back to let Liam and Tamara work together.

These two will make a good pair of doctors one day. She listens to them speak to the father and boy about how they check the cut and what their assessment is.

"Ms. Katharine, did you want to take a look?" asks Tamara.

Katharine moves over and examines the cleaned wound. She agrees with their assessment and tells the father so.

"The wound will be bandaged, and in a few days, we can come out and check on it and see if the bandage needs to be changed. I believe you're one of the workers from the shipyard, so you won't be able to bring him to us. Is that correct?"

"Yes, it is, and thank you, Ms. Katharine."

"No need to thank me. Liam and Tamara have done all the work."

The father smiles, grateful for the help.

EIGHTEEN

LATER IN THE afternoon, Katharine is gardening outside of the Stuart infirmary. She stands up to stretch from replanting some of the myrtle and heather around the building. Putting them near the infirmary will allow them easy access to make medicines for various ailments and help make the place look inviting, as it did in the photo Ethan had shown her.

Liam and Tamara are inside. She's about to yell for William when he comes up beside her with a tin cup full of water.

"Ms. Katie, would you like something to drink?"

"Yes, I would, William." She takes it, looks, and then asks, "Where did you get the water from, William?"

"The water container you brought with you."

"Thank you, William." She drinks all the water in the cup.

As she's about to return the cup to William, she hears horses' hooves approaching them. She turns and recognizes Ty as one rider, but the other she does not.

"Ms. Katharine, your assistance is needed. This is Ryan from the Young parish, our neighbours."

"Good day, Ms." Ryan nods. "If you'll follow me, our midwife has requested assistance."

"I will need to get my bag."

"I'm ahead of you there, Katharine." Ty dismounts and brings Tally over. On the side, he has secured her bag and cloak.

"Good man, Ty," she says as she puts on her cloak. Then she mounts Tally. "Please tell Liam and Tamara where I am and take William back to Mrs. Jones at the estate."

Ty nods and moves to the building.

Ryan lifts his hand to wave. Katharine turns to see Tamara in the window, waving at him.

"Lead the way, Ryan."

"Yes, Ms."

With both horses galloping, they soon arrive at the Young estate.

At the front of the estate home, Ryan and Katharine dismount. Two young men take the horses, and Ryan escorts her in. A maid immediately shows them to the bed chamber.

"Ryan, please stay outside the door. If I should require anything, I trust you will obtain it for me."

"Certainly, Ms. Katharine."

She nods, enters the bed chamber, and looks to the midwife. In a calm voice, Katharine greets the midwife: "Good morning, I'm Ms. Katharine. I was told you asked for me. How may I assist you?"

"I'm Mrs. Hannah. Thank you for coming. We heard—"

She can't finish the sentence, as a scream cuts through the room. Katharine's attention immediately turns to the woman in the bed.

"This is Ms. Grace. Her baby is early, and she's already miscarried twice," whispers Mrs. Hannah.

"Grace, my name is Katharine, and I'm here to assist in your birth."

"Please, please, please make the pain go away," she says as she twists in the bed.

"Grace, I'll need to examine you. May I have your permission to do so?"

"Aye, aye, please."

"Grace, I need you to take some deep breaths, like this." Katherine breathes in through her nose and then out through her mouth, and Grace follows suit.

"Very good; keep doing that until I tell you to stop."

Katharine removes her cloak, moves to her bag, and removes her apron and clothes. She sees no basin of water in the room.

"Mrs. Hannah, can you please get me clean water? Hot is preferred, or a bottle of alcohol, whichever is faster to obtain. I need them to wash up before I begin my examination. I'll also require you to do the same."

"We don't—"

Katharine holds up her hand. "I understand you may not do it, Mrs. Hannah, but I do. You've asked me to come to assist you. If you choose not to clean before you work with Ms. Grace, I must ask you to leave."

"I'll have a basin of water brought in." She moves out of the room.

"That's right, Grace, keep breathing. You're doing splendidly."

Mrs. Hannah returns with a basin of water. Katharine washes up quickly, dons her apron, and then moves to examine Grace. In her examination, she determines that Grace is carrying two babies. Her size and the fact that she hears two heartbeats are good signs. When she checks on the position, she finds that the first one is breech. It's not in the proper position to go head-first down the birth canal.

"Grace, the first babe isn't in the correct position to come through the birth canal; we'll have to reposition him."

Grace looks at her with a terrified expression. Then she looks at Mrs. Hannah.

"First babe? You mean there's more than one?"

"Yes, I heard two heartbeats when I examined you."

"Oh my goodness, how is this possible? No, it can't be twins; I'm not ready for twins."

Katharine takes Grace's hand and says, "You can do this. You have me and Mrs. Hannah." She looks up and sees that Mrs. Hannah is as frightened as Grace. "It will be difficult, Grace. I won't lie, but I've delivered twins before." She squeezes her hand and then moves to the foot of the bed. "Shall we get your son into position?"

"Son? How do you know?"

"I don't. He's being difficult, so I assume it's a boy. Are you ready?"

Katharine works slowly to adjust the babe into position. It's tedious, grueling, and taxing for Grace, but the babe is finally turned to the proper position.

"When I say push, Grace, you need to push."

"I can't," she says, exhausted from the repositioning.

"Yes, you can. Mrs. Hannah, when I say push, I need you to gently push down on Grace's belly when she pushes."

Twenty minutes later, the first babe is born, crying as he comes out.

"What did I tell you, Grace? A boy." The child lets out a wail. Grace is crying, a mix of joy and exhaustion. Katharine and Mrs. Hannah work together to deal with the first child. No sooner have they wrapped him and placed him in a maid's arms when Grace is screaming from the contraction for the second child, born five minutes later. Grace lies on the bed entirely and utterly exhausted. Her arms are to her sides, her head on the pillow, and tears spill down her face. A second maid has entered along with Tamara.

"I brought this for you, Ms. Katharine, to see if I could be of assistance," says Tamara as she places the basin of hot water on the side table.

Katharine looks at Tamara and nods. She reminds Katharine so much of herself at that age. She's willing to step in and help and learn more. She'll do well as a doctor on the Stuart estate.

"Tamara, could you help me and the maids with the babies?" Katharine checks each baby to ensure their health, and then Tamara works with the maids to clean the babies. Everything looks normal: lots of cries, and all fingers, toes, arms, and legs. Each one looks and feels good.

"Mrs. Hannah, I suggest you put them together for now. They're used to being together and will calm each other down. Tamara, why don't you tell Ryan that Mr. Young has a healthy baby boy and girl."

"Yes, Ms. Katharine."

"Mrs. Hannah, when Tamara returns, we'll show you how to look after Grace, if you like."

Mrs. Hannah nods to Katharine.

The babes have been laid together in a chest drawer.

"May I see them?" whispers Grace.

"Of course you can." Mrs. Hannah and a maid bring the chest drawer over. Grace moves her head to see them but is too tired to lift them.

"They're so beautiful," says Katharine. "If I may say so, Grace, you were brilliant in delivering these two rascals."

Grace starts to cry again.

Tamara returns to the room. "Ryan asked when Laird Young could see the babies and wife."

"Grace, are you up to seeing your husband?"

"No, yes, I don't know." She's still crying and moving her head back and forth.

"How about once we have you cleaned up, changed, and ready to show off your newborns, you can let us know?"

Grace nods and tries to stop crying.

"Tamara, may I ask you to assist Mrs. Hannah in looking after Ms. Grace."

"Certainly, Ms. Katharine."

Once Grace is looked after, she feels she can handle seeing her husband. He enters the room and moves directly over to Grace, who's sitting up. He kisses her forehead, and after a minute of just looking at her, he says, "My dear, how are you?"

"I'm exhausted, Gavin. But I wanted you to meet your children." She motions to the drawer. He moves over, and Mrs. Hannah is there to pick up the boy and give it to him.

"A boy and a girl, Laird."

"Oh my goodness, Grace."

"I know—it wasn't until Ms. Katharine here told us."

"I and my family are indebted to you, Ms. Katharine."

"There's no need for that, sir. Grace did most of the work; we just helped out. In any event, I should let you and your wife enjoy this time with your children."

"I'll have Ryan return you and Tamara to the Stuart estate."

"If it's all right with you and Mrs. Hannah, I'd like to come by tomorrow to check in on the patients—Grace and the children."

"We'll see you tomorrow," says Gavin.

Mrs. Hannah smiles and nods to Katharine as she delivers the girl to Grace to hold while her husband cradles their son.

Katharine returns the nod to Mrs. Hannah. She and Tamara collect their things and leave the room. Ryan is waiting by the stairs to escort them back to the Stuart estate.

On their way back, Ryan and Tamara engage in friendly banter. Katharine is quite surprised at how at ease they are with each other.

"This is open and free banter between you two. How long have you known each other?" Katharine asks.

They both look at each other, not sure how to answer.

"Ryan, you waved to Tamara, and she returned the wave before we departed the Stuart estate. This says you know each other. Well, come on, come on, let's have it."

"Since we were children, Ms. Katharine," answers Tamara.

"Tamara's mother and my mother are best friends," Ryan says.

"So even though you have different lairds, can you still interact with each other?"

"Yes, Ms. Katharine. We're neighbours and friends. We may not belong to the same clan, but we're not enemies."

"Then I should ask, do the Stuarts have enemy clans I should be aware of?"

"No, Ms. Katharine. The area's clans have learned that being good neighbours and working together is more beneficial than trying to take over all the time," says Tamara as she winks at Ryan.

"The Young and Stuart clan have gotten along for years, Ms. Katharine. Several clan members have married, so that also helps to keep the peace," injects Ryan.

"Knowing I don't have to worry about a clan war is a relief. Can you imagine the files we'd have to do, Tamara?"

Tamara and Katharine laugh heartily.

"I think this is a private joke I'm not getting," interjects Ryan.

"Aye, it is Ryan; I'll tell you later," finishes Tamara.

The conversation turns back to the bantering between Tamara and Ryan, with Katharine smiling as she listens to the quick, rapid exchanges. She had this with Poppy and has missed it so much. Listening to it gives her a memory to hold on to and joy in her heart.

The following day, Katharine and Tamara travel to the Young estate to check in with Grace and the newborns. Mrs. Hannah greets them when they arrive and explains that Grace struggles to feed the two babies. Katharine asks Tamara to help Mrs. Hannah prepare and bring a bottle to the bed chamber. As the two head to the kitchen to prepare the bottle, Katharine hears her name being called.

"Katharine, welcome; it's good to see you," says Gavin as he comes down the stairs.

"Aye, good morning," she replies.

"Grace is up in our room with the children. Did you need me to show you the way?"

"Please, if you wouldn't mind," says Katharine as she lifts her skirt to make her way up the stairs.

Gavin shows her the way. "Let me know if you need anything. I'll leave you to tend to my wife."

"Thank you, Laird Young."

"Please, call me Gavin."

"Gavin," she says as she nods and then turns the doorknob to enter. Katharine notices that Grace is struggling to feed the babe at her breast.

"Good morning, Grace. How are you doing this morning?" asks Katharine.

"I don't know what I'm doing wrong," cries Grace.

Katharine moves over to the chair where Grace is sitting. "May I?" she asks and takes the child from Grace. "As a brand-new mother to twins, I suggest that you conserve your energy and sanity by alternating between nursing one child and bottle-feeding the other one. It looks like this one has already been fed," Katharine says as she looks down at the one sound asleep in the crib beside the chair.

"Yes, about an hour ago," cries Grace as she buttons up her gown and wipes away tears.

"Grace, you had a difficult birth, and your body needs to heal and adjust. Right now, you can produce enough milk for one babe," says Katharine as a knock is heard on the door.

Tamara and Mrs. Hannah enter. "The bottle you asked for, Ms. Katharine," says Mrs. Hannah as she hands it to Katharine.

"Thank you, Mrs. Hannah," says Katharine as she takes the bottle.

"So today, this little one is going to be bottle-fed. Tomorrow, it will be that one." She nods to the crib and places the bottle in the baby's mouth. The baby begins to suck and take the bottle.

Grace lets out another cry and begins to sob uncontrollably.

"Tamara, can you finish feeding this little one?" Katharine directs as she moves to place the child in Tamara's arms.

"Mrs. Hannah, has Grace eaten anything yet this morning?" questions Katharine.

"Not that I know, Ms. Katharine," replies Mrs. Hannah.

"I think a nice cup of coffee and a good hearty breakfast would help Lady Young keep her strength up," says Katharine, signaling to Mrs. Hannah that Grace needs to be taken care of.

"I'll go speak to the cook and bring it up to you, my Lady," responds Mrs. Hannah as she leaves the room.

Katharine moves to kneel in front of Grace, like a child would before a parent. "Now, Grace, what's all this crying about?" she asks as she takes her hand.

"I don't know. I don't know. I feel so, so, so—"

Katharine squeezes her hand and says, "You don't need to or have to do it all, Grace. Mrs. Hannah is here, as are Tamara, myself, Gavin, and I'm sure many more."

"Thank you," says Grace as she squeezes Katharine's hand.

"Doctor's orders are that you must care for yourself as much as you do these two wee ones. Mrs. Hannah will be back with food and drink. It looks like this one is ready to join her brother," says Katharine as Tamara lays the child down in the crib.

"Have you decided on names for them?" asks Tamara.

"Yes, we have," says Gavin as he enters the room with a tray of food and a pot of coffee.

"Mrs. Hannah gave me strict orders to make sure you eat and drink to gain your strength," recites Gavin as he puts the tray on the table beside the chair and leans over to kiss his wife. "We've named them Frasier and Fiona. Frasier after my father, and Fiona after Grace's mother."

"Oh, that is so lovely," replies Katharine.

"Grace and I have something for you, Katharine." He takes a thistle brooch from the bureau drawer by the bed, with the Young tartan attached, and hands it to Katharine. "Thank you for ensuring the safe delivery of our children and taking good care of my Grace."

The beautiful piece of jewellery takes Katharine aback. "It's beautiful, but I can't accept it. It's my calling to heal and to use that healing to serve others."

"Katharine, please, we want you to have this. We've already given Mrs. Hannah something, and we truly want you to have it."

"I'll only accept this token of appreciation if, in return, you help me when I require it. This brooch will be our signal to each other."

"Aye, it's a deal," says Gavin.

Katharine takes the brooch, pins it to her dress, and then hugs Grace and Gavin. "I'll be in town at the shipyard next week working with Liam to get him situated with the workers there. I'll see you when I get back. If Mrs. Hannah needs assistance, please have Ryan get Tamara at the infirmary."

Katharine and Tamara take their leave to return to the Stuart estate to prepare for tomorrow. On their ride home, Katharine realizes that if she hadn't come to Scotland, Grace and the children may not have survived. "*'For I know the plans I have for you,'* *declares the Lord.*"[4] She closes her eyes and says, "Thank you, Father, for bringing me here."

"Are you all right, Ms. Katharine?" asks Tamara.

"I am very well and very blessed, Tamara," Katharine replies, smiling back at Tamara and continuing their journey home.

It's a wonderful early afternoon. The sun is shining and there's a warm breeze. The colour of green in different shades and tones, with a pop of purple, blue, and yellow here and there, make for a beautiful landscape to look at as Katharine rides back to the Stuart estate. Once at the stables, she dismounts and walks Tally into her stall. She turns Tally around with them facing the stall door when she catches movement and recognizes Mr. Holmes. You can't miss him with his distinctive Garrick coat.

"Good afternoon, Mr. Holmes," Katharine addresses as she removes her medical bag from the saddle horn and moves out of the stall, closing the door behind her.

He nods to her. Rather than returning the greeting, he responds, "Ms. Katharine, do you want to hear a joke?"

"Why not, Mr. Holmes?" she says, holding her medical bag in both hands.

"Why don't you run with bagpipes?"

Katharine takes a minute to ponder the comment. She tilts her head. Then she moves her right hand up to her chin, tapping it to make it look like she's trying to figure it out.

"I'm not familiar enough with bagpipes, Mr. Holmes. So why don't you run with bagpipes?"

"You could put an aye out, or worse yet, get kilt."

It takes her a moment to understand it using Scottish terms. She moves her hand to cover her mouth, but it doesn't stop the chuckle that escapes. She thinks this is one she needs to remember when she returns to England. The crew on the ship will enjoy it.

Mr. Holmes grins and says, "Aye lass, you got it, aye—eye, kilt—killed."

"Yes, I did get it, Mr. Holmes. It's a good one. I've left Tally in her stall. Can you take care of her for me? I need to get to the infirmary."

---

[4] Jeremiah 29:11

"Aye, that's what I'm here for, Ms. Katharine."

"Thank you," says Katharine as she leaves the stable and heads toward the infirmary. Mr. Holmes watches as she leaves. He moves into the stall to look after Tally. The grin on his face is not one of humour but of a more sinister thought. "She thinks she's so smart coming here to play doctor. An Englishwoman! What was Laird thinking? Nothing but trouble, I tell you, nothing but trouble. I'll have to make the Stuarts see that, won't I?"

"Talking to yourself, Mr. Holmes?" says Ethan as he stops on his way to Ty's office.

"Yes, Laird. Unless the horse developed a voice and is the one doing the talking."

Ethan chuckles at his quick wit. "Tally is back. Did Ms. Katharine go to the house or the infirmary?"

"She asked me to look after Tally, as she was off to the infirmary."

"Thank you, Holmes. Is Mr. Ty in his office?"

"He should be, Laird."

Ethan nods and continues toward the office.

"Now I'm a messenger boy on top of a stable boy," Mr. Holmes says under his breath as he pulls too tight on the stirrup to loosen it. Tally moves to show him that she doesn't appreciate the gesture. "Darn animals," he mutters under his breath and continues to tack the horse as requested.

"Ty, do you have a moment?"

"Of course, Ethan. What can I do for you?" asks Ty from behind his desk.

"I wanted to let you know that both Katharine and Liam will be coming to the shipyard tomorrow to start providing medical assistance to all the workers."

"You'll need an extra carriage for you three?"

"Yes."

"I assume you'll be staying with your brother, Reid."

"I need you to deliver our bags to the house."

"Consider it done. Does Reid know about Katharine?"

"I told him I'd have the doctor come in on Monday and that we'd stay with him. When I spoke with Katharine, she suggested Liam come along to be the man to deal with the workers, and she'd act as his nurse."

"So he has no idea that it's Katharine who'll be coming, or that Dr. Bennett is a woman?"

"No, I didn't tell him."

"I look forward to hearing all about his reaction. Too bad I won't be there to witness it," says Ty as he leans back in his chair.

"I think he'll be shocked at first, like we all were. But I also believe that he'll be fine once we explain what we'll be doing and he sees for himself that she is more than competent."

Ty decides it's not his place to speak on this and raises his eyes. "I'll have the carriage ready for you. I'll drive it and have Mr. Holmes look after the workers' wagon."

"Excellent, see you later this evening."

"Aye."

Ethan takes his leave, and as he passes by Tally's stall, he can still hear Holmes talking to either the horse or himself. He's unsure which one it is, but he could have sworn he heard Holmes say something like "an Englishwoman." He heads back to the house to tell Mrs. Jones that there will be three fewer people here next week.

NINETEEN

everyone gathers at the stables for their journey into town. Mr. Holmes drives the workers' wagon, while Ty drives the carriage carrying Ethan, Katharine, and Liam. Tally is attached to the back. Katharine looks at Tally and then turns to ask Ethan why she's coming.

"Just in case you need to be called back here. We did tell Tamara that if she requires you to let us know."

"I didn't think of that. Thank you, Ethan."

Ethan extends his hand to help Katharine into the carriage. She takes it and takes her seat opposite Liam. Ethan climbs in and sits beside Katharine. It takes about an hour to get to the shipyard. The workers immediately go to work, and Mr. Holmes leads the wagon back to the Stuart estate. Ethan assists Katharine out of the carriage and instructs Ty to deliver Tally to the horse livery nearby, and their belongings to Reid's home. Ethan, Katharine, and Liam head to the offices. Ms. Fanny, Ethan and Reid's secretary, stands at her desk to greet them as they enter.

"Good morning, Ms. Fanny."

"Good morning, Mr. Ethan; I see we have visitors."

"Yes. Ms. Fanny, I'd like you to meet Ms. Katharine and Mr. Liam. Liam will oversee the medical needs here at the shipyard, and Katharine is mentoring him."

Ms. Fanny tactfully nods to indicate that she understands. "Your brother is in his office expecting you." She gestures to his office and nods to Liam and Katharine as she sits back down to finish the correspondence she's working on.

"Follow me." Ethan leads them to the office ahead. He knocks and enters. "Good morning, brother. How are you this morning?"

"I'm doing well, brother." Reid comes around from behind his desk to hug Ethan.

"So how did things go with the new doctor?"

"Speaking of which, I'd like to present Ms. Katharine Bennett, our new doctor from England."

During the introduction, Katharine extends her hand to shake Reid's. Reid takes Katharine's hand and shakes it. Katharine immediately notices in his facial expression and handshake that he will not take too kindly to a woman in this role. Once he removes his hand, Reid says what she has heard so many times before.

"Ms. Bennett, no disrespect, but you're not what we expected. To be brutally honest, it's doubtful the men will come to you as a woman, playing doctor, for medical assistance."

Katharine smiles at Reid and with such grace says, "Yes, Mr. Stuart, I believe this is a discussion Mr. Ethan and I had a few days ago. That's why Mr. Ethan agreed it would be best if Liam were introduced as the person to whom the workers would be coming for medical assistance. Is that not right, Mr. Ethan?"

Ethan is a bit dumbfounded at how his brother has spoken and behaved. "Yes, Ms. Katharine, it is." It's said in a tone she hasn't heard before—stern and aggressive.

Katharine steps slightly back to be beside Liam. She puts her arm around Liam to guide him forward so Reid can see whom she is speaking of.

"Liam is not qualified as a doctor, so he will require someone to guide and assist him. As you know, Mr. Stuart, most of your workers are also tenants on the estate. They've been quite aware of who I am and what I can do since the day I arrived almost two months ago. But to ensure your workers receive the best medical attention, I can act as his nurse this week and mentor him through his appointments."

"Wise decision, Ms. Bennett."

"No, Mr. Stuart, years of experience."

You could cut the tension in the room with a knife. These two do not like each other at all. Ethan knows Katharine is as riled as she was when she dealt with Mr. Randall. He must get his brother alone to talk with him about his hostility toward Katharine.

"Liam, Katharine—Ms. Franny will show you to my office; I'll be there momentarily."

They leave Reid's office. Once the door is closed, Ethan turns to Reid and, in his controlled voice, says, "What was that all about, dear brother?"

"Seriously, Ethan," Reid says as he moves back behind his desk, "did you honestly think the men would respond to her as a doctor?"

Ethan moves to the desk, places his hands on it, and leans in. "Actually, I didn't think about it. It was Katharine who brought it to my attention. She said this would be the case. That's why we brought Liam. You didn't even give us a chance to explain; you took one look at her and … I have no words for your treatment; I know we were raised better than that, Reid."

"Ethan, you live in your world, and I live in mine. Maybe out in the fields they're more accepting of women doing a man's job, but here in town, it will not fly."

"Perhaps not, but after I witnessed how she dealt with Mr. Randall during the birth of his child on the day she arrived, I believe she can handle anything thrown at her, including these shipyard workers. As she said, I would also like to remind you that those tenant workers already know who she is and what she's capable of." He leans closer. "As much as I love you, Reid, I will not tolerate disrespect. Katharine has already proven herself to me, Bonnie, Ty, and Mrs. Jones. Several tenants, including shipyard workers, are indebted to her medical abilities. She has our support, and you will support her in getting Liam situated here as the doctor. Is that clear?"

"Yes, Ethan. You are clear."

"Good," he says, returning and taking his hands off the desk. "Please have Mr. McFarlane come to my office so we can inform him, as the supervisor on the floor, of what we intend to do so we can move forward in getting Liam established."

"I'll do that for you right now, Ethan."

"Oh, and Reid, you know we'll be staying at your home for the week. If you think this is going to be a problem, I will acquire rooms in the hotel."

"Ethan, that won't be necessary; there is plenty of room." He moves up beside Ethan. "I know I may have sounded harsh to Ms. Bennett."

"Reid, you were rude. Katharine may be used to this, but I am not. You will apologize to Katharine."

"So it's Ms. Bennett to me and Katharine to you?"

"Yes, Reid, because I see her as equal, not below me." Ethan leaves his office but doesn't do it quietly. He lets the door slam behind him as he leaves.

Reid is left standing with his mouth open as though to say something. He leans against his desk, crosses his legs, and pinches the bridge between nose and eyes, thinking this is not how this Monday was supposed to go. *Ethan and I have had our differences before; they've been worked out, or we've agreed to disagree. We'll have the opportunity to talk later this evening after supper.* In the meantime, he moves from his desk to the door. "Better get Mr. McFarlane and see if we can try and salvage this day."

Reid finds Mr. McFarlane on the floor. He brings him back to Ethan's office and returns to his own.

Ethan introduces Mr. McFarlane to Liam and Katharine. He explains the situation to Mr. McFarlane, who's not convinced this will work. However, Ethan is the boss, so he'll do as instructed.

"Ms. Bennett, Liam, if you follow me, I'll show you to the room Dr. Bell used to see anyone who required medical attention."

"Thank you, Mr. McFarlane," replies Katharine as she gestures to Liam to lead the way.

"If you need me, please come get me. I'll be in my office," says Ethan.

They both nod to him and then follow Mr. McFarlane out the door, who leads them down the flight of stairs to the work floor.

"This is my office," he says, pointing. "And this is the medical office." The medical office is right beside his. He opens the door and turns on the light. "It may need some cleaning, as it hasn't been used in quite some time."

"Thank you, Mr. McFarlane. May I ask where we can get a bucket, some rags, hot water, and soap to do a little cleaning?" Katharine says as she moves around the room.

"I can show you, Ms. Bennett."

"Ms. Katharine, why don't you look around further while Mr. McFarlane shows me where I can get those items. I think I may need a few trips for hot water," says Liam as he looks around the room himself.

"Excellent idea, Liam," she replies, noticing a coat rack in the corner. She pulls it out. "You'll work well for what I need right now." She hangs her bag from one of the hooks, removes her cloak, and hangs it on the rack. "All right, time to get to work," she says as she takes her apron from her bag. Once it's tied, she rolls up her sleeves. "Where to start?"

"Here we go, Ms. Katharine," says Liam as he returns with a bucket of water, soap, and rags. "I found this brush; it looks brand new. I asked, and they said we could use it."

"Well, Dr. Liam, since this is going to be your office, where would you like to start?"

The smile of confidence that spreads across Liam's face is enough for Katharine to see he appreciates her letting him take the lead. Katharine lets Liam show her how he wants the room set up. It takes them a few hours to clean, check the supplies, and organize them. The door is kept open while they work to air the room and allow others to see what's happening. Liam moves his desk and chair to be in front of the window so he can see out on the work floor. A chair is placed by his desk and just inside the door so a worker can come in and sit down.

"Excuse me, Ms., Mr. McFarlane said I should come to see you about this cut," the worker says as he holds a rag to his left hand.

"Yes, please come in." Katharine motions the worker to sit in the chair just to the left as he enters the door. "Liam, you have your first patient."

"What do we have here?" he asks as he moves to the desk chair. It has wheels, so he can move over to see about the hand while staying in the chair.

The worker removes the rag to show that his index finger has been cut from the tip to the knuckle.

"How did you do this?"

"I was sawing a piece, and the saw jumped when I finished. It caught the finger."

"I must clean it to get a better look, Ms. Katharine—"

"Here is clean water and disinfectant for you."

"Thank you."

"What's your name?" asks Katharine. She knows it's best to keep the worker preoccupied while Liam does his work.

"Callum, Ms."

"Callum. You're not one of the tenant workers, are you?"

"No, Ms. Ouch."

"Sorry, I should have warned you. The disinfectant stings," Liam says.

"Liam, can I be of assistance?"

"From what I can see, it looks like a clean cut. It's long but not deep." As he speaks, Katharine leans over to look for herself and nods.

"Can you get me some gauze and tape to bandage this up?"

"Certainly, Liam."

"Callum, I'm going to bandage up your finger. I'll be using your middle one to give support. I'll be here tomorrow and want you to see me before you start your shift so I can look at it and change the bandage. We don't want it to get infected."

"Yes, sir."

Liam completes the bandaging, and Callum returns to the work floor.

"You did well, Liam."

"Thank you, Ms. Katharine."

"Once you're finished with your patient notes, I suggest you take the list we made up for supplies to Mr. McFarlane to see if he can direct you to where to get them. If not, go see Ethan."

While Liam is out, Katharine finishes up the cleaning of the room. She has her back to the door when she hears someone speak to her.

"Spreading your cleanliness, are we?" says Ethan with a hint of sarcasm.

"Yes, I am." She smiles back.

"It looks good," Ethan says as he looks around.

"Liam has done a good job. He moved everything where he wants it. He also handled a patient this morning."

"Yes, he told me. That's why I'm here. I'll take you and Liam to the apothecary to get what you need, and then we'll call it a day."

"Aye."

"Learning a bit of our language, are we?"

Katharine tilts her head and wants to say aye again but decides not to.

"Let me take that bucket for you," Ethan says, taking it from her and heading toward the shed where Liam had gotten everything.

"Ms. Katharine, Mr. McFarlane has indicated he will have the two workers who sustained broken bones see us tomorrow. Mr. Ethan will take us to the apothecary and then to his brother's home" says Liam.

"Yes, he was just here to tell me so." As she speaks, Ethan returns. "Let me grab my cloak and bag. Liam, I'll get your coat too." She brings Liam's coat and hands it to him, along with her bag. "I think it would look better if you carried the bag. I'll give you the honour of turning off the lights and closing the door to your office."

The grin she saw earlier beams back as he takes her bag, moves over to turn off the light, and closes the door.

Ethan places his hand on Katharine's waist. "Shall we?" She moves with him, and Liam follows behind.

The walk to the apothecary allows Katharine to take in the view along the pier. It reminds her of the dock back home where her family's business is located. It has good and bad parts, but being by the water is calming. Ethan guides her, and she half listens to what he says while talking to Liam. She's too in her little world of the sounds and smells to interrupt.

They make their purchases and head toward Reid's house, where they'll stay until Friday morning. Katharine notices that they're walking downhill toward the water and that the wooden flat walkway by the harbour is now a twist and turn of cobblestone beneath their feet. She sees how the houses are all connected, with the door set in and the number attached to it so you can easily find which house is which. They turn the corner and come upon steps that lead down to a home on the corner.

"We're here," says Ethan, moving his head to indicate that the house before them is where they'll call home for the next week.

"My word, it's so ..." Katharine pauses momentarily because her first instinct is to say how haunting it looks. It's a magnificent home but sticks out compared to all the other row houses around it. She sees at least four levels from her quick look;

perhaps it's because it's so skinny and tall on the corner that it looks out of place. If you turn your head just the right way, it seems like it's leaning down, the way the path moves. She notices small balconies on the fourth floor. Maybe one of those rooms will be hers so that she can enjoy the morning out there. The only door she sees is right at a ninety-degree angle; it connects one side to the other. She needs a moment to take it in. The domes on the roof look like mushroom caps, but they remind her of a church steeple. If you think about it, it seems like the church is in the middle of the town square, with everyone living around it.

Thank goodness for Liam, who says, "Mr. Ethan, how did our bags get here?"

"I had Ty deliver them on his way back to the estate this morning. He parked at the end and walked them down."

"My goodness, that must have been a trek."

"No, the trek is Friday when he comes to pick them up and has to carry them up the lane," he replies as he motions up behind them.

Katharine knew how she felt while walking down the hill, but when she turns around, it's apparent how right she was. The cobblestone path, which moves like a snake, gives the impression that she was moving side to side, not down, but now she can see the incline.

"We'll certainly get our exercise this week, Liam," says Katharine as she turns to Liam and smiles.

"It's not as bad as it looks," says Ethan.

"Says the man who walks this way whenever he's in town. We're used to walking on open land and riding everywhere. But we'll persevere, won't we, Liam? It will make us good, hearty Scottish men," replies Katharine as she stomps her foot and swings her arm to show her newfound energy.

Ethan and Liam find her antics amusing, and she's rewarded with enthusiastic laughter.

"Liam, are you ready to find our living arrangements for the week?"

"Yes, Ms. Katharine, let's see what the Stuart townhouse looks like," he says as he takes the stairs ahead of them.

Ethan moves to the first step and turns back to say, "Katharine, this way." He extends his arm for her to take, and he'll help her down the stairs.

Katharine takes his arm, and as she does, they both feel the warmth from each other and the little spark that always seems to ignite when they touch. Liam reaches the front door ahead of them, and Ethan signals for him to enter; there's no need to knock. Ethan moves aside to allow Katharine to enter before him; as she turns to say thank you, she looks up to where they had stood. Two men with a ladder and a light are lighting the streetlights, cast like a beacon. It's her light that guides her home.

She smiles at the thought and then looks up, seeing the curiosity in Ethan's face. She nods and enters the house to see what lies ahead this evening.

Katharine has to put her emotions aside for dinner this evening. She's used to the type of response she received from Reid, so why is this one bothering her more? Maybe because as Ethan and Bonnie's brother, she expected him to accept her like they have. Those who live in the country seem to have a higher opinion of women. City people are different.

Having some time before dinner allows Katharine to settle in her room. It's on the fourth floor, opposite of what she saw while standing on the street by the stairs. She has a balcony, and you can see the mouth of the port from it. "It will be a beautiful sight in the morning," she says to herself. "I'll keep the curtains tied back so the morning sun will wake me."

The room is small; if she had to guess, she'd say it was a servant's room. Nonetheless, it has a bed, dresser, and bureau, and the colour is a soft peach. For what she needs, it will do. Liam is right across the hall from her. His room is the same, but in grey. She takes the time to unpack and put her stuff away. Since she has time before dinner, she pulls out her paper and pen to write a letter to her mother. She can mail it tomorrow. "I should see if I can telegram my brother this week," she says as she finishes the letter. She makes a mental note to ask Ethan if a telegram can be sent to him while they're in town, just to give him an update.

She finishes sealing the letter and sees by the clock on her desk that it's quarter to seven. My heavens, she has fifteen minutes to get downstairs for the meal. Quickly, she washes her face and hands, resets her hair, and ensures that her dress is acceptable after all the cleaning she and Liam did in the medical office that day.

"Oh dear, perhaps I was to dress up; no one said anything. We can hope for the best."

She quickly glances around the room to make sure everything is in order. Bad habit. She is so used to doing that at home. Out the door, she finds her way down to where they'll be eating. It's pretty straightforward. She follows the beautiful aromas and a large number of stairs. They'll be getting a workout from walking up and down the hill, from the house to work, and up and down from their rooms. *I wonder if Reid planned that*, she thinks to herself as she laughs.

At the bottom of the stairs, she hears voices and follows them until she finds Reid, Ethan, and Liam in a sitting room. She breathes a soft sigh of relief. They haven't changed from their daywear, so what she has on will be acceptable.

"Good evening, gentleman."

"Good evening," the men say in unison.

"Mr. Stuart, the aroma from your kitchen is mouth-watering. If I didn't know any better, I would have thought it was Mrs. Florence's roast chicken I smell."

"Mrs. Florence?" questions Reid.

"Oh, that's the name of our housekeeper back home. The aromas from her cooking are heavenly."

"I'll let the cook know you approve, Ms. Bennett. And you are correct—it is roast chicken. If you'll follow me into the dining room," Reid says, extending his arm to lead her, as Ethan had done to help her down the stairs.

Katharine is polite but declines to take his arm. Instead, she extends her hand to gesture and speaks, "Lead the way, Mr. Stuart."

Reid slightly bows and turns to lead her into the dining room. "Please, Ms. Bennett, you are a guest in my house, and I hope you'll call me Reid." He pulls out the chair to show her where she's to sit.

"Very well, Reid, and you may call me Katharine. However, when I work in the shipyard, I will address you as either Mr. Reid or Mr. Stuart. Just as I do the same for Ethan."

"Of course, Katharine."

Liam and Ethan have taken their seats. Liam is opposite her, and Ethan is opposite his brother at the foot of the table.

"Ethan, while I'm in town and have the opportunity, I'd like to send a telegram to my brother. I can give him an update on how things are going."

"Aye, we can do that tomorrow, Katharine."

The doors leading from the kitchen swing open. Out comes the cook carrying a platter with chicken and vegetables, and a maid with a plate of potatoes, a boat of gravy, and a basket of freshly made bread.

"It smells wonderful," compliments Katharine.

The cook looks at her, blushes slightly, and nods as she says, "Enjoy."

The cook returns to the kitchen. The maid moves to the side table to retrieve the decanter and proceeds to pour wine for the meal. Reid plates for himself and then passes to Katharine until everyone has what they need. It's an excellent meal, and they discuss how Liam and Katharine did at the shipyard.

Once coffee and dessert have been served, Reid clears his throat and addresses Katharine.

"Katharine, I must apologize for my rudeness to you this morning in my office. You were not what I expected. My big brother reminded me that we were raised better than I acted. You and Liam have my full support in any medical assistance you provide to our shipyard workers."

"Thank you, Reid," she says as she sips her coffee and then looks at Ethan, as though to say, "I know you made him do this."

"Liam and I would like to know if you know of any workers we need to see. Do you know of anyone who has been injured of late but was unable or unwilling to get treatment?"

"I can't say. The best person to ask is Mr. MacFarlane."

"I'll look after this inquiry tomorrow, Ms. Katharine," interjects Liam.

Katharine nods at him as she takes another sip of her coffee.

Reid provides Ethan with some updates to change the conversation, as he's done as requested and apologized.

"Gentlemen, if you'll excuse me, I want to retire for the evening." Katharine moves her chair back and rises. The men follow suit. "Reid, please let the cook know the meal was lovely."

"I will. Good night, Katharine. We'll see you at the shipyard tomorrow."

Katharine turns and leaves the room. There's a smile on her face. She knows Ethan made Reid apologize. She also knows he has yet to learn of her experience and background. It's not her job to convince him. It's her job to help those who require her medical attention. In her line of work, she has found that when the patient needs relief from pain or needs someone who knows what they're doing, at the moment they don't care who it is, just that it gets done. It's only afterwards that they have an issue with the fact that she's a woman. She takes her hand and uses the stair rail to ascend the numerous stairs. She will never take for granted again that she lives in a one-floor house.

As she steps, she hears her name spoken. She moves up one step and turns to see Ethan behind her. "Yes?"

With her hand still on the rail, Ethan places his hand on hers and says, "I wanted to reiterate what Reid said. While in the shipyard, please don't hesitate to contact Reid or me if you have any issues. We're both here to support you."

"I have no doubt, Ethan. As you said, happy workers mean happy customers. Liam and I will do our best to ensure you have happy workers."

"Thank you, Katharine. I want to leave around eight tomorrow morning. We can stop at the telegram office before we go to the shipyard. Liam will go in with Reid to stock the medical supplies and speak with Mr. MacFarlane."

"Excellent idea. Good night, Ethan."

"Good night, Katharine," he says as he squeezes her hand and then releases it.

She goes up the stairs as Ethan watches her until she's at the top and moves out of sight.

The days are long, but the week in town passes quickly. They wake early to get to work and arrive home late to eat and sleep. Half of the men who work permanently in town are opening up to Liam and Katharine. A few tenant workers have spoken of their excellent work under Katharine's supervision on the estate and how she saved Mrs. Randall's life. Mr. Randall hasn't said anything bad, but he also hasn't said anything good. This has piqued their curiosity, so even with minor scratches, they come in to see them. In the end, as Katharine said, they will figure it out for themselves and then decide if coming to get free medical assistance is to their benefit, no matter who is administering it.

There have only been minor injuries, and the two men with the broken limbs are evaluated. Katharine doesn't think the limbs were set incorrectly, but because of the casts they had to wear and not using them, they have to get the limbs back in shape. Each worker is instructed to do exercises to strengthen their limbs and is given work limitations. This is to ensure their safety and that of their coworkers.

At supper on Thursday evening, Reid discusses an issue with Ethan. Reid clears his throat and says, "This may not be the best topic to discuss at the dinner table."

"Reid, I'm not squeamish, if that's what you're concerned about," laughs Katharine as she takes a bite of her beef pie.

"Yes, I guess you're not. For a few weeks, we've had a rat problem on the pier."

"How bad?" asks Ethan as he sips his wine glass.

"Fortunately, we haven't had an infestation at the shipyard like some other businesses. We've had a few sightings, but no more than usual. Some workers indicated they saw a few in their barracks, but even then, they couldn't say if it was a mouse or a rat."

"No one has reported being bitten or anything, have they?" questions Liam.

"No. We've made it clear that if anyone is bitten, they must report it. They must also report any sightings: where, when, and those things. In any event, we're doing our best to fix holes and build them out, and we have a person who regularly checks the shipyard building and barracks to ensure they're clean," explains Reid, taking a bite of the food on his plate.

"You mentioned other businesses. How many?" asks Ethan.

"There have been four others. We made inquiries when the business to our right informed us. It seems they're going from one to the other. We've let the business on the left side know as well. However, since we haven't seen a significant increase, we'll continue to monitor and do what we can to keep it that way."

"Please let me—I mean, us—know if that changes. Liam and Katharine will need to be aware of any workers who get bitten so that they can set a course of action," instructs Ethan.

"Liam and I will work to have a procedure in place in case that happens when we're not here," says Katharine as she looks at Liam.

"Thank you, Katharine. I'm sure it won't be necessary," says Reid.

"I've seen how well you and your workers keep the shipyard floor clean and organized as best you can. However, when you have a rodent problem, being either rats or mice, it's not just one but many, and they can transmit diseases. I suggest we err on the side of caution and be prepared, just in case," Katharine politely responds.

"As you wish, Katharine." Reid nods to her as the maid brings out the coffee and dessert.

The topic changes, as it's their last night in the house for dinner, and tonight the cook has outdone herself by making petticoat tails (shortbread) and a wonderful raspberry cranachan (which is like a soft cheesecake with fresh fruit).

Once Katharine excuses herself for the evening, she returns to her room to pack for her return to the Stuart estate. She takes a moment to sit on the bench and looks out the window overlooking the water. It's been a productive week. Liam has done an excellent job establishing himself with the workers. There hasn't been any outright disdain, but there is an undercurrent that she's not welcome. Reid may have apologized and acted out the part, but he doesn't like her being here. The only person who has openly disapproved of her is Mr. Randall. He makes a point of scowling at her whenever they see each other.

I think he's just a bitter man. It's back to working with Tamara and Liam at the estate infirmary. She smiles and says, "Thank you, Lord, for a beautiful week in town. May we finish strong tomorrow."

Before Liam and Katharine leave the shipyard Friday evening, they arrange with Mr. McFarlane for someone to come to the estate and let them know if there is any need for serious medical assistance. Otherwise, having someone on the floor who can do minor treatments daily may be prudent. Mr. McFarlane has been doing that since Dr. Bell passed and will continue to do it regularly.

Ethan, Katharine, and Liam discuss how things went for the week to pass the time on the drive back to the estate from town. It's decided that in two weeks, Liam will return to the shipyard to spend a week providing medical assistance for the workers.

TWENTY

wagon with the workers and the carriage with Ethan, Katharine, and Liam return to the Stuart estate.

"It's nice to be home," sighs Katharine as she climbs out of the carriage with Ethan's help.

Ty takes the carriage to the stables.

"You consider this your home?" questions Ethan with a smirk.

"Until next July, yes, Ethan, this is my home," she says, smiling at him.

"I'll feel the same way when I come back on Friday. Reid likes town life; I, for one, am much more comfortable here," states Ethan.

"Ms. Katharine, do you want these supplies to go to the infirmary?" asks Liam.

"Yes, but we can do that tomorrow. We'll put them in the room at the back of the house and take them over tomorrow," instructs Katharine.

Ty approaches them from the stables. "Mr. Holmes is looking after the horses and wagons. Shall we see what Mrs. Jones has for supper this evening?" Ty says as he rubs his hands together.

"Yes, let's," says Ethan as he turns for Katharine to lead the way.

Halfway to the house, William comes out, running toward them. "Ms. Katie, Ms. Katie, you're back," William yells joyfully.

Katharine drops down to greet the boy with a hug, who runs straight into her, pushing her off balance, and over they go.

"I'm so glad you're happy to see me, William. I've missed you."

"Aye, me too, Ms. Katie."

"William, how about you let Mrs. Jones know we're back while I help Ms. Katie," smirks Ethan.

"Yes, Mr. Ethan, but will you tell me all about your time in town this evening, Ms. Katie?" pleads William as he moves away to hurry off toward the house.

"On one condition, William," she says as she moves back to squat so she is eye to eye with him. "Remember what I taught you about how to say my proper name."

William nods.

"Can you concentrate and say my proper name."

William nods.

Katharine tilts her head as though to say, "Well then?"

"Yes, Ms. Katharine," he says slowly and deliberately.

"Thank you, William. Now off you go as Mr. Ethan asked. We'll catch up."

He dashes off to the house. Ethan helps Katharine, but they need to catch up to Ty and Liam, whom William has already overtaken as he heads to the house.

"You have a way with William, Katharine. He lights up around you."

"He's a child full of joy, Ethan. Even though, in his few years, he's lost both his mother and father, he still maintains his childlike innocence. He's a breath of fresh air, and there are a few things I've noticed he needs some help with, like the pronunciation of certain words, like my proper name."

Ethan halts and puts his hand on Katharine's arm to stop her. "Now that you mention that, we just thought it was due to his age and what has happened to him."

"Things aren't always as they seem, Ethan."

"No, they're not Katharine; no, they're not."

There's a moment between them. They both feel the spark that takes place when one touches the other. Ethan doesn't release his hand from Katharine's arm, and Katharine doesn't release herself from his touch. The smells from the kitchen permeate through the door and pull them out of the moment. The sound of laughter is heard.

"This is what was missing at your brother's house, Ethan," says Katharine as she motions to the house. "Reid has people who work for him, but here you have a family; that makes it home."

"Aye, we may be brothers, but we're very different in how we live. Let's get inside and see what they're up to," Ethan says as he moves his hand to the small of her back.

"Yes, let's," she says, allowing him to guide her into his home. The warmth of the hearth and the people inside pull them through the door, and they finish the evening surrounded by friends and family.

It's been three months since Katharine arrived in Scotland. She came the first week of July, and it's now the first week of October. "My goodness, it will be December soon, which means Christmas," she says to herself. A smile comes across her face. Christmas is her favourite time of the year. She'll have to talk to Mrs. Jones to see if she can make a few items Mrs. Florence would have made at home. This allows her to share with them but also brings a little bit of home to her.

She looks up to see the light rain hitting the window, with the wind moving the branches on the shrubs and trees just outside. It's a brisk, rainy day. Snow isn't expected for another month, so perhaps a white Christmas. Her thoughts are interrupted by the arrival of Tamara and Liam. They've been out to visit some of the tenants to do checkups. She puts her pen back into the ink well and closes her notebook. The door opens to greet her with the cold from outside. In comes Liam with his arms around a young man, with a teenage boy behind him. Katharine moves over to help out.

"I brought them both in, Ms. Katharine. I thought you should look."

Right behind him is Tamara with Mrs. Carr. Tamara begins to explain the situation. "She has the same symptoms as they do, and she's home alone, so—"

"Let's get her over here on the exam table. Liam, can you get them into the chairs, and we'll take a look."

Each patient is checked to see the symptoms and stage they're at. Cold compresses are given to help bring the fever down, and sips of warm tea steeped with willow bark are encouraged to help break the fever and relieve the aches and pains.

They settle the patients, and then another young girl comes through the door, and about thirty minutes later, another young man.

"Ms. Katharine, this is the fifth person who's come to us with the same symptoms today. We don't have room for them all," exclaims Tamara as she looks around the room with trepidation.

"She's right. Some of these patients are from large families. We may see more in the coming days," responds Liam.

"I agree. Where do you suggest we start keeping them? It has to be large enough for the patients and us, but we can keep it isolated."

"The great hall," replies Tamara. "It has two fireplaces for warmth, and there's only one way in and out. We can shut down the entrance from the kitchen."

"Liam, can you please find Ms. Bonnie, Mr. Ty, and Mrs. Jones. However, it would be best if you kept your distance. Until we know what this is, we need to not spread it. Ask them to meet us in the kitchen in twenty minutes. Make sure they know it's urgent."

"Yes, Ms. Katharine." Liam dashes off to gather everyone in the kitchen.

"Tamara, come with me; in the meantime, we'll get what we need, and I'll have you stay with the patients until we can move them into the great hall."

Katharine and Tamara begin to gather the bare necessities. Tamara remains in the infirmary to look after the patients, and Katharine rushes into the kitchen to give the news to the group. Their great hall will be turned into a makeshift infirmary for the foreseeable future.

Katharine had Liam explain the situation, and all three listen carefully. When he's finished, Bonnie turns to Katharine and says, "Are you sure this isn't just a cold due to the change in weather?"

"No, each of the patients is from a different family, all with similar symptoms, and all of them came to us today to tell me it's more than just a cold. It's a sign we have something on our hands that we need to deal with now rather than later.

"Liam is right. Four of the patients are from large families; if sick, the rest could get sick, and so on. We must look after them and ensure we don't spread what they have. Until we determined what's happening, the best defence is to stay away. That's why I've asked you to stay over there, and we're here. Tamara, Liam, and I are already exposed. We need everyone in this house to stay out of the great room. We can look after the main entrance, but this door has to be locked, and only one of us or one of you is to open it. We'll need to let the families know that they must stay in their homes, and if one gets sick, come here to be looked after."

Ty indicates that as Mrs. Carr lives alone, he will go to the homes of the other four patients. Liam provides Ty with the list of families he needs to visit. Ty indicates that he'll have two men inform the rest of the tenants of what's happening so they know that if anyone becomes sick to come to the main house.

"If you notice any of them sick, please let me know so I can go out and check. But make sure you try to convince them to come to the main house so we can help them. Please don't bring them in. It would be best if you kept your distance. We need you out here and healthy."

"I will, Katharine." He moves out the back door toward the stable to talk to the other men visiting the estate tenants.

"Mrs. Jones, can I ask for the stove to be filled with pots so that there's always hot water available? We'll need to clean each patient as they come into the room. We'll do our best to keep the blankets for one person, but they must be washed afterward. I realize it will be more work, but—"

"Aye, it will be, Ms. Katharine, but we must do what we must. We'll do our best."

"That's all I can ask. Bonnie, it may be best to inform your neighbours of what's happening. At this point, it's as a precaution. With us living out here in the rural areas, I hope it's easy enough to keep what this is at bay. But if people are unaware of what's happening, they could come in contact with it or spread it without knowing. Once Ty is back, I'll have him inform the Youngs and McDonalds. Do either of them have doctors in their parish?"

"Aye," says Bonnie.

"When Ty sees them, be sure he indicates that they need to be informed. I'm sure the families will, but—"

"Better to be safe than sorry."

"Yes."

"I'll let him know."

"Thank you, Bonnie."

"Let us know what you need, Katharine."

"Is there someone who could be our messenger? William, of course. If I give him instructions and he delivers them to you, we can continue to do our job here, if that works for you."

"We can certainly try it, Katharine."

"Very well. Liam, you and I will help Tamara get the patients into the great hall. Mrs. Jones, please lock this door behind us so we know no one will be coming in."

"Yes, Ms. Katharine."

They enter the hall through the kitchen door and hear the lock click as they walk across.

"We might as well start putting them all here. Liam, help me move these chairs."

They make an area open for the patients. Liam and Katharine go to the infirmary and work as a team to bring each person into the great hall. Just as they enter with the first patient, they hear William yelling, "Ms. Katie, Ms. Katie."

Katharine turns around and raises her hand. "William, stop." He does just that. Liam takes the patient in, and Katharine moves to bring her full attention to William. She bends down so she is at his eye level. "William, it's essential that you listen to what I have to say and do as I tell you."

"Yes, Ms. Katie."

"I have a very important assignment for you, William. I need you to be my messenger to take messages to Mrs. Jones, Ms. Bonnie, or Mr. Ty. They know that if you're coming, it's because we asked you to. Do you understand?"

He nods.

"Thank you, William. To do this, I'll need you to get your chair and place it under the shield on the wall. We can call it your messenger office, and we'll know where to find you."

William looks at where he's to put his chair and is so excited. "I'll go do that right now, Ms. Katie."

"Thank you, William. I'm sure we'll have a message for you soon." Katharine rises and turns to assist Liam.

The first patient is stripped to one layer before being naked, and then washed, put down on the makeshift bed, and tucked in, and you can hear them breathe a sigh of relief.

"Oh my, I just realized we can't do this to everyone without some privacy," says Katharine.

"How about for now, we bring in the next two male patients, and the other two females can be done in the exam room and brought here. Then we can decide what to do from here on in. We may have to make a changeroom, so to speak," suggests Liam.

"Yes, excellent idea, Liam. Oh, and each person's clothes must be washed before we put them back on or near them."

"Give me a minute; I'll fold his clothes and put them at the foot of his bed so we know who's who."

They're brought in one by one. Getting the fifth patient in the great hall takes about two hours.

William sets up his messenger office. It's out of their way but close enough that they can give him his orders if they need him.

The first patient says, "Excuse me, miss, may I have something to drink?"

"Yes, I'll get you some water, or do you want to try some tea?"

"Oh, I think I could do with some tea."

"Give us a few, and we should have that for you. Tamara, can you—"

"Yes, Ms. Katharine." Tamara moves to the door and calls William. "I need you to go find Mrs. Jones and have her make a pot of tea and give us five cups. Tell her to place it by the kitchen door, knock, and then leave. We'll retrieve it."

"Yes, Ms. Tamara."

"William, can you repeat what I said back to me?"

He does it verbatim.

"Excellent."

"I'll be right back, Ms. Tamara. I have to go find Mrs. Jones for you." And off he goes. William returns to say he delivered the message and that Mrs. Jones is working on it.

Twenty minutes later, a knock and then the click of the lock is heard on the door leading into the great hall from the kitchen. Katharine opens the door to retrieve the tray with the pot of tea and five cups. She also sees another tray with what looks like stew on it. She looks up to see Bonnie and Mrs. Jones.

"You three need to keep your strength up. I expect to see three empty bowls, Ms. Katharine," says Mrs. Jones.

"Thank you, Mrs. Jones. Tamara, can you please help me?"

Tamara comes over to take the first tray, and Katharine takes the second. Once they close the door and start to walk across the hall, the click of the lock signals that it's been locked.

Once all the patients have been tended to, Liam, Tamara, and Katharine take a few minutes to sit in silence by the large fireplace. The food smells delicious, but they're too tired to eat. Katharine suggests they eat the food provided by Mrs. Jones and reiterates what she had said.

"In that case, I think we'd better eat the stew," says Liam as he lifts his bowl. He begins stirring it and blows on it to help cool it down. Tamara and Katharine follow suit. As Katharine eats, she looks up into Liam's and Tamara's tired eyes. She knows it's been a long day, but this can't be put off any longer.

"Liam and Tamara, can you tell me the common symptoms for each patient?"

Taking a minute between bites of their stew, they scan the room to study each patient.

Tamara is the first to respond. "They each have a fever and then get the chills."

"Three have a dry cough and a rash," adds Liam.

"Very well. I'll have William ask Ty to retrieve supplies from the infirmary office, and we'll begin to keep a record of each person and their symptoms. I suggest we look out for nausea and vomiting. We need to take shifts. I'll do the first. Liam, you can take the second, and Tamara, you do the third."

They finish their meal. Liam and Tamara take the two trays back to the door by the kitchen. Katharine instructs William to let Mrs. Jones know that she can retrieve the trays from the room. When the trays are retrieved, William and Ty set the supplies Katharine requested in a box at the door. She takes the box, closes the door, and waits for the click to signal that the door is locked. If she's going to do the first watch, she better keep herself busy so she doesn't fall asleep.

She moves a table and chair between the door and fireplace in the nook. William thought she would need these, so he got them without asking. In an hour, Katharine checks on the patients. She feels that she needs to check all of them for a rash. On the first patient, there's nothing as bad as on the second, but when she does a physical examination on the next three, she sees what looks like little bite marks. She ensures each one is comfortable, breathing regularly, and well. Katharine returns to her desk, makes the notes, and takes a moment to pray. She finishes and hears William in the hall say, "Good night, Ms. Katie." She rises and moves to the door so he can see her. There is Mrs. Jones with William in hand.

Katharine waves and says, "Good night, William." She nods to Mrs. Jones.

"Oh, I hope so, William. I hope it will be a good night," she says as she returns to the desk to finish her shift.

TWENTY-ONE

EARLY THE FOLLOWING day, a woman cries, "Help me, please help me." She comes in with what looks like a rag doll in her arms.

Tamara reaches the door first. "Mrs. McDougall!"

"It's Mary. She was like this morning, and after Mr. Ty's visit, I came right here."

"Ms. Katharine, this is Mrs. McDougall. She's here with her youngest, and her second oldest is Owen over there."

Katharine moves over and Tamara takes the child behind the curtains to check on her and complete the process for everyone.

"Mrs. McDougall, do you have other children at home?" Katharine inquires, her voice filled with concern.

"Yes, my oldest is with her two younger ones. Why?' Mrs. McDougall's eyes dart around the room.

"Mrs. McDougall, you weren't supposed to enter this room. Now that you have, we can't take the chance of you carrying whatever this is back to your family or anyone else. I'm sorry, but you'll have to stay here with us," Katharine explains.

"I have two here who are sick and three healthy at home. What can I do to help?" says Mrs. McDougall.

Katharine shows her over to the area where they wash and clean. She's given a new apron and goes to her son to see how he's doing. Liam takes Mary and places her on a cot; Mrs. McDougall asks that she be brought over with Owen so she can tend to them both. Katharine tells her they can't; each is in a different stage, and she doesn't want to make either of them worse. The first five patients are two days ahead of Mary and the other three who have come in, all of whom are vomiting. It's essential to have each group together.

Katharine asks William to tell Ms. Bonnie to find the books she needs in the study and to let Mr. Ty know he will need to go to the McDougall family and let them know their mom and sister are at the main house. As is the routine now, when William is asked to do something, he repeats it back, and then he's off on his merry little way to complete the assignment.

Ethan returns with the workers early on Friday. Bonnie and Ty greet him and explain what has happened in the last few days. He's angry and upset.

"Why didn't you send for me?"

Ty says, "Because, Laird, our priority was to ensure the safety and well-being of those who were and are sick. Inform the other tenants and neighbours."

"Aye. It was my call, Ethan," says Bonnie sternly. "We didn't have the time or the manpower to go in and get you. We knew you would be home today, so we left it until now."

He sighs, breathes, pinches his nose, looks up at his sister, grabs her, hugs her, and says, "You did the right thing. I apologize, and you too, Ty. How are things?"

Bonnie steps back from his hug and looks at Ty. They suggest they go to his study and talk.

"I'll meet you there in fifteen minutes. I'd like to see Katharine first."

"Um, no, you can't."

He looks at Ty like he has two heads.

"Katharine, Liam, and Tamara are confined to the great hall where all the patients are. We can't go in. They only come out to use Katharine's room as a bathroom and to change clothes. This is why we wanted to talk to you in the study."

"Let's go then so that I can get the whole picture. I think I'll need a drink for this conversation."

Bonnie whispers to Ty, "I think all of us will need one."

Thirty minutes later, Ethan has been updated on what has happened in the last two days.

"I'll remain here until this is over. Ty, can you please inform Reid."

"Yes, Ethan."

"Bonnie—"

There's a soft but audible knock at the door. "Come in," all three say.

William barely pushes the door open. He pops his head in and says, "Ms. Bonnie, Ms. Katie is asking for some books."

"I'll get them for you, William," says Ethan. "Can you tell me what books she was asking for?"

William repeats what Katharine told him. Ethan locates the books and is about to take them himself, but William stops him and says, "No, Laird, Ms. Katie asked me to bring them to her." He lifts his hands to Ethan's to say, "Give me the books, please."

"Of course, William," he says as he hands him the books. "May I come with you?"

"It's your house, Laird," says William as he shrugs his shoulders.

"So it is, William. Let's get these to Ms. Katharine, shall we?"

"Aye, Laird."

They leave the study together, followed by Bonnie and Ty, who goes to the kitchen.

William arrives at the designated spot to leave things for Katharine. She sees William with the books and smiles.

"Thank you, my little man." Then she spots Ethan moving in behind William. "Ethan, you're home."

"Yes, it's Friday. I came home with the other shipbuilders for the weekend."

"Is it Friday?" she asks.

Ethan looks down at William, who looks up at him. "Why don't you see what Mrs. Jones has for supper in the kitchen while I talk with Ms. Katharine for a bit."

"Aye, Laird. Bye, Ms. Katie."

"Bye, William."

"So it would seem there has been quite the excitement around here."

"Not the word I would use, but it is nice to see you."

"Aye. What can I do, Katharine?"

"If you could move back, I can grab these books and double-check my findings."

He returns from the table and says, "You think you know what it might be?"

Katharine moves to the table to retrieve the books. "I think. Until I have a chance to discuss with Liam and Tamara and review these books, I don't want to make an assumption."

He nods.

As she picks up the books, she looks at Ethan and says, "We could use some more firewood for the fireplaces, however. That would be helpful."

"I'll find William; he can help me get that for you."

"He would love it, Ethan."

"Why does he get to call you Ms. Katie and I don't?"

"Because he's a child, and when he calls me Ms. Katie, I'm reminded of my mother. Her pet name for me is Katie."

"So does Ms. Katie help remind you of home?"

"Yes, it does, and the way William says it brings joy to my heart, so I let him."

She takes the books and brings them up to herself to hug them. As she does, you can see the pain on her face. Ethan wants to reach across the table and hug her like she's hugging the books. Instead, he nods and says, "We'll be back with the firewood you need." He takes his leave.

The fires are stoked after William and Ethan deliver the firewood that evening. Each patient has been checked. There are sixteen in total; seven new ones came just today. The two books Katharine had William bring to her are divided between Liam and Tamara.

"I'd like you both to check to see if you can find what might be the culprit."

"Do you know?"

"I believe so. However, you also need to be able to come to the same conclusion as I have."

While they read by the fire, Katharine moves over to where Mrs. McDougall is beside her daughter, Mary, who hasn't been doing well.

"Mrs. McDougall, you need to get some rest. We don't want you getting this."

"Nay."

"Owen is doing well; if Mary changes, I'll wake you. I promise."

"Aye, Ms. Katharine. I'll get a wee bit of shut-eye."

"Good."

Mrs. McDougall moves over to Katharine's cot and lies down. Katharine moves over to where Mrs. McDougall sits beside Mary. She's holding her own but weak, and her fever isn't breaking like her brother's did. As Katharine sweeps the hair from her forehead, she whispers a silent prayer.

While Liam and Tamara conference over the books, Katharine again checks on two new patients in the same condition as Mary, which is alarming to Katharine. She doesn't want to upset Mrs. McDougall or the other patients, so she'll let the others know they're the ones to pay more attention to. On the good side, three of the first five are doing well, including Owen, Mary's brother. Liam and Tamara motion Katharine over. She moves from her spot beside Mary.

"So what we can determine with the symptoms is that we're more than likely dealing with typhus, but we can't figure out how they got it," whispers Liam to ensure the patients can't hear their discussion.

As the evening progresses, there's further discussion. Liam and Tamara determined that the common denominator is that each sick person comes from a tenant whose father is a shipyard worker. They are the carriers. They take Mrs. Carr out of the equation, because she lives alone but does visit other tenants regularly.

"William, please get Mr. Ethan for us immediately," says Katharine. No sooner has she said the words when a scream penetrates the room.

Mary is rolling back and forth, holding her head and screaming. All three run to her, Katharine arriving first. "Mary, is it your head? Does your head hurt?"

"Make it stop, make it stop! Mama, it hurts."

Mrs. McDougall rushes over to cradle her. "It's okay, baby," she says, beginning to rock her back and forth.

"Mrs. McDougall, I need to check her eyes."

She won't release her.

"Mrs. McDougall, you need to let me—"

Mary goes lifeless; her hands drop from her head, and her head turns into her mother's arm.

"It's okay, baby; it's okay, baby." They can do nothing but watch as she rocks her child in her arms and tears fall from her eyes. Both Liam and Tamara try to hold back the tears in theirs.

"Mrs. McDougall," says Katharine as she tries to release Mary from her mother's arms. It's like she's not hearing Katharine.

Katharine feels a hand on her shoulder and turns to see that it's Ethan. "Let me, Katharine," says Ethan, and without thinking, Katharine rises to move out of the way.

"Heather, look at me," says Ethan very gently and lovingly. He takes his hands and places them on her arms. She looks up at him. "Heather, please release her to my care."

"Why, Ethan, why?"

"I can't answer that, Heather." He squeezes her arms gently. "We need to take care of her."

"Yes, Ethan."

She releases Mary. Ethan moves in to take the child. He lifts her and then turns to Katharine.

"Come with me," she says. She moves to the kitchen door, knocks, waits a minute, unlocks, and leaves the great hall. No one is there. She motions to her room in the back. Mary is gently laid on her bed. "I'll handle this, but you may ask Mrs. McDougall if she wishes to assist."

"It's best if you handle this, Katharine," says Ethan in a cracked voice.

She nods to acknowledge what she must do. Katharine takes hold of his arm as he leaves the room and says, "Since you entered the great hall, it will be necessary for you to be confined to the great hall."

He places his other hand on hers, which holds him. "You will find me there when you're finished."

"May I ask something? You called her by her first name?"

"Heather and I grew up together. If she hadn't fallen in love with her husband while I was away learning the business, we probably would have been married with as many children by now." His eyes drift to Mary on the bed.

"I see."

"When you're finished."

"Yes, I'll return to the room."

"Here, take this key and lock the door behind you. I'll knock to get back in."

She turns to begin the process she has done many times before back home, but it's the first time here in Scotland.

An hour later, a knock echoes in the great hall. Ethan motions to Liam to get it as Heather sleeps in his arms. Tamara has been sitting with Owen, who could do nothing but watch while his sister died in her mother's arms. Katharine enters the room and nods to Ethan. She quickly talks with Liam, and they move to check the two other patients in the same condition as Mary. Their fevers haven't broken either, and their eyes are checked to ensure they're not dilated, indicating the onset of Mary's unexpected headache. So far, so good, but since the onset with Mary was sudden, they'll be monitored more regularly. When Mrs. McDougall awakes, she asks to move beside Owen. She's still unsettled and needs to be by her child. Ethan helps her over, and then he and Tamara move to the fire with Katharine and Liam.

Ethan sees the exhaustion in their faces. "Katharine, the three of you can't continue at this pace. There will be more, and it will be too much for just you. If we use everyone in the house to help and they stay in the house, would that work for you?"

"Yes."

"Very well. I'll ensure Ty is the only one who doesn't enter and keeps his distance. He's my right hand to the outside, so I require him not to be part of this."

"Thank you, Ethan. It would help if we could all move freely through the house and keep the sick here. I don't know how I didn't think of that," she says as she puts her hand on her forehead to try and rub away the weariness.

"You have more important things to consider," he says. "William brought me here because he said you had something to tell me. What was it?"

Tamara informs Ethan that they have figured out it's typhus they're dealing with, and it's more than likely the workers from the shipyard who brought it to the parish.

"So if the workers brought this back, how did they get it?"

Katharine interjects, "When we were in town a few weeks ago, you and Reid were discussing the fact that due to the weather for the late summer/early fall being warmer than usual, there has been a rat problem down by the waterfront."

"Yes, but how?"

"Those rats may have or did have fleas. If the rats come in contact with a worker, say in the barracks they live in, those fleas could get on them. I've seen where they live during the week, and it can easily be transmitted from one coat to another. I don't mean to say that your workers live in bad conditions, Ethan, but rats are survivors, and they find their way in and out of places so quickly that the men may never have been aware of them, but they left their trace."

"I see," says Ethan as he pinches the bridge between his nose and eyes.

"Then the workers travel back here on Friday with the clothes with fleas on them and spread it to their families, and we have this."

"So we have to quarantine the workers?"

"Yes."

"They're not going to like that they can't work."

"No, they can work," says Katharine. "You quarantine them in town. Their living quarters should also be cleaned. Holes and cracks should be checked anywhere a rat could get in. Build them out. The workers can work; they can't return here until we tell them. You may also want to ensure that they're confined to their housing for the next while. We don't want to spread this in town or anywhere else. In the meantime, the tenants here on the estate will need to clean their homes and wash all their clothes. Until this outbreak is dealt with, they will have minimum contact with each other."

"Got it. I'll have Ty inform Reid immediately."

Ethan asks William to send Ty a message. Ty writes it out, gives it to William, and off he goes.

TWENTY-TWO

ETHAN INDICATES THAT the tenants need to be informed about the situation. He tells Bonnie, "Since we know what we're dealing with, we can let the tenants know."

"Yes, it's been a long time, but a community gathering will be needed. We're all in this together, and it's important that we support each other during this time," replies Bonnie.

"Do you have the space for everyone?" questions Ethan.

"We could have everyone meet us around the infirmary. We'll make it work, Ethan," responds Bonnie.

"I'll need you and Liam to be with me to answer questions," Ethan addresses Katharine. "The men won't mind going into town to work. We'll make sure they stay there. As for the wives and children left behind, it might be a different story."

On Ethan's instructions, Ty rushes into town that evening to advise Reid about what's happening back at the estate. Ty ensures Reid knows what needs to be done regarding the twelve workers who stay in town. They must be confined to their lodgings until they've been cleaned from top to bottom, their clothes laundered, and any cracks or holes in the lodgings boarded up to build the mice out. Once that's been completed, Mr. McFarlane, who's responsible for overseeing what needs to be done, will check everything. Before returning to the Stuart estate, Ty calls upon the doctor in town to make sure he's aware of the circumstances and arranges for him to do a medical check of the workers for any signs of typhus.

Back at the estate, all the tenants gathered the next day outside the infirmary, as Laird Stuart requested. Ethan, Katharine, and Liam stand on the back of the wagon.

After a quick head count, Ethan shouts, "Thank you, everyone, for coming. I want to advise everyone of the situation that has arisen."

There's discussion among the tenants, and Ethan continues by shouting, "Our medical staff has ascertained that we're dealing with typhus. Every household must follow the instructions I give you. Firstly, if anyone feels poorly, they're to come to the main house so proper medical attention can be given. You are now to return to your home and stay there. Your homes, shops, carts, and even clothes must be cleaned. Those who work at the shipyard will go in on Monday, but you won't return to the estate until we tell you to. The estate farmers will continue to work as they have, each family looking after their own, with the restriction of no visiting each other."

The tenants roar with grumbling and complaining. Ethan continues, "There has already been one death, a child, with the potential for many more. Make no mistakes—I will do what is necessary to protect everyone on the Stuart estate. Am I clear?"

The tenants are unhappy but realize they have no choice but to do as instructed. With their continued grumbling and complaining, most leave the gathering and return home. A few strays stay behind to ask questions, which Katharine or Liam are able to answer. Ethan keeps a watchful eye on the tenants as they leave to gauge any disgruntled or unruly ones.

Back at the main house, Katharine pulls Ethan aside. She suggests to him that the Young family may be of assistance to them.

Ethan asks, "Do you think so? Ty will need some extra hands to check on the tenants regularly."

"I believe so. Do you trust me?" responds Katharine.

"Yes."

"Then if I may, I'll have Ty deliver this to the Young family." Katharine retrieves the thistle brooch she has kept in her skirt pocket. "It was given to me when I assisted in the birth of Grace's twins. I took it on the condition that if or when I required assistance, it would be delivered to them, and they would come. As you said, we'll require more hands than we currently have, Ethan."

"We can ask; it doesn't mean they will accept," says Ethan.

"Perhaps, but we must at least try."

"Agreed. Have them meet us at the bottom of the main house's front stairs. We can speak to them there," replies Ethan.

"Whatever you wish, Ethan."

"Let me write a note to Gavin," says Ethan. He runs to his study, quickly writes a note, and then returns to Katharine. "May I have the brooch, Katharine? I'll give it to Ty to deliver to Laird Young with the note," he says as he waves the paper in his hand.

"Yes, here you go," Katharine says as she places the brooch in her hand; Ethan is holding his note.

Ethan takes a moment to squeeze her hand and then says, "Thank you. I've asked for them to arrive tomorrow by 10:00 a.m. Does that work for you?"

"It should unless there's an issue with a patient, but I believe Liam and Tamara can handle it. We'll need to speak to them for the time."

"I'll find Ty so he can deliver these," says Ethan as he nods to Katharine and turns to head to the kitchen and out the back door to the stables.

As requested, Gavin and Ryan arrived at the front of the Stuart home promptly at 10:00 a.m. the following day. Ethan and Gavin acknowledge each other with a nod.

"We received your message, Ms. Katharine, along with your note, Laird Stuart," says Gavin as he nods to Ethan and moves his hand over the brooch pinned to his tartan. "How may we be of assistance?"

Ethan defers the explanation of the situation to Katharine, who efficiently explains what aid they're asking for.

"I'll need to speak with Grace first, Katharine. I don't see a problem in providing you with extra hands. We need to figure out who will come." He looks to Ryan. "How many do you require?"

"I would say about six more: three women to work in the house to help with meals and laundry, and three men to work outside and be able to go from house to house to see how things are going and help on the farms if necessary."

"Can you give me a day or two?"

"Of course," say Ethan and Katharine together as they look at each other.

"Laird Young, truly, I can't thank you enough," responds Ethan as he steps back.

"Ethan, if not for Katharine, I may not have my children or wife. I will always be eternally indebted to her. I'll send word once we have the people for you and know when they'll be here."

"Thank you," respond Ethan and Katharine together again.

Gavin confirms that six extra hands will be arriving in two days. Ryan volunteers to be close to Tamara and two young men—Taylor, sixteen, and Sean, eighteen. They've worked under Ryan for years; he trusts them, and they're hard workers. Three young ladies—Brigette, sixteen, Colleen, seventeen, and Lily, nineteen—come to work in the home for Mrs. Jones.

With the extra hands from the Young family, the burden is lifted off everyone except Katharine, Liam, and Tamara, but mostly Katharine. However, people are still coming in to be treated, which is disconcerting to Katharine. With the men staying in town and the tenants keeping to themselves, it doesn't make sense that they still have people coming in sick.

"What have I missed?" says Katharine as she sits at her desk, looking around the great hall and the paperwork in front of her.

"Ms. Katharine, what are you still doing here?" Liam asks as he finishes his round of the hall. "You need to get out and have some rest."

"I know, Liam, I just—"

Shaking his head, Liam moves in and takes Katharine's arm to aid in lifting her out of the chair. "I am prescribing what you tell both Tamara and I. Get out, get some fresh air, rest, and return when I tell you to. So I am telling you, Ms. Katharine, for your good and for those who need you in this room, that you don't come back until after supper this evening. I'll be letting Tamara know when she relieves me," informs Liam.

"I—"

"Aye it is," says Liam as he leads her to the door into the kitchen.

Katharine stands at the door and looks at Liam but can't say anything. Liam crosses his arms and says, "Please don't make me speak to Laird Stuart, Ms. Katharine, because I will, and he'll make you stay out of this room longer than me."

"Very well, Liam, I'll be back this evening after supper." She reaches to squeeze his arm. Katharine knows he's right; she would have done the same to him if the shoe were on the other foot. He has learned on his own that sometimes you must take matters into your own hands. "Well done, Liam; well done indeed," she says as she moves through the kitchen to her room.

Her body and brain are too wired to go to sleep. She grabs her Bible and notebook and heads toward the glen, where she always finds peace. Finding a spot, she sits, closes her eyes, takes a deep breath, and slowly releases it. As she opens her eyes, she sees the beauty all around her, which is so majestic, and she bursts into tears. Laying the items in her hand aside, she lifts her hands to her face and sobs. The tears she's held back for several weeks will no longer be suppressed. Crying helps to heal; right now, she needs all the healing she can get. "Why, Lord, why?" she mumbles as she takes her sleeve to wipe away the tears. "I'm at a loss. What more can I do? Please help me—us—Father," she squeaks out as another wave of tears flows.

Unknown to Katharine, Ethan has come to the glen to speak with her. He hears her cries and walks up from behind Katharine and says, "Katharine," so she knows it's him. He kneels as he puts his hand on her shoulder. Without looking at Ethan, Katharine takes her hand, places it upon his, and leans her head down on their hands. They say nothing for quite some time. Ethan wants Katharine to know he's there for her. Once Katharine's crying has subsided, she moves her head and looks at Ethan.

"I don't know what more I can do. It should be subsiding, but it isn't," she confesses.

Ethan squeezes her shoulder and says, "We know this, Katharine. You, Liam, Tamara, all of us are doing everything we can. We'll have to let it run its course."

"I know, Ethan, but I feel overwhelmed and helpless. I've never dealt with this amount of sick people at the same time," she says.

Ethan moves his hand from her shoulder and takes her hand in his. "Katharine, everyone knows you, Liam, and Tamara are doing the best you can. Some more cases may still be coming in, but not to the extent it was. We've gotten this far. Tell me if you need more assistance." He responds by squeezing her hand.

"Thank you, Ethan. We could use more people in the infirmary to help look after everyone." Katharine breathes profoundly and exhales, saying, "Perhaps we could see if a few of the people who are just getting over the sickness would be helpers. They're immune and know what to expect. They'd be vital in assisting the others."

"Aye, we'll start there," says Ethan. "From now on, Katharine, if you need anything, please come to me."

"I will, Ethan," she says, squeezing his hand.

Ethan smiles back. "Funny how I was coming to speak to you on this matter. Liam informed me you were instructed not to return to the great hall until after supper."

"Yes, he did," she says sheepishly. "He also said you would have made me stay away longer."

"He's right. You're training them well, Katharine."

"That wasn't my training, Ethan; that was all Liam, and yes, they are doing extraordinarily well, considering the circumstances," she says as she adjusts her seat.

Ethan sees her Bible and notes in the grass beside her, and William pops his head through the bushes to say, "Ms. Katie, I found you."

"Yes, William, you have found me."

"You don't come to the glen this time of day, do you, Ms. Katie?" he says as he falls beside her.

Chuckling and looking at Ethan, she says, "No, William, I don't."

"May I sit with you, Ms. Katie?" William asks as he plays with the grass in front of him.

"Yes, you may, William. I was just going to read and write."

"I'll leave you to it, Katharine," says Ethan as he squeezes her hand one last time and rises.

"William, you take good care of Ms. Katharine," he says as he ruffles his hair.

"Yes, Laird," responds William.

"I'll see you at supper," Ethan says to them both as he leaves the glen.

William begins to recite the Scottish poem he says daily with Katharine at the glen. As Katharine turns to lift her Bible and journal, she begins to recite what William is saying: "If there be righteousness in the heart, there will be beauty in the character. If there be beauty in the character, there will be harmony in the house. If there be harmony in the house, there will be order in the nation. If there is order in the nation, there will be peace in the world."

A few days later, it's the evening shift in the great hall. The room is warm, and the crackle of the two fireplaces can be heard echoing. Tonight is different from the ones before. Peace and calmness have settled in the room. Everyone is either reading, chatting softly among themselves, or sleeping. Katharine looks up from her desk, and what she sees is hope. It's been a battle to fight the typhus. There have been losses—four children and three adults—but many more survived. No new cases have come in for the past seven days. She scans the great hall, checking to see if anyone needs her. She returns to her notes to complete the page.

A few coughs are heard. Katharine rises from her chair to attend to them. As she begins her nightly routine of going around from cot to cot, she senses the peacefulness of the night. There are about twenty patients in the great hall this evening; tomorrow, there will be three less. Katharine takes her time to visit and check in on each patient. Unbeknownst to them on her visit, she prays over them and gives them a tender touch.

Katharine is finishing with her last two patients as Ethan enters the great hall. He pauses, leans against the door frame, crosses his arms, and watches her. He's not sure the losses wouldn't have been more significant without Katharine, as they quickly caught it. The community lost seven, but he doesn't wish to think about what it could have been. Katharine, Liam, and Tamara have done an amazing job, and the community and his neighbours stepped up to do what they could. Watching Katharine, he's reminded of his mother, who would come to tuck them in before bed. She too looks like a mother putting her children to bed. It's an image he likes, and he can't help but smile. There is love in what she does, as well as compassion. She has poured so much of herself into caring for the sick. When Katharine finishes sweeping the room and returns to her desk, she looks up to catch Ethan leaning in the doorway. She smiles and nods to him. He pushes off the door and moves toward her.

"I'm here to assist before I retire for the evening."

She motions to the pile of wood kept by the fireplaces. "If you could tend to the fires for Tamara and Ryan, who will be taking the next shift."

Ethan nods and walks over to the fireplace furthest from them. He stokes the fire, adds a log, and then checks for the supply. Katharine moves behind her desk and begins to finish the notes on the patients for Tamara when she takes over.

The other fireplace is close to her desk, and as Ethan looks after it, he asks, "How are things this evening?"

Katharine says, "It looks like everyone is on the mend. There have been no newer cases; a few will leave the great hall tomorrow. If we can stay the course by next week, those here now should be ready. Then the great hall can return to being a dining hall instead of an infirmary."

Ethan sits with his back to the fire but faces her. "You mean this is done?"

"I wouldn't say that, Ethan. We need no new cases; all those here are over the isolation period. So until next week, let's pray this is over." She gets up and moves to her desk.

"I will. When will Tamara and Ryan relieve you?"

"In about thirty minutes. Why?"

"May I stay and keep you company until they get here? I wanted to speak to you about something."

"Of course. What did you want to speak to me about?"

Ethan moves to take a chair and puts it beside Katharine. "So we can talk more quietly and not disturb them," he tells her, but truthfully, he wants to be close to her. "When the great hall is returned to its regular function, I thought it would be good to celebrate getting through this ordeal. It would be for the community, and we'll invite the Young family as well, since they have been vital in helping us get through this. It would be a way to thank everyone who helped, celebrate those who made it, and mourn those who did not. As we weren't able to have proper burials, it will allow everyone a chance to grieve."

Katharine likes the idea so much that she tenderly moves in and hugs him without thinking. "It's a splendid idea, Ethan. I know the families who lost their loved ones will appreciate it."

Ethan moves his arms around to hold her in the hug longer. "I'm glad you approve. We'll have to make sure the room is well-cleaned beforehand, but I'm sure you, Liam, and Tamara will look after that."

Katharine moves out of the embrace, a bit embarrassed by what she's done. She blushes slightly, but she won't lie. She enjoyed the hug. "So will Mrs. Jones. She's so used to having hot water pots boiling all day long that she'll use them to scour everything in here."

Ethan chuckles. "Yes, I'm sure she will. I'll let you finish your patient notes, Katharine." He takes her hand between his, squeezes, and then rises. Before he leaves, he leans in and kisses her forehead. "I'll see you tomorrow. Good night, Katharine."

"Good night, Ethan," she responds. She keeps her eyes closed to hold the memory and feeling of his touch, both by his lips and arms, and the warmth from his body from the hug.

TWENTY-THREE

IT TOOK A few days longer than Katharine had estimated, but the outbreak has run its course. The last patients in the great hall are healthy enough to go home. The first two days after the last patients are released, the great hall is kept hot, with the two fireplaces burning non-stop. Branches from the rowan and juniper trees are used to keep the fires burning. The heat will help kill anything, and the smoke is an old custom of cleaning away bad feelings and luck, called "redding the house."

They take two days to open all the windows and air the great hall out. Only then are Mrs. Jones and her brigade allowed to start setting things right for the celebration. With the help of the Randall children and a few others, it takes another five days before the entire room is cleaned and decorated for a celebration. As is a custom in Scotland, candles are placed in the windows and decorated with greenery and berries. This is the traditional way of welcoming a stranger. By honouring the visit of a stranger in the night, you honour the Holy Family, who searched for shelter the night of Christ's birth. This year, a candle for every life lost due to the outbreak is added to the windows throughout the great hall, to be lit on the gathering night.

With the children's help, Ty lets the tenants know a community celebration dinner is being held in the great hall. Ryan delivers the announcement to the Young family, and Ethan and Katharine speak directly to the families who lost loved ones during the outbreak. These families are asked to arrive earlier than the other guests for a special event.

Several musicians in the community volunteer to perform at the celebration. Bonnie and Mrs. Jones suggest they set up in one corner and play hymns during the lighting ceremony and then more lively dancing music for the celebration.

As each family who lost a family member enters the great hall, they're greeted by Laird Stuart and his family. Once inside the great hall, Katharine, Ty, Liam, Tamara, and Mrs. Jones assist in the candle-lighting ceremony. Once all the other guests arrive and are assembled for the celebration, Ethan steps forward into the middle of the great hall, and the music stops. Ethan motions for Mrs. Jones's brigade to deliver trays of drinks to the guests for toasts. They start with him and then proceed around the room. As they do, Ethan begins to speak.

"Good evening to you all. My family and I are thankful for your presence with us this evening. It's been a challenging time for all of us these past months. As you look around, you will notice the candles lit in the windows this evening. Each one is in loving memory of those who are not here today but are forever present in our hearts. Tonight, we remember them. Let's not forget what happened, but it's time to step forward and welcome a new beginning." Ethan raises his glass to signify that they may take a drink. "I will now ask my sister, Bonnie, to pray before we partake in the evening meal." He moves aside as Bonnie moves to where he stood.

Bonnie nods to Ethan, clears her throat, and says, "Let us all pray." She bows and begins. "Lord, we thank you for this night of celebration. We thank you for getting us through this time of sickness. Allow your love to fall on the families who have lost a loved one and guide them in this time of grief. May your presence be with us this evening as we remember your promise never to leave or forsake us. May we take that promise with us this evening and in the coming days. We ask you to bless the food that has been so lovingly prepared and bless it to our bodies. Amen."

A chorus of "Amen" is heard through the hall, and all bowed heads are raised.

"I invite you to enjoy the food, the music, and each other's company this evening," says Bonnie.

The food is served in a banquet style, which allows everyone to enjoy refreshments and socialize. A few tables are set up for those who wish to sit, and the children sit along the walls, where they can eat and play without getting in the way.

After an hour, the music stops, and Ty steps forward. "May I have everyone's attention, please. I want to take this opportunity on behalf of the Stuart family to thank our neighbours, the Youngs. Their generosity in providing extra hands to work here in the estate home, helping care for the sick, and extra hands for the tenants to bring in their crops was very much appreciated. To the Youngs," he says as he raises his glass and drinks. The guests repeat the sentiment. "I'd also like to thank the Stuart community for rising to the occasion and being open and willing to take help from the Youngs. It was hard work to ensure everyone stayed safe and did what needed to be done. To the Stuart community," praises Ty and again raises his glass and takes a drink.

"Here, here," is repeated throughout the hall.

"Now, my friends, if you're not too full from the wonderful food Mrs. Jones prepared for us," says Ty as he pats his stomach (laughter can be heard in agreement), "the musicians are ready to play dancing music. Grab your partner and have fun."

The music starts. The children are the first to get out on the dance floor, followed by the adults. Ty, Bonnie, Ryan, and Tamara join in.

Ethan spots Katharine beside Mrs. Jones and William and asks, "Katharine, may I have this dance?"

She nods and says, "Yes, you may, Ethan."

Ethan leads her onto the dance floor, and they circle the room together.

When the song ends and another one starts, Ethan and Katharine stay on the dance floor. But when another song begins, William moves across the dance floor to Ethan and Katharine. He tugs on Katharine's skirt.

"Ms. Katharine, may I have this dance?"

She looks at Ethan, who smiles and nods. He looks at William and says, "Remember, you have to lead, William."

"Yes, sir."

"I would love to dance with you, William; thank you."

William moves in and takes her hand. She puts her hand on his shoulder, and he holds on to her arm. He leads her around the floor, or so he thinks. You can see them both laughing and having fun.

Ethan moves to stand beside Mrs. Jones. He watches as William and Katharine dance.

"I see you let someone else have a turn," whispers Mrs. Jones.

"He spoke her proper name. I didn't stand a chance," he replies.

"Oh, you have a chance, Laird." She winks at him. "But it was still kind of you."

Ethan smiles and gazes around the room. Two months earlier, sickness and death were present in this room. Now there is dancing and laughter. They have much to celebrate this coming New Year, which will be here in a few weeks. Right now, Ethan is grateful for everyone who did their part during this outbreak, but most of all, Katharine. If she wasn't here, what could have happened? "I won't think of that," says Ethan, moving over to offer his hand to Mrs. Jones for a dance to celebrate.

While Katharine helps with the clean-up from the night before, the chatter is about the New Year celebration.

"What about Christmas?" asks Katharine.

Mrs. Jones responds, "Christmas is not an observed holiday here, Katharine."

"Really? I didn't realize you wouldn't be celebrating Christmas." She's surprised and can't imagine not celebrating her favourite time of the year. "Would it be possible, Mrs. Jones, if I did a family tradition to celebrate Christmas here?"

"What did you have in mind, lass?" asks Mrs. Jones.

"My mother, Mrs. Florence, Lois, and I would prepare a big Christmas breakfast. We would all sit together, exchange gifts, and enjoy the day. I usually help prepare the meal, so—"

"It sounds like a lovely idea. If you can make a list of what you need, we can ensure we have it for you. Right, Mrs. Jones?" says Bonnie.

"Aye, sounds good, lass," replies Mrs. Jones.

Katharine grabs paper and a pen from her room. She starts by making a menu and listing the ingredients they need.

"How many people will be here to participate?" asks Katharine.

"You, me, Mrs. Jones, William, Ethan, and Ty," says Bonnie.

"What about Liam and Tamara?" says Katharine.

"Oh yes, add them too," says Mrs. Jones.

"The menu will be simple, Mrs. Jones, and if there are leftovers, they can be used throughout the day. That's what we usually do," says Katharine as she hands the list to Bonnie. "Some of the items can be made a few days ahead. Most of it can be done the day before. I'll speak to Tamara and Liam to make sure they can look after the infirmary on Christmas Eve, and I can come and get everything prepared."

"I'll check the pantry and larder for you, Katharine, to ensure we have what you need," says Bonnie.

"Thank you. I'll go speak to Tamara and Liam," says Katharine. She's excited to bring some family traditions to the Stuarts for Christmas.

On Christmas Eve, Katharine leaves Tamara and Liam to look after the few people who have come to the infirmary. With the help of Mrs. Jones and Bonnie, the Christmas breakfast is prepared as much as possible. Some last-minute things can only be done just before they eat. It's a lovely time in the kitchen working with Mrs. Jones and Bonnie. It's almost as if she was home helping Mrs. Florence and Lois.

Katharine finishes when William comes into the kitchen and asks about Christmas.

"I have a story I can read to you. Meet me in the study, William," says Katharine.

"Yes, Ms. Katie," he says as he runs off.

Katharine laughs. She slips into her room to grab her Bible. As she enters the study, she finds William sitting by the fireplace hearth. She opens her Bible and begins to read, "In those days …" Once she has read the passage, Katharine explains to William about the birth of Jesus and how he is the greatest gift given to them.

Unknown to Katharine or William, Ethan has entered the study. The picture before him of a woman and child huddled together around the warmth of the fire and showing love to each other causes him to catch his breath. The scene he sees is one he hopes to have for himself one day. He moves forward to let them know he's there when, from behind, he hears Mrs. Jones saying, "William, it's time for bed."

"I have to go, Ms. Katie. I'll see you in the morning," says William.

"Yes, you will. Happy Christmas, William."

"Happy Christmas, Ms. Katie."

William gets up, hugs her, and kisses her on the cheek.

"Happy Christmas, Laird," he says as he runs past and out the door.

Katharine laughs, and so does Ethan.

"He's excited."

"Yes. He's looking forward to the Christmas breakfast tomorrow."

"As we all are, Katharine."

"I'm excited to share some of my Christmas traditions with you and the family, Ethan."

Ethan moves over to take his seat by the fire.

Katharine continues. "I understand that Christmas is not the big day in Scotland, but New Year's is considered the big celebration. Is that correct?"

"Yes. We do the reverse of what you do in England. I'm sure Christmas is celebrated with all the trimmings, and I believe you have December 26 too. In Scotland, we celebrate New Year's with all the trimmings, and the season up to January 2. A popular custom is the gathering of people outside. They cross arms and join hands while singing "Auld Lang Syne" in unison. It's to ring in a new beginning."

Katharine nods.

"On New Year's Day, the traditional meal depends on what part of Scotland you're from. It may be wild salmon, pheasant, venison, or wild boar. Desserts can be a trifle, shortbread, mincemeat pies, or pudding. Mrs. Jones does a brilliant job. Usually we have an open house on January 1 for the community. Since we just had a celebration, we've decided to forego that this year and allow everyone to celebrate at home."

"I look forward to experiencing your New Year's celebration," replies Katharine.

"We'll be able to appreciate each other's traditions this year," says Ethan.

Katharine tries to hide a yawn. "If I want to be ready for tomorrow, I should retire for the evening. Mrs. Jones has offered to help me with the Christmas breakfast, but I want her to have a day where she doesn't have to cook."

"You cook too? Is there anything you can't do?"

"Sew. I may be able to stitch up a cut, but put a piece of fabric in my hand, and I have no idea what to do."

Ethan's genuine hearty laugh is music to Katharine's ear.

"I bid you good night, Katharine. I'm looking forward to the Christmas breakfast tomorrow. Until then."

"Until then, Ethan. Happy Christmas."

"Happy Christmas, Katharine."

Christmas morning is very festive in the Stuart home this year. Katharine gets up early to finish the meal prep and add special touches to the table. She marks each person's place with a colourful bundle and a handwritten name tag attached.

"Ms. Katie, what are these?" asks William as he examines the bundle with his name on it.

"William, please put that back. Once the meal is over, everyone gets to open their bundle."

"I'm not hungry—"

"William, you heard Ms. Katharine. Now put it back, son," says Ty.

"Yes, Mr. Ty," says William as he begrudgingly puts the bundle back.

"Katharine, can William and I help?" asks Ty.

"Yes, can you go and find everyone? The last of the items should be done in ten minutes. We'll be ready to eat and then open bundles," she says as she winks to William.

Everyone is located and arrives in the kitchen to take their place at the table. Bonnie helps Katharine get everything on the table. Ethan says grace, and a fantastic English Christmas breakfast is enjoyed.

"Ms. Katharine, that was lovely," says Mrs. Jones as she enjoys her cup of tea. "If you decide to give up doctoring, you'd be welcome in my kitchen any day, lass."

"Thank you, Mrs. Jones."

"Can we open our bundles now, Ms. Katie?"

"You have no patience, do you, little one?" says Ty as he messes up his hair.

William looks at him and moves his head to the side to indicate "No, I do not."

"Everyone is welcome to open their bundles. Our tradition is to give each person a small token of our love. Usually, it's handmade, but unfortunately—"

Ethan places his hand on hers and says, "It's all right, Katharine; we know where your time has been spent."

She squeezes his hand, and then he removes it to open his bundle.

Each person finds something inside with a note attached.

Mrs. Jones gets new wooden spoons. They're needed to ensure the meals are prepared and to keep everyone in line. It's a running joke in the home. Mrs. Jones talks with her spoons, not her hands.

William receives a kite, to keep him busy playing outside.

Liam and Tamara both receive a leather-bound journal. Inside each journal, it says, "To: Liam, To: Tamara, From: Katharine, Date: December 25, 1830. Something to keep your thoughts in."

Bonnie gets a shawl, to keep a bonnie lass warm walking back and forth from the stable all year.

Ty receives a pair of leather gloves. He's a hard worker who must protect his hands from the elements.

Ethan's gift is a thistle pin. This is to ensure Laird Stuart has his tartan appropriately pinned.

"Katharine, these are wonderful, but we have nothing for you," says Bonnie.

"Bonnie, I'm giving you a glimpse into my English tradition. I don't expect anything in return. You'll show me the Scottish New Year in the next few days. This time of year is about giving, and we each are doing that uniquely," she responds as she looks to Ethan to acknowledge their discussion last night in the study.

"I, for one, can say I like this tradition. Thank you, Katharine. How about we all pitch in to help clean this up and enjoy the rest of our day?" says Mrs. Jones.

"Yes, let's," says William, pushing his chair back and running out the back door to use his new kite.

"I'll go make sure he doesn't fly away," says Ty as he gets up from his chair before following William out the back door. He bends down, kisses Bonnie on the forehead, and squeezes her shoulder. He winks at Katharine, puts on his gloves, and goes out the door.

"Did the two of you want to try and make a run for it too?" Katharine asks as she looks to Liam and Ethan.

Liam looks at Ethan, and Ethan looks at Liam.

"I can't speak for Laird Stuart, but I'm good. It's the least I can do, Ms. Katharine, for the wonderful meal you made."

"Did you want to take some back to your family for the day?" asks Katharine.

"Aye, that would be grand," responds Liam as he looks at Ethan.

"Feel free to take what you need, Liam. The same goes for you, Tamara. You both can share Katharine's English traditions with them," replies Ethan as he rises to start taking some of the plates off the table.

It doesn't take long to pack some of the extra food for Liam and Tamara to take home, and the rest is put away to be used throughout the day by those who want it.

Katharine bids Liam and Tamara a happy Christmas as they leave. She reminds them that she put a note on the infirmary door asking anyone to come to her at the estate if they need assistance that day. She'll look after anything that comes up, giving them a day off. They're happy to know that they'll be spending the day with their families.

Katharine watches Ty and William play with the kite. She feels a wonderful sense of peace and joy. William and Ty are having a lovely time keeping the kite flying. She smiles and turns to go back into the kitchen but hits what feels like a wall. Nope, it's Ethan, who's been standing behind her.

"Oh dear, I am sorry, Ethan. I didn't realize you were behind me."

"I was trying to see how Ty and William were doing with the kite and didn't want to disturb you, as you seemed to be doing the same."

"Why don't you go out and have fun with them?"

"I might do that, Katharine. I wanted to thank you for this morning. It was nice to sit as a family and learn a new tradition. I also wanted to thank you for the pin for my tartan. How did you know I needed one?"

"Your sister mentioned it when you wore your kilt for the community celebration, so I asked Gavin if he could help me get something appropriate."

"I'll have to speak to Gavin about where he finds such an amazing silversmith. The workmanship is outstanding. I'll wear it for the New Year's celebration."

"I'm glad you like it. It will be something you can wear and remember me by."

"I will always remember you, Katharine."

Laughter could be heard from William and Ty.

"I think I should get out there while I can. Thank you again, Katharine." Ethan moves in and kisses her forehead, just as Ty did with Bonnie. Then he steps past and out the door to join in the fun of trying to fly the kite.

Katharine turns slightly to watch Ethan leave and join in the antics outside. The love she sees and feels makes her feel so content. "Happy Christmas it is," she says to herself and proceeds into the house to see what Mrs. Jones and Bonnie are up to.

"My goodness," says Katharine as she sits with her tea. "Do you do this every year?"

"Yes. Part of the Hogmanay tradition is that the house is cleaned from top to bottom," replies Mrs. Jones as she moves to the table to sit with Katharine and take her coffee.

"Since we did a thorough cleaning to prepare the house for the celebration after the outbreak, we just want to do a few rooms," inserts Bonnie as she joins the ladies.

"No wonder you have to start so early; it will take you days," says Katharine.

"We usually start a week before, but as Bonnie said, we've already done most of it," says Mrs. Jones as she sips her coffee.

"It was decided this year that since we recently had the community celebration, each family would have their own New Year celebration and not have a big party here like we usually do," says Bonnie.

"With Liam and Tamara handling medical issues, I'm happy to learn the Stuart traditions, even if it is house cleaning," chuckles Katharine.

"Tomorrow, we'll start the food preparation for New Year's Eve. On New Year's Day and the second, we keep the meals simple so we can enjoy the days off," giggles Mrs. Jones.

"She usually has too much to drink on New Year's Eve," responds Bonnie.

"Mrs. Jones, I never would have guessed," gasps Katharine.

"Aye, lass, once a year I let my hair down and have some fun," winks Mrs. Jones as she finishes her coffee. "Till then, it's back to work we go."

For the remainder of the day, the three work to clean the rooms that require cleaning. The next day, Katharine helps make three-cornered biscuits, known as "Hogmanay" and the meat pies they will enjoy on New Year's Day. Working in the kitchen with Mrs. Jones and Bonnie, as she did for Christmas, reminds Katharine of home, where Mrs. Florence and Lois chat while they worked.

In no time at all, it's New Year's Eve. The table in the great hall is set for the six who will enjoy the evening meal.

"This looks lovely, Mrs. Jones. Can I help you with anything?" Katharine asks as she admires the table's simple elegance.

"Aye, lass, if you could get those wine glasses off the side table." Mrs. Jones nods as she finishes the centrepiece.

"I have the wine, Mrs. Jones," states Ethan as he enters the great hall with two bottles.

Katharine is finishing putting the last wine glasses on the table when she sees Ethan in his kilt, wearing the pin she gave him for Christmas and a jacket with his tartan over it. She gasps at how handsome he is.

"Good evening, Katharine," he says.

"Good evening, Ethan," responds Katharine. "You look very Scottish. I'm looking forward to the festivities this evening."

"You look very English this evening, Katharine," he replies. "We look forward to sharing our Scottish traditions as you did your English with us for Christmas."

The evening meal is full of merriment. At five minutes to midnight, Ethan, Katharine, Mrs. Jones, William, Ty, and Bonnie go outside. They all join hands in a circle and, at the stroke of midnight, begin to sing "Auld Lang Syne." Ty kisses Bonnie, Mrs. Jones kisses William, and Ethan says, "Happy New Year, Katharine," and kisses her.

"Katharine, part of our tradition here on the Stuart estate is to 'sain,' or bless, the livestock," interrupts Ty. "Follow me to the stables."

Everyone walks to the stables. A pitcher of water and glasses are on Ty's desk in his office. He pours water into a glass, takes a drink, and then moves over to a horse's stall, where he sprinkles it with the water to bless it.

"Katharine, you bless Tally, as she's your horse," says Ethan as he pours her a glass of water.

"Thank you, Ethan," she says as she takes the water and drinks. Then she moves to Tally's stall to bless her.

Bonnie and Ethan follow suit, and soon all of the horses in the stable have been blessed.

"We have one more tradition for you, Katharine," says Bonnie.

With Ty accompanying Bonnie, Ethan leads Katharine to the house. A pounding sound is heard once they're back in the great hall.

"Come, Katharine. We'll answer the door," says Ethan as he escorts her to the front door. Ethan opens the door, and Liam and Tamara stand with their families. In unison, they all shout, "Happy New Year."

"Welcome, friends; please come in," says Ethan.

Liam is the first to walk through the door and hands Katharine a bottle of whiskey. Tamara walks through and subsequently deposits what looks like a fruit cake, and then both parents give her a lump of coal.

Katharine looks up to Ethan. He chuckles as he closes the door.

"This is called first-footing, Katharine. The goal is to be the first foot to enter the home that year, hoping to bring the household good luck for the year ahead."

"But what of these?" asks Katharine as she holds the items in her arms.

"Whiskey is for good cheer, cake is for an abundance of food, and coal is for warmth," says Ethan.

"I think you might want to put the whiskey in a safe place; Mrs. Jones is already more than tipsy," says Katharine.

Ethan laughs. He takes the items from Katharine's arm. "I'll make sure these find good homes," he says, motioning Katharine to follow the neighbours into the great hall to continue the celebrations.

TWENTY-FOUR

IT'S THE FIRST Friday of the new year. With the outbreak behind them and the start of the new year, it's a welcome, joyful, and peaceful evening around the kitchen hearth. It's been quite some time since Mrs. Jones, Bonnie, Ty, and Ethan have been able to partake in this ritual. The kitchen has always been their gathering place. Tonight, instead of the usual coffee or tea, a treat of homemade spiced apple cider with a splash of Scottish whiskey helps to keep the dampness of the evening at bay. Laughter fills the room.

"It's good to have the sound of laughter back in the house," Mrs. Jones declares as she raises her cup to take a sip.

"Aye, it is, Mrs. Jones," salutes Ty as he raises his cup and takes a sip.

Just as Ethan and Ty would sit up in the study and stare into the fire, so do the four stare into the hearth in quiet contemplation.

Bonnie sits with her cup in her hand, holding it like the only heat source.

"I'm truly grateful for Katharine, Liam, and Tamara. If they hadn't isolated the sick, determined what it was, how it was spread, and most of all, how to stop it, I shudder to think where we might be." She lifts her cup to take a drink to soothe her felt chill.

"I agree, sister. I'm also thankful for the community's support. At first, they didn't like it," Ethan says, sipping his cup. "But everyone ensured that anyone who came in contact with the shipbuilders did the proper cleaning, even Mr. Holmes."

"Mr. Holmes?" questions Mrs. Jones.

"Mr. Holmes assured me he washed his clothes and cleaned the wagon used to transport the workers," says Ty.

Mrs. Jones almost chokes on her drink. She puts her cup down on the table. "That can't be, Ty. He may have told you that he did it, but I can tell you he didn't."

Stunned by Mrs. Jones's statement, Ty replies, "Mrs. Jones, are you sure? You would be calling Mr. Holmes a liar?"

"Aye, I am. I usually do his washing. I can tell you, I did wash his clothes. However, I have never washed the outer coat he wears everywhere. If I've never washed it, you can bet he hasn't. Unless he thinks getting it wet on rainy days counts as a wash." She gets up. "As for the wagon, you can check with William. He hasn't been out to help Mr. Holmes wash the wagon in some time."

"Mr. Holmes gets William to help wash the wagon?" questions Ty as he sits down his cup.

"Nay, William washes it, and he just tells him the places he misses. William always comes to tell me where he is. I don't recall the last time he told me he was helping Mr. Holmes."

"Do you know where William is?"

"Yes, I believe he's studying with Katharine. Let me go fetch him for you."

Mrs. Jones goes off to get William from the study.

Ty and Ethan exchange glances, but both reserve commenting until they have heard from William.

Mrs. Jones returns with William in hand. Ty moves over in front of William and then squats down. "William, can you tell me when you last helped Mr. Holmes wash down the wagon that takes the men into town?"

William nods yes.

"Can you tell me when that was, William?"

He takes a moment to look up at Mrs. Jones. "It's all right, William. Tell Mr. Ty," she says.

"It was when Colin Randall stayed with us, Mr. Ty. We both went out to do the cleaning for Mr. Holmes. It was nice to have someone to help me. We had fun."

"You're sure? You haven't helped Mr. Holmes since?"

William shakes his head no.

"Thank you, William. You've been most helpful." Ty squeezes his shoulder to indicate he has done well.

"May I return to the study, Mrs. Jones?"

"Yes, you may, William. You can say good night to Ms. Katharine; it's almost bedtime."

"Yes, Mrs. Jones." Off he runs to the study to say good night to Katharine.

"I'll clean the wagon tomorrow from top to bottom so it's ready to return the workers to the shipyard on Monday," says Ty.

"Be sure to mention to Mr. Holmes that his coat is to be given to Mrs. Jones to be washed and dried so he has it for work on Monday."

Ethan turns to address Mrs. Jones. "If he hasn't come to give you his coat by mid-meal tomorrow, you can get it from him. Be sure to take Ty with you."

"Yes, Laird."

"Ethan, I'm so sorry. I should have checked, but with everything going on. For Mr. Holmes to disregard my orders, I will—"

As if he was slapped upside the head, it hits Ethan: "Oh my goodness, he's the one."

"The one what?" says Bonnie.

"The one who's been causing all the little problems, incidents, accidents, you name it, both here and in town. He has access. He has free rein. How did I not see this before?" He brings his fist to his forehead.

"What's going on?" says Mrs. Jones.

"Remember back when William's father was killed? Mr. Holmes was injured in the same accident. It would have been a preventable accident if he had secured the scaffold properly. We arranged for him to get paid a shipbuilder's wage to do 'farm work,' as he called it, here. It was better than the alternative of nothing. I thought, we thought"—he gestures to Ty.

"You're right, Ethan." Ty moves beside Ethan. "It was almost three months after he started here when the little incidents started to happen. He deliberately made them look like accidents at first, so we thought nothing of it.

Bonnie is now confused and angry. "I'm not sure what you're both talking about, but I think you had better explain."

"As you know, there have been some incidents here on the estate, but nothing serious. We were chalking them up to accidents," states Ethan as he begins to pace in front of the hearth.

"Yes, I'm aware of that. You said something about him being responsible for an accident in town. If he was responsible, why have you not dealt with him?"

"We've had no proof, but he's the common denominator. How is it that we haven't seen this before? It was right there before us, and we missed it."

Ty pipes in, "The doctor, Ethan. Mr. Holmes was the one in charge of saddling Dr. Bell's horse. He was also the one who said he found the burr on the saddle blanket. We took his word for it. Didn't think anything of it. Who's to say he didn't put the burr under the blanket. As Dr. Bell rode out to the tenant's house that day, it irritated the horse so badly that it threw him and caused his death.

"Why would he do that?" say Bonnie and Mrs. Jones together.

"Mr. Holmes blamed Dr. Bell for the injury to his leg not healing properly. This meant he couldn't return to the shipyard. Instead, he had to stay here and work on the farm."

"I know he didn't like the arrangement, but I would never think he had that much malice toward Dr. Bell," says Bonnie.

"It started with Dr. Bell, but I think it was more about the Stuart family. Mr. Holmes has always had a chip on his shoulder regarding us. Father said he would have been promoted if Mr. Holmes had a better work ethic. His lack of integrity and callousness toward his co-workers were things Father could not and did not overlook. I remember Father saying he discussed his concerns with Mr. Holmes, but nothing came of it. Mr. Holmes believed he was entitled to a promotion. He didn't have to earn it."

"What are we to do?" questions Bonnie.

"If what you say is true, he's already killed two people and all those who could have been saved from the spread of typhus," adds Mrs. Jones.

"Hang him!" says Ty. "I'm sorry. I said that out loud, didn't I?"

"Yes, my friend, you did. I agree, but unless we can prove what we suspect, it's his word against ours. For now, we'll keep an eye on Mr. Holmes. Ty, have one of your most trusted men move into the stables with him. Mr. Holmes is not to be left alone. Everything Mr. Holmes does is to be double-checked, especially all horses saddled for Liam, Tamara, and Katharine."

Ethan takes a few minutes to pace in front of the hearth. "Tomorrow we'll all assemble in my study. We'll start from the beginning and look at each incident or accident since Mr. Holmes's arrival on the Stuart estate. We mustn't show our hand but treat him the same."

"How do you treat a viper?" spits out Ty.

"Very carefully, my friend. In the meantime, we do what we can to ensure he causes no harm to anyone else, whether on the estate or in town at the shipyard. Agreed?"

"Agreed," reply the other three in unison.

"What about Katharine?" says Bonnie. "Should she not be in on this discovery and discussion?"

"For now, we'll leave her out of this. She's concentrating on mentoring Liam and Tamara and getting the parish to trust them for medical purposes. Besides, this is an issue from before she arrived, and it's family business. It doesn't concern her."

"As you wish, Ethan. But I'd like to say I think it's a bad idea and she should be told."

"Thank you, Bonnie. I appreciate your concern."

Mrs. Jones bids good night to get William and put him to bed. Bonnie nods good night to both Ethan and Ty and heads toward her room.

"I have to agree with Bonnie and Ethan. Katharine should be aware of what's going on."

"Once we know more. As I said, Ty, for now, all we have is a common denominator, and until we can put the puzzle of Mr. Holmes together piece by piece, I would prefer not to put this weight on her as well. The community is beginning to accept her, especially with what she's done through the outbreak. That's why she's here, Ty. I need her to concentrate on that, not this."

"Aye, Ethan. I understand. But at some point, you'll need to talk to her to see if we can assemble the puzzle."

"Aye. I pray we're wrong, but my gut tells me we're not."

"Good night, Ethan," says Ty as he leaves the kitchen to return to the stables.

"Good night isn't exactly what I would call this, Ty," says Ethan as he falls into his chair and stares into the glowing embers.

Katharine lays her pen down and moves to stretch from all the reading and writing she's been doing. She feels the breeze from the window, and it beckons her over. She gets onto the bench to open the window further to let in more airflow. Night has fallen. The moon shines brightly through the clouds, which move quickly. The breeze touches her face. She closes her eyes to breathe in the warm, salty air. She moves to her tiptoes to see further out the window. The clouds are shaped like hands surrounding the moon. It reminds her of someone looking down on her.

She smiles. "I know you're watching over me."

"Who is watching over you?" speaks Ethan as he enters the study.

Katharine is startled, putting her off balance, and she falls back off the bench. Ethan rushes over in time to catch her.

"You startled me," states Katharine as she lies in Ethan's arms.

"Are you falling for me, Katharine?" replies Ethan.

Laughing, Katharine moves out of his arms and points to the moon, which is gone now. "With the clouds around the moon, it looked like someone was looking down on me."

With Ethan so close, Katharine feels his breath upon her neck; she closes her eyes and breathes in his scent. "The breeze is quite warm. It will be nice to air out the room now that the weather is changing; there's no need for a fire tonight," she says.

He reaches out his hand to assist Katharine when he gets to his feet. They feel that spark again. This time, Ethan notices that Katharine's eyes have turned black. He smiles. The spark between them is enough for this evening. "You're correct, Katharine. I don't think we'll require a fire this evening."

As Katharine isn't removing her hand from his, Ethan asks, "I have about an hour of work before I retire. Would you care to join me for a sherry?"

Katharine releases her hand, and Ethan moves behind his desk to pour himself a glass. He turns to Katharine.

"Yes, I think I'll have a glass with you."

He's a bit surprised and lifts his brow. He pours a small amount into the glass and takes it over to her. Katharine takes the glass, and his fingers graze hers as he releases it. Katharine tries to hide the warmth running up her arm, and her instinctual intake of breath is noticed.

"Are you cold, Katharine? Do I need to close the window?"

"No, I'm fine, thank you."

She takes the sherry glass and moves back to her desk so Ethan can't see the redness on her face from his touch. Ethan smiles, takes a sip, and returns to his desk chair. Katharine takes a sip, takes a deep breath, and works on patient notes. Ethan looks over at her. He knows she felt the spark between them. She can deny it all she wants, but there's something there.

Once Katharine retires for the evening, Mrs. Jones, Ty, and Bonnie sneak into the study and sit around Ethan's desk.

"I truly don't feel right not letting Katharine in on this," states Bonnie.

"Duly noted, sister. For now, this is to be kept between us four. The fewer who know, the better," replies Ethan as he pulls his chair up to the desk. "So I've been going over what we discussed the other night. Since Mr. Holmes's arrival here at the estate, I've noted about ten incidents, not including the death of Dr. Bell. As for the outbreak, I don't think we say it's entirely Mr. Holmes's responsibility. However, his disregard for our orders could have contributed to some of the deaths from it."

"When you mean incidents, what are you referring to?" questions Bonnie.

"Remember when we had those horses that got sick, and we determined it was something that had gotten into the feed? We had equipment that broke in the fields while being used; upon inspection, we learned that the damage hadn't be done by the fieldwork. Mr. Holmes was in charge of feeding the horses and taking the equipment out to the tenants," explains Ty. "There were also the bags of seeds for planting crops. The holes were small enough not to be noticed then, but once sowing started, it was realized that about five farms had a quarter of a field that wasn't seeded. Mr. Holmes was the one to deliver those seed bags to each tenant."

"If you ask me, these things sound innocent enough to happen daily on a farm," pipes up Mrs. Jones.

"You are correct, Mrs. Jones," says Ethan. "That is why we didn't think anything of them. But when you start adding them up and seeing how Mr. Holmes is the common factor, it makes you stop and think. Why is he doing this?"

"That was going to be my question," interrupts Bonnie.

"I think he started doing these small things to see if he could get away with it. The horses are to help the tenants work the land; if they had been lost, then our crops that year would have been lost, along with revenue. I think you get the picture. When that didn't work, he moved to other avenues."

"Thank goodness no one got hurt," says Mrs. Jones.

"Unfortunately, Dr. Bell did, and he paid for it with his life," inserts Ty.

"Yes, I do believe it was Mr. Holmes who instigated that; whether he expected to kill him or just have him thrown from the horse, we'll never know," states Ethan as he gets up from the desk.

"I don't understand. If Mr. Holmes is trying to ruin us financially, that affects him. Does he not see that?" states Bonnie.

"I chalked it up to the fact that he had an injury that pained him. However, Mr. Holmes is a bitter man who thinks he's above working here as a farm hand," replies Ty. He made it clear from day one that he didn't want to come but wouldn't give up the wage he was getting. To think if we had done something earlier—"

"We can't change the past, my friend. But we can do what we can to ensure he doesn't cause further harm," replies Ethan.

"What do you suggest we do? Can we not just let him go?" answers Bonnie.

"Yes, we could. Then we'd have an even more disgruntled ex-employee on our hands and no way of keeping an eye on him. Right now, Ty has Fergus working with him. We informed Mr. Holmes that we wanted Fergus to learn his duties so they could share the burden, and he seemed to go for it. For now, we keep him under a watchful eye and try not to tip our hand that we're on to him," explains Ethan.

"I say get rid of the garbage. No offense, Laird," says Mrs. Jones.

"We will, Mrs. Jones, but we have to do this so that when he acts again, we catch him, and then the law can look after him," Ethan replies as he looks at Ty.

"Do we need to speak to Reid on this matter?" asks Bonnie.

"I'll check with Reid to see if there have been any issues at the shipyard since he left. It's my understanding that there haven't been. He takes the workers in and comes back. With Fergus going in with him until further notice, I don't think there will be a need to raise concerns."

"I'll go in on Monday instead of Fergus and speak to Reid if that works for you, Ethan," says Ty.

"Yes, good idea, Ty," replies Ethan. "For now, we keep a close watch over him. He'll try to do something again, and when he does, we'll catch him in the act."

"Aye," say Ty, Bonnie, and Mrs. Jones in unison.

TWENTY-FIVE

ONE MORNING, A few days later, Ty sees Fergus saddling Tally. "Is Ms. Katharine going out?" he asks.

"Yes, she came into the stables earlier asking Mr. Holmes to get Tally ready and bring her to the infirmary. He said he had something else to do, so he gave me her to deliver. I was double-checking and noticed the saddle straps were too loose. If Ms. Katharine had needed to gallop, she would have fallen off," Fergus informs Ty.

"Thank you, Fergus. I'm sure Ms. Katharine would have checked herself, but I appreciate you doing it instead."

"If I may say, sir, I don't like that man, and for what it's worth, he does the bare minimum to say he did it."

"Keep watch, Fergus; I'll report this to Laird Stuart," says Ty as he pats Fergus on the shoulder and heads toward the house.

Ty finds Ethan in the kitchen having coffee with Mrs. Jones and Bonnie. "I have some information, Ethan," says Ty as he grabs a cup. "Fergus tells me Mr. Holmes did not properly saddle Tally for Katharine this morning."

"What?" chokes Ethan as he's taking a drink.

"Katharine came to the stables this morning, asking Mr. Holmes to saddle and bring Tally to the infirmary for her. Mr. Holmes gave the horse to Fergus to deliver, and he had the foresight to double-check, which he did and adjusted the saddle correctly."

"My heavens," exclaims Mrs. Jones.

"He is too bold," says Bonnie.

"This also means he has no idea he's being watched. We now have the upper hand," replies Ethan.

"Now that we see he's targeting Katharine, I think we need to speak to her on this, Ethan," Bonnie reiterates.

Ethan takes another sip from his coffee and stares out the window as he sees Fergus walking Tally over to the infirmary.

"Not yet. Katharine is doing a wonderful job with Liam and Tamara. The community respects her because of the care she provided during the outbreak. Let them do their jobs, and we'll look after Mr. Holmes."

"But Ethan," says Bonnie, but Ty touches her shoulder to signal that now is not the time. They may not like his decision, but as Laird, he decides to make it.

"As you say, Ethan," responds Ty. He moves to kiss Bonnie on the forehead, puts his cup on the counter, and returns to the stable. Mrs. Jones moves to get back to the bread she was making. Bonnie takes the last swallow of coffee from her cup, gets up, and puts it on the counter. She comes to stand beside Ethan. She looks out the window where he's gazing and whispers, "I know you are Laird, brother, and I will follow your instructions. As your sister, I must tell you that your feelings for Katharine cloud your judgement. You're making a mistake by not speaking to her about this issue. I will say no more on this matter." She leans in to kiss him and leaves the room to continue her morning chores.

"I should have delivered the horse to the English doctor myself," says Mr. Holmes as he sharpens his dirk. "That Fergus double-checked the saddle straps. Who does he think he is?" he mutters as he wipes the blade and returns it to the strap on his leg. "Next time—there is always a next time," he says as he looks around. "They think they're so smart, those Stuarts, but who is the smart one? Me, that's who. Sooner or later, I will ensure they get what is coming, just like I did with Dr. Bell." He removes his garish coat and throws it up on the wagon seat. "I best make it look like I'm busy; otherwise, they'll have something else for me to do," he says as he walks to the tool room.

Ty is coming back from the house when he thinks he hears voices, so he stops to listen. He overhears everything Holmes has been saying to himself. "You snake," Ty says as he walks into the stables.

Out of the tool room comes Mr. Holmes; he sees Ty, nods, and says, "Was going to oil up the front left wheel; it's been squeaking."

"Good idea, and while you're at it, do the other three," instructs Ty as he pats the wagon and moves to his office.

"Aye, sir," grumbles Mr. Holmes.

Once Ty gets to his office, he turns to watch Mr. Holmes and sees Fergus enter through the stable door. "Fergus, please give Mr. Holmes a hand oiling all four wheels on the wagon."

"Aye, sir." Fergus nods as he moves over to help Mr. Holmes.

Ty sits at his desk and writes down what he overheard to reiterate it to Ethan later. Going back to the house so soon after coming from it may be suspicious. Besides, Fergus is shadowing him for now. Ty heard Holmes confess that he was the one who handled Dr. Bell and that he was after the Stuart family. "Aye, Holmes, there will be a next time, and it will be your last," says Ty as he puts the paper he wrote on in the inside pocket of his coat. "Might as well try and get some work done this morning," Ty says, reaching for his folder of invoices requiring his attention.

Since Katharine is visiting tenants during the noon meal, Ty decides to tell everyone what he overheard in the stables. He explains what transpired and hands the note to Ethan.

"It's still his word against ours," says Ty.

"Yes, but it's something," responds Ethan. "I'll visit the parish constable this afternoon. I think it's best to let him know what we suspect and are doing."

"I think that's a brilliant idea, brother. You should take all of your notes regarding the incidents and the one Ty just gave you," informs Bonnie.

"Aye, that's a good idea, sister."

"Fergus is keeping a close eye on Mr. Holmes for now," states Ty.

They finish their noon meal by discussing the estate business that needs addressing. Then Ethan gathers the information to take to the parish constable; Ty returns to the stable; Bonnie and Mrs. Jones clear the meal, and they return to the household duties for the day.

It's been a week since Mr. Holmes tried to sabotage Katharine's horse and Ethan visited the parish constable. The constable had taken the information and cautioned Ethan to be careful. If Mr. Holmes has done what they suspected, he's a danger and needs to be stopped; however, they need actual proof or to catch him in the act of harming another. Nothing Ethan and the others don't already know. It's time to lay the groundwork to catch him at his game.

Katharine is doing her usual inventory at the infirmary when she hears a knock at the door. She sees Mr. Holmes standing at the door with a plant.

"Good day, Ms. Bennett. I thought you might like these to plant around the infirmary to add colour. They're beginning to grow along the road to and from the shipyard," he says.

"It's quite a nice purple colour, isn't it?" she says as she inspects it. "Do you know what it is, Mr. Holmes?"

"Nay, lass, I'm not good with that, but it looked so pretty."

"Thank you, Mr. Holmes. Let me take it, and we'll see if we can figure it out," she says as she takes the plant from his hand. She touches the lovely flowers that look like bells.

Mr. Holmes nods, smiles, and turns, leaving the infirmary. As he walks away, he begins to whistle to himself.

Katharine watches as Mr. Holmes leaves and hears him whistling as he goes. She takes the plant and puts it on the window sill until she can check to see what it is. As she removes her hand, she gets a splinter and instinctively puts it in her mouth. "Ouch, that hurt," she says to herself. Katharine checks her finger and sees the sliver of wood. She gets out the magnifying glass and tweezers to remove it herself. She then washes her hands, cleans the wound, and continues with her work.

At supper that evening, while Katharine eats, Bonnie notices a rash on her hand. She asks, "Katharine, what happened to your hand?"

Katharine looks down and sees the rash. "I put a plant on the window sill in the infirmary and got a sliver. The finger has been sore, which is to be expected, but I didn't notice that a rash has started," she says as she moves her hand around to investigate.

"You said you put a plant on the window sill? Which one was it?" asks Bonnie again.

"I don't know. Mr. Holmes brought it to me. He said he thought it would add colour to the infirmary's gardens. He couldn't tell me what it was, so I put it there until I investigated what it was," she says as she moves her hand to her head.

"Does this plant have purple bell-shaped flowers?" Bonnie inquires.

"Yes. Do you know what it is?" replies Katharine as she rubs her head.

"Katharine, do you have a headache?" interrupts Ethan.

"Yes, it started a few hours ago."

Bonnie and Ethan exchange glances, then Bonnie continues, "It could be one of two plants, but with the rash and the headache, it's likely foxglove. It can be poisonous if ingested."

"I touched the flowers, as they were so lovely, and when I got the sliver, I"—she shows them what she did.

"Aye," is heard from Ethan, Bonnie, and Ty.

Bonnie puts her hands on Katharine's arm and says, "The rash is isolated to your hand, where the sliver was. Your headache is more than likely because you ingested a small quantity of the poison."

"Let me go get the plant so we can be sure of what it is," says Ty as he excuses himself from the table to retrieve it from the infirmary. When he returns, everyone confirms it is foxglove.

"If you wish, Katharine, I can show you a book indicating other possible symptoms, but that's usually if a large amount is ingested. Unfortunately, it's a beautiful plant but can be dangerous, so most people stay clear if they don't know," continues Bonnie.

"I'll take a look just to be sure, Bonnie. Thank you. But I agree. My rash is isolated to the wound area, and I have a slight headache. Nothing that would alarm me. I see you have done some doctoring yourself, Bonnie."

"Aye, I have, Katharine. Come, I'll show you the book," says Bonnie as she leaves the table with Katharine following behind.

"He knew what that plant was," Ethan says through gritted teeth as he slams the table.

"I'll check with Fergus about how this happened, Ethan, but we need to figure something out. We can't have someone with him day and night, and now we can be sure he's targeting Katharine, and possibly even Liam or Tamara," states Ty.

"Let's sleep on it, my friend, and see what we come up with. I'll inform the parish constable tomorrow so he's kept apprised of what's happening and that it looks like things are escalating," says Ethan as he gets up from the table and heads to the study. Ty goes to the stable to speak to Fergus.

Once Katharine has reviewed the book and determined her symptoms are minor, she returns to the kitchen with Bonnie to assist Mrs. Jones in cleaning up from the evening meal.

TWENTY-SIX

FOLLOWING WHAT TRANSPIRED with Katharine, Ethan decides to stay on the estate. On Monday morning, Ty accompanies Mr. Holmes to take the workers to the shipyard. Ty informs Reid of why Ethan won't be in this week. While they're away in town, Ethan visits the parish constable to let him know about the latest incident.

On the drive back to the estate, Ty says to Mr. Holmes, "Those purple flowers that grow along the path here"—he points to them—"are called foxglove. Although they're pretty, they can also be poisonous."

Mr. Holmes stays quiet and drives the team back to the estate.

"I understand you gave some to Ms. Katharine the other day. It would be best for you not to give Ms. Katharine, Liam, or Tamara a plant you don't recognize. We wouldn't want anyone to come to harm, would we, Mr. Holmes?"

He nods and says, "Aye," but doesn't look at Ty.

Once back at the stable, Ty goes to his office, and Fergus assists Mr. Holmes in unhitching the horses and dealing with the wagon. While Fergus is busy doing his job, Mr. Holmes thinks, *Mr. Ty made it clear they know about the poisonous plant I gave Ms. Katharine. I must be much more careful, as they know what I did. I may have to wait a while before I try something else. Besides, that will give me time to figure out a way to shake off my shadow.* He looks over to Fergus, who's putting a horse in her stall. "I've been able to get away with so much already; I need to be more cunning in my next move. I may have to change my strategy."

"Sorry, Holmes, did you say something?" asks Fergus as he walks by.

"Nay, I was just talking to myself," replies Holmes.

"Aye," says Fergus, leading the second horse into her stall.

Now, who dislikes Ms. Katharine? Aye, Mr. Randall, of course. He's made it clear that he disdains her, as she's English, and he doesn't like that she acts like she deserves to be treated equally to him, a man. Aye, that's the way to go, he thinks maliciously as he plans how to set in play his next move.

Knowing that Mr. Holmes is aware that his trick with the poisonous plant was caught, the Stuarts are confident that he'll behave for a little while. Besides, they have Fergus sticking to him like glue. Mr. Holmes isn't making a move without Fergus right there with him.

In the coming weeks, as is the routine, Mr. Holmes and Fergus take the workers in when Ethan goes in for the week. However, this week, Ethan is staying back at the estate, so Ty goes in with Mr. Holmes.

Ty speaks to Reid and then returns to the estate. On Monday morning, upon their return, instead of Ty going to his office, he tells both Mr. Holmes and Fergus, "If you need me, I'll be up at the house with Ms. Bonnie and Laird Stuart to discuss farm issues."

They nod in unison and say "Aye" and return to dealing with the horses and wagon.

"Good morning, everyone. Liam and Tamara are both at the infirmary; no house visits are scheduled. If anyone needs me, I'll be down at the glen," Katharine tells them as she walks through the kitchen and out the back.

"Aye, Ms. Katharine. If you see William, tell him to come see me, please," says Mrs. Jones.

"I will," responds Katharine. "Good morning, Ty," she says as she passes him going to the house.

"Good morning, Katharine. Off to the glen?" says Ty.

"Yes, how did you know?" asks Katharine.

"You have your journal and Bible," responds Ty.

Katharine looks down at her hands and realizes that she usually has those items when she goes to the glen. "Good guess, Ty. Oh, if you see William, let him know Mrs. Jones is looking for him," replies Katharine as she continues her walk to the glen.

"Aye," replies Ty as he waves to her and continues to the house.

Ethan and Bonnie are sitting at the kitchen table when Ty comes in. He helps himself to a cup of coffee and sits at the table with them.

"How goes it?" asks Ty.

"This situation with Mr. Holmes is like trying to play chess. Not knowing what his next move is makes it difficult to know how we move," states Ethan.

"Aye, and we know how much you love a game of chess," Bonnie says sarcastically as she smiles at both men.

"Part of the chess game is patience and strategy, my friend," says Ty. "We're a move ahead of him. I don't believe Mr. Holmes knows how much we've pieced together."

Bonnie asks, "You don't think speaking to him about the foxglove might have tipped him off?"

"No. I think it's bought us some time. I think he'll lie low for a while to regroup, as he didn't get away with this last one," replies Ty.

"Let's hope that's the case, Ty. I wouldn't have said Mr. Holmes is smart, but from what we've learned, he is much more cunning and malicious than we ever gave him credit for. We must stay ahead of him," interjects Ethan as he sips his coffee.

As Katharine passes by the stable, its doors wide open, she waves to Fergus and Mr. Holmes, who are working inside.

"She's off to the glen," says Mr. Holmes.

As they pass, a lone rider tips his hat to Ms. Katharine and makes his way toward the Stuart stable.

"Good morning to you," waves the parish constable riding toward the stable. He halts his horse, dismounts, and walks over to tie it at the rail.

"Good morning, sir," replies Fergus as he emerges from the stable, wiping his hands on a rag.

"I'm here to see Laird Stuart," says the parish constable.

"Aye, if you follow that path, you'll come to the back of the house. Open the door, announce yourself, and walk through the mud room, which takes you into the kitchen." Fergus points to the house.

"Aye, thank you," says the parish constable, who notices a man standing behind Fergus inside the stable. He follows the path and directions Fergus gave him to get to the house.

"Wonder why the parish constable is here?" asks Mr. Holmes as he moves closer to Fergus.

"Nay, no idea," replies Fergus.

The constable lets himself in and is welcomed by Mrs. Jones. He's shown to the table where everyone else sits, and Mrs. Jones gives him a coffee.

"What brings you here, Constable?" asks Ethan.

He drinks from his cup and nods to Mrs. Jones. "Aye, a good cup of coffee, thank you." He then directs his attention to Ethan. "Perhaps we should have this discussion in a more private room."

"Anything you have to say can be said in front of all of us, Constable," instructs Ethan.

"Very well. I've been investigating Mr. Holmes. I thought it would be best to start at the beginning. I talked with the constables in town regarding the accident at the shipyard. Once I had their information and authorization, I spoke to two witnesses. They were reluctant at the time to say anything, but their conscience got the better of them as time passed. I have two sworn statements confirming that Mr. Holmes didn't do what he was instructed to do to erect the scaffold safely. This resulted in his injuries and the death of the other man."

"Are you telling me I have two workers who knew what he did and didn't say anything?" Ethan asks in controlled anger.

"They are no longer employed with you, sir, but one grows a conscience with time. They both will still be charged with providing false information, which is a small fine. The big picture is I have two witnesses with corroborating details."

"You mean we can arrest Mr. Holmes now?" asks Ty as he rises from the table.

"Yes, with the witnesses, Ty's recollection of what he overheard Mr. Holmes say, and the detailed documentation provided, I believe there's enough evidence against Mr. Holmes to put him behind bars."

The room is silent, and they're shocked to know the game is over.

At the stable, Fergus notices that the constable's horse isn't standing correctly. He checks, and the left hind horseshoe has lost a nail. It will need a new one to keep it in place. Fergus can fix it and asks Mr. Holmes to go and let the constable know. Mr. Holmes reluctantly goes to the house, saying, "Again, I'm a messenger boy." Mr. Holmes comes through the back door and is in the mud room area when he overhears the words of the constable, indicating he's there to arrest Mr. Holmes. He is livid, turns, leaves the house, and, in a rage, heads toward the glen where Katharine is.

"Watch where you're going, boy," says Mr. Holmes as he knocks William over. William dusts himself off and runs to the door. "Mrs. Jones, Ms. Katharine said you wanted to see me," he says as he stops in front of Mrs. Jones.

"I did, William. My goodness, boy, what happened to you?" asks Mrs. Jones when she sees the dirt on his pants and shirt.

"Mr. Holmes pushed me down the path as he came from the house. He's not in a good mood," William says as he tries to dust off more of the dirt from his clothes. With William's statement, everyone realizes Mr. Holmes must have overheard their conversation.

"Oh dear," Bonnie whispers.

"William, do you know which direction he was headed?" questions Ty.

"Aye, the glen," replies William.

"Katharine," say all four in unison.

Chairs scrape across the floor as Ethan, Ty, and the constable rush out the door after him. When William sees the three running out the door, he takes off. With his tiny legs and energy, he overtakes them all. Fergus looks up from finishing with the horse hoof; he sees William fly by, and then all three men running toward the glen. *This can't be good*, he thinks, dropping everything to follow.

"If that woman doctor hadn't come, they would never have realized what I'd done. She's the reason I've been found out." Convincing himself that Katharine is the problem to be dealt with, Mr. Holmes enters the glen and approaches Katharine. Her back is to him as she's reading her Bible. He takes out his dirk, moving quietly and quickly at her. Sensing something isn't right, Katharine lifts her head, turns around, and sees Mr. Holmes coming at her with a knife in his hand. "Jesus!" she shouts, raising the Bible in her hand.

Everything moves in slow motion. William comes rushing through the bushes, running to Katharine to hug her. Mr. Holmes doesn't stop his attack but plunges the dirk down at Katharine. However, he stabs William, not Katharine. Screams are heard as everyone else comes through the bushes to witness Mr. Holmes stepping back and pulling his dirk out of William's lifeless body. He stumbles back, realizing he didn't get the person he was after.

"Grab him," yells the constable as he and Fergus restrain Mr. Holmes.

"I will take that," says the constable as he removes the dirk from Mr. Holmes's hand. You, sir, are under arrest," he says, leading him away with Fergus's help.

Yelling, Mr. Holmes says, "I did nothing wrong. This is all the Stuarts' fault; they made me do it."

Liam, Tamara, and Ryan come through the bushes. They had watched from the infirmary as everyone ran past it, and they followed to see what was happening.

"No, no, no," wails Katharine as she holds William in her arms and rocks back and forth. Everyone around her is stunned. It seems like forever before anyone approaches the distraught Katharine. The sight of a limp little boy with a blood-stained shirt in the arms of a wailing Katharine hits them like a bolt of lightning. Ryan quietly walks through the group toward her. He kneels before Katharine and places both of his hands on Katharine's upper arms.

"Ms. Katharine," he says to draw her attention to himself. She doesn't waver her gaze from William. Ryan shakes her slightly this time, saying, "Ms. Katharine, look at me."

The shaking registers, and she lifts her head to look at Ryan.

"Let me take William from you."

She doesn't hear him. She sits and rocks the little man in her arms.

"Ms. Katharine," speaks Ryan more firmly as he squeezes her arms.

She looks up at Ryan with tears streaming down her face and then back down at William. She begins to whisper into William's ear, "If there be righteousness in the heart, there will be beauty in the character. If there be beauty in the character, there will be harmony in the house. If there be harmony in the house, there will be order in the nation. If there is order in the nation, there will be peace in the world. May you find peace where you go, William." She kisses his head, saying, "I love you, little man." Her gaze returns to Ryan, who hasn't moved from his spot.

"I'll take him back to the infirmary for you."

She releases William into Ryan's care. Ryan manoeuvres William away from Katharine and begins his walk back to the infirmary. Katharine watches Ryan go, as though he's carrying a sleeping child to bed. Katharine remains motionless. Ethan moves toward her. Ty, however, holds him back and quietly says, "No, Ethan."

Ty looks to Liam and Tamara and motions for them to go to her. Liam comes over and kneels before Katharine, just like Ryan had. "Ms. Katharine, let us help you."

Liam offers her his hand. She sits for a moment, not entirely sure of what to do.

Liam says again, "Ms. Katharine, let us help you." He moves both hands in front for her to take. She looks up and sees him but doesn't fully register what he asked. Those looking on watch as the woman they knew not to be fazed by circumstances and who had the strength to endure sits hopelessly and lost at what just transpired. Katharine sees Liam's hands extended forward to assist. She follows his lead and takes his hands, and he helps her get up. Tamara moves beside and puts her arm around her as Liam moves to the other side—the three walk side by side back to the estate infirmary, following where Ryan had tread.

Only after he's sure that they're far enough away not to hear does Ethan say, "What have we done, Ty?"

"I have no answer for you, my friend. This mistake will haunt us for the rest of our lives."

Ethan paces like a caged lion, ready to spring. He feels lost and out of control. If there were walls to pound on, he would do it now. All he can do is beat himself up instead.

"Come, my friend, we must find Mrs. Jones."

Now another blow hits Ethan. "Ty, how do I tell her she has lost another."

"Together, Ethan, together."

His head down, as the weight of the evening is too much, Ty takes his arm and puts it around his beloved friend to be the support he will need to get back to the estate and tell Mrs. Jones and Bonnie that William has died.

The cries heard from the estate are screams of "No, no, no." The agony from both Bonnie and Mrs. Jones is the undoing of Ethan. His tears of loss, regret, and love flow as he hugs Mrs. Jones. Ty consoles Bonnie. Ethan knows he's responsible for William's death as much as if he was the one who had plunged the knife into his chest himself. In his arrogance to protect his people and the woman he has grown to love, he was blinded to what was right before him. It's a mistake when someone else pays the consequences for his actions.

After Mrs. Jones's tears subside, Bonnie looks up into Ty's eyes with the unspoken words, "What have we done?" He nods to her. She moves out of Ty's hug to go over and take Mrs. Jones from Ethan. She assists her back to her room and spends the night with her.

Ethan turns to go to his study. "I need to be alone, Ty."

"Are you sure, Ethan?"

"No, Ty, I am not sure of anything anymore."

Ethan enters his study and pours himself a drink. He goes to sit in his chair but decides to stand instead; he looks at his drink, then the fire. He closes his eyes, lifts his head, and lets out a roar. He throws the drink into the fire and drops to the floor, crying repeatedly, "I am so sorry, William. Forgive me, William, for what I have done. Forgive me, Father; please forgive me, Father."

The Stuart estate is mourning the loss of William. His burial is set for Sunday afternoon. This allows most, if not all, of the community to attend. Everyone knew William or had known his parents. Liam and Tamara are tasked with preparing him for burial. He's wrapped in "death clothes" and placed in a coffin that Ty and Ethan built themselves. A wooden plate is laid on William's chest in keeping with Scottish tradition. On the plate is a handful of earth, representing that the body is being returned to the earth from whence it came. A handful of salt represents the eternal soul, and at Katharine's request, blades of grass are added to the plate, which William would always play with when they were at the glen. After the Sunday church service, William is laid to rest with his parents in the community cemetery on the Stuart estate.

Following William's burial, a community dinner is held in the great hall. During this dinner, Ethan explains to the community what transpired regarding Mr. Holmes. As Katharine listens, it becomes clear that the core members of the Stuart family were aware of what was going on, and she was not informed. You can see it on her face. The shock of knowing the ones closest to her—Ethan, Bonnie, Mrs. Jones, Ty—all knew, and no one told her. A righteous anger is fueled within Katharine on hearing this news. She looks at Liam and Tamara; they too have the same look of shock on their faces. They didn't know. All three of them were left in the dark. William's death could have been prevented if they had trusted her, Liam, and Tamara enough to know what was going on when it came to Mr. Holmes.

Ethan speaks to the three of them, saying, "I know I was wrong not to say anything to you. As Laird, it was my decision. I am responsible for William's death, and I will have to live with that for the rest of my life."

Katharine stands up from the table. In a hurt and angry tone, she says, "Why would you not tell me, Ethan? When have I ever given you cause to think I couldn't or wouldn't help you in this regard?"

Ethan moves back to walk toward her. She is not finished.

"I have done everything asked of me. I spent two months or more caring for your sick during the outbreak." She looks around at the community people. "I have fought for your people, with you, beside you, and for you. I have shown all of you that I was on your side. I felt like I was a member of this family."

Bonnie and Ty slide back their chairs to add to the conversation. Katharine raises her hands to signal that they aren't to interrupt her. "Instead, everything I have done was for naught. From the first day I arrived, I have fought to show you that I am more than a filthy Englishman." She looks directly at Mr. Randall, who lowers his eyes. "I am an outsider and always will be."

"Katharine …" starts Bonnie.

Katharine bows her head, clenches her hands beside her body, closes her eyes, and says a silent prayer. She releases her hands, opens her eyes, looks up, and finds Ethan across the room. She sees his eyes to hold his gaze.

She speaks in a weak, almost ready-to-crack-from-tears voice. "If I may, Laird Stuart, for the duration of my commitment here, I will keep to my room when I am not in the infirmary." She turns and nods toward Liam and Tamara. "Liam and Tamara can handle most, if not all, situations without me. I will be available for consultation, but from this day until my departure, all medical assistance will be through them. I will devote most of my time to completing the reference books and updating all of the medical records for them." With a large intake of breath, she says, "If I may, Laird, I would like to retire to my room for the evening." She is barely keeping it together.

"Aye, as you wish, Katharine."

She will do something she has never done before. She bows her head and does a quick courtesy. When she rises, she lifts her skirt and turns to leave the room. Those in attendance are silent. They are dumbfounded at what just happened. Katharine did something most of his people rarely do. It was to say, "I know my place, and it is beneath you. I wouldn't say I like it, but I will submit to the authority above me."

There is murmuring from the crowd.

"Mrs. Jones has one of William's favourite desserts for us to enjoy; please help yourselves." Ty motions to the table along the side, where the chocolate pudding is ready for those who wish to partake.

Ethan moves to place his hand on Ty's shoulder to say "Thank you, my friend," and he moves to his place of sanctuary. His study.

Ty turns to Bonnie, takes hold of her arm, and asks, "Will you be okay here by yourself for a while?"

"Aye, take care of him, will you?"

"Aye, my love, I will." He bends to kiss her on the cheek.

Ty follows Ethan into the study to have a little conversation with him. Ty knows Ethan is in love with Katharine, even if he doesn't say it. Katharine won him over the first evening, when she dealt with Mr. Randall.

"We all know she's hurt and angry, Ethan, but she'll come around."

"I don't know, Ty. She called me Laird and bowed. For Katharine, that's a sign of surrender. I've never seen her back down before."

"I would suggest, my friend, that you give her some space the next few days and then speak to her. She's still trying to take in the death of William, as we all are."

"What do I say to her? She's right, Ty. I was selfish in not letting her, Liam, and Tamara know about what we discovered about Mr. Holmes."

"You're only human, Ethan. Don't let Mr. Holmes take more from us than he already has. Katharine is hurting, and rightly so. You, Bonnie, Mrs. Jones, and I didn't tell her even when we thought we should. She feels betrayed. We will all have to account to her for this, Ethan, not just you."

"Aye, but ultimately, everything is my decision as Laird, and she knows that." He moves to the fireplace and bends down to stoke the embers.

"Katharine has a heart too full of love to let anger and bitterness overtake it. We all need to give her room to process what has happened and then talk"

"We can't lose her, Ty," speaks Ethan as he gets up from the fire.

"You won't lose her, Ethan. You have to let her work this out for herself. Stay close and show her you're not going anywhere and are there for her."

"How?"

"She's at the glen most mornings. Be there, sit quietly with her just as William did. Sometimes it's not the words, my friend, but the actions that speak louder."

"You are a wise man, Ty, and a good and loyal friend."

Ty pours a glass of whiskey for both himself and Ethan. He comes over, hands it to him, and says, "To not lose what we love." He taps Ethan's glass and drinks his whiskey. Ethan does the same. "If you'll excuse me, Ethan, I want to return to Bonnie."

"Of course, Ty; good night, my friend."

Ty nods, sets the glass on the table, and quietly leaves the room.

"To not lose what we love. Losing William is the only loss I can take right now. I don't intend to lose you too, Katharine," he says as he sits in front of the fire growing from the embers he has stirred.

It seems like it takes forever for Katharine to return to her room. As it's her habit to turn to say thank you to William for walking her to her door every night, she goes to do so, but he isn't there. She pushes the door open, closes it, and locks it. Turning slowly, she slides down the door and ends up in a heap on the floor. She begins to weep for her little man, William, but mainly for the feeling of betrayal by those she's called family for the last eleven months and the lack of trust from a man she has grown to love. She thought all she had to do was come here, do a job, and go home. How did things get so complicated? Others would hear her cries if they passed by her room. She cries so hard and for so long that she falls asleep against the door.

TWENTY-SEVEN

AS IS HER routine, Katharine arises the following day and needs to be somewhere to give her comfort, so she goes to the glen. Today she allows the tears to flow as she sits and looks at the beauty around her and listens to the water as it travels from one end to the other in the glen.

She has been sitting for a moment when she hears rustling behind her. She doesn't think to look because she thinks it will be William, who would always find her a little while after she arrived. But she realizes it can't be him. When she turns to look, she sees Ethan; he has come through the entrance and sat quietly down from her, with his knees up and his hands around them to hold them in. She looks at him with surprise in her eyes. Why is he here? She turns to the glen, closes her eyes, breathes, and gives up a silent prayer. They both sit in quiet contemplation. Neither speaks, but they know they are each there.

For the next several days, Ethan comes to the glen to sit quietly with Katharine. On the fifth day, Ethan speaks.

"You don't come to the study in the evenings to do your paperwork." She doesn't respond. "I've grown accustomed to having you in the study at night; it doesn't seem the same." No response. "I realize you're angry and upset, Katharine. I can't undo what has been done. All I can ask for is your forgiveness."

She nods to him, then turns back to gaze at the glen.

Ethan continues to sit with her, and he too turns his gaze to the glen. "What more can I do?" he says to himself. "She won't speak to me." He sighs and begins to get up.

Katharine turns to him and says, "I need time to process what has happened."

He nods at her and leaves. She talked to him. That's a start. He'll be back tomorrow and as often as it takes to get his Katharine back.

After her morning on the glen, Katharine stops by the infirmary to let Liam and Tamara know she will be at the Young estate. Instead of going to the house, she goes to the stables to saddle Tally. She tells Fergus where she is going and sets off for the neighbours.

When she arrives, she sees Gavin.

"Katharine, this is a surprise. Is everything all right?" questions Gavin.

"Yes and no."

"Come in, lass. Grace is still having her breakfast."

"Thank you, Gavin."

Gavin opens the door to allow Katharine access.

"I would also like to speak with you. Do you have a moment?"

"Aye, I do, lass. Let's go and see Grace together," he says as he comes in and closes the door.

Katharine nods and moves to the breakfast room. She hears Grace's voice talking to someone; when she enters, she sees Grace holding one of the babes and talking to her. Katharine smiles at the sweet sight she sees before her. Grace lifts her head to see Katharine enter and smiles at her.

"Good morning, Katharine; what a nice surprise."

"I said the same thing, my dear," Gavin replies, kissing his wife and taking the baby from her arms. "Katharine would like to speak to us," he adds.

"Oh, is everything all right?"

"I will explain. May I?" she asks as she sits at the table.

"Of course. Do you wish for tea or coffee?"

Katharine takes a seat at the table. "Maybe a whiskey." She laughs.

Gavin raises his eyes to say, "Oh dear." Grace looks at Gavin as if to say, "This is not good."

"I was only joking; a coffee would be lovely, thank you."

"Let me get that for you, Katharine. I'll get one for you too, my dear."

"I still have mine here, love; thank you anyway."

Gavin goes over to the counter to pour himself and Katharine their coffees. He brings the cups to the table and then sits beside Grace.

"Now, Katharine, what brings you here to speak with us both?"

"I'm sure you're both aware that my one-year commitment with the Stuarts ends in a little more than a month."

Grace and Gavin nod.

PATRICIA CORLIS

Katharine goes to take a drink from her coffee cup, but her hands are too shaky, so she returns it to the saucer. She pauses for a moment.

"Katharine," says Grace, moving her hand over to cover hers, "what can we do to help you, my friend?"

The tears she's been holding back pour out. "I am so sorry. I'm usually composed and not prone to this kind of outburst." She takes a few moments to compose herself and uses the napkin to wipe away the tears.

"Take your time, Katharine. We know the loss of William has hit you hard," says Gavin.

"Are you also aware that Bonnie, Ty, Mrs. Jones, and Ethan knew about Mr. Holmes but didn't tell me or Liam and Tamara?" she says as she wrings the napkin.

"Aye."

The look on Katharine's face is one of complete shock.

Gavin holds up his hand. "I meant to say that Tamara learned about Mr. Holmes the night you did. She too felt betrayed and spoke to Ryan. He's the one who spoke with me. He wanted to know how he could support Tamara."

"And what did you tell him?"

"As a Laird, it's up to us to protect our people. We make the best decisions we can. We are human, Katharine, and we do make mistakes. We must live with them; sometimes our actions have consequences that others pay the price for. I know it's hard for you to see or hear it, but Ethan was doing what he thought was in the best interest of the Stuart community. It had nothing to do with trust; it had everything to do with protection. He knew Mr. Holmes was a threat to the community and was doing what he could to keep everyone safe."

Katharine closes her eyes and sighs. "My head says I should understand. You're right, Gavin. It's the heart that's not letting me due to the hurt. Seeing, hearing, and understanding your words is hard for me. I have a wound I can't seem to heal, and I'm the doctor," she squeaks out.

Gavin moves to take her other hand. She allows him, even though she could use it to wipe away tears. She squeezes their hands as to signal "Thank you."

"The reason I came is to ask you for help." She lets go of their hands and takes the brooch from her dress pocket. She then lays it on the table before Gavin.

"What do you require assistance for?" Gavin asks as he takes the brooch from the table.

"I must stay somewhere once my one-year commitment with the Stuarts is completed. I will make arrangements with my brother, but until I know when the ship will be here to pick me up, I'll need—"

"Of course, you can stay here with us," Grace pipes up, "for as long as you need."

172

"I'll let my brother know he can reach me here when the ship arrives after the one-year commitment." With a deep breath and a feeling of less weight, Katharine smiles at them both. "Thank you so much. You have no idea how much I appreciate this."

"I believe Ryan was going to be going over to see Tamara. How about I have him ride back with you?" offers Gavin.

"Aye, Gavin, that's a wonderful idea," responds Katharine.

They all laugh at Katharine's attempt to sound Scottish.

"Let me go see where he is. I'll be back."

Katharine, with renewed strength, takes a sip from her cup.

"Can I assume, Katharine, that you haven't spoken to Ethan about everything that has happened or your decision to come here?"

She puts her cup back down. "No. I've been too angry and hurt to speak to him. My head says I need to, but my heart says not yet."

"Ethan cares deeply for you, Katharine. He would never intentionally do anything to hurt you; you need to believe that."

She nods. "I'm still processing it all, Grace. It's one thing to try and save the life of someone, but William ... he died in my arms, Grace, and I could do nothing to save him. Nothing, nothing, nothing." She weeps uncontrollably with her face in her hands.

Grace pushes back her chair to come around to comfort Katharine as she would her own crying child. She feels a little lighter after she cries with Grace and knowing she has their support.

Gavin returns to let Katharine know Ryan will be ready to accompany her back to the Stuart estate in an hour. This allows Katharine to spend time with Grace, talk, and enjoy quality time with the twins.

A burden has been lifted off Katharine now that she knows she has a place to stay once her one-year commitment is completed. In the mornings, she continues to go to the glen to spend time with herself. In quiet contemplation, she forgives Ethan, Ty, Bonnie, and Mrs. Jones. Part of the process is writing letters to each person. When she's not in the glen, she spends time in her room working on the reference book for Liam and Tamara and reviewing files to ensure her notes are up to date for when she leaves. Although it's been a struggle, Katharine does participate in the evening meals.

Liam and Tamara are asked to attend this particular Friday dinner. To ease the tension, Ethan begins with, "Thank you for coming," to Liam and Tamara. "I know you and Katharine are all still reeling from the events that transpired with Mr. Holmes. I want to apologize for the personal hurt I have caused you. My actions had nothing to do with not trusting you." He takes a moment to move forward in his chair and continues. "I did what I thought was best for the community. I am proud of you both and grateful for what you've learned in the past year under Katharine's mentorship. You are all extremely valued persons to the Stuart family."

"Aye. You both have truly grown in this past year," Bonnie inserts. "I also want to extend an apology to you on behalf of myself, Ty, and Mrs. Jones. We did what we did, as Ethan said, to protect you and the community."

"I appreciate your apology," says Liam as he nods to Ethan and Bonnie. "I can't speak for Tamara or Ms. Katharine; I understand what you're saying, but"—both Tamara and Katharine nod in agreement with what Liam says—"if you trust us with the lives of the people in this community, then by informing us of what was going on, we may have been able to intervene. Tamara and I saw Mr. Holmes heading toward the glen where Ms. Katharine was ..." He can't continue, as he becomes emotional.

"Liam, I can't change the past. What I can do is give you all the time needed to find it in your hearts to forgive us for our mistakes," states Ethan.

"Aye" is heard in unison from Liam and Tamara.

Katharine looks at Ethan and says "Aye" as she nods.

"Very well. Now how about we enjoy the fruits of Mrs. Jones's labour?" Ty inserts as he picks up a tray of meat to pass around the table.

"Aye" is heard from everyone. The heavy atmosphere surrounding the table when everyone first sat down has been lifted, and cheerfulness has taken over.

Two days before Katharine is to finish her one-year commitment, she's summoned to assist with a difficult birth. Liam urgently arrives back at the Stuart estate and explains to Katharine that it's Mrs. Randall. Neither he nor Tamara is confident about how things are going. Katharine is stunned. Mrs. Randall is the woman who gave birth the first night she arrived, and now, just before she leaves, she's giving birth again. She had no idea she was pregnant.

"How far along is she, Liam?"

"I believe she said she had another month. Something is very wrong, Ms. Katharine. Please, we need your help."

"Of course, Liam. I'll grab my bag and be right with you." Katharine grabs her bag but doesn't take the cloak. She hasn't worn it since William died in her arms. She looks at it and leaves it hanging on the hook by the door as she moves outside. When Liam and Katharine enter the stables, Katharine catches Ty.

"Ty, Liam and I are heading to the Randall home. It would be best to bring the wagon, as it will be needed."

Ty looks to Liam, who nods. "Right away, Katharine. I won't be far behind."

"Thank you."

Liam and Katharine work together to get Tally saddled and on their way.

Ethan hears the horses galloping off from the stables and then hears Ty working with his men to prepare the wagon. He goes to the stable to find out what the commotion is about.

"Katharine left with Liam to go to the Randalls'. She's asked for the wagon."

"I'll come with you, Ty. Let me tell Mrs. Jones and Bonnie that we'll have the Randall children again."

Katharine and Liam arrive at the Randall house. It's much too quiet. Liam stays behind with the horses and waits for Ty to arrive. Katharine enters to see the children all in the kitchen by the hearth. The older ones are trying to comfort the younger ones. She doesn't stop to do her usual routine. She enters the bedroom, where Tamara is beside Mrs. Randall.

"Tamara, can you gather the children and then take them outside? Liam is there with the horses. Mr. Ty will be here shortly with the wagon to take them to the Stuart estate.

"Yes, Ms. Katharine. We didn't know what else to do—"

"It is well, Tamara. You and Liam must care for the children."

Tamara nods and leaves the room, sure to close the door behind her.

Katharine moves to where Tamara had been sitting beside Mrs. Randall. She is still. You can see the paleness in her face, the blue around her lips and nose, and hear the laboured breathing. Katharine silently prays, "Lord, give me strength. Mrs. Randall, it's me, Ms. Katharine," she says as she kneels beside the bed. She sees Mrs. Randall's lips moving. She moves closer to check for a pulse, which is extremely weak. She strains to hear what she's saying.

"Please forgive me" is what she can understand from reading her lips.

"Mrs. Randall, can you hear me?" She doesn't respond, and her lips stop moving.

Katharine grabs her bag, takes the stethoscope, and checks for a heartbeat. She can't find one. She moves to the baby and whispers, "Please, God." She takes several minutes to poke and prod. There is no movement, and she can't find a heartbeat either. As Katharine closes Mrs. Randall's eyes, she says, "May you find the peace you deserve. Into God's hands, we commend you." She takes a few minutes to say a prayer.

Lifting her head, she rises from kneeling at the side of the bed. Katharine turns and finds Mr. Randall standing in the bedroom doorway, with his hat in his hand rung tightly. He sees his wife lying on the bed. His face has a look of panic. Katharine moves toward him, and you can see him cringing. "Mr. Randall, your wife and child are gone."

Ethan enters the home, and she sees him standing just behind Mr. Randall by the front door. She looks past Mr. Randall and says, "Mr. Stuart, it is my medical opinion that, with the loss of Mrs. Randall, it would be in the children's best interest if they are taken into your care."

Ethan looks over Mr. Randall's shoulder and says, "Liam and Tamara have the children settled in the wagon Ty brought, as you requested. They will be taken back to the estate and cared for until I say otherwise."

"Thank you."

Katharine moves to the bed. She pulls the bed covers up and over Mrs. Randall. She retrieves her bag and moves toward Mr. Randall to leave the room.

"Wait, what am I to do?" Mr. Randall says as he points to the bed.

In a calm voice, Katharine looks at him and says, "Mr. Randall, you paid no heed to the medical advice I gave you and your wife. You paid no respect to your wife to get her with child again, to the unborn child, and certainly not to the children you already have. Perhaps now you could take the time to show them the respect they deserve. I leave them in your hands, sir. Good day."

She picks up her skirt, flees the room, and leaves the cottage. Mr. Randall looks at Ethan. Ethan nods, and he too leaves the home. Mr. Randall is left standing in his bedroom alone, looking at the bed where his wife and unborn child took their last breaths.

Many tears are shed on the way back to the Stuart estate. All of the children are, in one form or another, crying over the loss of their mother. Liam, Tamara, and Katharine do their best to comfort them. Katharine weeps with them, for the unnecessary loss of a woman and child but also for the grief of losing William. She can openly cry, and no one will know what the tears are for. Ty and Ethan can hear the cries of the children and the adults trying to comfort them. They dare not look back, for they too may succumb to tears.

Bonnie and Mrs. Jones are there to greet them when they enter the estate courtyard. Everyone works together to get the children inside, beside the kitchen fire, to warm them up and get food and something hot to drink. Katharine, Liam, and Tamara stay with the children while Mrs. Jones and Bonnie go off to get their room ready for them.

"Ms. Katharine."

"Yes, Lucas."

Lucas moves from his chair up into Katharine's lap. "Will we ever see our father again?"

"Yes, Lucas, of course you will."

"Why did you take us away?"

"Do you remember the last time I came when your mother gave birth to your brother, James?"

"Yes."

"Do you remember I said that you and your siblings were brought here to the estate to give your mother a chance to recuperate from giving birth to your brother?"

Lucas shakes his head to say no.

"This time, Lucas, you were taken away to allow your father time to make all the necessary arrangements for your mother's and unborn sibling's burials. We brought you back here so that Liam, Tamara, Mr. Ty, Mrs. Jones, Ms. Bonnie, and Mr. Ethan can all be here for you if you need us."

"I want my mommy back," cries Bree.

"I would return her to you if I could, Bree." She moves her hand down to caress her little cheek. Katharine looks at all the children and says, "There is one place your mother will always be." She presses her hand against her chest where her heart beats. "Here in each of your hearts. Right now, it hurts. Your mother loved every one of you. She wouldn't want you to be sad forever. A little piece of your heart will always hurt from the loss of your mother. Someday, you'll be able to laugh because you remember something your mother used to do or how she would do something, but most of all, she raised each of you to be the amazing child you are. Never forget that. She may not be here for you to touch and see, but she's never far from you because she will always be in your heart."

Mrs. Jones wipes her eyes and blows her nose. "That was lovely, Ms. Katharine. Children, your room is ready. Let's get you sorted out, aye."

The older ones help the younger ones, and Tamara takes the babe, who has fallen asleep in her arms. As Lucas climbs out of Katharine's lap and takes his sister's hand to be led to the room, Katharine turns to watch them leave and catches sight of Ethan in the corner.

He has been sitting off to the side, out of sight of Katharine. He heard what she was saying to the children. He knows she was speaking the truth to them about their mother, but he also realizes she was talking to herself about William. He will always have a piece of their hearts, too. Their eyes meet, and they can see the hurt in each other. Katharine lets the tears she's been holding back fall. Ethan rises from his seat, with tears falling down his face, too; he follows the children to their room as he wipes the tears away.

Knowing she has to speak with Ethan, Kathleen takes the lead and goes to the study. She knocks and enters. Ethan is sitting by the fire and doesn't bother to look when he says, "Not tonight, Ty."

"It's not Ty," she answers.

He turns around and hears Katharine's voice, so he gets out of his chair.

"Might I have a word with you?"

"Of course, Katharine; please have a seat."

She crosses the room to sit in the chair opposite him at the fire.

Ethan sits back down and stares at her. He misses having her here to study at night. He doesn't think he'll get this chance again.

"I," they both say simultaneously as they look at each other.

"You came to me, Katharine; please go first."

She nods to acknowledge what he said. "I'd like to apologize for my behaviour. I was hurt first by the loss of William and then to find out what you had done and the feeling of betrayal. It was like one cut on top of another. It wasn't just you but Bonnie, Ty, and Mrs. Jones. It was like my family had turned their backs on me, and also to have lost William …" She turns to look into the fire and places her hand over her mouth to stop the hurt from seeping through.

"Katharine, if I could do it all over again …" He moves forward to reach for her hand.

She turns to look into his eyes. "That's just it, Ethan. You can't do it over again. I have seen and understood your responsibilities to this community as their Laird. Every day, you and I have to make decisions that affect others." She squeezes his hand and then releases it. "I wanted to speak to you first. I've contacted my brother regarding when the ship will arrive in Scotland to return me to England."

Ethan releases her hand and falls back into his chair. *Hopefully, she'll have to stay longer than the one year*, he thinks to himself.

"The ship will come to get me on its way back from its current voyage. It will be another three weeks."

A smile comes across his face. That will give him time to build back the trust.

"With my commitment ending in a few days, I've arranged to stay with the Young family until the ship arrives. My brother will contact me there."

At this point, Ethan looks at Katharine and can see her mouth moving, but he hears nothing.

"I want to be the one to tell Bonnie, Ty, Mrs. Jones." She turns her head to look at Ethan, who is dazed.

"Ethan, are you all right?"

"No, Katharine, I am not all right." He gets up from his chair and moves behind his desk. "I had hoped to ask you to forgive me and to let you know how much I respect and trust you. If you had neither of them from me, you wouldn't have been here for the past year. You are determined to finish your commitment and take your leave. I will have a letter of recommendation for you." He sits to begin writing. "I am sure Bonnie, Mrs. Jones, and Ty will appreciate hearing your decision directly from you. Be sure to speak with Ty about any necessary arrangements to take you to the Youngs."

Katharine is still trying to figure out how to react. He is angry. Why is he angry? She's doing what she's supposed to be doing—finishing the commitment and leaving. "I will," she says shakenly. "I'll see if Mrs. Jones is in the kitchen."

"I think you will find her in the Randall room with the children," directs Ethan.

She leaves the room, not feeling as good as when she entered. Ethan waits until she has left before he slams his fists on the desk in frustration.

TWENTY-EIGHT

KATHARINE FINDS MRS. Jones in the kitchen with Bonnie. *That's good; I can talk to them both simultaneously.*

"Mrs. Jones, Bonnie, may I speak with you briefly?"

They both nod and smile.

"Can we sit at the table?"

"Aye," says Bonnie as they all move over.

"I was just up to see Ethan and speak with him. I wanted to apologize to you both for my behaviour these past few weeks. It wasn't professional and—"

"Ms. Katharine, there is no need to apologize," interrupts Mrs. Jones.

"Yes, there is. First of all, I'm here to do a job. Although I have been doing it, I haven't done it to the best of my ability, which is unacceptable. I hope you will both forgive me."

"I can't speak for Mrs. Jones, but there is nothing to forgive. I should be asking you to forgive me. I was one of Ethan's confidants who didn't tell you about our plan," says Bonnie.

Katharine moves her hands from her lap and takes each one's hand. "It has taken me this time to realize that all of you did what you thought was best. I can now see that. I also wanted to tell you that, with the year-long commitment finishing in a few days, I will stay with the Young family until the ship arrives in another three weeks."

Both Bonnie and Mrs. Jones squeeze her hand but say nothing.

A cry is heard from the Randall room. "I'll go and see," says Mrs. Jones, who excuses herself to investigate.

In a few moments, Bonnie says, "And you told Ethan this?"

"Yes, I did."

They both look at each other.

"What would you like for your going away meal, lass?" Mrs. Jones asks as she returns to the table.

"Nothing, Mrs. Jones. I want to leave much quieter than I arrived."

"But"—says Mrs. Jones.

"Nothing, Mrs. Jones. It's hard enough as it is. Please."

"Aye, lass, as you wish," says Mrs. Jones. She turns to return to the stove, where a stew is simmering for tomorrow's meal.

"You will be missed, Katharine. Are you sure we can't convince you to stay with us?"

"I think it would be best to finish the commitment to the Stuart family, as set out in the contract, and await my return to England with the Youngs."

"Very well, Katharine. But if we wanted to visit, you wouldn't turn us away, would you?"

"No, Bonnie, I wouldn't turn away a visit."

"Aye, then we'll have a visit." She squeezes her hand again.

"I need to speak to Ty. Is he in the stable?"

"Aye, I believe he is."

"Thank you, Bonnie. I'll go see if I can find him."

"If I see him, I'll tell him you're looking for him."

"And if I see him, I'll tell him I found him." They laugh as Bonnie returns to the kitchen to help Mrs. Jones, and Katharine heads to the stables.

"Ty. Ty, it's me, Katharine. Are you here?"

"I'm in my office, Katharine," shouts Ty as he sticks his head out the door. "It's good to see you. What can I do for you?"

Katharine begins her apology like with the others. Ty listens. When Katharine is finished, he asks her to come in and take a seat. Once she's seated, Ty moves over to his desk. He takes a seat and then opens the bottom cabinet of his desk. He brings out two glasses and pulls out a bottle of Scottish whiskey. He doesn't ask if she would like some; he pours an amount into each. He then places one at the end of the desk for her to take. He keeps his in his hands and leans back in his chair.

"The blessing you spoke over William the night he died, Katharine. Where did you learn it from?"

"William. He would say it whenever we were at the glen together."

"Do you know who taught him?"

"Yes, William said his mother."

"His mother taught him, just as our mother taught us," he whispered, swirling the scotch in his glass.

"His mother, your mother—wait, you were related to William?"

"Aye, I was, lass."

"But you, William, Ethan ... no one said."

"Because it wasn't something anyone knew about, Katharine. The sins of the mother should not be held accountable to the child. My mother's indiscretion was covered up, and the baby was given to another family, who raised it as their own. The irony is that my mother watched her child grow every day and could do nothing about it. The only stipulation my mother asked was that the child learn that blessing. The family didn't oppose it. When I heard Talon, William's mother, recite it one day, I asked where she'd learned it from. She knew she was adopted, as her mother was unable to carry a child. She told me her birth mother asked that she learn it. I was old enough to put two and two together."

"Ty, I had no idea."

"Neither does Ethan, Bonnie, or Mrs. Jones. You see, Katharine, I understand how you feel. I also understand Ethan's decision as Laird to deal with Mr. Holmes, who would have continued to harm this community. We all carry burdens, Katharine. Some days they're too heavy to carry, and some days they're light enough to go miles. However, along the way you find people to help you carry them; that's the greatest gift." He takes a swig of his scotch. Leaning forward, he speaks again. "Katharine, we are human, make mistakes, hope to God we learn from them, and have friends and family to get us through. Take the glass, Katharine."

She picks up her glass and holds it. Ty brings his over to hers and says, "To William, who has found peace. May we find ours and know that one day we will see him again."

They both take the scotch and swig it back. Katharine coughs a little, Ty laughs, and they sit together in the rustle of the stable's sounds.

"Before I go, Ty, I did want to ask you if you'd arrange for me to take Tally to the Young family. I'll stay with them until the ship arrives in port to take me back to England. Ryan has indicated that he will escort me; I need a wagon to take me and my things."

"Of course. Just let me know when."

"I will. Thank you, Ty." She gets up to leave but then turns back and says, "William would have been over the moon to know you were his uncle, Ty."

"I was so happy when he was brought here for Mrs. Jones to look after him. I may not have ever been called Uncle Ty, but hearing him say Mr. Ty was just as good."

"I hope one day you'll be able to tell Ethan, and especially Bonnie."

"One day. My mother is still alive, and it's her secret to tell until she passes."

"I understand, Ty. No one will hear it from me."

Ty nods, and she leaves the office.

Caring for the five Randall children occupies Katharine for her remaining time at the Stuart estate. On her last night after supper, she sneaks out to the infirmary after the children have been put to bed. Taking her cloak, she hangs in on the coat rack and places her medical bag on the desk with two handwritten notes with each of their names on them. She has said her goodbyes earlier this evening and doesn't have the strength to give them the items or notes. She leaves it for them to find in the morning when she's gone.

"I must get back to the house," she says as she quietly leaves the infirmary for the last time. Back in her room, she prepares her trunk for the trip. She hears a knock on her door. "Yes," she answers.

Ty walks in. "Aye, Katharine, I came to get the trunk for you."

"Yes, I just finished. It's all ready."

Ty nods and moves over to deal with the trunk. "When you're ready, Katharine, Ryan and I will be at the stable."

"Thank you, Ty."

He takes the trunk and moves out of the room. Katharine looks around at the room she has called hers for the last year. "I will not cry," she says to herself. "I have completed the year commitment, and now it's time to go." She grabs the other letters she wrote from her bed and the small bag she used as a purse. Her first stop is the study. She doesn't expect Ethan to be up. This evening, she makes a point to speak to each person individually to say goodbye. She quietly opens the door and sees that he's asleep by the fire in his "thinking" chair. She moves in as far as his desk and places the note addressed to him up against his inkwell. In a calm voice, she says, "Mar sin leat," Scottish Gaelic for goodbye (pronounced "mar-shin-lat). She leaves as quietly as she came in.

Now the tears she said she wasn't going to shed start. Down to the kitchen she goes. She leaves a note for Mrs. Jones and Bonnie by the coffee and tea. "Do not look back," she says as she passes through the kitchen to make her way to the stable. She stops at the door to breathe and wipe away the tears. Then it's out into the darkness of the night.

TWENTY-NINE

KATHARINE ARRIVES AT the stables. Ryan has his mount, and Ty has her trunk ready in the wagon.

"Are we ready?" she asks.

"Whenever you are, Ms. Katharine," replies Ryan.

"Very well, it is time," she says. Ty takes her hand to help her into the wagon. Ryan mounts his horse, and Ty takes the driver's seat. Before he pulls away, he looks up to see Ethan standing at the study window, looking down. He nods. Katharine sees the exchange, and when she looks up, she sees Ethan standing in the window watching them. It takes everything she has to smile and wave to him. He raises his hand back to her and smiles. It's so much easier when there's distance between them. Ty makes a sound and lightly snaps the reins. The horses start the trek to the Young family, with Ryan beside them.

Turning from the window, Ethan drags himself to his desk and flops into his chair. *You bloody made a mess of this. You fell asleep.* He moves forward to put his face in his hands. He takes a deep breath and then rubs his face. When he sits back, he notices the envelope with his name on it. *That's Katharine's handwriting.* He rolls the chair over to grab it and then walks over to his chair by the fire. He turns it over to open it. It's not sealed. He carefully takes out the stationery and unfolds it to begin reading the handwritten note she left for him.

"Dear Ethan,

My year at the Stuart estate has been full of joy. Watching Liam and Tamara grow in their capacity to care for their community has been professionally and personally rewarding. I am confident, as I know you will be, that they can handle the care of the people daily. If any challenging situations arise, Dr. Morris from town is available to assist. Thank you for supporting me as the community's doctor during my stay. It hasn't been an easy year, losing people to the outbreak and then William. There are no words to describe my loss, but it was an even more significant loss for you. I only saw from my point of view and didn't allow you to speak of yours. For that, I ask you to forgive me for my selfishness. You have a heart that protects those in your care, including myself. I didn't see that then, but it's clear that what you did was for the greater good. You asked me in the glen to forgive you. I never responded to you. I want you to know I do and have forgiven you. I will cherish my time here at the Stuart estate and hold a particular part of Scotland in my heart. Be blessed, Ethan,

With love and respect, Katharine"

A tear falls on the note, and the ink blurs. He moves the note so no more tears fall onto it as he wipes one away. "What do I do? I can't let her go. She's only with the neighbours for at least a few weeks." He gets up and returns to his desk to put the note in his top drawer. As he opens it, he sees the letter of reference he has for her. "Yes, of course. I can take it over to her, as I said I would make sure she had one. Tomorrow. I will do it tomorrow," he says to himself.

A knock is heard at the door.

"Come in."

"Ethan, Ty is taking Katharine to the Youngs," says Bonnie.

"Aye, I saw them from the window." He points to it.

Bonnie moves over to the desk in front of him and crosses her arms in front of her. "My dear brother, I love you very much, but sometimes I think you are your worst enemy. I will speak for myself when I know you love that woman. Why are you not fighting harder for her?"

"Because I thought she hated me and blamed me for William's death, just as I do."

"Ethan—"

"I know, Bonnie, I know, but I will always carry the weight of his death on my shoulders. However, after reading Katharine's note, I see I was wrong and have to do something. I have her letter of reference that I was going to give to her before she left. However, I fell asleep when she came to see me, so she left it here. I might go over tomorrow and visit with her to give her the letter."

Releasing her arms and dropping her hands to the desk, she says, "Now that's a grand idea, brother. When I spoke with her as she was leaving, she said she wouldn't refuse a visit. So how about we both go over tomorrow?"

Ethan comes around from his desk and draws his sister into a hug.

"I love you, Bonnie. Thank you."

Bonnie takes her arms and wraps them around Ethan. "I love you too, brother. Now, how about you save some of this for Katharine?"

They both laugh but stay hugging each other.

It's a tranquil ride to the Young estate. When they arrive, both Gavin and Grace are there to welcome them. Gavin assists Katharine out of the wagon.

"Ryan, can you assist Ty with Katharine's trunk? You know which room she'll stay in."

"Aye, Laird."

Ty locks the wagon and jumps from the driver's seat to assist Ryan.

"Ty, before I go in, I wanted to give you this." She takes the envelope out of her bag. He sees it's a letter with his name written on it. "All I ask is that you wait until you're back in your office with a glass of scotch before you read it."

"Aye, Ms. Katharine, I will."

"I remember when we first met one year ago, Ty. I told you then we were going to get along."

"Aye, and that we have, Katharine."

"Aye, and that we have, Ty. Take care, my friend, and take care of the others, especially Ethan," she whispers as she steps in, tiptoes up, kisses him on the cheek, and squeezes his arm. He squeezes her hand as he moves around and helps Ryan remove the trunk from the wagon.

"Thank you again, Gavin and Grace."

"Let's go inside, shall we?" Grace says as she wraps her sweater around herself and motions for Katharine to follow.

Into the house she goes, starting a new chapter in her life.

Back on the estate, after dealing with the horse and wagon, Ty goes into his office. He takes out his glass of whiskey, opens Katharine's note, and reads it. When he finishes, he looks up to find Bonnie standing in the doorway.

"Ty."

He doesn't hesitate. He gets up and moves across the room, taking Bonnie in his arms, kissing her, and then holding her.

She returns the hug and holds on to him.

"What is it with you men this evening?" she says as she lifts her head and looks up to Ty. "Wait, was that a letter from Katharine?"

"Aye, it was," says Ty with a hint of curiosity.

"Ethan read the one she left for him earlier, and I ended up in a bear hug with him for several minutes. Now here I am with you. I'll have to thank her when I see her tomorrow."

He gives her a look and says, "What are you up to, Bonnie?"

She moves her arms so that they're now around Ty and moves in closer. "You know as well as I do that Ethan and Katharine are in love with each other. Ethan has already told me as much now. We need to get Katharine on board."

"So matchmaking will be your job, will it?" he jokes as he kisses her forehead.

"It worked for us, didn't it?"

"Aye, it has. In the meantime, lass, I think it's time I talked with your brother about asking for your hand in marriage."

"Ty, you know it's yours."

"Aye, that I do, my love." He bends down and kisses her. "But as the Laird, my friend, your brother, I would like to do it right and be sure we have his blessing."

"And what if he doesn't give it?"

Ty looks at her questioningly then says, "He will."

"I know he will. I'm just kidding with you, my dear. I'm keeping you on your toes."

"I love you, Bonnie Stuart." He kisses her again and then moves to turn off the light in the office and leads her out the door and back to the house.

Tamara and Liam arrive at the infirmary in the morning. Liam unlocks the door. He lets Tamara enter first, and then he follows. They take a minute to get situated, and then Tamara notices Katharine's cloak hanging on the coat rack, and her medical bag on the desk with two handwritten notes.

"Liam," she says as she bends to pick up the notes. She hands the one to Liam.

Liam looks over and then takes the note from Tamara. "Ms. Katharine didn't take them with her?"

Tamara opens her note and begins to read.

"My dear Tamara,

Watching you blossom into the healer you are has been a joy. You remind me so much of myself at your age. Confident and determined, yet gentle and patient. My aunt gave me this cloak to signify that I was ready to take on the role of a healer and to protect me from the ailments of the day. To me, it became like a suit of armour. I leave it to you, Tamara, to let you know you are more than ready and capable of tending to the people of the Stuart community. Wear it with love—love for what you do and the people you tend to. I hope you, too, will see it as your suit of armour. Be blessed, Tamara.

With love, Katharine"

Tamara picks up the cloak and puts it on. It's heavier than it looks, but she will wear it honourably.

"What does yours say, Liam?"

Liam opens his note to read.

"My dear Liam,

You were the one I was most concerned about when I came to the Stuart community a year ago. Is healing your calling? But day by day, you gained confidence and showed the ability to adapt calmly to the situation, always looking to ensure the person you were treating was comfortable. I think it was when you took the reins at the shipyard that I began to see just how good you are at this, and when allowed to take on the role of doctor, you flourished. This medical bag was from my uncle, a doctor in his community. I leave it for you to use in your community. Serve them well, Liam.

With love, Katharine"

Liam moves over to pick up the medical bag. When he looks inside, he sees she has also left her instruments. Liam looks at Tamara and holds the bag before her so she can peer in.

"She left us everything that was hers?"

They look at each other, perplexed, wondering why she left them her most prized possessions yet honoured them simultaneously.

"She's only over at the Young place. Can we visit and ask?"

"Aye, that we can," responds Tamara. She looks up to see Mrs. Carr coming to the infirmary. "Duty calls, Liam," she says as she points to the window. He turns to see Mrs. Carr as well. Tamara removes the cloak and hangs it on the cloak rack by the door. Liam puts the bag under the desk to look at it later.

That same morning, Ethan and Bonnie ride over to the Young estate. While Ethan is securing the mounts, they're both greeted by Ryan, who's on his way to speak to Gavin.

"I was just on my way to speak to Laird Young. I'll let them know you're here. Please come in, out of the chill."

Ryan motions for them to come into the home and closes the door. "I will be but a moment."

"I'm beginning to think this was a bad idea, sister," whispers Ethan to Bonnie.

"Trust me, Ethan, this will be fine. I—"

"Laird Stuart, Ms. Stuart, welcome," greets Grace. "Please come in. Can I offer you a cup of coffee this morning?"

"Oh, that would be lovely; thank you, Mrs. Young," replies Bonnie.

"We're neighbours; please call me Grace."

"And I am Bonnie."

"Laird."

"If I am to call you Grace, please call me Ethan, neighbour."

Grace laughs, as she's been caught. "Very well, Ethan. Coffee for you too?"

"Yes, please."

"Follow me to the sitting room, and we can enjoy each other's company there. Gavin will be in soon, as he has to speak to Ryan on a matter."

"We thought we might be able to see Katharine," inquires Bonnie.

"Certainly. I'll get her after I let the kitchen know we have guests for coffee this morning. Please make yourselves at home. I'll be back."

After stopping to let the cook know they have guests in the sitting room and coffee for five will be needed, Grace heads straight to Katharine's room.

"Katharine, are you up?" says Grace as she knocks and opens the door.

"Yes, for quite some time," laughs Katharine as she sits at the table reading a book.

"Well, I thought you might enjoy coming to the sitting room and having coffee with visitors."

Katharine looks at her, waiting for some indication of who these visitors are.

"Don't just sit there, Katharine. Come on, let's go," says Grace as she moves her arms to say get out the door.

Katharine follows Grace into the sitting room to find Ethan and Gavin standing by the fire, talking; Bonnie is in the chair enjoying a cup of coffee.

Katharine is surprised but smiles and says, "Good morning."

Bonnie gets up to hug Katharine. "You said you wouldn't refuse a visit."

"Yes, I said that," she says as she looks up at Ethan, who nods. "Is everything all right? I've only been gone for a few hours."

"Everything is fine; we both had something to tell you," Bonnie states excitedly.

Ethan moves from the fireplace to Katharine and takes an envelope out of his pocket. "I promised you this letter of reference, Katharine. I apologize for not having it ready when you left. I wanted you to have it." He hands it to her. She takes it, and they both hold the note together, unwilling to let go.

"Thank you, Ethan," she says as she takes his note.

Grace and Gavin look at each other and nod, as if to speak to each other without words.

"If you will excuse Grace and me for a moment, we have the twins to look in on. We'll be back; please take your time." Gavin comes across the room, takes Grace in his arms, and walks toward the stairs leading up to the twins' room.

To break the spell between them, Katharine takes the chair opposite Bonnie and says, "Bonnie, you said you had news."

Bonnie looks to Ethan and then back to Katharine.

"Go ahead and tell her; I know you're dying to do so," jokes Ethan as he returns to the fireplace to retrieve his coffee cup.

"Ty asked me to marry him, and I said yes."

Katharine scurries from her chair to hug Bonnie. "Bonnie, I'm so happy for you. Ty is a wonderful man, and you are very blessed to have him."

"Aye, I know, as he knows he is blessed to be getting me too."

They both laugh, and so does Ethan.

"I told him as much when he came to see me about asking for her hand in marriage," pipes in Ethan.

"I can assume you said yes then," Katharine asks Ethan.

"Aye, I did. Bonnie and Ty love and respect each other. They make a good team. Besides, it was only my blessing he was asking for. Ultimately, it's Bonnie's decision as to whom she marries."

"When will the wedding be?"

"Ty and I haven't discussed that yet, but we hope soon. I wanted to tell you so you know."

"And I am so happy you did. Please let me know if I can do anything while here."

"I will. Oh, Mrs. Jones sent over something for you. I left it in my pack. I'll go and get it." She leaves the room to get Katharine's parcel.

"She is so happy."

"Aye, it's good to have something to celebrate."

"Aye, it is," says Katharine back to him.

"Before she comes back," he says as he eyes the door, "Ty hopes to be married within the next few weeks."

"But Bonnie said—"

"We have a surprise for her. Ty and I are working together on this. I'll be at the estate for the next few weeks, helping him out. I may need to call upon you for your assistance to get a woman's perspective on things. Can I ask that of you, Katharine?"

"Please do, Ethan," she says as she places her hand on his arm.

Bonnie enters the room to see the tender touch between the two but doesn't let on she sees it. She hands Katharine the parcel of Mrs. Jones's baked goods for Katharine and the Youngs to enjoy. Right behind Bonnie comes Grace and Gavin back into the room.

"Do I smell something?" says Grace.

"Yes," says Katharine as she unwraps the parcel to show Mrs. Jones's scones.

"Feel free to come over anytime if you're going to bring those. Ryan is always telling us about them. He gets them from Tamara. I've had a sample, and my goodness! Don't tell our cook, but these are better," jokes Gavin.

"Bonnie, we should get back," says Ethan.

"Oh yes, Ethan, of course. Katharine, we'll talk later."

"Yes, we will, Bonnie."

"Thank you, Gavin, Grace, Katharine. Good day," says Ethan as he nods to them and then leads Bonnie out of the room and down the hall to the front door.

THIRTY

"Yes, sister, it most certainly did."

They smile at each other, not realizing they each have different agendas for coming to see Katharine, which will surprise each other in the days ahead.

It would seem love is in the air. A few days later, Katharine discovers that Ryan proposed to Tamara, and she said yes. The Stuarts are not the only ones doing some matchmaking. Gavin and Grace decide to host a small celebration for Ryan and Tamara's engagement. It's a small gathering of Ryan's family, Tamara's family, and, of course, the Stuarts. Katharine helps Grace with the arrangements, and Mrs. Jones and the Youngs' cook work together to prepare the celebration meal.

Katharine is coming out of the dining room when she sees that Tamara and Liam have arrived. Tamara is wearing the cloak she left her, and Liam is carrying the medical bag. When Liam sees Katharine, he lifts the bag and says, "We were always taught to be prepared."

Katharine nods and responds, "I like this teacher. Anyone I know?"

They laugh among themselves. Ryan comes out of the room where everyone is gathering.

"Mo Ghradh," which means "my love" in Scottish Gaelic (pronounced mo gehrai), he says as he bends in to kiss Tamara's cheek. "Let me take your cloak."

Ryan takes her cloak and hangs it on the hook by the door. Liam takes his coat off and places it on the hook and bag.

Katharine takes Liam's arm. "Why don't you two take a minute so we can get into the room, and then you can enter together?"

Ryan nods. "Aye, good idea, Ms. Katharine."

Liam escorts Katharine into the room, and they move beside Grace, Gavin, Ethan, Bonnie, and Ty.

Ryan and Tamara enter the room a few minutes later to a round of applause. It's a very informal gathering of family and friends.

"It would seem love is in the air. Ty and Bonnie and now Ryan and Tamara," says Grace as she takes Katharine's arm.

"Who will make it a lucky three?" Bonnie replies as she moves over with Grace and Katharine.

"Lucky three?" questioned Katharine.

"Aye, engagements and weddings usually come in three, so we need one more," giggles Grace as she looks at Liam.

Liam raises his hand and says, "Count me out, Lady Young. I am not courting anyone. Besides, with Katharine leaving and Tamara getting married, I'll be the only doctor for a while."

"Really, would Tamara not be able to continue to work with you, Liam?" questions a concerned Katharine.

Ethan interrupts the conversation. "It's up to Tamara and Ryan. You've taught them well, Katharine. Tamara may come here to the Young estate, and then you'll have them both handling two communities."

"Ethan is correct; it's up to Tamara and Ryan. She would be welcomed here," says Gavin.

"Whatever they decide, they'll do what's best for their communities," states Katharine as she looks at the happy couple talking with friends.

"Aye, they will, my friend, they will indeed," replies Grace.

Bonnie returns to the Young estate a few days after her first visit to see Katharine. When she arrives, she's taken to the dining room, where Grace and Katharine enjoy their morning coffee and breakfast together.

"Good morning, Katharine, Grace," says Bonnie as she enters the dining room.

Katharine hugs Bonnie and says, "Good morning to you too. What brings you here so soon after your last visit?"

"I'm in a bit of a fluster, Katharine. Ty wants us to be married as soon as possible." She winks at Katharine.

Katharine and Grace laugh.

"I agree with him completely," she says as she sits at the table. "We hope to have it on Friday the sixteenth, three weeks from now."

"My goodness, that is quick," says Grace.

"Aye, Ethan is going to be Ty's witness, Reid is going to give me away, and I would ask you, Katharine, to be my witness."

"Bonnie, I would be honoured," says Katharine as she reaches over to take Bonnie's hand.

"You indicated that the ship wasn't due in port until the twentieth, so you'll be here to support me and participate in the ceremony."

"Yes, that's what my brother indicated in his last telegram. But can we get it all done by then, Bonnie?" asks Katharine.

"Aye, all I'm tasked with is to look after the dresses, flowers, and food. We already know Mrs. Jones will handle the food, so I thought I could discuss my wedding and your dress with you. They will be simple but elegant."

"What about everything else?" asks Grace, very interested in the answer.

"Ty and Ethan have indicated they'll look after all of that. Remember, they tell me what they think to ensure I approve. So far, I'm impressed."

"Really?" say Grace and Katharine in unison as they look at each other.

"Yes, Ty and Ethan are arranging the ceremony outside the house. It's large enough to hold the number of people we expect to come. It will be in the late afternoon; the community is invited, of course, and we plan to have a buffet of cold foods, and also drinks and music. We don't usually get rain this time of year, but if there is, we'll move everything to the great hall. Ty and I don't need anything fancy; we want a day to celebrate with our family and friends."

"Aye, this sounds wonderful, Bonnie. If you need help sewing the dresses, I and a few of my ladies are available," says Grace.

"Don't look at me, Bonnie; sewing is the one thing I am terrible at," inserts Katharine as she surrenders her hands.

Laughter echoes through the room.

"Aye, I know, Katharine." Reaching into the pouch she has with her, she pulls out some papers. "I've brought some clippings to show you what I was thinking of for the dresses, to see what we can decide."

"Excuse me, I'll check on the children, get some more refreshments, and be back to help in any way you may need," says Grace as she moves from her chair.

Katharine and Bonnie pull closer together to look at the various clippings.

A few days later as Gavin enters the dining room, he announces, "Katharine, you have a visitor."

"My goodness, I didn't get this many visits from patients at the Stuart estate daily. Who is it, Gavin?" comments Katharine as she finishes her coffee.

"It's Laird Stuart," says Gavin as he winks at his wife.

"He's probably here to ask about wedding plans. If you'll excuse me," says Katharine as she gets up from the table and finds Ethan in the living room.

"Should we wager, my dear, on why Laird Stuart is here?" says Grace.

"We both know he's here to call on Katharine and use the pretense of wedding preparations," Gavin replies as he kisses her.

"Aye, we do indeed, love," says Grace as she finishes her breakfast.

Katharine enters the living room, and Ethan stands out from the side window. "Good morning, Ethan," says Katharine.

Ethan turns around. "Good morning, Katharine." A smile brightens his face. "I was hoping you had a few minutes to discuss the wedding preparations."

"Certainly," she says as she directs him to a chair by the sofa. "Can I get you a coffee?"

"Nay, I had already, but thank you," he says as he takes the chair offered. Katharine sits beside him.

"I understand you will be Bonnie's witness?"

"Yes. We picked the dresses, and she's working on the flowers."

"Aye. We knew those were areas she'd want to look after. Ty and I are doing everything else. We've told Bonnie some things we're doing, but not everything," he says mischievously.

"Aye, she said. How can I be of assistance, Ethan?"

"Ty and I will have a trellis made for them and the minister to stand under as they exchange vows. I was hoping to get you to decorate it."

Katharine nods. "Of course, Ethan. I could get Grace and Tamara to help out with that too, once I know what flowers she's picked," she says. Ethan nods in agreement.

Ethan opens his jacket and removes a neatly folded cloth from the inside pocket. "Part of the ceremony is handfasting, or tying the knot. This is the Stuart tartan. Do you think Grace could help you make the ribbon for the handfasting from our family tartan?" he asks as he hands it to Katharine.

As Katharine takes the tartan, the spark that's always there when they touch strikes again. This time, they both look at each other but do nothing to remove their hands from each other. Katharine says, "Grace has already offered to help with the dresses, so I'm sure this won't be a problem, Ethan."

"Thank you, Katharine," says Ethan as he squeezes her hand.

"Was there anything else, Ethan?" she says.

"Katharine, it would seem you get more visitors in our home than we do," says Gavin as he enters the doorway.

"What?" says Katharine as she looks to Gavin.

"Bonnie is here with the fabric to get started on the dresses, and something about flowers."

Ethan stands up, releasing Katharine's hand. "Bonnie is here. She can't see me," he says.

"Why can't she see you?" questions Gavin.

"I told her I would see the parish constable to get an update on Mr. Holmes's trial. She doesn't know I'm here to talk to Katharine about wedding plans. If she does, I'll never hear the end of it, about how we can't even organize a wedding ourselves, let alone that I lied to her about where I was going."

You hear Bonnie yelling from the hallway, "Katharine, I have the dress fabric."

On instinct, Ethan dashes behind the sofa to hide. Knowing the tartan in her hand will give something away, Katharine lifts the sofa cushion, slides it under, and sits on it. Just as she does, Bonnie, with Grace, comes in.

"Good morning, Bonnie. You have fabric for the dresses; that was quick."

"It's not the exact colour we were looking for, but I think it will work. Here, let me show you," says Bonnie as she moves over to the sofa.

Katharine gets up from the sofa and meets Bonnie halfway across the room. She looks to Grace as if to say, "Please don't say anything."

"Bonnie, why don't we take these upstairs to my room? There's a full-length mirror there, so we can see how the fabric looks and get started on what we'll need," says Katharine as she guides her toward the door.

"Aye, that's an excellent idea."

"Grace, could you bring some coffee to my room?" asks Katharine.

Grace is bewildered by the fact that Ethan isn't in the room, the face Katharine made at her, and her rushing Bonnie out of the room. However, she automatically responds, "Aye," and watches as they leave the room.

The door closes, leaving Gavin to tell Ethan, "You can come out of your hiding place now, Laird Stuart."

Ethan pops his head up over the sofa, and Grace laughs. "What is going on?"

"It would seem Laird Stuart didn't want to be caught in a lie by his sister," laughs Gavin as he moves to the sofa to take what Katharine put under the pillow.

"I gave that to Katharine to see if you could help her make the ribbons for the handfasting," says Ethan to Grace as he gets up from behind the sofa.

"I'll take it and put it somewhere so Bonnie doesn't see it," says Grace as she moves over and takes it from Gavin. You may want to give yourself a few minutes before leaving. Katharine's room faces the entrance. I'll go up and distract them so Bonnie doesn't see you leaving." She chuckles as she leaves the room.

"The things we do for family," says Ethan as he moves from behind the sofa toward Gavin.

"Yes, the things we do for love, my friend," says Gavin as he pats Ethan's shoulder and accompanies him out the door.

"Well done, Mrs. Hannah," says Katharine. As a thank you to Gavin and Grace for allowing her to stay with them until she returns to England, she's been working with Mrs. Hannah to improve her medical skills.

"Katharine," says Grace as she comes into the room, "Ty is here to see you; he says it's urgent."

Katharine gets up quickly to meet with Ty.

"Good morning, Katharine. I wanted you to have this immediately." He hands her a telegram. "I was in the telegraph office today and I was given this. I guess because you only received messages from the Stuarts, they filed it under our name, not the Youngs'. I wanted you to have it immediately."

"Thank you, Ty." Katharine opens the telegram to see a message from her brother. The *Olympia* will arrive in port on the fifteenth to pick her up. "My goodness, that's tomorrow," she says as she moves her hand to her mouth.

"Katharine?" questions Ty.

"The ship will be in port tomorrow to pick me up. This is earlier than expected."

"Does it say how long they'll be in port?"

"No, it just says it will arrive in port on the fifteenth to pick me up."

"The wedding is on Friday, Katharine."

"I know, Ty." She looks at him with a fallen face of disappointment. "I need to speak with Gavin to make arrangements. When I'm finished, I'll come over to see you both."

"I'll go and tell Bonnie," he says as he releases the brake and snaps the reins to signal the horses to move forward.

When Katharine enters the Young home, she asks Ryan if he's seen Gavin. He indicates he is in his study. She goes to the door and knocks.

"Come in."

"Good morn, Gavin," she says as she enters.

"Good morn, Katharine. How can I help?"

"I just received word from my brother," she says as she holds up the telegram. "The ship that's to pick me up is scheduled to arrive tomorrow."

"Tomorrow?"

"Yes, tomorrow."

"I'll speak with Ryan. He'll see when the ship arrives, speak to the captain, and get the details."

"Thank you, Gavin. I think it might be best if Ty goes with Ryan. The captain knows Ty, so it may work better if—"

"Of course, Katharine. Don't worry, we'll ensure the ship doesn't leave without you, unless you want it to."

"No, no. Well, you know Bonnie and Ty are getting married on Friday. We've worked so hard, and I—"

"Want to be there for them."

"Yes."

Gavin gets up from his desk and moves around to stand before Katharine.

"Katharine, things happen for a reason. We can't control how fast the winds blow a ship so that it arrives earlier than expected. They may be in port on the fifteenth, but that doesn't mean they'll leave then."

"Yes, of course, you're right."

"You get what you need ready, and then we'll go from there."

"Usually I take control in situations," says Katharine.

Grace comes into the study and asks, "Is everything okay?"

"Katharine told me the ship to take her back home to England is to arrive tomorrow. I reassured her we would make sure she got on the ship."

"Oh dear, that's earlier than expected," responds Grace.

Katharine smiles at her and says, "I said the same thing."

"It will be fine, Katharine. Let me talk with Ryan. In the meantime, I suggest you prepare your trunk and anything else." He squeezes her arms. He moves over to kiss his wife and leaves to find Ryan.

"Well then, my friend, let's get you packed and organized for your travels home," she says as she moves over to Katharine and hugs her.

"I'm sad to leave for many reasons but excited to go home. Does that make sense?"

Grace pulls back and looks at her. "Yes, it does. Follow your heart, my dear. Things happen for a reason."

"Gavin just said the same thing."

"Did he now? I married a wise man." They both laugh. Arm in arm, they leave the study to go and ensure Katharine is prepared for tomorrow.

THIRTY-ONE

RYAN RIDES TO the Stuart estate to go with Ty into town to check on the ship's status. When Ty and Ryan approached the ship, they ask to speak to the captain.

"You asked to speak to me, sir," says the captain, extending his hand to Ty.

"I did. It's good to see you, Captain," replies Ty. "There was a bit of confusion when I received the telegram that you would be in port, and Ms. Katharine wasn't aware you would be here so early to pick her up."

"We're in port for the next week, Mr. Ty, for repairs to the bow," the captain states with some confusion.

"This is wonderful news, Captain. I am to be married tomorrow, and Ms. Katharine will be at the wedding. We were upset to know she might not be able to be here," sighs Ty.

"Rest assured, sir. We'll give you at least a day's notice when we're leaving. At this time, we have estimated a week to complete the repairs, but we both know that could be longer."

"Yes, we do, sir. Thank you so much. I'll return and let Ms. Katharine know the good news. She's staying at the Young estate. This is Ryan, Laird Young's man. He'll give you the information to ensure she knows when she'll be leaving."

Ryan and the captain speak. Then Ty and Ryan leave to return to the estates to relay the information provided.

Ty goes directly to the Stuart estate to let Bonnie know there is no need to worry; Katharine will be able to attend the wedding. Ty enters the house and shouts, "Bonnie, my dear."

"Aye, I'm here," she replies as she enters the kitchen.

"I have wonderful news," he says as he moves in to kiss her. "Katharine will be here for the wedding. The ship is in for at least a week of repairs."

"Oh, thank goodness." She jumps into Ty's arms for a hug. "We must tell Ethan. He's upset thinking she is to leave today."

"Aye, I will, lass. Is he in his office?"

"Aye, he is. Let's tell him together," says Bonnie as she grabs Ty's hand, and off they go.

Upon Ryan's return to the Young estate, Gavin, Grace, and Katharine meet him at the front door. He doesn't even get off his mount. "Ms. Katharine, I have excellent news. The captain has indicated that the ship will be in port for at least a week for repairs. You are not leaving today. You'll be here for the wedding tomorrow," he informs them.

"Oh, thank goodness," says Katharine as she turns to hug Grace.

"Aye, lass, I told you, didn't I?" states Gavin as he claps his hands together.

"Aye, you did, Laird Young," replies Katharine with a wink.

"Come now, we still have many things to get done for the wedding," says Grace.

"I was going to get the wagon ready to take you and anything you have to the Stuart estate," says Ryan as he looks at Katharine.

"Thank you, Ryan, that would be wonderful."

He nods to Katharine and then to the Laird.

"Please let Ethan, Bonnie, and Ty know that if they require extra hands, we're here to assist," says Grace as she turns to walk with Katharine into the house.

"I'll let them know, but there is one thing you can do for them," says Katharine.

"Aye, what is it, my dear?" replies Grace.

"You can pray for good weather, as the wedding is happening outside," smiles Katharine. "I know they can do it in the great hall if they have to, but they want it outside."

"Consider it done, Katharine," says Grace, and into the house they go.

Katharine, Grace, and Tamara are able to decorate the trellis, and there's a scurry of activity to get as much done as possible before tomorrow's wedding.

"It's good that we don't have to worry about—"

Mrs. Jones interrupts Tamara. "Don't even say it, lass," she says as she helps set up the chairs.

"Aye, Mrs. Jones," says Tamara as she winks at Katharine.

"Katharine, I must get home to the twins. I'll see you tomorrow around one," informs Grace as she moves to the stable to find Ryan to take her back home.

"What else do you need us to do, Mrs. Jones?" asks Katharine.

"I think we're finished for now, my dear. Grace has the three young ladies who assisted during the outbreak coming over tomorrow to help me with the wedding buffet. They'll look after the kitchen while I attend the wedding. I can't believe my wee Bonnie is getting married," cries Mrs. Jones.

"Aye, Mrs. Jones, but she's not leaving you. They'll be going away for a honeymoon. Then she'll be back with you at the house doing what she has always done," Katharine encourages her as she hugs her.

"I know, lass. I've watched them grow into wonderful adults and feel like they're my own."

"And the feeling is mutual, Mrs. Jones," says Tamara as she hugs Katharine and Mrs. Jones.

"All right, all right, we have what we can do for today. Let's go in and get ready for supper. It's a simple meal this evening," Mrs. Jones informs as she moves out of the group hug and up toward the house.

"You are staying this evening, Ms. Katharine?" asks Tamara.

"Aye. Bonnie wanted me to be here to prepare for the ceremony, and if Mrs. Jones requires anything, then I'm here to help."

"Aye, I'll see you tomorrow then, Ms. Katharine. It's good to have you back, if only for a few days," says Tamara as she squeezes her hand and walks toward the house.

"It's good to be back, my dear," says Katharine as she looks around to critique their work to transform the area into a beautiful setting for tomorrow's wedding.

With her back to the house, Katharine doesn't see or hear as Ethan walks up behind her. He stands and looks at the decorated trellis and the chairs in a semi-circle with a path down the middle for the bride to walk down. "I see you've been hard at work," he whispers in her ear.

Katharine turns slightly to look up at Ethan and smiles. "Aye, we have. There are final touches to put on tomorrow, but for now, it looks good."

"Aye, it does, Katharine. Bonnie and Ty will have a beautiful wedding tomorrow," says Ethan as he moves beside her. Taking Katharine's hand, he says, "You have become the sister Bonnie has always wanted. Thank you for all of your help."

"I can say the same about Bonnie, Ethan."

"Aye."

They look out onto the decorated lawn with smiles, and hands held together, ready for a wedding.

The following day, the sun is shining, and the final preparations for the wedding are taking place. There's a buzz in the air like a bunch of bees busy in the hive, but in this case, it's people moving around, ensuring all last-minute touches are put into place. Mrs. Jones has the girls working with her to set up the tables outside and get as much done beforehand as possible. The wedding is at 4:00 p.m., so everyone keeps a close watch on the weather, as it can change quickly, but as the day progresses, it's clear skies. The wedding won't have to be moved to the great hall. Ethan, Ty, and Katharine have done a walk-through to ensure everything is in place before getting ready.

"It looks like we are set to go," says Ty.

"Yes, and the weather seems to agree with us today," states Katharine.

"Aye, it does indeed," inserts Ethan.

"Everything looks lovely, Katharine; Bonnie will be pleased," responds Ty.

"It could rain cats and dogs, Ty, and she'd be over the moon to be marrying you out here or in the great hall," replies Katharine as she moves in to hug him. "Take good care of her, my friend."

"Aye, I will, Katharine," he says as he returns the hug.

"As everything is under control, I'll head back to the house to prepare for the wedding. I will see you both then," says Katharine as she moves out of Ty's embrace and turns to squeeze Ethan's arm, saying, "I will see you later."

Ethan turns to Ty and says, "In a few hours, I can call you brother, my friend."

"Aye, you will, and somehow I don't think Reid will like that too much." Ty chuckles as they head toward the house so they can prepare for the wedding.

"Aye, it's true, but I see more of you than I do him, so you move up the ladder," replies Ethan as he gives Ty a quick hug, and they begin their walk into the house.

At 4:00 p.m., the community gathers with both families in the estate's back yard. Ty and Ethan take their place with the minister by the trellis.

"Are you ready, Ty?" whispers Ethan.

"Aye, very ready, Ethan."

Bagpipes begin to play. Their attention is drawn to a figure at the top of the hill leading down to them. Katharine is standing in a simple blue dress, which happens to be a colour from the Stuart tartan. Her hair is up with strands of heather throughout it, and loose pieces fall along the sides. The bouquet she carries contains heather, thistle, and primrose. The colours complement the gown but also reflect the Stuart tartan colours. She looks so different from her everyday attire, and it shows when everyone turns to watch her.

Katharine takes a deep breath. She's not used to being the centre of attention. She looks straight ahead at Ty and Ethan. She nods and begins walking down the aisle. She takes her time and acknowledges those in the audience. Grace and Gavin, Ryan and Tamara, Liam and Mrs. Jones. The bagpipes change the tune once she has joined Ty and Ethan at the trellis. All rise to a signal that the bride is about to proceed.

At the top of the hill, Bonnie stands in her cream-coloured dress, and the bouquet she carries is grander than Katharine's but has the same flowers. Her brother Reid takes his hand and places it over hers.

"Are you ready, my dear?" he asks with love.

"Aye, brother, I am more than ready," she replies.

Reid accompanies Bonnie down the path to Ty. When they arrive, Ethan moves over to Bonnie's other side. The minister asks, "Who gives this woman in marriage?"

In unison, Reid and Ethan reply, "We do." Ethan takes Bonnie's hand, squeezes it, and then kisses her. He moves back beside Ty. Reid does the same and sits beside Mrs. Jones in the front. Katharine takes Bonnie's bouquet, and the minister begins.

"Bonnie and Ty will be binding their lives together, and as such, they will be participating in an old Scottish ritual of handfasting or, as some would say, tying the knot. May I have the ribbon?"

Katharine steps forward and hands the minister the ribbon she and Grace made from the Stuart tartan Ethan had given her.

"I invite the couple to join hands. This symbolizes their free will to enter this union and demonstrates the act of physically coming together."

Bonnie and Ty face each other and join their right hands. The minister takes the ribbon, wraps it around their hands, and ties them together. He steps back and begins the ceremony. When the vows are complete, he says, "Ty, you may now kiss your bride."

Ty leans in and kisses Bonnie tenderly and lovely.

The minister moves toward them and releases the ribbon from their hands. "Ladies and gentlemen, this completes the wedding ceremony. The bride and groom will lead the way to the wedding festivities."

There's a round of applause as Katharine gives Bonnie her bouquet. Ty offers Bonnie his arm as they lead the way to the wedding buffet. Ethan holds out his arm for Katharine to take as they follow behind. The minister stops to offer his arm to Mrs. Jones, and the rest of the guests follow.

Mrs. Jones and her team outdid themselves with the wedding buffet. The food is plentiful, as is the wine and whiskey. Her best work was left for the two-tiered wedding cake made of fruit cake with a brandy flavour. The evening is filled with love and laughter. The music is lively, and several couples and children are dancing.

"Katharine, I have someone I'd like you to meet," says Ty as he moves toward Katharine.

"Oh, yes, of course," responds Katharine.

Ty leads Katharine to an older woman enjoying the festivities from her seat at the table.

"Mother, I'd like to introduce you to Ms. Katharine Bennett. She's been on the Stuart estate for the past year mentoring Liam and Tamara."

"It's a pleasure to meet you," says Katharine as she stretches her hand.

"Aye, my dear. The pleasure is all mine. I've heard nothing but good things about you from my Ty," she says to Katharine while looking at her son.

"You've raised a good man," says Katharine.

"Aye, he has turned out well and found a bonnie wife too," Ty's mother says as she winks at Katharine.

"Oh, I get it, Bonnie as in pretty wife, not as in the name of Bonnie," laughs Katharine. "Now I know where Ty gets his sense of humour from."

"What's so funny?" asks Bonnie as she comes over to see what's happening, taking Ty's hand and kissing him.

"Ty's mother made a joke, and I got it," informs Katharine.

"She is a quick one, that's for sure," says Bonnie. "Did you want to join in the dance?" Bonnie asks Ty's mother.

"Aye, but on one condition, lass."

"What's that?"

"Could you call me Màthair (pronounced Mah-hir)?"

"I would be honoured to call you Màthair," says Bonnie as she moves in to hug her. "Well then, Màthair, let's show them what Scottish dancing looks like."

"Aye, lass, let's." And off they go.

"Does Màthair mean mother?" asks Katharine.

"Aye, it's Scottish Gaelic. My mother was concerned that with Bonnie having lost her mathair, she might not want to call her it, but—"

"Bonnie is the daughter she lost, and your mother is the màthair Bonnie lost. They have each found something they lost, Ty."

"Aye, they have, haven't they? Thank you, Katharine."

Ty and Katharine watch Bonnie and Ty's mother dance together as the bagpipes play.

Later, Ethan approaches Katharine. "Katharine, Bonnie and Ty are leaving, so we'll need to say goodbye," he says as he leads her to the couple.

"Yes, of course," responds Katharine.

Katharine gives Bonnie and Ty a hug. "You're off to start your new life together. I may not be here when you return. I'll write to you as soon as I can, and if you should want to visit me in England, Bonnie, you'd be welcome."

Bonnie hugs her and says, "Aye, I will hold you to that, my friend."

Ty hugs her again and says, "Safe travels, my dear. I too will hold you to the fact that we can visit you in England."

Ty helps Bonnie up into the carriage and then gets in himself. Fergus flips the reins to signal that the horses can move, and they slowly move out of sight. Bonnie and Ty plan to spend a few days in town and then travel to Edinburgh for a few weeks before returning home.

With the wedding festivities closing, Mrs. Jones convinces Katharine to spend the evening at the house.

"Lass, there's no sense in you going to the Young estate, then turning around and coming back here in the morning to help clean up. The girls are also staying," she says as she waves to her helpers.

"Aye, Katharine, Mrs. Jones is right. You can take Bonnie's room, since you used it to get ready for the wedding," interrupts Ethan.

"Well, yes, it is late, and you're right, Mrs. Jones. It makes more sense for me to stay and be here to help in the morning. Let me go tell Gavin and Grace," says Katharine as she turns to find her friends.

Ethan moves over to Mrs. Jones and whispers, "Thank you, Mrs. Jones." He hugs her.

"She belongs here; we both know that, don't we?" replies Mrs. Jones.

"Aye, we do," responds Ethan.

Katharine walks back to the two. "I let Grace know I will be staying this evening to help clean up in the morning. Is there anything I can do now?"

"No, lass. The girls have dealt with all of the food and drinks. We can deal with anything else tomorrow," Mrs. Jones informs her.

Ethan moves between Mrs. Jones and Katharine. He raises his arms to each and says, "If I may, ladies, let us retire for the evening."

They both take his arm, and he leads them to the house, finishing a beautiful evening.

THIRTY-TWO

"WHY DOES IT seem like it took longer to get all of the wedding decorations up," inquires Katharine as she removes the last of flowers from the trellis.

"Aye, it did, didn't it?" replies Ethan.

"What will you do with the trellis?" asks Mrs. Jones.

"I think we'll keep it there for now. Bonnie and Ty may want it for their own home one day," says Ethan.

"It looked so lovely with the ribbons and flowers. It might make a nice place for afternoon tea," says Katharine. "Oh, sorry, did I say that out loud?"

"Aye, lass, you did. In Scotland, it may not be afternoon tea, instead a cup of coffee in the morning," replies Mrs. Jones.

"Aye, or either tea or coffee in the evening after one of your excellent meals, Mrs. Jones," comments Ethan.

"Aye, it is a place to gather together," says Katharine.

"I never thought of it like that, but aye, it certainly is, Katharine," responds Ethan as he moves beside her.

"Katharine, you've given me an idea. You two bring that table over here with some chairs. I'll take this box into the house. The girls and I will be out shortly with breakfast and coffee to enjoy around our new gathering place," says Mrs. Jones as she turns toward the house with a skip in her step.

Ethan and Katharine look at each other to say, "I think we'd better do what she says." They work together to move the table and chairs as instructed and finish up the last of the cleaning outside. About twenty minutes later, Mrs. Jones, the girls, and

Fergus arrive with breakfast and coffee. This morning, the usual people who enjoy breakfast in the morning are away, so instead, Mrs. Jones and new faces gather to enjoy time together.

Katharine helps Mrs. Jones and the girls take everything back to the house after their morning breakfast by the trellis. Once in the house, she goes to her room to pack and return to the Young estate with the girls. When she's ready, she heads downstairs. Ethan and Fergus have the wagon ready to take everyone back.

With Fergus driving, Ethan assists each girl into the wagon and ensures her belongings are safely packed away for the ride. When it's Katharine's turn, he extends his hand to assist her, but as she moves up and into the wagon, he moves his hand to her back to guide her up and in.

Katharine looks at Ethan and says, "Thank you, Ethan."

Ethan nods to acknowledge her words and secures her belongings like the others. He climbs beside Fergus, and they're off to the Young estate.

When they arrive, Fergus helps with the girls. It seems he has taken a shine to Brigette, so they linger near the wagon to talk while Ethan escorts Katharine to the house.

Before Katharine enters, Ethan gently takes her elbow and says, "Katharine, I will be home at the estate this week with Bonnie and Ty away. Please let me know when you hear from the captain about your departure day. I want to be the one to take you to town to catch the ship back home."

"I'd like that very much, Ethan. I'll send Ryan over and let you know," replies Katharine.

"Aye, now let me help you with these bags."

Katharine opens the door, and they enter together. Ethan puts the bags down by the table, and as he does, Gavin comes walking toward them with Ryan.

"So you have returned to us, have you, Katharine?" Gavin asks sarcastically.

"Aye, I have," says Katharine in a terrible Scottish accent.

Everyone laughs at her attempt. "Ethan, do you have time for a coffee? I wanted to discuss something with you now that the wedding is over," asks Gavin.

"Aye," replies Ethan.

"I'll go and let the cook know, Gavin, and find Grace," says Katharine.

"Thank you, Katharine. We'll be in my office," says Gavin as he leads Ethan and Ryan to his office.

Ethan and Katharine smile at each other, and then Katharine moves toward the kitchen to speak to the cook and find Grace.

Monday morning, a rider delivers a message to the Young estate.

"Ms. Katharine, I have a message for you," Ryan says as he enters the dining room. He hands the message to her. Katharine puts her coffee cup down, takes the message from Ryan, and begins to read.

After a minute, Grace asks, "What does it say, Katharine?"

"My apologies, Grace. The captain is letting me know that the repairs to the ship are scheduled to be completed on time and that the ship will be leaving port at noon on Friday. I'm to be on the ship by 10:00 a.m."

"He is a man of his word. He has given you more than enough time to get packed and be there on time," says Grace.

"Aye, he has," says Katharine.

Looking at Ryan, Katharine asks, "Ryan, are you going to see Tamara today?"

"Aye, Ms. Katharine. Is there something you need me to do?"

"Aye, can you let Ethan know the ship is scheduled to leave on Friday, and I will need to be there before 10:00 a.m.? He asked to take me, and I said yes."

Ryan and Grace exchange looks, and then he replies, "Aye, I can do that for you, Ms. Katharine. I'll let you know what Laird Stuart's reply is."

"Thank you, Ryan."

Ryan nods to both ladies and leaves the room.

"Good thing I'm already packed. I have four days before I leave for home. What will we do?"

"I know you didn't want a big send-off when you left after your one-year commitment, Katharine," says Grace as she reaches over to take her hand, "but I'd like to have a farewell dinner for you here. It will be small. I considered inviting Ethan, Ryan, Tamara, Liam, and Mrs. Jones."

"I don't know, Grace."

"Katharine, you may not want it, but perhaps they need it. I sense that with you leaving like you did, neither you nor they could get closure. It won't be fancy. I'll have a nice meal with friends to say farewell."

"How can I say no to that, Grace?"

"You can't. That's good. I'll catch Ryan to ensure he extends the invitations," says Grace as she gets up from the table to look for Ryan.

Katharine takes a moment to contemplate how her time in Scotland is ending and how she feels about it.

Ryan returns from the Stuart estate to indicate everyone has accepted the invitation to a Thursday evening farewell dinner at the Youngs'. As Katharine is mostly packed for the trip, there are just a few last-minute items to be dealt with so that she can assist Grace with the preparation.

As Grace had indicated, it's a tiny and intimate dinner for those Katharine dealt with for most of her time at the Stuart estate to say goodbye. Katharine is slightly sad that Bonnie and Ty aren't there, but she had already said her goodbyes to them. Katharine realizes she needs this to close this chapter in her life and is grateful.

As everyone is enjoying their coffee and dessert, Ethan uses his spoon to hit the side of his coffee cup to bring everyone's attention to him. He moves back, looks at Gavin, and then at Katharine. "As Katharine wouldn't like us to make a big deal out of her leaving, I would like to say a few words. Katharine, the Stuart family is indebted to you for your mentoring with Liam and Tamara. They have flourished. I and Gavin have discussed this with both Tamara and Liam." He nods to each as he continues. "With Ryan and Tamara marrying in the new year, we thought it best to pool our resources. Tamara and Liam will work with Gavin's team so that both estates can work together and share their responsibilities."

"My goodness, this is wonderful news," says Katharine as she takes Tamara's and Liam's hands.

"It was Liam's idea," inserts Gavin.

"Yes, I thought that with Tamara marrying Ryan, it might be better if both estates worked together. Since we have an established infirmary, and with me there and Tamara here, it seemed like a good idea," interjects Liam.

"Aye, it is," say Gavin and Ethan in unison.

There is laughter. "I am so happy to know that both estates will be in good hands," replies Katharine.

"Aye, they will, Ms. Katharine, and we have you to thank for this. If you hadn't asked the Youngs for assistance during the outbreak, Liam may not have considered joining estates," inserts Tamara.

"So this is what you two were discussing earlier this week?" asks Katharine.

"Aye, it is," says Gavin as he stands with Ethan.

"Katharine, as you know, my family will always be indebted to you. Your short time here will forever be in our hearts and in the Stuart family's. We know you don't like attention, but we also wanted you to know you will be missed."

"I couldn't have said it better, Gavin. Sometimes the simple things are the most effective. Tapadh leat (pronounced tapa lay-at), which is Gaelic for thank you, from our hearts to yours," speaks Ethan.

Katharine nods, as she's not able to speak due to her emotions.

"Now that we have that out of the way, how about we move to the living room, where we can finish our evening?" says Grace as she sees Katharine getting very emotional.

When it's time to leave, everyone takes a moment to hug Katharine and say goodbye. Liam is the first, then Tamara. When Ethan says goodbye, he reminds her that he will be there at 9:00 a.m. tomorrow to pick her up and take her to the pier to catch the ship home. "Until tomorrow then, Katharine," and he squeezes her hand.

"Till tomorrow, Ethan," Katharine replies.

Ethan arrives early the following day to take Katharine into town to catch the ship back to England. While Gavin assists Ethan in loading her belongings into the wagon, Katharine says her final goodbyes to Grace.

"Please let us know you arrived home safely, Katharine," Grace asks as she moves out of the hug.

"Of course, I will," responds Katharine as she moves to give Gavin one final hug.

"Aye, lass, safe travels home. And remember, you're always welcome here," informs Gavin as he returns the hug.

"Aye," she replies and moves out of the hug. "Goodbye, my friends."

Katharine moves to the wagon. Ethan helps her up into the seat beside him. He turns and nods to both Gavin and Grace. He takes his seat and then signals the horses to begin their travels into town. Ethan and Katharine chit-chat on the way to town, but Katharine takes the opportunity to look at the surroundings she has called home for the past year. Once Ethan pulls up to the pier, Katharine closes her eyes to take a visual of what she has seen so she can remember when she gets home.

"Katharine, are you all right?" Ethan asks as he moves his hand over hers, his voice concerned.

"Yes, no. I mean, yes, I am good, Ethan. I was putting a picture in my head to remember everything."

"I'm glad you want to remember. I want to reiterate what Gavin said to you. You are always welcome, Katharine. I know everyone would love to have you come back and visit."

"Aye."

They both laugh. Ethan gets down and then assists Katharine.

"Let's see the captain and get you settled on the ship," says Ethan, taking her elbow to guide her down the pier toward the ship.

Kennedy sees Katharine and begins to wave. "Good morning, Ms. Katharine."

Katharine returns the wave and replies, "Good Morning, Kennedy. Is the captain available? Mr. Stuart is here to see him."

"I'll go and find him, Ms. Katharine. In the meantime, if you bring your belongings, I'll make sure they get into your cabin. It's the same as when you arrived," says Kennedy as he moves away to get the captain.

"I'll go and get your things, Katharine; wait here for the captain," instructs Ethan.

"Yes, of course, Ethan."

"Ms. Bennett, it's good to see you again. How was your stay in Scotland?" the captain asks as he walks the gangway toward her.

"It's been eventful, Captain. Mr. Stuart is just getting my things. He'll be here in a moment."

"I understand Ty, his steward, was married last week."

"Yes, it was a lovely wedding. Oh, here he comes now."

Ethan places Katharine's luggage where Kennedy indicates and then walks over to both of them. Ethan outstretches his hand to shake the captain's. "Captain, it's a pleasure to meet you."

"As it is for me, Mr. Stuart. This is a fine ship, sir."

"Thank you."

With an awkward pause, the captain says, "Ms. Bennett, now that we know you're here, you may take your time getting on the ship."

"Yes, Captain. Kennedy indicated he would get my bags and put them in the room I was in before."

"Very well, Ms. Bennett. The crew hasn't changed since the last time you were on. I'll see you later. Mr. Stuart," he says as he bows and then returns to the ship.

Once the captain is back on board, Kennedy comes down the gangway, grabs Katharine's bags, and takes them on board.

Katharine turns to Ethan. Taking his hands, she says, "As I indicated to Grace, I'll let them know I arrived safely back home and will have them relay the message to you as well. Mar sin leat, Ethan," she says.

Ethan smiles at her and asks, "May I hug you to say Mar sin leat, Katharine?"

"Aye, you may."

Ethan moves in to hug her, and Katharine returns the hug. They stand holding each other for a while. Ethan pulls away and says, "I should let you get on the ship and settled before you have to leave."

"Aye, I mean, yes, I should. Then I can sit up to watch as we leave port later."

"Aye."

One last time, Katharine takes Ethan's hand and squeezes it. As she turns to walk the gangway onto the ship, Ethan walks with her, not letting go of her hand until he has to. She makes her way onto the ship and then turns to wave to Ethan. He returns the wave and quietly says, "Fare thee well, love," as she moves away from the ship's side.

Katharine has to move away before Ethan sees her crying. She goes to her cabin, and the tears start flowing. Katharine is excited to be returning home. She has missed her mother, Mrs. Florence, and Lois, yet a part of her feels lost leaving Scotland.

When she was here, Katharine made friends and was intertwined with the Stuart and Young families. This is something she has never had back home. Yes, there is Poppy, who is like a sister, but here in Scotland, the everyday interaction with Bonnie, Ty, Liam, Tamara, Mrs. Jones, Gavin, Grace, and, of course, William, her little man, taught her that she needs to have a better life and work balance. Being able to mentor Liam and Tamara allowed her to shoulder the burden with them and opened her eyes to how she needs to make changes when she gets back to England.

Ethan, if she's going to be honest with herself, is the one who has shown her the most. As much as she was hurt and angry at his actions, she has the utmost respect for him. Like her, he has the responsibility of so many others on his shoulders and does his best. She can't fault him for that. She also knows that during her time on the Stuart estate, she grew to have deep feelings for him, but with her leaving after a year, she didn't want to act upon them. She knows that Ethan, too, feels the same way, with his discreet touch, look, or how he speaks to her. Yet again, with her leaving, he may have held back for that reason. Ethan, along with William and everyone else on the Isle of Skye, Scotland, will always have a piece of her heart.

Wiping away tears, Katharine decides to take the time to unpack a little and then make her way up top to watch as the ship leaves port. When the time comes for the ship to sail, she watches the crew as they work to set sail. As the wind moves the ship out of the harbour, she quietly smiles. "Farewell, Scotland, until we meet again."

THIRTY-THREE

TRAVEL BACK TO England is much more turbulent than going to Scotland. When Katharine asks about it, she's told that it's due to the time of year in which they're sailing. Although it's rough, it's tolerable. Katharine has to remember what she was taught on the last trip to help her with seasickness.

The crew is interested in her adventures in Scotland, so the evenings are spent telling them her stories. It's an excellent way to finish the evenings. It reminds her greatly of her evening meetings with Ethan. During the day, when she's mostly on her own, she has time to reflect and pray on things she's thinking of changing when she returns home. By leaving her cloak and medical bag with Tamara and Liam, she feels she needs to pivot in her calling. For now, she'll take a step back from doctoring full-time and leave Ian in charge of looking after the community of Brookville. She'll help out when necessary. Katharine believes she needs to move to the estate her uncle left her, live there, and begin growing medicinal plants and flowers for the communities around her. Seeing how much this helped in Scotland gave her this idea. She has the funds to renovate the estate as she would like, and there's even a medical wing from where her uncle practised. With a plan in place, Katharine feels prepared for when she returns home.

When she arrives in port, Walter meets the ship to take Katharine back to the estate.

"Katharine, it is so good to see you," Walter says lovingly as he hugs her. "You look different. Scotland agrees with you, or do you agree with Scotland?"

"Aye, it does," laughs Katharine.

"And you talk like one too."

"It's good to see you, Walter. How are you?" Katharine asks as Kennedy brings down her bags. "Thank you, Kennedy," says Katharine.

"Ms. Katharine," he says as he tips his hat and returns to the ship.

"This is all you have? This is nothing to what you took."

"Aye, I mean, yes, it is, Walter. One of the trunks was medical supplies, and I left that there along with a few other things."

Walter has one of his men take the bags to the carriage.

"I look forward to hearing about your adventures in Scotland, Katharine. When you are ready."

"Yes, I think an evening of family and friends is a splendid idea, Walter."

Walter leads Katharine to the carriage, where her belongings have been packed away, and helps her into it. As Walter gets in to sit opposite her, Katharine says, "Walter, can we stop at the telegram office to send one to the Young family? I promised them I'd let them know I arrived home safe and sound."

"Certainly, it's on our way." He hits the ceiling of the carriage and says, "Driver, please take us to the telegraph office."

"Yes, Mr. Bennett," replies the driver.

With the telegram sent, Walter and Katharine chat on their way home. When they arrive, Walter drops Katharine off at her mother's cottage, where all three are outside waiting for her.

Katharine steps out of the carriage and runs into her mother's arms. "Katie, oh Katie, it's so good to see you, my dear. You look tired."

"I am, Mother. The trip home was a bit rough, but I persevered."

"Mrs. Florence, Lois, oh, how I have missed you both," she says as she hugs them.

"It's good to have you home, child," says Mrs. Florence, and Lois nods.

"I'll leave you to catch up. I'll be in touch to set up an evening to hear about Scotland," he says to Katharine, and then turns to tip his hat to the ladies.

The driver has removed her belongings from the carriage and placed them by the cottage door.

"Come, let's get you inside. Have a cuppa tea and hear all about your time away," says Katharine's mother, taking her around the waist and leading her into the cottage.

A week after Katharine's return, Walter holds a small family and friend gathering at the Bennett estate to welcome her back and hear about her time in Scotland.

"Katharine, my dear, it is so good to have you back," Dr. Roger Wylie says as he and his wife hug her.

"Aye, I mean, yes, it's nice to be back," replies Katharine.

Chuckling, Ian says, "Aye, see you have picked up some Scottish language."

Everyone laughs at the joke.

"Ian, do you have a moment? I want to speak with you."

"Of course, Katharine," he says as they move to a corner for a private conversation.

"I wanted to ask you: Do you think you could continue looking after the community indefinitely?"

"I can, but Katharine, is everything all right?" he says, concerned.

"There are some things I haven't spoken about this evening that happened in Scotland. It has made me take a look at things in a different light. I feel I'm being called in a different direction. I want to discuss it with you at greater length. Do you have time tomorrow?"

"I'm not scheduled to go out to see anyone until 11:00. How about I meet you in the office at around 9:30 tomorrow, and we can talk then."

Katharine nods to Ian, and they both move back to the group to finish the delightful evening.

"I have to say, Katharine, this is a wonderful idea. Growing flowers, plants, herbs, and the like for medicinal use here in our back yards," says Ian the next day.

"I know. This is one of the things I learned in my year of mentoring in Scotland. We had a wonderful garden full of plants, herbs, and flowers outside the infirmary to use whenever needed. I want to get this going on my estate so that Brookville and surrounding communities can benefit from their use."

"I will continue to care for Brookville, Katharine. However, you have been missed. You should make the rounds and let your community know what you have in store. That will keep the gossip at bay. Besides, I don't think you could ever give up caring for others. It's who you are, and it's truly a gift."

"Thank you, Ian. Let me know your schedule next week, and we can do a few days of going to houses and telling people. Besides, I'll need to ensure I have Mr. McCloud and Mrs. Theo's approval to get the rest of the community on board," laughs Katharine.

Ian and Katharine chuckle at the reference to when Katharine did the same for Ian a year ago. They work out a schedule for next week.

In the meantime, Katharine plans to move to her estate and get things going over there. Her mother is unhappy with Katharine moving out of the cottage and away from her, but she knows it's time. Katharine has changed since returning from Scotland. It was like she left as a caterpillar and became a butterfly in Scotland. Katharine tells her mother everything about what happened in Scotland, especially the loss of William and her love for Ethan. The world she had worked in tilted and has not yet been set upright, but perhaps that was for a reason. Katharine tells her mother that she's being called to take a different direction down the healing path. Here in England, she feels the weight of the community on her shoulders; in Scotland, she learned to share the burden, and now she wants to do that here too. Ian and Dr. Roger will continue to look after the community; she will help out when needed, but she will concentrate on her new passion, growing gardens full of medicine.

With the assistance of Mr. Robert, Katharine is soon installed into her estate. It takes a little while before she builds a good relationship with the workers on the estate. She learns what Ethan had told her: "Take care of the workers, and the workers will take care of everything else." She is hands-on in getting involved in planning the gardens. Her steward is an excellent artist and designs each section of the garden, including the layout of where each plant, herb, and flower will go and what will be planted with each other. Katharine finds it interesting that he suggests that thistles be used as borders to keep some smaller animals away. It's funny how the thistle, a symbol associated with Scotland, will protect her English garden.

THIRTY-FOUR

IT'S BEEN A month since Katharine has been gone. Ethan goes about his routine, but you can see he misses Katharine. One evening, Mrs. Jones, Bonnie, and Ty go to his study to tell him that he has to do something. His moping around is not going to bring her back.

Mrs. Jones says, "Laird, I thought you had better sense than to let the best thing in your life slip through your fingers. How did you let her get on that ship and sail away?"

Ethan responds, "What did you want me to do? Pick her up and carry her back here."

"Aye, Laird, it might have worked. At least she would have known how you felt," says Mrs. Jones as she crosses her arms.

"Aye, Mrs. Jones."

"Did you even tell her how you felt about her, Ethan?" asks Bonnie.

"Nay, I did not. She was determined to leave this place and put everything that happened behind her."

"She's stronger than you give her credit for, Ethan. She has a heart full of love, compassion, and forgiveness. She would have stayed if she knew you wanted her to," pipes up Ty.

"Well, brother, what do you intend to do about it?"

"What do you want me to do, sail to England and get her back?"

"Aye," all three say in unison.

"You are the owner of a shipbuilding company. There has to be a ship in port that you built for someone, and they could take you there. Besides, we can't continue to deal with you like you are, Laird. You make decisions for your community, for your business, and for everyone else all the time. How about you decide for yourself and you alone, my friend? I can tell you having the woman you love beside you is the best decision you can ever make," says Ty, taking Bonnie's hand and kissing her.

"I don't think—"

"That is your problem—your thinking. Don't think. Do. You're holding back because the last time you made a decision, it cost us dearly, and you're afraid to make another one, brother. We can't bring back any of the people Mr. Holmes took from us, but there may have been more if we hadn't done what we did. Can you honestly look me in the eye and tell me that you think he wouldn't have continued to harm others?"

"Nay, I cannot."

"Good. We can't change the past, Ethan, but you choose what happens in the future; don't let it cloud your judgement."

He pinches his nose. He twitches his eyes and takes a moment before responding. "Very well. I'll look into setting sail for England. However, there are a few things I'll need to take with me before I go. Are you all willing to help me?"

"Aye, we are."

Ethan secures passage on a cargo ship to England. He calls in a favour from his best customer, and they have a ship sailing to where Ethan needs to go. In the meantime, both the Stuart and Young estates work together to get what he needs to take with him.

His voyage to England is rough, and it takes two extra days to reach shore, but he finally makes it. After a bumpy journey, Ethan settles in at his lodgings and takes a few days to get his land legs and settle his sickness.

After the third day, Ethan feels much better after a good night's sleep. He's up early that morning to visit the Bennett Import & Export Trading Business office and get directions to the Bennett estate to see Katharine. With the directions secured and assistance as to a place to rent a mount, Ethan is off by mid-morning.

He arrives at the Bennett estate and asks to speak with Katharine. The butler informs Ethan that Ms. Katharine doesn't live at the estate but instead resides with her mother, who lives in the cottage on the estate. The butler directs Ethan to where he needs to go. Ethan arrives at the small but quaint cottage. It may not be much to look at, but you can feel the warmth of those living there. He knocks at the door.

Lois answers by asking, "Who's calling?"

"I'm here to see Ms. Katharine Bennett." Lois immediately hears the accent and knows that this is Mr. Stuart from Scotland, where Ms. Katharine had been for the last year.

"I'm sorry, sir. Ms. Katharine is not at home. May I ask who's calling?"

"It is Ethan Stuart. Ms. Bennett worked for me as a doctor last year."

"Yes, sir, I figured from the accent, sir."

"Do you know when she will be back?"

"I think you should come in, Mr. Stuart, and speak to Ms. Katharine's mother, who can better explain."

"Thank you, Lois."

"How do you know my name, sir?"

"Ms. Bennett—I mean, Katharine—spoke of you and your mother, Mrs. Florence, often and lovingly."

Lois blushes. "She's a wonderful lady, Ms. Katharine."

"Yes, she is," replies Ethan in a whisper.

"If you would wait here, Mr. Stuart, I'll let Mrs. Bennett know you are here."

"Of course." Ethan sits by the door as he awaits Lois's return.

"Mr. Stuart, if you follow me, Mrs. Bennett will see you."

Ethan rises and follows Lois to the sitting room.

"Mrs. Bennett, Mr. Stuart," says Lois as she leads Ethan into the room.

Ethan comes over to stand in front of Mrs. Bennett. She looks up to take stock of the man who has won her daughter's heart. "Good day, Mr. Stuart."

"Mrs. Bennett. If I may?" He turns to the chair beside her.

"Please. May I get you a cup of tea or coffee?"

"No, I'm fine, thank you."

Mrs. Bennett looks at Lois. Lois nods and leaves the room.

Ethan sits in the chair, and there are a few minutes of silence as they try to decide which one is to speak first.

Mrs. Bennett continues to knit, and she starts the conversation once she has finished her row.

"Mr. Stuart, I am sure it is not I whom you are here to see but Katharine."

"Aye, I am."

"And the purpose of your visit is—"

"I'm not sure how much Katharine told you about what happened during her year at the Stuart estate in Scotland—"

"Enough for me to know that my daughter has not returned to her medical duties in this community upon her return. She has extended her leave for another six months and has taken up residence in her estate to start a farm to grow medicine." Ethan can see that her hands have not stopped knitting but have picked up speed while she speaks.

"If I may speak with Ms. Katharine, perhaps I could help."

"My daughter has returned a changed person, Mr. Stuart. Most of it is good, but there is still a sadness she is trying to mend."

Ethan leans forward in his chair. "When Katharine left, I didn't tell her how I felt about her. I love your daughter, Mrs. Bennett. I need to have the opportunity to tell her that."

"I know she loves you too, Mr. Stuart. I can see it in her eyes when any of us mention you or when she speaks of you. I think it would be best that the two of you have the opportunity to tell each other this."

"I have something for her, and she will understand." Ethan reaches into his coat pocket and takes out the brooch the Young family had given to her.

"Oh, my, Katharine told me about this. You can take the brooch to Katharine, Mr. Stuart. Lois will ensure you have the proper information and everything you need to find her," informs Mrs. Bennett.

"Thank you, Mrs. Bennett."

Unknown to Ethan, Lois is standing by the door. "Mr. Stuart, if you follow me, I'll provide you with the information Mrs. Bennett indicated."

Ethan nods to Mrs. Bennett and leaves to follow Lois.

Late that afternoon, Katharine is tending to the garden patches they have cultivated to begin the fall planting. They only have three to start, but there will be more next year. She notices that the wind has picked up. She lifts her head to see the clouds moving quickly, changing from white to grey. Black ones are following close behind. Now she hears thunder but not from the sky. When she turns toward the path, she sees a rider fast approaching. She doesn't recognize who it is until he pulls back his mount to stop and she hears her name called with a familiar accent.

"Katharine!"

"Ethan, is that you?"

"Aye, it is."

"Why, how?"

"Your mother."

With hands on her hips, Katharine says, "What did you tell my mother to convince her to tell you where I was?"

Ethan dismounts. Keeping the reins in his hands, he walks over to Katharine. He puts the reins up around the horn on the saddle to give the horse the ability to eat the grass as they talk. Ethan reaches into his pocket, takes out the brooch, and holds it in his hand for her to see.

Katharine takes the brooch and looks up at Ethan. "Why do the Youngs require my assistance?"

"Grace is with child, and she has made it clear that you and only you are to be with her when she gives birth."

"I cannot—"

"Katie." Ethan moves even closer to her.

Katharine looks up with tears, as the last person to say her nickname with a Scottish accent was William.

"Katie, my dear, I have travelled all this way to tell the woman I love that I love her and to ask her to marry me." As the last word leaves his mouth, Ethan reaches for Katharine. He takes her head in his hands and softly kisses her lips.

When Katharine opens her eyes, she looks straight into Ethan's beautiful blue eyes.

"Ethan, I love you too. I've been lost since I returned and—"

Ethan doesn't let her finish but kisses her again. "We've both been lost," he speaks as he gently strokes her right cheek with his thumb.

Katharine takes a moment to look up into Ethan's eyes. She sees he speaks the truth.

"Wait before you answer that." He releases her and moves to the horse. He moves to the satchel and pulls out a package and brings it over to her. "The Stuart family is not happy that you're gone. The Young family is not happy that you're gone, but most of all, I am not happy that you're gone. I know I made a mistake in not telling you about my plan to deal with Mr. Holmes. It cost us dearly. Not a day goes by that I don't think of William. I hope that from this day forward, there will be no secrets between us. I want to earn your respect and trust; please let me."

"Ethan, I forgave you and anyone I held unforgiveness toward before I left Scotland."

"I was asked to give this to you when I found you and asked you to marry me. So Katharine Bennett, will you marry me?"

He hands her the package. Katharine unwraps the package to find a new cloak inside. She lifts the cloak to inspect it and sees the Stuart family's tartan colours sewn into the creases on one side. When she turns it over to see inside, she sees the same has been done with the tartan colours of the Young family.

"Ethan, this is beautiful," she says as she flips it over her shoulders and buttons it up.

"Yes, it is quite something. Many women from both families worked to make this for you."

"I don't know what to say," she says as she slips her arms through the holes. Ethan takes the brooch from her hand and pins it to her new cloak.

"I would love to hear a yes."

"Yes, Ethan, I will marry you." Katharine moves in to circle her arms around Ethan and leans up to kiss him. When the kiss is broken, Katharine looks up and says, "For the record, my dear, it was the cloak that sealed the deal."

"I'll be sure to have more made for you, Katie—many more." Light rain starts to fall. Ethan kisses her quickly and looks to see the storm is fast approaching. "We should find shelter quickly."

Katharine looks up and agrees. "Yes, we should."

Ethan mounts his horse, leans down, and offers his hand to Katharine. She looks up and, without hesitation, takes his hand and swings up behind him. He turns the horse and heads back to the house. The cloak moves to and fro, like the waves of the ocean. As it cascades, you see the colours of both tartans moving together as one.